Marianne Kusma was born and grew up in the city of Lincoln and at the time was the middle child of three girls. She moved to Devon at the age of fourteen and since then moved around the country at various stages in her life, resettling back in Devon where she married and brought up her family of five children. Marianne is also a grandmother and enjoys spending her time with the children and writing whenever she finds a few hours.

Marianne Kusma

UNLOCKING THE WILLOW

AUSTIN MACAULEY PUBLISHERS™

LONDON • CAMBRIDGE • NEW YORK • SHARJAH

A CIP catalogue record for this title is available from the British Library.

ISBN 9781788780674 (Paperback)
ISBN 9781788780681 (Hardback)
ISBN 9781528969437 (ePub e-book)

www.austinmacauley.com

First Published (2021)
Austin Macauley Publishers Ltd
25 Canada Square
Canary Wharf
London
E14 5LQ

For my sisters, Michelle and Maria, and for my brother, Paul, who along with myself learned how to live again. And for my husband, Neil, my best friend who believed in me enough to become a writer's widower while I spent hours and hours with my mind stuck in *Unlocking the Willow*. Thank you.

A massive thank you to my daughter, Rachael James, for her superb artwork on the cover of this, my first book.

Chapter One

The Beginning Is Best

"If you'd like to follow me dear, we can have our little chat."

There was that awful word again – 'Dear'.

Scarlet shuddered at its unnerving sound and tried to dismiss it. There was a lot to discuss if she wanted justice for her family. Allowing words to control her emotions now would not serve any benefit.

"My name is Pam Starling," she said soothingly when they entered the room. "Take a seat Scarlet – make yourself comfortable."

Scarlet scanned the gloomy room. At some point, somebody had painted it a warm, peachy colour, perhaps in a failed attempt to try and make it look less dismal, but other than this, nothing contributed in making it feel welcoming. The blinds in the windows had been completely closed, allowing the room to relish in its melancholy, casting an inky depression over the already greyed carpet tiles, which had seen better days. Two tatty, brown, leather sofas faced each other, separated in the middle by an old, heavily stained, coffee table.

"I work with the Lincolnshire Children's Mental Health Services, I'm one of the psychologists here…"

"And the social services asked you for your, *professional,* opinion," said Scarlet condescendingly, stopping Pam short of her sentence.

"Yes, that's right. The social services did indeed ask for my opinion, but only because they were concerned with your story of events leading up to where we are. They said your story was, erm… well, extraordinary." She smiled awkwardly. "Perhaps we can work together to find an answer to what's been going on."

Pam gazed at Scarlet sympathetically as if trying to fathom what could cause such deranged symptoms to such a severe degree; this case was going to be tricky.

Scarlet knew it was going to be difficult to get her to believe her story. It did seem far-fetched after all, even to her, but there was only the truth, no matter how unbelievable it sounded.

Scarlet stared back with wide eyes, uncertain of where to begin. The police hadn't known what to make of it all and had passed the case over to the social services, who in turn had their own dilemma of what should be done.

"I know why the social services asked you to speak to me. They think I'm crazy, don't they?" Scarlet bit back instinctively.

"Well, crazy is a word used by people when things can't be explained. Most of the time though, there is a logical explanation for strange happenings. I tell you what – why don't you tell me what happened, and I can be the judge of whether I think you're crazy or not."

Scarlet sighed cynically. "I don't know where to start."

"I always find that the beginning is best. Just take your time Scarlet, there's no rush."

Pam smiled again with the same sickly look that Scarlet interpreted to mean she had already made up her mind, perhaps even decided which pills she ought to be taking.

"Wha' about my brother and sisters? Will they 'ave to be interviewed too?"

"Somebody else will see them shortly. Don't worry about that though, just focus on your account of events and I'm sure we can piece everything together afterwards. When you're ready Scarlet."

Scarlet dug her hand into her pocket; her fingers found the warmth of her turquoise stone as it tumbled between them, soothing her nerves. She could use it right now, that would show her. There'd be no doubting her story then.

Deciding against it, Scarlet took a deep breath in and let the strange words flow…

"Life used to be wonderful once. We were a happy normal family. I have a sister a year older than me called Ruby, one younger by two years called Rose – I used to have a Mum and I used to have a Dad . . ."

She stopped short and pushed away a tear which had welled up in the corner of her eye. Pam stopped taking notes while observing her furtive behaviour, before quickly jotting something else down.

"Wha' ya writin' everythin' down for?" snapped Scarlet, shifting uncomfortably in her seat.

"I'm writing a story for you so that later when we go over it, if you don't like how somethings been interpreted, we can change it. The courts like to see everything written down. There's nothing to worry about."

Scarlet stared sceptically at her.

"You mean so that ya can analyse my behaviour an' use it against me later on!"

"You have huge trust issues Scarlet! I'm here to help, that's all. Perhaps if we can get some more information from you, we might be able to understand where that has all stemmed from. Tell me about your dad, what was he like?"

Scarlet's eyes glazed over and her lips curled into a warm smile.

"Dad was called Ben. He had amazingly sharp, blue eyes, like those hyacinth flowers you see in the spring. He had thick, jet black hair, and he was funny. He used to make us laugh, if there were ever any problems, Dad would be there to make it all better again." Scarlet smiled as she reminisced, unaware of the tears that had once again appeared in her eyes.

"It sounds as though you had a good relationship with your dad," said Pam probing gently into her mind. "What did he do Scarlet?"

Scarlet, suddenly aware of the wetness pricking her face brushed her cheek with the back of her hand and sighed.

"Dad was a pilot; he kept his flight manuals and other documentation downstairs in the basement. He stored some of the files in big cardboard boxes, but the majority of them were stacked on big, heavy, metal shelving. Mum was… Is called Matilda, but nobody knows if she's alive. She had long blonde hair like all us girls do. We all look quite similar actually, same blue eyes, same build, same everythin' really."

Pam stopped her.

"Scarlet, I think from here on in, I'd like to refer to you as 'Scarlet' on paper as I'm taking notes of our discussion. You know, like in a third person narrative. It makes the whole account easier to digest if you can see this through the eyes of another person, plus, it takes away the trauma you might feel after reading it back to yourself at a later date if you are able to distance yourself from the situation a bit. Does that make sense?"

"Yeah. I guess so," she answered timidly, shrugging her shoulders in a manner which suggested she didn't care.

*****

The family lived happily in a small detached house with a small garden, but number 19 Normandy Street was to be the home which turned the family's settled life into one which would never be the same again.

Just a few doors down on the other side of the street at number 30, was a man named Dennis who lived with his young son of around 8 years old. Dennis was recently divorced and had not long moved into the house, but it wasn't long before Matilda and Ben quickly became acquainted with him.

Dennis was a strange looking individual, he seemed nice enough and friendly, but his appearance was just a little bit weird. I say weird but I guess everybody looks different in their own way – I mean what's weird really unless you regard the wearing of a waistcoat with a pair of jeans and open toed sandals on his tatty, socked feet unusual? Or the fact that his hair seemed to lift from off his head in one piece when the wind caught the slightest sniff of it?

The girls just found him to be strange, they didn't feel easy around him, but even so, he and his son Jamie were familiar visitors and the two older girls in particular enjoyed Jamie's company.

He was a genius when it came to building with Lego bricks. His talents were way beyond a child of his age, he could build anything with the added complication of moving parts, all without instructions. He would simply have an idea and *bang,* the masterpiece would almost leap from his imagination and materialise within minutes.

The girls' appearances were completely different to Jamie's. Where they were pretty much paraded around as though they had just left the set of Little House on the Prairie with their matching handmade frocks, buckled shoes, white socks and their hair neatly braided and tied with ribbons, Jamie was not so well groomed.

His father did the best he could to take care of him, but being a father had never come naturally. His poor dress sense was obvious enough without having to worry about what an eight-year-old boy should wear and how he ought to be groomed. Instead, Jamie was pretty much left to fend for himself, choosing to wear ripped jeans and oversized shirts almost on a daily basis without appearing much different to how he looked the day before. It wouldn't have been so bad if his clothes had at least looked like they had been made for a young child, but in Matilda's and Ben's opinion, they were sure the shirts had once belonged to Dennis.

Ben had had some similar in design when big collars and large, colourful, paisley patterns had been all the rage, but on Jamie, Ben wondered how they had ever been passed as fashionable in the seventies.

The over-sized pointed collars seemed to hang limply around his scrawny little neck like tormented animals sewn in place to prevent them from running away, and the sleeves had been turned up at least six or seven times in order to expose his hands.

His blonde shaggy hair had the same grace as a haystack with strands dragged out on end by a crow looking for suitable nest material. But underneath his overgrown hair, the most sparkling, light blue emeralds shone out like precious gems in the sunlight. His laugh was contagious; he had the ability to make anyone smile who came near him. Jamie's bright attitude was one the girls loved; he was an easy-going boy with a love of life that couldn't be faltered.

Ben was a gentle man who didn't see the bad in others. He had a good heart and pitied Dennis for the situation life had thrown at him, and it was this that ultimately led to the downfall and unfortunate circumstances which were to take place so soon.

The night of the fire was no different to any other night. Matilda had put the girls to bed and Ben had read them all a story as he always did. The girls slept in a room they all shared, across the landing from where their parents slept. Thankfully, they were young enough to still enjoy each other's company which was just as well since there was no other room available. Ruby was 7, Scarlet 6 and Rose just 4.

Matilda knew that Ben was going to be late to bed that night, he had said something earlier to her about finding some old manuals from the basement; Apparently, he needed them for work the next day and didn't know how long he would be digging them out.

Several hours after the girls had gone to sleep, and with Ben still rooting through his files, Matilda got up from the sofa, put the mug of tea she had been keeping her hands warm with onto the glass coffee table and popped her nose around the basement door. The glow and smell of paraffin lamps enveloped her as it opened – they had used these lamps ever since moving into the house, supposedly as a temporary measure until more permanent lighting could be installed, but they just hadn't got around to fixing it.

"Honey," she called from the top of the wooden staircase.

"Yeah, what's up?" Ben called back without stopping.

"I'm going up for a shower now. When d'ya think you'll be finished?"

"Maybe another few hours darlin'. Don't worry about me, I'll be up soon," he called back.

Matilda shut the door leaving Ben to finish off and quietly slipped upstairs to the en suite in her bedroom and turned the shower on. Her life was perfect; she had a good, hardworking husband, three lovely little girls and an exceptionally happy family home. Matilda stood under the jet of water as she mulled over her life, it was just one of those moments when she felt completely overwhelmed with happiness, like nothing could ever go wrong.

She grabbed a towel from off the door hook and wrapped it around herself before checking in on the girls. They were still sound asleep; soft cooing snores of peaceful slumber twittered in the room like the ticking of a clock counting down the seconds of their perfect life.

Matilda pulled the bedroom door leaving a small gap between it and the frame then stealthily, tiptoed away back into her room and slipped beneath her bed covers. Within minutes, Matilda had dozed off and fallen into a deep sleep.

A sudden CRASH jolted her abruptly from her sleep.

In blind panic, Matilda threw back her bedding and leapt out of bed in a confused state of terror. Her heart had mysteriously managed to lodge itself in her throat so that she could hardly swallow back the panic which had escaped from the darkest depths of her nightmares.

She had dreamed that someone had been frantically trying to get her attention through a downstairs window just before the explosive noise had coincided with her nightmare. She had had this dream before, but this was the first time it had overlapped with a noise from the other side.

Matilda threw the curtains open expecting to see the traumatic aftermath of a road accident, but the road was silent, nothing outside seemed to be out of place or unusual. Then her thoughts turned to the safety of the girls, perhaps one of them had fallen out of bed.

Matilda rushed across the landing and pushed the bedroom door open, but the girls slept soundly, unfazed by their mother's overactive imagination.

Slightly confused, but relieved and heavy from sleep, Matilda pulled the girls' door ajar and returned wearily to bed. Ben's side of the bed was still made up and untouched, he must still be busy she assumed as she glanced over at the bright numbers on the alarm clock; it was 1:30am.

Matilda sighed with concern. She knew Ben didn't like to be disturbed when he had work to do, but in all fairness, he needed to get some sleep too. Her eyes flickered as she thought about him downstairs and gently her melatonin filled mind took over, swiftly taking her back into an unintentional slumber.

As if something or someone had shaken Matilda from her sleep, she suddenly woke up in alarm. The distinct, acrid smell of smoke creeping into her body through her nostrils forced her to finally realise what had alerted her from her sleep earlier, but somehow, she was unable to move.

A plume of inky black crept under the bedroom door, surreptitiously gliding like silk up the other side until it reached the ceiling. Then its maleficent shadow curled over the bed, spreading its form above her like a ravenous beast.

Choking, Matilda was suddenly released from the grips of terror as her body and mind rushed to respond. Within seconds, several towels Matilda had ironically used to dry herself with earlier that evening were plunged under a jet of water from the shower, drenching them as fast as she was able.

Her mind raced as her shaking hands tried to keep up. Right now, the only thing that mattered was getting the girls out of the house as quickly and as safely as possible, she would try to find Ben as soon as she could, but the girls had to come first, she told herself.

The towels had only been immersed for a few seconds, but to Matilda it seemed like a lot longer as she waiting for them to soak up the life-saving fluid. She squeezed one lightly, expelling some of the water before wrapping it around her face then grabbed the others, wringing them as she ran. The wall of black smoke hit her as she opened her bedroom door, and although it seemed to intentionally seek out her eyes, Matilda ignored its effects and burst through into the girls' room.

It was worse than Matilda suspected. In the little time it had taken her to be alerted and prepared to help the girls, the smoky monster had already filled their room with its toxic breath and penetrated the sleeping children's lungs. The sound of pained hacking stifled the darkened room so that although Matilda couldn't make out the silhouette of where the girls were positioned, she could sense where they were, purely by detecting their desperate gasps for air.

"GIRLS, I'VE GOT SOME WET TOWELS HERE," she shouted over the panicked cries of the children as she fumbled her way through the dark to where they were.

"IT'S GOING TO BE OKAY, WRAP THEM ROUND YER FACES AN' DON'T TAKE THEM OFF UNTILL WE GET OUTSIDE. STAY WITH ME AND KEEP MOVING. DO YA HEAR WHAT I'M TELLIN' YA? STAY CLOSE."

Matilda practically threw the wet towels at the girls, but they didn't care. They snatched them automatically, scrabbling to tie them in place, being sure to cover their mouths as their mother had instructed. It made a difference instantly, but they knew time was still of the essence as their home continued to be consumed.

They followed their mother through the house clinging to her dressing gown as she led the way. The smoke was thicker out on the landing as it climbed steadily up the stairs, almost as if it were deliberately trying to barricade them inside the building.

"KEEP COMIN'. WE WILL BE OUT SOON," shouted Matilda courageously over her shoulder.

The walls felt hot to the touch as the children fumbled through the dark, frantically clinging to anything which offered even the slightest hope of guiding them out.

As they reached the bottom of the stairs it became obvious where the fire had started.

Even through the already smoky room, the family could clearly see great, black plumes being pumped into the house under the basement door like a thick swarm of flies.

Matilda's heart sank immediately as she instantly understood the meaning of the explosive noise earlier. It must have had something to do with those damn paraffin lamps; they were hardly safe, but both she and Ben had still used them.

Her guilt suddenly overwhelmed her; if only she had investigated the noise earlier, she might have saved him, but now Ben was behind that door, trapped in a furnace and there was nothing she could do to help him. Opening the door would almost certainly mean a death sentence for both her and the children; the chance of actually getting to her husband and saving the children was an exceptionally slim one.

Still, Matilda felt a compelling urge to call out for Ben, there was the faintest chance he might answer back… But apart from the cacophonous crackling of burning furniture and spitting wood there was no response at all.

Scarlet tugged on her mother's sleeve drawing her attention back to their plight.

"WE HAVE TO GET OUT MUM," she shouted over the raucous sizzling as she pointed towards an unexpected sight.

The back door was unlocked and slightly ajar making the darkness outside appear brighter than normal. The dark light poured in through the small gap signalling their escape route, which although being oddly unusual to be left open, gave no time for Matilda to question its state.

Without hesitation, the children and Matilda ran towards it, half asleep and half intoxicated with fumes, they pushed their way out, literally stumbling into a heap on the other side, coughing and choking before snatching the fresh, sweet air the still night offered.

The exchange of toxic smoke for the clean air almost burned as much as the smoke had done. Only now, the combined cocktail of safety mixing with the agreeable, chilled air overwhelmed the girls, causing a sudden rush of dizziness – and then there was nothing…

The pending sound of the fire engines siren waking up the night didn't stir the children; the promise of protection it brought fell upon deaf ears.

"Good girl, nice deep breaths now."

Scarlet's eyes flickered open. A smiling paramedic stood over her, firmly holding an oxygen mask over her face.

"You're okay now sweetheart. We're going to take good care of ya, jus' keep breathin'."

Scarlet anxiously pushed the mask from her face and tried to sit up.

"Where's Daddy?" she mumbled through a broken, weak and croaky voice.

In a panic her eyes darted around the ambulance, and then to the illuminated sky outside.

The bright orange flames lit up the night as they licked the insides of the house, its tongue frantically lapping the walls as each flame searched for something not yet touched by the beast raging inside.

"It's okay sweetheart," said the paramedic sensing what was troubling her. "We'll find yer daddy if he's still in there. The firefighters have already gone in to make sure everyone is out. Try not to worry, just lie down and breathe."

Releasing the weight from her shoulders, Scarlet collapsed back onto the stretcher, relieved that her father wasn't alone.

Her mother and sisters were in different ambulances she assumed since she was being treated alone where she was. She could hear the paramedics talking gently to her mother in the ambulance next to her, although she couldn't quite make out what they were saying; they sounded muffled. But then another louder, angry, concerned voice erupted over the top.

"Wha'd'ya mean, Ben's in there? Where in there?" said the voice she recognised instantly to be Dennis'.

For the first time Dennis stepped away from the other ambulance enabling him to be seen through the open door. He seemed very anxious as he stepped first backwards, then forwards again. His hand reached to his head, his fingers ruffled his normally stuck down hair, dragging it forward through his stocky fingers like they had been transformed into a comb.

"A dun understand! How can 'e still be in there?"

"We're doin' all we can sir – sorry, I didn't catch ya name, are you a relation?"

"Dennis – me name's Dennis. I'm a – a family friend," he answered in a daze.

"Well Dennis, a couple o' the lads 'ave gone in to look for 'im. If he's in there, we'll find 'im."

He smiled as if trying to convince him it was under control, but in fairness they were no more certain of the situation than anyone else.

A window suddenly exploded under the pressure which had been building inside, sending shards of broken glass showering down onto the ground outside like crystals of ice. The smoke which bellowed out, escaped into the sky, a breath from Death evading the home it had callously consumed.

It was almost mesmerising to watch hadn't it been for the fact that it was so distressing. Everything they owned, all their possessions completely destroyed forever, but the worst was still to unfold.

A few moments later, two firemen came out of the house with a figure draped over one of the men's shoulders like a rag doll. They carefully laid him on a stretcher before rushing him away in a waiting ambulance. The blue lights flickered in the dark, illuminating their presence, while the ear-splitting siren signalled its emergency.

"Now yer daddy's gone to 'ospital, we can go an' get ya checked out too," said the paramedic in a constrained, calm voice while he cupped Scarlet's small hand tenderly in his own, almost as though he were trying to shield her from what was happening.

Scarlet smiled slightly under her mask.

"Is Mummy comin' as well?"

"Yes sweetheart, you're all goin'."

The paramedic didn't let go of Scarlet's hand, he kept it encapsulated in his own for the entire journey as the ambulances rushed in convoy to the hospital. It didn't take long to arrive at the accident and emergency department, and it didn't take long for the children or Matilda to be checked over before being discharged.

The doctor talked gently to Matilda, his voice sounded monotonous and soothing, lulling Scarlet's mind into a peaceful daze. Her eyes wondered across the medical room, focusing on the dark window. It looked like a mirror the way everything reflected back, almost like there was a parallel world through that glass, and she wondered for a few brief moments if the images which imitated the figures in the room were simply following the people here, or if they were living a similar life on the other side, but with slightly different outcomes.

"You'll be okay," said the doctor to Matilda in a somewhat altered tone, suddenly yanking Scarlet back into the room.

"You were all very lucky to have got out when you did, otherwise the outcome could have been quite different. If you or the children have any difficulties with breathing over the next 24 hours Mrs Hartman, please don't hesitate coming back."

His attention turned to the other doctor waiting patiently by the door. "This is Doctor Lilly Woodward; she will take you down to see your husband."

The doctor smiled in a concluding kind of way then left the room, leaving the family and Dennis with Doctor Woodward.

"Is my husband okay?" asked Matilda anxiously.

"Mrs Hartman, your husband came into us in a very bad way. He was very lucky to be taken out of the house alive considering the trauma his body incurred. As it stands at the moment, well…"

"Well what? What's the matter" asked Matilda, beginning to sense that things weren't as well as she had hoped.

Doctor Woodward's eyes glazed over sympathetically.

"Well, he wasn't doing so well, so we decided he would be more comfortable if we put him into an induced coma. You need to understand that he won't be responsive. I'm sorry to say that you need to be prepared for the worst Mrs

Hartman." Doctor Woodward rested her hand supportively on Matilda's shoulder. "I'm terribly sorry."

Matilda grasped Dennis by his hand, stopping him from assuming his role as some sort of comforting escort to her husband's side.

"Dennis – I'm sorry, but I need to do this by myself. I realise I must sound terribly rude right now, but I need to be left alone with my husband – if you don't mind?"

Dennis took Matilda's hand in his own and tried his best to look empathetic, nodding with understanding.

"Of course Matilda. I'm sorry, I should've realised ya need to be by his side without someone like me faffing around. But if ya do need me, ya will ask won't ya?" He smiled with concern, his hands cupping hers in a nurturing kind of way.

"Actually, now you mention it, there is somethin' you can do to help," she answered. "I know I'm asking a lot and if it's too much I'll understand, but would ya mind takin' the girls home with you tonight? I want to stay with Ben; I can't leave 'im and it's not good for the girls to see their dad like this?"

"Matilda!" he said in a way that suggested she might as well have slapped in the face. "Nothin' is too much for you. Ya know I'd do anythin' to help. After all – what are friends for?"

"Oh, thank you Dennis. It means so much to me to know the girls will be looked after, you really are so kind."

"Honestly Matilda, it's the least I can do. Don't ya worry about the girls, they're safe with me. If and when Ben comes round, tell 'im I'm thinkin' of 'im will ya love?"

"Of course I will. Thank you," she smiled half-heartedly trying to put on a brave face.

"I'll see ya soon then," he said, leaning forward to gently kiss Matilda on her cheek before carefully placing her hand back to her side as though he thought she were made of porcelain. "I'm 'ere for you an' the girls. Just know that okay."

Matilda smiled awkwardly.

"You're a good friend Dennis. Thanks."

"Mrs Hartman," said Doctor Woodward gently. "Please, if you'll come this way."

Dennis smiled smugly before turning to leave, leading the girls away, with Rose securely tucked in his arms, bundled in her smoky smelling blanket.

"C'mon girls – Jamie, let's get 'ome shall we?"

18

Chapter Two
30 Normandy Street

Dennis gripped Scarlet's hand tightly, while Ruby walked slowly behind with Jamie. The night air felt colder than it had done earlier, perhaps because they had all been in shock, but now it seemed to find its way through the children's thin night dresses as if searching for their sensitive skin. Scarlet shivered, which in turn set off a chain reaction in the other two older children. Jamie who was also scantily clad in only his pyjamas rubbed his arms automatically.

"The car's only over there." Dennis pointed to a silver Cortina parked just a few paces away. "We will be 'ome and warm again real soon. It'll all work out just fine ya know, you'll see," he assured them with a gentle smile.

Scarlet returned the smile, but didn't think anything was going to be okay. Everyone kept telling them it would be, but from her perspective, all she could see was her daddy in intensive care and a house that had been burnt down. It didn't feel at all as if things would ever be okay again.

Dennis unlocked the driver's side then leaned over from the inside, lifting a button to unlock the other doors.

Jamie opened the back-passenger door and the girls climbed in. The journey home went by in a blur, the street lights flashed by quickly making bright lines of white in Scarlet's eyes as they drove, reminding her very much of the way the ambulance lights had flashed when they had followed their father to the hospital.

It was hard to take her mind off her father and the recollection of the smoke-filled house. She relived the blinding walk down the stairs as she stumbled alongside her mother, desperately searching for the exit. She could still smell the toxic smoke over everyone's clothes. She hadn't noticed the small waterfall which had started trickling down her cheeks and she didn't notice when the car suddenly stopped on Dennis's drive.

Dennis turned to look over his shoulder smiling broadly like he had achieved something extraordinary.

"We're 'ome," he grinned. "C'mon let's get inside and get some sleep hey."

The children scrambled out of the car, following Dennis and Jamie up the small path to the front door.

The firemen, just a few doors over the other side of the road were still busy extinguishing the remaining flames from the house and the smell of smoke still hung heavy in the air.

Ruby and Scarlet stood fixed to Dennis's front door without moving as they stared helplessly, traumatised at the charred, skeletal, remains of their home.

Scarlet was suddenly aware of a heavy hand clamp down on her shoulder. "Best not to get too upset Scarlet, it's only an 'ouse," said Dennis through a toothy grin.

"It was our house though," retorted Ruby angrily.

"Yeah I know – but there will be others. Come in outta the cold now."

Ruby, Scarlet and Rose turned away from their house in frustration and stomped through the front door while Dennis lingered a moment longer, staring at the beautiful burnt ruins before locking the door for the night… and chuckled.

"The room is made up for yer all and there's an airbed on the floor next to the double bed fer Rose to sleep on," explained Dennis proudly.

He led the girls upstairs into Jamie's room. The bed had been freshly made up with a pink bedspread, and the airbed had a pretty, blue flowered throw, neatly covering the sheets beneath.

"Where will Jamie sleep?" asked Ruby suddenly realising that there was no room left for him.

"That's okay, don't worry about Jamie, he can share with me for as long as we need the extra space," answered Dennis.

A lamp in the shape of a little toadstool house stood on a small white bedside table casting a bright light into the room making it look rather welcoming. Dennis noticed Rose's attention turn to the novelty lamp and smiled at her.

"Ya like it Rose? I bought it today fer yer when I popped into town. I thought as soon as I saw it, *I know some lill girls who'd like tha'*. Anyway, see if yer can get some sleep then eh."

The girls didn't sleep well for the remainder of that night, but the few moments they did drift to sleep, upsetting images played in their heads like recordings. Their house was fine one moment, and the next, flames were pouring out of every window, and then from the flames their dad appeared, gliding almost like mist so that the fire had no effect on him.

He knelt down at their sides and draped his arm around their shoulders, smiling apologetically with tears shining in his eyes.

"Hey baby," he said touching Scarlet's face gently with his finger.

"Hello Daddy," she choked through a throat full of tears.

"Hey – don't cry flower. It's all gonna be jus' fine, really it will."

He brushed her tears away with his soft finger, pinching her cheek playfully as he wiped it dry.

"You know I can't stay don't ya?" he asked, holding her hand tightly in his own.

"But you must remember, I love you all so much. I'm sorry I can't be there to see you grow up, but you know what?"

"What Daddy?" she sniffed.

"No matter what happens, I will always be with you right here, in your memories, in your heart, in everything you do or see, I will be watching. When you look up at night and see the stars, you can be sure I will be seeing them too. Love is everlasting and all that love and all those memories we made together stay with us too. Stay strong and take care of each other."

Then slowly he stood tall from his crouched position, gently kissed them goodbye on their foreheads and disappeared back into the flames.

Scarlet woke with a start to see Ruby sitting bolt upright with the same dazed look on her face.

"Did you dream of Daddy too, Ruby?"

Ruby slowly turned to her sister, silent tears rolled down her face.

"Yeah. He said goodbye Scarlet. D'ya think it might've bin real?"

Scarlet shrugged her shoulders.

"It was just a dream. Anyway, I don't wanna talk about it," she sobbed, dismissively wiping away the wet trail from her face as she tried to push the dream from her thoughts.

Just then a gentle knock was heard on the door.

"Are you awake? May I come in?"

"Yes, we're awake," answered Ruby sniffing back her emotions quickly.

Dennis entered cautiously and peeped around the door.

"You know, Jamie was asking abou' ya, he's just outside. Can 'e come in?"

"Yeh that's okay," Ruby answered shyly.

Jamie poked his nose around the door and grinned.

"Hello," he said gingerly.

Ruby and Scarlet smiled back and Rose scrambled up from her air bed onto Scarlet's.

"I'll let you lot talk then shall a?" said Dennis uneasily, realising the girls didn't want to talk to him.

He pulled the bedroom door closed behind him leaving the children in peace. The children looked blankly at each other for a few moments before giggling their nerves away.

"I'm sorry about yer 'ouse," Jamie started. "D' yer think yer dad'll be okay?"

Scarlet looked down uncomfortably as she remembered her dream.

"I dunno, but Mummy should be comin' back soon."

Ruby laid her arm around her sister's shoulder and Rose tucked herself between them both.

"It'll be okay," she said gently, realising what had upset Scarlet again.

Her own dream reverberated in her head making her feel uneasy, particularly since she hadn't been the only one to have had the same dream. It felt too real to be anything other than just that.

"D'ya really think Daddy'll be okay Ruby?" asked Rose beginning to cry also.

In honesty, Ruby wasn't entirely sure either. While she had enjoyed seeing her father in her dream looking well, his purpose in visiting wasn't a welcome one; he'd come to say goodbye.

She didn't answer this time. She felt that by reassuring Rose, she might be making things a whole lot harder to deal with if the worst should happen. Rose was younger, how could she be expected to understand that the dream had been one of farewell?

"D'ya wanna play with Lego before breakfast? Dad said we have time if you wanted to," said Jamie hoping to lift the girls' mood a bit and in a desperate bid to change the sorry conversation.

He pulled out the box which was stored under his bed, dragging it into the middle of the room.

"I can build you a nice house, better than the one you had. You could pretend it will be like the new one you get to live in next."

He smiled cautiously at Scarlet, unsure that he had said the right thing, but hoped they didn't think him to be unthoughtful or cruel.

The girls seized the opportunity to lift their spirits and slipped off the bed. The Lego bricks had been scattered all over the carpet where Jamie had quite literally emptied the contents of the box out.

"You can sort the colours into piles for me if you want," said Jamie hopefully. "It will make it easier to build the house if I can see what I need."

The girls were only too glad to help. There were a lot of intricate pieces to sift through, different sizes, different colours and shapes not to mention decorative pieces, including little taps and flowers and window shutters. It took the girls minds off the events from the night before long enough to be called down for some cereal.

The girls weren't long into eating when a knock was heard on the door and their mother stepped inside. Her eyes were swollen red and her hands trembled, but she wore a slight smile on her face in an awkwardly strained way.

The girls jumped up from the table and ran to her side, hugging her tightly.

"How is he Matilda?" asked Dennis almost in a whisper.

She glanced up at him and shook her head slowly, brushing away the persistent tears.

"Come and sit with me a moment," she whispered to the girls. "There's something I need to talk to you about."

"D'ya want to use the back-room love?" asked Dennis, sensing that this would be the talk he was hoping for.

"Yes, if you wouldn't mind," she answered, forcing another brave smile on her obviously pained face before taking the girls by their hands and leading them into the back room.

Matilda pushed the door closed while taking the opportunity to catch her breath and discreetly wipe her face dry whilst her back was turned.

"Take as long as yer need love," shouted Dennis from the other side of the door.

Matilda sighed deeply then turned to face her children.

"Come and sit with me a minute," she said as she seated herself on the sofa, patting the cushions next to her with her hand indicating where the children were to sit.

"You know, Daddy was very poorly when the firemen took him out of the house last night," began Matilda carefully. "Well, sometimes even the best medicine and the best doctors can't help when someone is as poorly as Daddy

23

was." She gulped hard swallowing back her tears, fighting the lump in her throat which had surfaced again.

"Daddy left us early this morning. He couldn't stay, he tried, he wanted to," she croaked, desperate to hold back her tears, "But he was in so much pain. I told him it was okay to go – and he did."

"He was so brave. Your daddy would want you all to be brave too, just like him. But now that Daddy isn't here, we are going to have to stay strong and take care of each other, just like we always have done. We'll have lots of days where we feel sad and when we'll miss him, but those are the days that we have to remember how lucky we were to have had him in our lives at all."

Matilda burst into tears; it sounded so much more factual hearing herself saying the words out loud.

"I'm sorry," she whispered through her tears, "It's hard for me to tell you because I know how much we all loved him. I'm really going to miss him, we all will."

"You mean he's dead, don't you?" said Ruby in a matter of fact way. Her eyes welled up at her understanding.

"Yes sweetheart, he's dead," sniffed Matilda, looking at her daughter through glazed eyes.

For a brief moment, time stopped, while the reality of Bens death hit home, and then the emotions seemed to break free from their constraints. Matilda held the girls tightly in her arms while the family huddled together in grief.

"We will go and live with Grandad and Grandma until we find a new place to live," sniffed Matilda, pulling herself together for the children and breaking the embrace. "You will like it there; especially with the lovely arboretum on the doorstep. You know how much Grandad and Grandma love you and they have lots of space to play in don't they!"

This cheered the girls slightly. The house was a beautiful big Edwardian building set over five levels with tall ceilings and fancy ornate covings which ran around the perimeters of the rooms. It was a house which to the girls was like an Aladdin's cave where their imaginations could run free.

"Come on," she said bravely, drying her eyes with the back of her hand. "Let's get goin'." Matilda stood up and together hand in hand they left the room, returning to where Dennis was waiting.

"Ya alright love?" he croaked, as he watched her and the girls return.

24

"Yeah, we'll be okay," she replied firmly. "We have a plan which should help us move forward, don't we girls?" she said, smiling bravely at the children as she slipped on her shoes. "You'll need to put these on," she continued brightly, handing the girls a pair of soft flat shoes each. "I hope they fit, I had to pick them up quickly from the shop before comin' back from the hospital."

The girls slipped the shoes on to their bare feet and walked to the door.

"Thanks for everything Dennis," said Matilda turning back to face him before leaving the house. "You've been such a good friend. I don't know what I'd 'ave done without ya." Leaning forward she gently pecked Dennis on the cheek. "We'll see you soon Dennis."

Chapter Three
Memories

The taxi stopped outside the elegant house. Its roof seemed to touch the sky and the chimneys appeared to stick out from the roof in all directions. The white painted walls looked bright in the sun welcoming them to a home of peace and love.

The gardens which the house stood in were tranquil. Tall trees and perfect flower beds decorated the grounds and the sound of birds singing their songs seemed to make the move easier, almost as if they were singing just for them.

Grandma opened the door to them. She always wore a blue and white butcher apron whose long strings tied twice around her slim waist before finally being tied in a neat bow at the front.

She was a dear lady whose silver hair tucked short and neat behind her ears. Distant, pale blue eyes sparkled lost in thought, and her soft peachy skin resembled an over ripe apricot. She smiled warmly at her family and hustled them indoors.

"Come in come in," she said in her unforgettable Austrian accent.

She had come to live in England just after World War Two with the children's Latvian grandad. He stood behind Grandma as they were welcomed inside, fussing over the children as he always did.

He was a tall strong man whose hair seemed to defy age, apart from an odd streak of white which had forced its way through creating an unusual effect, especially when it fell in front of his left eye. Every so often, Grandad seemed to notice it had rebelliously slipped off the top of his head and would try to make it stay in place by combing it through his fingers, almost trying to firmly press it back. He had the kindest warm grey, blue eyes with a glimmer of adventure hidden behind them.

His face beamed when he saw the children, the light in his eyes leapt out like little flames which had been bellowed up from cooling embers.

"My goodness, you've all grown again. I hope you're not too big for chocolate biscuits or I don't know what I'll do with them." He chuckled to himself when he saw the girls' reaction.

This house had the most amazing pantry which Grandad liked to call his shop. It was situated under the first set of stairs behind a small, painted oak door. The pantry itself took up the whole of the basement and was filled with lots of exciting, foreign foods as well as sweet things that the children were most interested in.

A blackened metal key hung on an old nail above the small basement door. It was as though this door was the entrance to a magical world where beyond it, anything was possible.

Grandad took down the key and placed it into the lock.

"Who wants to open the door today?" he asked with the same usual childish beam across his face.

"ME, ME. I DO GRANDAD CHOOSE ME," shouted Scarlet in excitement.

Opening that door had a way of making the children feel a mixture of elation and anxiety, both at the same time. The smells which promised to pour out were almost too overwhelming, but still the need to open it always triumphed.

Scarlet turned the key, the sound of heavy clunking in the sturdy mechanism rasped as it clicked into place, and the door creaked open on its old hinges.

The expected promised smell wafted out like a magic potion. A combined aroma of spicy sausage, mixed herbs and sweet confectionary mixed together beautifully with the scent of garlic radiating from the tied bulbs strung together, plaited with their own stems.

Grandad turned the light on so that the pantry shone brightly, allowing all its hidden treasures to be seen.

Three worn granite steps provided access into the room and carefully the girls followed Grandad down into the basement.

No matter how many times the girls had seen this room it never became less exciting. Rows upon rows of tinned fruit, piles of dried herbs and jars of sweets lined the shelves, almost begging to be chosen. Under the bottom shelves Grandad stored cardboard boxes filled with fresh fruit from his allotment, Victoria Plums, Coxes Apples and Williams Pears all waited, beckoning the girls to peer inside.

Their eyes rested on the jars of colourful sweets which were perched on the third shelf. A string of brown paper bags hung on a small hook next to them.

"Which ones do you want?" Grandad asked, his voice giving away the same excitement the girls felt.

"Those ones up there. The red ones," said Ruby pointing up to some red cubed sweets.

Grandad reached up and brought them down. Opening the jar, he scooped out a good amount with a brass serving scoop, tipping them into one of the paper bags before handing it to Ruby.

"What about you?" he asked looking at Scarlet.

Scarlet had already decided on the ones which she liked the look of, and like her sister pointed to a jar, this time filled with white chocolate mice.

"Can I have the mouses please?"

Grandad laughed heartily. "Of course ya can," he answered as he reached for the jar, bringing it down to her height so she could peer inside.

Scarlet watched as Grandad tantalisingly unscrewed the lid the same way he had done for Ruby, a strong smell of sugary milk emanated from the contents.

His smile seemed to be glued to his face as he collected a good scoopful of the chocolate mice from the glass jar. The clinking sound as the scoop tapped the chocolate added to the excitement involved with serving up sweeties, and the gentle pitter-patter of them as they were tipped into the paper bag, amplified the entire experience from something quite ordinary into something quite special.

"Here you are," he said, pushing the bag into Scarlet's hand. And then his attention turned to Rose and he laughed. She was already pointing at the flying saucers in the clear jar, her face was filled with such ecstasy it looked like she might burst with excitement at any given moment.

Grandad took them down and served her with the same enthusiasm he had shown the other two girls. He was a child trapped in an old man's body, but his eyes were still young and his heart still youthful.

"Now what about some fruit?" he asked, setting his mind onto something healthier.

That's when it was apparent that Grandad wasn't a child; otherwise he'd have known that the girls were more than happy with their sweets. He had already started scuffling in one of the fruit boxes under the shelves before he had barely let go of Rose's flying saucers.

"Ah there they are," he said at last, pulling a box out covered with old newspapers and producing three fat, juicy looking plums. "Right c'mon then, let's lock the shop back up for now."

He handed the girls each a plum who then followed him back up the stone steps and out of the door. Grandad turned the key, locking it back up again, keeping the secrets it held safely on the other side.

Grandad had a way of making the girls feel special every time they visited, but now it seemed so much nicer knowing they would be staying with their grandparents for a little while. The house itself was big enough for the children and more, but having so much space to play in allowed their imaginations to open up and expand.

The ground floor consisted of a long kitchen which quite normally in those days also had a bath situated in the kitchen itself. This opened out into a large dining room where an Aga sat against the far wall. There was always a copper kettle filled with hot water which sat on one of the four hotplates on the top.

Next to the kettle, it was almost guaranteed there would be another large pot which constantly simmered with different vegetables and leftover food. Whenever there was too much of something, it would get thrown into the pot adding to the flavour. A huge amount of garlic radiated from the mixture; it was as if the hotpot were some kind of cauldron the way it gently bubbled. Every so often, Grandma wobbled over to the pot, threw in an extra ingredient, added a twist of sea salt then gave it all a stir with an oversized wooden spoon before replacing its lid.

Off from the dining room and through the door was the hall which housed the staircase and the unforgettable magic pantry, and from here another door opened into the sitting room. This room was generally a lot cooler since it fell under the shadows of the tall pine trees in the arboretum.

Even so it held its own charm in a different way, for on the wall of this room the most beautiful, elegant, handmade cuckoo clock took the limelight.

It was a walnut clock, carved with the most intricate and elaborate decorations. Small carved squirrels chased each other around the sides, and if you looked closely, a number of hidden animals and birds were disguised within the carved trees.

The chains were embellished with realistic looking pine cones and on the hour, every hour, a painted cuckoo bird burst through the wooden door above the clock face and tweeted according to the hour registered.

For hours the girls sat and watched, waiting for it to make an appearance and when it did, they squealed with laughter.

Up the first set of stairs were three large bedrooms. The girls' grandparents occupied the one at the far end of the landing, their mother Matilda took the middle one, and the girls were given the one to the left. This is the one which was directly above the sitting room and so had the most spectacular views over the Arboretum.

In the evening the girls listened to the calls of the owls and watched for the flashes of fiery red foxes as they dashed around on the well-kept lawns. It was a delightful room, one which kept the children's mind off the terrible, tragic death of their father.

From the landing another set of majestic stairs stood, which stepped up onto another floor. This was an identical lay out of the floor below but was used for storage. Boxes and boxes lined these rooms like large building bricks filled with treasures from years gone by. Old leather photo albums and old china tea sets were neatly stacked inside as though they might be used again one day.

The girls took complete advantage of these, playing around and hiding between them. From this floor another set of stairs spiralled up into the attic and it was in this particular space the girls' imaginations sparked the most.

The attic was a huge area which stretched over the entire ground space of the house. It was filled with wonderful toys and other items which had again been stored in boxes for safe keeping. In particular though there was one toy which Scarlet became particularly attached to.

A wooden grey horse, blotched with black and white spotted paint on its rear, stood over a wooden frame. It was fastened with a swinging bracket which allowed it to sway back and forth over its attachment. Both its mane and tail were made with real white horse hair and its bridle and saddle were made with leather. It was the most elegant, antique, rocking horse imaginable, and up in this attic, it was Scarlet's pride and joy.

In the few weeks that passed, Scarlet found herself in this attic for hours at a time imagining herself to be riding among the clouds high in the sky. From this pinnacle of the house, the attic had several large windows which lent themselves to be the starting point where Scarlet dreamt up her stories, and where her day dreams stretched right into the night.

Chapter Four
The Police Interview

It was easy to forget the house which burnt, but the memories of their father would never fade – that was until the police knocked on their grandparent's door a few weeks after the family had moved in.

"Good morning ma'am we're here to see Mrs Hartman if she's around. There are a few questions we need to ask her."

Grandma let the two policemen in and hurried off to find Matilda.

"Matilda! There are two policemen here asking for you. They're in the sitting room."

Matilda was a little taken back.

"Here! For me! Why?"

"Well go find out. It's probably just some routine questions they need to ask."

Matilda clasped her hands together tightly, twisting her fingers awkwardly as she walked anxiously into the sitting room where the police were waiting for her, and she closed the door.

"How can I help you?" she asked boldly, taking a deep breath in.

"Mrs Hartman, I'm inspector Whitehouse and this is my colleague Inspector Gallagher. We just need to ask a few questions about the night of the fire and your late husband's death. We appreciate you've had a lot to deal with, and your emotions are still running high, but the coroner's report suggests that your late husband had a head injury before he died consistent with force you'd expect to see from a blunt instrument. Is there any explanation you might be able to think of as to what led up to the fire and how your husband may have come about receiving such injuries?"

Matilda's jaw dropped.

"Head injuries? What d'ya mean, head injuries?"

"There was a deep cut to the skin and a large fracture on the bone just above his right temple area. It suggests he may have had an accident or attained an injury from something before he died from the smoke inhalation. There was very little smoke damage in his lungs which is very unusual considering the length of time your husband was actually in the building. It suggests he might not have been breathing properly; so you see, we can't rule out that someone wasn't perhaps responsible. Is there any way you can think of how this may have happened?"

Matilda stared into space in shock. Now that the police had mentioned the cut, the memory of him laying in the hospital bed surfaced again. At the time, she didn't think much about it, assuming it was probably due to him stumbling about in the smoke, but now it seemed to be evidence of foul play.

"I – I don't know," she stuttered. "Are you sayin' someone murdered my husband?"

"Well as we said Mrs Hartman, we can't rule out that possibility from our enquiries just yet. I know it's probably hard for you to take on board right now. But was there anyone who had a quarrel with yourself or your husband?"

"No…no, nobody had any problem with either of us. I don't understand what you're trying to tell me," she stuttered nervously.

The police looked at each other suspiciously; a small nod from inspector Whitehouse indicated his intention to pursue the questioning.

"And the fire? Do you know how it may have started? The fire crew say it started in the basement where your husband was found. They did give us an idea of what the likely cause was, but if we can have your thoughts on the matter, we can hopefully verify what they have suggested and perhaps clear this up quickly."

Matilda glanced quickly from one inspector to the other, her hands continued to twist and writhe in anguish.

"You think I had somethin' to do with my husband's death, don't you?" her voice was sharp and accusing.

The police didn't say anything. Their glare stayed focused on Matilda in a way that suggested she might hang herself if they gave her enough rope.

"I didn't do anythin'," she protested. "I was asleep when the fire broke out. We barely got out the house as it was."

"But you did get out!" probed Inspector Gallagher.

"Well of course we got out, but that's only because the back door was slightly open."

The police glanced at each other with the same suspicious look.

"Open you say? Is the back door *always* left open at night Mrs Hartman?"

"No of course not, but…"

"But that night it was conveniently left not just unlocked, but open for you. Is that what you'd have us believe? You didn't even think it was strange apparently, otherwise you would have mentioned it sooner of course." continued Inspector Gallagher.

"I don't know why the door was open. I didn't open it. Maybe Ben had to go out and left it that way," she spluttered innocently, almost in tears.

"So, you don't know what may have started the fire then? No idea at all?" he pushed relentlessly.

Matilda dried her eyes and cleared her throat, the image of that back door burnt in her mind's eye, resurfaced as clearly as it had done on the night of the fire.

"Well, I can guess. We didn't have a proper electricity supply to the basement, so we had to use either candles or an oil lamp whenever we went down there." She glanced up at the inspector. "Ben said he was goin' to have proper lights fitted down there, but he never got round…"

"Thank you Mrs Hartman. The fire department confirmed it probably started with paraffin from a lamp. There was evidence of a flammable substance in the basement when they investigated the scene, but your explanation clears that question up sufficiently."

"Yes, of course," said Matilda blankly as the visions of the back door surrounded with dark light pouring through, froze in her mind like a haunting from a bad dream.

"So, what about his injuries Mrs Hartman?" asked Inspector Gallagher, noticing that Matilda appeared to be pre-occupied thinking about something more. "Can you think of any way how these may have occurred?"

"You're asking me what I think would cause a deep, blunt injury, like I know what happened. Well I don't," she snapped defensively.

The police glanced at each other, unsure of Matilda's innocence, a little extra push couldn't hurt if she really was as innocent as she would have them believe.

"Are you sure there was no one who had a quarrel with Ben?"

"Why d'ya keep saying such awful things?" snapped Matilda uneasily. "No – he had no quarrels with anyone, and no one had any quarrels with him, or me?" Matilda's eyes flashed around now from one inspector to the other with confusion. "My husband was a good man; nobody had any reason to hurt him – nobody."

"Were there any visitors to the house that evening?" continued Inspector Gallagher, pushing ruthlessly.

"No. I put the girls to bed and Ben told me he needed to finish looking for something in the basement. He told me he'd be up shortly and I left him to it. The next thing I remember was waking up to the smell of smoke and that's when I realised the house was on fire."

"But nobody came into the house that evening after you went to bed?"

"No, for crying out loud. Nobody came in that night. There was no murderer in our house. If there was, then why wasn't I or the girls attacked and killed at the same time?"

"Did Ben say he was expecting a friend to come over? Anything at all that you remember could help!"

Matilda sighed with exasperation.

"Ben didn't say he was expecting any visitors, not that I'm aware of anyway. Besides, our friends wouldn't 'ave come by of an evening without checking first. Normally our friends visit in the day anyway."

Matilda stopped talking and for a few moments there was silence in the room while the inspectors allowed Matilda a few minutes to think.

"He may have slipped," she said thoughtfully, suddenly remembering the relevance of the explosion she had heard. Only it wasn't an explosion, it was Ben falling over the shelving – she was sure of it now.

"Sorry Mrs Hartman, what was that?"

"He may have slipped or stumbled over somethin', hit his head on the corner of the shelf and knocked over the lamp when he fell. You said he had a deep cut on his temple. Perhaps he hurt himself when he fell over." She looked directly at the inspector; her eyes wide open as if she had suddenly been given insight to what had happened.

Inspector Whitehouse nodded and looked at his colleague for his approval. "That sounds plausible Mrs Hartman. Okay, well I think we're done here, but if you do remember anything unusual from that night please let us know.

Otherwise, please accept our condolences for your husband's death and we will leave you to grieve in peace. Thank you – we'll see ourselves out."

Chapter Five
A Time for Farewells

The girls who had been sitting on the stairs had heard the conversation and ran to their mother the moment the police left.

"Why were the policemen asking lots of things about Daddy, Mummy?" asked Scarlet.

"They have to darling. Sometimes accidents might not always be accidents, so they sometimes ask questions. But don't you worry, it's all okay."

Matilda gently laid her hands over the girls' shoulders and patted them reassuringly.

The police had no reason to come back, the case was closed and recorded as an accident leaving the family free to bury their dad and husband. It was a sad day even with the spring in the air, but even the sound of bird song did nothing to lift their spirits.

The burial place was in a grave yard in the grounds of Mary Magdalene Church. The grounds had been planted out with flowering cherry trees and every spring, huge plumes of pale pink blossoms decorated the grounds like confetti when at last the petals fell.

Slowly the coffin was lowered into the ground, the sound of birds seemed to vanish leaving a respectful silence as he came to rest at the bottom.

Dennis stood close to Matilda, extending his arm around her waist as she sobbed, while Jamie tucked in among the girls as though they had already regrouped their family unit.

"Ya know, I hope ya don' min' me bein' so forth coming," began Dennis after the burial service had concluded, "But if ya want, yer all welcome to stay with me until ya get a place sorted ou'. Of course, I understand if you'd rather stay with yer parents."

Dennis held Matilda's hand gently in his own hoping he hadn't over stepped the mark, waiting for her facial response to determine if he had or not.

The girls looked at each other with screwed up faces. Of course they didn't want to stay with Dennis, his house was nothing like their grandparents and besides, he wasn't their dad and he certainly had no right behaving like he was.

Matilda took a moment to read the girl's faces before answering.

"Oh Dennis, that's so kind of you but I'd prefer to stay with my parents, for the time being anyway. You don't mind, do you?" Without waiting for a response, Matilda pulled her hand from his clasp and hustled the girls away. "We will see you soon Dennis," she called over her shoulder as she hurried off.

The silence in the car on the way home was so heavy it could almost be cut up. Matilda's thoughts whirled round and round, her mind whispering ideas to her that things might not have been as they appeared. Why was that back door open that night? What if things hadn't played out the way she had told the police?

The girls however were having trouble dealing with the fact their father had now passed away and his burial seemed to make it all the more real. He wasn't coming back.

The girls were glad when their grandparent's house came into view. It promised adventure and love and a chance to help their minds escape the funeral. Thankfully their grandparents had arrived home before them and had prepared hot tea and cinnamon buns for their return.

The next morning Matilda gathered the girls together and told them they were going to say goodbye to their old house and try to move on with their lives now that the funeral was over.

It felt strange driving towards the place they used to call home, almost as if they were going back there to live, as if they could just walk back through the front door the way they had done so many times before, and things would be exactly the same as they once had been.

Dad would be waiting in the front room and Mum would start cooking tea. But as they approached, the burnt, ashy remains lay scattered on the ground as though the building had actually died and been forgotten about, reminding them that their desires of a past life was firmly out of reach. It was upsetting to see it like this, blackened and smouldered with a thick blanket of ash covering the ground around it, almost mimicking the building's spilled blood.

The family got out the taxi and stood silently in front of the house for a few moments. The girls, unsure initially of why exactly their mother wanted to do this, almost immediately understood. This was another funeral. It seemed like an eternity just standing and looking, like a darkness drawing out their energy, leaving only deep sadness, absorbing their strength while it slowly weakened their spirits.

"How long do we have to stand here, Mummy?" asked Scarlet quietly after a little while.

"I'm sorry darling, I just needed to see it one last time to say goodbye. Anyway, I thought you migh' like to see Jamie, and I need to thank Dennis personally for his help when I really needed him."

She smiled down at the girls, then together they slowly walked the few doors up to Dennis's house and knocked on the door.

The door swung open almost immediately as if he had been expecting them.

"Matilda, girls, how wonderful to see you," he said, wrapping his arms around Matilda and greeting her with a kiss on both cheeks. "Come in; Jamie will be so glad to see you."

Scarlet didn't like his over familiar attitude. Her father hadn't long died and seeing Dennis embrace her mother so tenderly made her feel quite unwell. She turned away repulsed, doing her best to ignore it and waited for Jamie to come downstairs.

A little face peered round from the top of the stairs. He didn't seem his usual self. He was normally quite fun loving and cheeky, but today he looked subdued and frightened. Perhaps she mistook these emotions for empathy.

"Ya can go up and play if ya want," said Dennis. "Make sure ya be'ave," he warned Jamie in a harsh tone, giving him a stern glare before turning away to help Matilda with her coat.

"Le' me take tha' for ya duck," he said, in a way that made Scarlet's skin crawl. His hands quivering in the relish of taking a layer of clothing from her, but thankfully escaped Matilda's notice. "Matilda, I'm very sorry if I overstepped the mark yesterday at the funeral. I didn't mean to cause ya any more upset. It was clumsy and unthoughtful of me, forgive me."

None of the girls particularly liked the way Dennis looked, his appearance was hardly attractive, but this sudden over friendly attitude sat uncomfortably with them despite their young ages.

"Ya don't need to apologise Dennis. It was really kind of you."

He smiled at her apologetically, relieved that he hadn't blown his chances, before rushing in nervously with polite small talk.

"D'ya wanna cuppa duck? The kettle's not long boiled!"

The girls followed Jamie into his room leaving the adults downstairs. He pulled out the Lego, but even over the sound of the plastic bricks being pushed around, the children could still hear parts of the conversation downstairs.

"I can't help feeling a bit strange about it though Dennis. The police asked me to tell them if I remembered anything unusual that night…"

Dennis looked up from his tea as nonchalantly as he was able.

"And do you?" he asked quietly.

"I don't know. I'm just worried that the door might 'ave bin open for some other reason. I 'ad a job tryin' to convince them I had nothin' to do with it as it was. Now I'm afraid if I start doubting my explanation, they'll start accusing me again."

"It's probably best you don't say anythin' else about it then, unless ya wan' them sniffin' around again. There's any number of reasons that the door might've bin open slightly, but if you go shou'in' about it – well you're likely to start causing suspicion. I should just keep quiet love."

"But I didn't have anythin' to do with the fire Dennis," she pleaded innocently. "What if it's of more relevance than I thought?"

"Look duck, it's up to you, but if ya wan' my opinion I'd keep quiet. They don' know ya like I do, ya wouldn't want them to start asking questions again would ya? And to be honest love, if I were the police and you'd started to doubt what you remembered, I'd be on ya case until ya admitted you knew more than you were lettin' on. I'm jus' sayin'."

"But I didn't do anything Dennis. They have to believe me."

"Course they don' 'ave to believe ya Matilda! Think abou' it! A man is dead from a head injury, you manage to ge' out from a burnin' 'ouse with three kids, in the dark, and the door is conveniently left open fer ya to escape, and you wan' to tell me that sounds perfectly plausible do ya?"

There was a moment of complete silence downstairs as Matilda began to understand the implications.

"You don't think I killed Ben, do you?" she sounded hurt now and confused.

"No, of course I don't," he sighed, realising that perhaps he was being too hard on her. "But if ya look at the evidence it looks bad enough withou' you goin' around yapping abou' doors bein' left open fer ya, while your 'usband is conveniently knocked out and trapped in the basement. It doesn't sound good

39

does it? It's all a meant. You're a beautiful, kind and caring lady Matilda, but the police don't care about hurting you if it means they have answers."

Matilda sighed. "I guess you're right. I just feel terrible, there might be something I'm completely overlooking, but ya right, I'll stay quiet about it. It's time it was laid to rest."

The children played quietly, listening as best they could, but the awkward and odd behaviour from Jamie didn't make it easy. He seemed so different today, more restricted and distant with a general quietness which seemed to strain him, causing the girls to believe something was wrong.

His eyes barely left the floor even when the girls spoke to him, as if he were petrified to speak. They were pleased when it was time to go, it had been difficult for them to try and cheer him up, but even when they were going, his mood didn't lift.

"Come again soon Matilda, I'm sure Jamie would love the company too, wouldn't ya boy?" he nudged Jamie's arm sharply and he nodded in agreement, but his eyes still remained glued to the ground.

"Of course we will." This time Matilda leant forward and kissed Dennis gently on the lips. "Thank you for your advice Dennis."

Almost every day for the next few weeks they returned, the familiarity of Matilda and Dennis becoming ever more obvious while the girls became increasingly annoyed with this new apparent relationship. And then it happened, the part which the children had seen coming for a while. Dennis announced that he and Matilda were officially a couple and Jamie was as good as their step-brother.

For the time being Matilda stayed with the girls' grandparents, so at least for the moment they still had their space to believe and imagine whatever they wanted.

Grandad being Grandad noticed the girls becoming despondent and tried to cheer them up. The arboretum being so close became the usual grounds where he would take the girls to play. It was a wonderful place to walk in, relax, or to run off some of the children's energy, but what's more, over the time they had spent there, it had already been added to Scarlet's magical imagination. She was sure it had once been the garden belonging to a palace, because at the top of the arboretum were several stretches of long, wide stone steps, set on two levels.

To either side of the steps, a stone statue carved into a grand looking lion, sat majestically on a pedestal. The steps cascaded upwards, reaching onto a long, gravel footpath which led to a children's play park.

Scarlet had thought that at the top of the steps, there should have been a beautiful palace with tall towers, like the ones in a fairy tale book, but there wasn't a castle there. There was however, a very beautiful, romantic looking old house which had been built further up the hill.

Over the years it had been separated from the grounds, divorcing it completely from its former gardens. The house had now been sectioned off into separate, individual dwellings, turning it into an apartment building. It was easy to imagine how beautiful it would have been when it was used as a single house, complete with the entire estate.

It didn't stop the girls from imagining what they believed should have been there. They would run up and down the flights of stone stairs, pretending to be princesses on their way to a dance, just the way they remembered them from their stories.

Down in the centre of the park were two magnificent bandstands. They were both round and painted in very bright, elegant colours. One was painted a forest green with gold details. A twisted, steel Victorian rail ran around the perimeter of it encircling the embellished, elaborately patterned, mosaic tiles laid in the floor.

The other was painted a bright cherry red, again finished with gold touches which helped the decoration stand out beautifully. The floor was laid with long, oak, varnished floor boards which ran the length of the bandstand. The girls thought they had once been carousels, like the ones they'd seen at the fair ground with fancy ornamental horses.

The girls took great delight as they ran down to the bandstands from the top of the park, pretending they were the missing horses galloping around the outside as fast as they could go, until they were out of breath, and laughing.

There were some lovely ponds in the arboretum too. Big water lilies and bull rushes grew in them, spreading their plate like leaves across the ponds surface, providing cover for water boatmen, and sticklebacks.

The girls dipped their fishing nets in these ponds sometimes, hoping to catch some of the pond life, particularly the sticklebacks. They were odd looking fish, with huge golden or blue eyes, and as their name suggested, had two sharp looking protrusions sticking out from their backs.

41

In the centre, and on the far side of the pond, there were two huge water fountains. The children loved watching as gallons of water were sucked into the pumps, casting it high into the air, before finally allowing it to come splashing back down, cascading into droplets that rained onto the surface. They could watch this cycle forever, each drop making a perfectly round ripple, which then spread out wider and wider, descending further and further until it almost petered away completely.

Around the neatly cut and maintained lawns were stunning flower beds. In the spring, hyacinth bulbs pushed their way through the soil in a wide variety of colours blooming from half way up the stems, covering the area with thick, weighty blossoms. They had a heavy scent to them, one which was so fragrant they had the ability to make the girls feel drowsy just by breathing in the intoxicating perfume.

These were some of the last, relatively happy moments the children had. Life should have got better after this, but I'm sad to say, it was quite the opposite.

Chapter Six

Dennis

At last, the day came several months later that the council got in touch with Matilda; they had a new house where she and the girls could live.

It wasn't like their old house nor as grand as their grandparent's house, but it was theirs, and it was a place to settle again and call home.

The girls were just about to look around the house when a small knock disturbed their adventures.

Matilda smiled expectantly and turned to open the door. Dennis stood there with Jamie as bold as brass holding out a bunch of flowers for Matilda.

"Dennis, you shouldn't 'ave done." She held them to her nose inhaling their delicate perfume. "They're beautiful, thank you."

"Well, you deserve them darling," he said, kissing her lightly on the cheek.

"How rude of me, come in," said Matilda suddenly becoming aware that she had not invited them inside. "I'll pop these in some water and then ya can give me a hand to unpack if you don't mind Dennis. Hopefully it won't be long before we find the kettle in among these boxes. I'm only glad I had our things brought here yesterday."

There weren't many boxes, everything they had owned before had been destroyed, but there were a few boxes that Matilda had managed to fill with new clothes and a few other accessories for the house.

She laughed suddenly, "Well it won't take very long I suppose, I guess that's the brighter side to all of this mess."

Dennis's eyes met hers for a moment before Matilda realised the children were still watching,

"Why don't you take Jamie upstairs girls, show him your new bedroom and perhaps you could put a few things away if you wanted to."

The children reluctantly went upstairs leaving their mother alone with *him;* deciding that if he was going to be there for a while, they may as well explore the house a little. It was while they were in their bedroom that something peculiar happened, something that would change the way the children viewed the world forever.

"Who's tha' lady in the garden Scarlet?" said Ruby, staring out into the back garden.

Her eyes were firmly fixed on something and her face said it was something she didn't quite understand.

The other children went to the window to see what had caught Ruby's attention. The younger two of the children were just a bit shorter than Jamie and Ruby so couldn't quite see over the window sill.

"Lift up Scarlet and I'll lift Rose Jamie, then they can see too," commanded Ruby in a sisterly way.

Their little faces peeped over the top of the sill and scanned the lawn below.

"There's nothin' out there Ruby," said Jamie after a few seconds of searching. "I don't see anyone. Where ya looking?"

"She's right on the grass; ya should be able to see 'er," replied Ruby in confusion.

"I see her Ruby, she's very pretty. Look at her silvery cloak, it's beautiful," said Scarlet excitedly.

"Silver? It's not *silver,* stupid. It's black. She has long black hair and a black cloak with a big hood and she's got purple eyes."

Scarlet peeped over again convinced she had seen correctly, but there she stood, the same beautiful lady, clad in a silvery white cloak and a hood which covered most of her white shiny hair. Her eyes were light green like those of a cat caught in headlights.

"Well she doesn't look like that to me. I think you must be blind," Scarlet snapped in frustration.

"Well I don't know what either of you are looking at," said Jamie sounding annoyed, "Cos I can't see anyone. I think you're both making up a load of rubbish."

Scarlet and Ruby eyed each other up, both of them just as exasperated as each other.

"I'm going to tell Mummy you're lying," said Scarlet suddenly. "Mummy will see her, then she will tell you off for being a big, fat liar."

With that Scarlet hurried off down the stairs only to be confronted with a scene she didn't expect. There in the kitchen, Dennis held her mother in a tight embrace, his arms were wrapped tenderly around her waist.

"Honey come in," said Matilda when she caught sight of Scarlet's surprised face. "We have something we want to tell ya all. Call down the others, then we'll tell ya altogether."

Scarlet didn't need telling. She already knew what they were going to say and she didn't like it. Turning sharp on her heel she sped back up the stairs to where her siblings were still staring out of the window.

"Mummy says we all have to go down. Dennis and her want to tell us somethin'."

"Like what?" sneered Ruby. "Did you tell Mummy about your lies?"

"I'm not lying, you are," she bit back in anger, stamping her foot hard on the floor. "If ya don't come, I'm goin' to tell Mummy you're all being naughty."

"Fine! We're comin'!" answered Jamie who thought it best not to aggravate the situation any more than it already was.

Together the children went down to see what it was that they needed to be told, but they too didn't really need telling. The second they saw Matilda sitting next to Dennis on the sofa hand in hand it was pretty obvious.

"Come in kids, we want ya all to share our good news and thought ya should know first," said Dennis, eyeing them for a moment, but long enough to let the children see he meant business and that this was no request.

"Yer mum and me 'ave decided tha' a new house would be a good way for us all to begin again. I know it's bin very 'ard for ya all since yer father's death, bu' we 'ave to move forward. Wouldn't ya agree?"

This was no question; the decision had already been made. This was merely a formality to let them know what was going to happen.

"Muuum…" began Scarlet, hoping their mother might correct Dennis from misunderstanding the situation, tell him that he'd never be able to replace Dad, but before she had chance to question it, Matilda interrupted her.

"I think wha' Dennis is trying to tell ya, is that I have agreed for us all to live together now. Dennis has asked me to marry him, and I've accepted." She smiled sweetly. "It makes perfect sense if we all move in together so tha' we can make this work properly."

Matilda smiled again as though it was the most wonderful news she could think of. It didn't seem to matter that the children's father hadn't long died, and the girls weren't too pleased at the idea of their mother moving on so quickly.

"Wha' about Daddy though?" asked Scarlet quietly.

"Daddy died Scarlet, you know that. I need Dennis to help me through. If it wasn't for him, I don't know how I'd have coped. We all 'ave to look to the future now."

There was no answer to this. It was very clear they had already finalised these plans and nothing the children could say or do was going to change how they felt.

Matilda, now content that the children knew the arrangements melted back into Dennis's arms and became lost in the moment, oblivious to the girls' exasperation.

It hadn't really occurred to the girls how much they disliked Dennis until now. They had never paid too much attention to his mannerisms or thought too hard about his fashion sense, but now that their mother had dictated what was going to happen, Dennis almost immediately stirred up a sense of anger and hatred within them. It was outrageous the way he sat there looking so proud of himself, and so smug. His appearance suddenly became ridiculously hideous and completely annoying, more than it had ever done before.

"It won't be for a few years yet girls," said Dennis suddenly, almost as if he could hear or feel their disgust. "We're not goin' to rush into it so don't worry. We'll all 'ave plenty of time to ge' used to each other."

He smiled arrogantly over the top of Matilda's neatly tucked in head, his yellow teeth gaped through his lips like Colorado Beetles adding to Scarlet's disgust and irritation.

The children were a little older when Matilda and Dennis finally decided on a date for their momentous occasion. Rose was aged 7, Scarlet 9, Ruby aged 10 and Jamie aged 11.

Right up to the wedding day the girls couldn't understand what their mother saw in Dennis; she could have had her pick of men to choose from since she was a very beautiful woman, but nonetheless, it was Dennis she chose.

He still didn't sit right in the girls' minds of how it should be and he still came across as strange in both his looks and manners. At least by now though they had begun to get used to him being around the house, and Jamie was a welcome addition even though he was strange from time to time, but thankfully he wasn't nearly as weird as he had been a few years previously. Perhaps he had also just needed time to adjust; after all, he had also been through some difficult times.

Even so, regardless of what the girls failed to see in Dennis, Matilda must have seen something special, although what, would have been anyone's guess. She must have thought him to be a charming man, perhaps thinking he would be a super replacement for the children's natural father, or it may have been just a natural progression which developed over the course of time.

The wedding day finally arrived. The pair had a quiet registry office wedding without any fuss. It was a normal day really; Matilda wore a pastel green dress which covered her entire neck almost like a polo style cut, and the girls wore hand-made matching blue dresses, while Jamie was made to wear a pale blue shirt and jeans in an effort to at least try and blend in. After the wedding a few photographs of the ecstatic day were taken to record the exciting, unforgettable occasion.

There was no honeymoon. In fact, how they could afford to get married at all was amazing since Dennis refused to work. Ben had always worked to support the family, but somehow this was not a problem to Matilda now. It wasn't as if Dennis had a mountain of wealth or anything which would otherwise keep his family cared for, while the very idea of him ever finding a job remained unthinkable. However, he seemed very good at pretending he was busy, doing nothing all day left him incredibly exhausted.

"Put the kettle on will ya," he'd say every half an hour through the day. "I'm knackered."

It remained a mystery as to what caused him such fatigue, but it seemed to be a question better left unanswered; the girls assumed it could have only been the amount of effort he put in to drink so much tea.

Over the time that followed after the wedding, Dennis's true colours slowly unfurled, exposing him for the monster he really was. Even his attitude and behaviour towards Jamie seemed to become more strained despite him being his own biological son.

The girls couldn't quite put their finger on what it was that bothered them so much to begin with, there was just something which made them feel uncomfortable.

As the girls settled into their new lifestyle, their opinion of him lowered if there was any change toward him at all. The moody, stern looks they had been accustomed to before the wedding, now seemed perfectly sweet as his ugly side appeared. They found him to be a very unkind person, often showing an intensely cruel and wicked persona.

Dennis was a man who took great delight in, and strongly believed in harsh, corporal punishments. He actually enjoyed inflicting any kind of pain that manifest in his head, reminding the children on a daily basis of his golden rule. His eyes hardened as he glared intensely at the children.

"Remember! I don't want to 'ear a peep out of any of yer. If ya stay outta ma sight and don't get under ma feet it will be easier for us all. Y'all know the rule. Children should be seen and not 'eard, or better still, not seen or 'eard."

He had small, cold, hard, grey piggy eyes which he wrinkled up when he stared down at the lower life forms he knew as children. A horrible, wiry moustache which followed the top of his lip, hung untidily over it like a spider's legs. His head was shiny and bald like it had been polished time and time again by an over enthusiastic cleaner with OCD, afraid that microscopic specs of dust might settle there again if it wasn't regularly maintained.

In order to compensate for this loss of hair, he dragged the remaining lanky, lengths from the sides of his head placing them strategically and with impeccable precision over his immaculately polished head before spraying them down heavily with hairspray; gluing them firmly in place so as to stop them also from somehow escaping.

Scarlet was certain that he alone must have been responsible for the world's climate change with the amount of CFC gasses he discharged into the atmosphere from his hairspray cans. There had been a lot of media coverage on the news recently about the damage caused from these spray cans, and she was very aware how many Dennis used.

The cacophonous hissing and clonking coming from that room every morning was enough to convince anyone who didn't know better that it was alive with serpents. The finished result was one that could only be seen to be believed. When the wind caught his hardened hair, it would suddenly breathe life into the previously unanimated object, giving it the life it deserved.

Leaping into the air, the wild, scared animal now danced around on the top of his head, urgently trying to escape its fate. If it had moved any more than it did, the scientists behind the theory of evolution would finally have had the conclusive evidence they needed to support the idea that animals did indeed evolve.

Small legs would have grown out from the skirts of his hair and the wretched creature would have desperately clawed itself free, disassociating itself from him completely, flatly denying it had ever been a part of his head, before escaping from its shameful and embarrassing situation.

He would spend at least an hour every morning in the bathroom trying to perfect his ridiculous style, obviously believing he looked amazing and a vision of delight. When he finally paraded himself from the smelly, unbreathable, toxic bathroom, normally letting off a few loud, wet farts as he walked, a trail of Old Spice aftershave followed in his wake.

The stench followed faithfully down the stairs attached to its owner, then hung over him like a shadow as he finally plonked his behind into a dining chair.

"Make me a coffee will ya," he'd grunt, beckoning to one of the girls to serve him his over sweetened morning beverage.

His teeth were disgusting, stained a revolting yellowy brown colour and crooked. His breath was stagnant with the smell of old cigarettes and ash, despite his claim that he didn't smoke. In fact, his entire demeanour was so overbearingly vile that Scarlet was convinced his insides would have been just as revolting if she were unfortunate enough to have been given a glimpse inside of him.

Her mind conjured up a brief image in her mind's eye of a dirty, run down old engine smothered in thick, black, sticky tar which had accumulated like congealed oil and blood. His once pink lungs now oozed with thick masses of the sticky stuff sporadically dripping the gunk into his stomach and coating his rotting, yellow organs in its offensive waste.

Freaky looking tattoos covered the lengths of his arms and hands. Some kind of strange mythical creature adorned his left arm spreading its tentacles across the skin over his hand, and to his right arm and hand, he was inked with what looked like blackish, blue panthers. Their mouths were painted open, exposing sharp, blood dipped fangs. The artist had cleverly portrayed these beasts to give the impression that they were running down from his arm, then leaping off at his hand.

Occasionally he'd catch a glimpse of one of the girls furtively looking at his horrific tattoos and chose that opportunity to tease them, pulling up the sleeve of his shirt and thrusting his arm into their face.

"Ya like my pets?" he'd spit, his face twisted with spite.

Jamie had recently begun to grow a little in confidence, but after the wedding he seemed to crawl back into his shell. It was as if something awful had been rekindled from his past and was now hanging onto his soul like a parasite draining away any kind of happiness he might have had.

Regardless of this, he did his best to make life easier for everyone in the house. The children were all set chores which had to be done to a very high standard, failure to comply with the regulations set would mean a beating was in order for them.

The girls weren't sure if he was trying to be so nice because he felt guilty for the way his father behaved, perhaps over compensating for this unfortunate fact, or if he was just trying to make an extra vigilant effort to act normal.

It didn't occur to them to ask why he was always so moody in the first place, but if they had, Jamie may have revealed some of the true horrors and secrets that he had kept hidden from the rest of the world.

Perhaps it was his way of protecting the girls from the strange things he had seen happening with his father before they moved in together as a family, but whatever the motives for his sweet, generous nature, the children's bond as brother and sisters was not hindered.

Unfortunately to the girls' utter frustration, Matilda had been completely captivated by Dennis. Everything she had promised them after their father had died seemed to have died and been buried alongside him.

She still thought Dennis was a wonderful man, going along with him and his abhorrent behaviour, condoning anything he deemed fit, believing it was the best way to keep the family running in a controlled manner.

If Dennis had decided that the children should all jump off a cliff, Matilda would more than likely have agreed with him, believing that it was probably a good idea. Even so, making sure that Matilda conformed to his way of thinking was only the beginning.

The children were far too young to realise what Dennis was up to, and if they had, they might have understood the dangers that they faced.

Chapter Seven
Conforming

With Ben out of the way, Dennis had free reign to manipulate the children and a wife who adored and obsessed over him. But still this wasn't enough.

What Dennis really craved for, more than anything, was the power to have subjects submissive to him, treating him as though he were a god, or a king, obeying him, worshipping him even. And so with this in mind, he found a way to gain the kind of power he desired. It came in the form of something quite unusual. It was a strange, strict, religion known as a sect.

This wasn't any ordinary religion where the children would go off for a Sunday school meeting and listen to bible stories, or where learning came in the form of painting scenes from Noah's ark. Instead, children were expected to sit quietly without interrupting, preferably taking notes from the meeting and listening intently.

This sect was like no normal family church. This one allowed, even encouraged the kind of discipline that Dennis relished, where corporal punishment was used as a matter of course.

"Remember what the bible says," he'd grin nastily. "Proverbs 13 verse 24, God says use the rod, it is what constitutes love, and discipline is a gift from the almighty that gives every parent hope of shaping our children. By accepting this discipline and loving God's word, makes you worthy of being saved."

Everybody in the congregation would meet three times a week for two solid hours of study. Some of the children were allowed by their parents, to bring books to read or scribble in, some even had a small toy to help keep them from getting too distracted and causing a disruption, but not these children though.

The only book they were allowed to bring, on top of their usual study books, were the ones you use to make notes with, ensuring that they were listening one hundred per cent to the scriptures which detailed how children were to behave, and what would happen if they disobeyed their religion.

Subordination was an absolute must if evil, demonic spirits were to be kept at bay. Children who disobeyed their parents, no matter how cruel or unfair they thought they were being, were at risk of being possessed.

When the children got home in the evening at about 9.30, they had to discuss what they had learned, relaying to Dennis and Matilda why they were so happy to be a part of this wonderful organisation.

If Dennis thought they hadn't learnt enough, or if they didn't say the right things, they would be punished; normally that consisted of a beating since that wonderful scripture made it clear in Dennis's mind, that this was love.

Despite the outward appearance of being a happy family, the children could feel tension building between Matilda and Dennis. At first, Matilda had periods of staying quiet and withdrawn, this was closely followed by heated arguments that seemed to last forever.

The children were always sent away when they fought, but that didn't mean that they were completely in the dark about their disagreements.

The children by now were a few years older. Jamie was now 12, Ruby had turned 11, Scarlet 10 and Rose was now 8, and this was another one of those nights which would be very hard to forget.

Matilda sent the children away; and once upstairs the raised voices began to permeate through the floorboards.

"I just think we should tell the police about the door. It's bothered me for years Dennis; ya know how it's troubled me. What if someone did come in that night? What if Ben was attacked tha' night and whoever it was left the door open on the way out?"

"YA STUPID WOMAN," he shouted angrily. "YA REALLY THINK GOIN' TO THE POLICE NOW AFTER ALL THIS TIME THAT THEY'LL 'ELP YA. YOU'LL BE LOCKED AWAY FER MURDER YA WILL." He stopped for a moment to calm himself and then tried to reason with her again.

"Ya reckon you'll convince the police after all this time tha' ya knew nothin', then suddenly ou' the blue, you just 'appened to remember somethin' unusual. They'll point the finger at you then arrest ya fer his murder. Go on then! Go runnin' to the police an' see where it gets ya, but don' be bothering me with yer problems when yer in too deep."

"I know Dennis. It sounds bad, but I was too frightened to say anythin' before because of how suspicious it appeared, even to me. You've bin good to me, bu' I have to tell them that I might have made a mistake. Ben wouldn't have left the door open, he was too busy to have had any reason to go outside. Maybe he wasn't alone that night after all. I can't keep on with my guilt. The Bible says God won't forgive if I've done something wrong an' don't come clean."

"Listen woman! If you go blabbing now, we'll all be in trouble. Did you ever just stop an' think that things worked out the way they did cause that's wha' was s'posed to 'ave 'appened?"

"What d'ya mean, supposed to 'ave 'appened?" said Matilda with confusion. "It was an accident. Accidents aren't meant to happen. That's why they're called accidents…"

There was a sudden silence and then Matilda said something that none of the children would ever be able to forget.

"It *was* an accident – wasn't it, Dennis? You – had nothing to do with the fire – Did you?"

The silence of the accusation seemed to drag on forever.

"Course I didn't. How could I 'ave 'ad owt to do with it?" said Dennis at last quietly.

"You know, thinking back, ya didn't seem too bothered when Ben died. You even managed to sort Jamie's room out for the girls in the blink of an eye. Ya could have easily popped in that night after I'd gone to bed and…"

"And what?" interrupted Dennis angrily. "Jus' listen to yerself woman. Yer talking absolute rubbish an' ya know you are. Ben was my mate, ya know that. It didn't take long to make the room up when you asked me to take the girls in. I was bein' a friend, I dint expect ya to throw it back in me face years later."

"Well then there's no problem tellin' the police if no one's to blame," replied Matilda trying to ease the situation. "I know ya don't want me to, bu' I'll pop in first thing tomorrow mornin'."

"Agh, do wha' ya want," he spat. "I've 'eard enough of this rubbish for tonigh'; I'm goin' to ma shed fer a bit."

The back door slammed and Dennis dragged his heavy broken-down shoes across the concrete paving outside to his shed.

The house fell silent as the night crept in. The children heard Matilda's soft footsteps a few hours later as she made her way to her bedroom, signalling it was time for them to also be in bed.

The next morning the children woke expecting to hear the familiar noises from their mother as she busied herself in the kitchen. Her normal humming to the radio's tunes and the clattering of plates, but this morning there was very little sound coming from downstairs at all.

Chapter Eight
What Was That Dear?

Shuffling downstairs to see what was going on, or rather what wasn't going on, the children were a little surprised to see their mother drearily gazing out of the kitchen window. Her hands were in a bowl of soapy water and a few peculiar objects were bobbing about in the water, things that she had decided needed to be washed.

"G'mornin' Mum," said Scarlet, waiting for her to respond and wake from her trance, but instead she remained motionless as she stared absent-mindedly into the garden.

Scarlet turned to the window, scanning the garden to see what was so captivating, but there was nothing that she could see out there. She shrugged her shoulders and whispered to Jamie,

"What's wrong with her?"

"Dunno," he answered with a frown on his face.

Jamie clicked his fingers in a bid to break the spell, then waved comically in front of her face, but Matilda was oblivious to any of it.

"MUMMY," shouted Rose in fright. "WAKE UP."

It was like watching a wind-up toy in slow motion as she slowly turned her head to see Rose pulling at her arm. It was actually rather creepy, like something straight out of a horror film. Her face was white and vacant and her expression lifeless.

"What's the matter with you Mummy?" whimpered Rose almost in tears.

"There's nothing the matter with her," interrupted Dennis, suddenly appearing in the kitchen unnoticed, snapping her out of the trance instantly, "Is there Tilly?"

"Me? Something wrong! Don't be silly, now why would ya think something's wrong?"

She laughed, her tone sounding slightly confused as though her performance had all been some sort of absurd joke, but the children remained unconvinced. It was as if Dennis had her on strings, commanding her to move or speak at his will, like a puppet.

"Now, where was I?" she said, dismissing their concerns as an over-reaction. Matilda plunged her hands back into the water and fished out the unfamiliar object which the children had seen floating at the surface a few minutes earlier. It had now sunk to the bottom of the washing bowl weighted down with what appeared to be saturated garden soil.

Matilda huffed as she studied the remains of one of her houseplants. Its roots hung loosely to what was left of its compost and its once succulent leaves now hung pitifully over her fingers like a soggy lettuce.

"What the devil happened here?" she asked, frowning with absolute bemusement.

Her free hand dipped back into the water reappearing this time with a brown plastic plant pot, the last of the soil poured from the holes in the bottom.

"It was going to flower this year," she said sadly. "I waited ten years for this to actually do something, now look at it, it's ruined," she explained, holding up the dead orchid for everyone to see. The emotion on her face had swiftly changed from bewilderment to downright disappointment.

"How did it end up in the dish water?" asked Jamie in a perplexed, empathetic way, hoping to stir her memory.

"Well, it's hardly my idea of fun is it?" said Matilda in defence. "Which leaves me wondering which one of you might think this kind of thing is funny!" Her eyes glanced over the children accusingly hoping that at least one of them might know what had happened.

"Hush now Tilly. Calm yourself; tis just a plant," said Dennis gliding over to Matilda with intention. He clasped her face in his hands as he spoke slowly and purposefully. "Sshhh, my love. Calm – there's nothin' to worry about."

By the time Dennis had released her face, the Matilda the children knew, had vanished. Her expressionless face reappeared and her eyes glazed over, blinking back the disappointment and hurt she had just experienced, before nonchalantly dropping the limp orchid on the work surface.

"Whatever was I thinking?" she said suddenly, glancing dismissively at the wretched plant before turning her attention back to the children, accepting it as just one of those unexplained moments in time. "Anyway, what do you want for breakfast this morning? There's egg, toast, cereal or yoghurt."

"Erm, just egg and toast please Mum," said the confused girls almost together.

"And you Jamie?"

"The same thanks. If you're sure you're up to it though?"

"Of course I'm up to it, why wouldn't I be? Can I get you anythin' darlin'?"

Her sweet, obliging questioning was now aimed at Dennis. It was as if the disagreement the pair had had the night before had been erased from her mind. There was no sign of insubordination from her; in fact, her behaviour was more in line with someone who was under some kind of mind control.

"Nah, I will eat later ta," he answered flippantly.

The children sat down at the table and watched carefully as Matilda resumed her work. It wasn't long before it became quite obvious something really was amiss when Matilda suddenly began humming an odd tune to herself.

It was nothing like the children had ever heard before, it was rather repetitive and dreary, consisting of only a few notes which became increasingly annoying the more she continued. Ruby rolled her eyes in frustration, but nobody said anything.

She called him darling. She hadn't called him that for years, and he had called her Tilly. He'd never called her Tilly before, and what was all that business about with the washing of garden plants? thought Scarlet, losing herself in deep concentration, before a plate suddenly landed in front of her.

"There you go Julie," said Matilda smiling proudly at Scarlet as she slapped a slice of dry, untoasted bread on her plate. "I will get your egg in a minute."

Scarlet looked in surprise at the soft, pale bread before glancing at the others for their reaction without moving her head. The smallest hint of a smile curled on Jamie's lips – it was a bit funny after all.

He didn't have long to gloat, within seconds Matilda had whirled round again and doled everyone else a slice of the same untoasted bread.

"What d'ya say?" she demanded firmly when nobody recognised her offerings as edible material.

The children were taken back at her request for thanks. Under normal circumstances they were usually forthcoming with their manners, but this morning they were caught off guard and a bit surprised.

"Erm – sorry. Thanks Mum!" answered Ruby quickly on behalf of everyone, smiling graciously as best she could.

"I should think so too. I'll just get the eggs, give me a minute."

Matilda was still humming her jolly little tune to herself as she placed an egg from the saucepan in front of each of the children.

"There you go. Enjoy! Now I'll just make some tea, then I can get on with the housework."

She turned away and began preparing the teapot, dropping in a few teabags and pouring some milk into a small creamer. The children thought nothing more on it, deciding to make the best of a bad situation; perhaps she would feel better as the day progressed.

Ruby tapped on the shell to expose the top, expecting to see a firm, cooked egg. She had been looking forward to dipping her bread into the soft, creamy yolk and taste the warm, delicate flavour on her tongue, but what greeted her was far from her delicious expectations.

The crack made its way down the egg shell, allowing the entire form to collapse in on itself like a small implosion. The sticky, raw contents spilled out through the sides almost crawling over the bread like a slug, trailing its slime over everything it touched.

"Just the way you like them Georgina," said Matilda who was now stood over Ruby watching in anticipation for the delight which was bound to appear at any given moment across her face.

The girls stared in horror at each other; she couldn't be serious – could she? And who the devil was Georgina anyway?

"Mum. The eggs are raw!" said Ruby in confused disgust.

Deciding they had better investigate the state of their own eggs, the others tapped open theirs also, only to discover that they too had been presented with cold, uncooked eggs straight from a pan of cold water.

The slimy mess oozed out, slipping its way down the side of the egg cup, slopping into small, gloopy ponds on their plates.

Matilda wasn't giving anything away if this was a prank; no smirk, no giggle, nothing. Her face remained straight as she returned to making the tea. She wondered over to the tap and filled up the teapot with cold water, merrily humming the same monotonous tune over and over again like some sort of weird incantation.

Stirring the tea briskly with a spoon, she replaced the lid.

"Did you say something Lucy?" she asked Ruby, staring at her through blank, lost eyes, as if everything was perfectly normal.

"My name's Ruby Mum. Not Lucy. Not Georgina. And I said – the eggs are raw. And why didn't you boil the kettle for the tea? If this is a joke, it's not funny."

"That's nice dear," answered Matilda absentmindedly, before she began pouring the unbrewed, cold, tea stained water into cups, still merrily humming the little tune to herself.

Ruby's mouth dropped open in bewilderment. Her mother wasn't making any sense at all, neither in her actions nor in her dialogue. It was impossible to draw any conclusions to her apparent sudden onset of madness. The children were still not entirely convinced that this wasn't an elaborate and cruel joke, or if she was suffering from some form of amnesia.

They watched her for a while longer, hoping to see either an improvement if she was in fact feeling unwell, or a slight hiccup in the drama if she was indeed acting it all out.

"Are you finished eating Luke?" she asked, whisking Jamie's plate of uneaten soggy bread and raw eggs away, scraping the contents into the kitchen sink before he'd had time to respond.

Her clean up certainly suggested she really was having a problem developing in her mind, and more scarily, the severity of it seemed to be more in line with a person who had been suffering with dementia for quite some years, not one you'd expect from a person who was perfectly well the day before.

Matilda opened the cupboard and began stacking the unwashed dishes in among the clean ones, unaware that she was doing anything unusual, before setting her mind back to the task of making the cold tea. If the children were looking for confirmation that their mother was unwell, this was it. Matilda had always been a scrupulous woman; putting unwashed dishes in with clean ones was not something she would have ever done, not even for a joke. But in her own head, she saw nothing out of the ordinary.

It was like watching a strange comedy on stage, only this was a show where the children weren't sure if they were supposed to laugh, or call for a doctor.

Matilda hummed her strange repetitive tune while she continued to make the tea, adding some milk to the cold concoction before proudly placing a cup in front of each child. By now her behaviour was getting very tedious to observe and the irritating tune was becoming infuriating.

Scarlet suddenly tutted very loudly, as if the cork holding back her frustration was abruptly blown out.

"Mum, just sit down for a minute will you," she snapped sharply.

Matilda stopped in her tracks like a toy whose batteries had instantly run flat. Her tune was cut short of the last annoying few notes and her eyes looked worryingly vacant, but her facial expression suggested that she was being chastised.

"Did I do something wrong?" she asked, obediently taking a seat next to her daughter as if *she* were the child.

Scarlet felt instantly guilty. She hadn't meant to sound so angry; she had only meant to stop her mother from acting so strangely.

"I'm sorry Mum," she apologised sheepishly. "We were just worried about you; you're not acting like you normally do," she explained.

"Aww, that's nice dear?" replied Matilda with a renewed smile. Her eyes twinkled with contentment despite her mind being in complete tatters. There was absolutely nothing troubling her at all, her eyes mimicked how she felt like windows to her soul.

"Are you feeling okay Mum?" Scarlet tried again, this time taking a slightly different approach. "Only, you seem a bit forgetful this morning. Have you noticed... anything at all?"

She felt her cheeks flush pink at asking such an obnoxious, impertinent question. She was simply trying to distinguish if her mother was feeling unwell, but yet again, it suddenly dawned on her how rude she had inadvertently sounded.

"Of course I'm okay Pamela, what a strange question. I couldn't feel better actually," she answered, sounding more like an adult again, despite calling Scarlet, Pamela. "Please all of you though, stop the questions now. I feel perfectly well and actually very... well – free today. It's really rather lovely. You know, I don't remember the last time I felt so stress free and relaxed."

Her eyes sparkled in the light, catching the sun as it radiated through the kitchen window. It seemed pointless asking her anything else; she obviously didn't believe there was a problem. She hadn't even seemed to notice her memory was falling short as far as the children's names were concerned, let alone anything else. It seemed wrong to make her feel uncomfortable when she showed such good form as far as her emotional wellbeing was concerned.

"Okay Mum, that's good then," said Scarlet, withdrawing her concern reluctantly.

The fact that Matilda didn't notice anything out of the ordinary didn't make the children feel any less concerned for their mother. There was something terribly wrong and there was nothing they could do about it. It was hard not to watch her; she was now recklessly sabotaging another poor house plant, feeding it with a solution of washing up liquid and soluble paracetamol.

She'll be furious when she realises what she's done, thought Scarlet.

Dennis got up from his chair and gently pecked Matilda on the cheek giving an arrogant sideways smirk at the children.

"Would you like the radio on Mum? You usually like to listen to it in the mornin'," said Ruby in an attempt to turn her frustration away from the sneers of Dennis.

"Yes. Now there's a good idea. Would ya like some music on Tilly?" he mocked, smiling again at Ruby with the same disgusting look which suggested he knew only too well what was going on.

"No darling, I'm okay. Thank you for asking though. Really, none of ya need to worry; I'm feeling remarkably well and very light today," she smiled again reassuringly. "Now – enough of this silliness. Who wants some breakfast? I will make ya all some lovely eggs. I know how much ya all like 'em."

Unaware of the abhorrent mess she had already made with her last attempts, she waited expectantly for the children's requests. A second serving of this repugnant offering was the last thing the children wanted to see slopped up in front of them again. Scarlet heaved at just the thought of a second helping, quickly moving her hand in front of her mouth just to hold back the urge to vomit.

"No, we're all good, thanks Mum," said Ruby, understanding the sheer look of horror in her sibling's faces. "We have to be gettin' to school anyway."

The children were sure that Dennis had something to do with this. He hadn't wanted her to go running to the police with her stories today. This was all a bit too convenient.

"When ya come 'ome this afternoon, I want to take y'all into town," she called after the children before they stepped out of the front door. "It'll be nice to spend a few hours together, don't ya think?"

The children didn't quite know how to respond to this sudden, lovely gesture. She hadn't shown this much generosity since their father had died four years ago, but as extraordinary as it seemed, the children were not about to let their mother forget her suggested trip when they returned home.

The children rushed home after school that day. Strangely enough, Matilda hadn't forgotten her promise. Perhaps it was something she really had set her heart on doing, or better still, the children hoped her earlier amnesia had worn off.

They caught the bus into town and together they walked around, browsing from one shop to another looking at all the lovely items displayed in the windows. Everything seemed to be so expensive, not that it mattered to the children. Spending time together felt much more important than buying anything anyway. It almost felt that Matilda was trying to make up for the time in recent years that had been lost. This was a moment for just the children and her, leaving Dennis behind where he belonged.

Chapter Nine
A Trip into Town

They had just wondered up through the town towards Stokes, an old fashioned tea room which had been built on a bridge over the River Witham, when Ruby noticed her mother's face beginning to appear vague again. There was a sudden look of emptiness in her eyes that suggested she didn't have a clue where she was.

"Mum, I'm here!" said Ruby, catching her mother's attention, drawing her wondering eyes back in to meet her own. "Shall we go and sit down for a while?"

"Yes, let's sit down," she repeated childishly back to Ruby.

Pushing the door open, Jamie led the way into the café and pulled a chair out for Matilda to sit down on. A pretty waitress with brown hair tied neatly in a bun came over after a short while.

"Good afternoon ma'am, what can I get you?" she asked, addressing her question at Matilda.

Ruby was just about to apologise for taking up space and explain that their mum was feeling a bit out of sorts, when Matilda spoke up, cutting her short.

"Ooohh – how exciting! What a lovely girl you are, how very kind. Well – I think I would like a cappuccino and the children can all have a thick, chocolate milkshake. Thank you."

The waitress smiled nervously before turning away with her order, leaving Matilda sitting patiently with the confounded children at the table.

Of course, neither the waitress nor Matilda had any idea what had just taken place, but the children understood very well that their mother had just ordered a very special treat without realising that she would have to pay for this extravagance.

"Mum! You do know that this'll cost a small fortune, don't you?" whispered Jamie, when he was certain the waitress was out of ear shot.

"Oh, it'll be okay. I have a few pounds in my purse I think – if it comes to that. Anyway, I don't think the nice lady wants any money. You heard her ask what we wanted didn't you?"

Jamie looked at his sisters and sighed. He only hoped that Matilda had enough to pay for this, otherwise it could be quite embarrassing.

A few minutes later the waitress came back carrying a tray of chocolate thick shakes and Matilda's coffee.

"Is there anything else I can get for you?" she asked politely, poising with her pen in her right hand ready to take an order for anything else.

Scarlet was very quick this time to decline the offer before her mother decided it would be a good idea to order caviar and crackers with the best champagne.

"No. Thank you very much. We're okay now." She smiled at the waitress who nodded, then turned swiftly away, sensing that something wasn't quite right.

"Why did ya tell her no? I'd 'ave liked some carrot cake or some of that strawberry gateau in the fridge over there," said Matilda sounding extremely disappointed. She pointed towards the glass refrigerated counter filled with lots of well decorated cakes. "You never let me have anything nice, it's not fair."

Jamie's eyebrows rose into his forehead and his jaw dropped in synchronisation.

"You'd have to pay for all that Mum. Why would the waitress just let you have it for nothin'? This is a café not yer friend's house," he explained as best as he could in a hushed voice, trying to remain as discreet as possible without drawing any unwanted or embarrassing attention to themselves from the other customers.

"I'm hungry though!" She protested immaturely.

"You're only hungry because you've seen the cake. If ya hadn't seen it, you'd not be bothered. Wait till we get home Mum, it's cheaper," he explained, realising he was starting to sound more like her father than her son.

Matilda scowled angrily at Jamie, adamant that she really was hungry. She had just been about to argue again when Ruby diverted her attention, grabbing her hand tightly in her own.

"Let's just have our drinks Mum, when we get home you can have some cake."

Matilda huffed in defeat. "Okay, but I don't know why I can't just have some now." Her eyes glazed over as she continued to stare hungrily at the chilled desserts.

"Come on then, let's get goin' if we are all finished," said Jamie impatiently, just as soon as Matilda had finished sipping her coffee. "Before Mum does something even more embarrassing."

Everyone was in agreement with this; Matilda was becoming troublesome, and trying to dictate what she might do next was causing the children to become quite anxious.

Helping Matilda to her feet, the children paid the bill and left the café, pushing Matilda out the door first, but her mind was distracted again almost immediately at the sight of a pretty little gift shop. It was a quaint little shop built in Tudor times with traditional black timber frames and a croaked black door. They had passed this shop many times in years gone by without going inside, but today, Matilda was captivated by the goods on display in the shop's window.

"I want to look in there," she said, making a bee line straight for the entrance.

The children panicked in alarm. It had taken all their effort to convince her to leave the café; allowing her to walk freely into another pretty shop hardly seemed like a good idea.

"No, I don't think so Mum," said Ruby nervously, grabbing Matilda by the sleeve of her coat before she was able to disappear into the shop.

There was a reason they had never ventured inside before, even they knew that beautiful hand-made items came with a price, and that price was normally one they couldn't afford.

"What if she thinks that she can just put anything that takes her fancy straight into her handbag?" she continued, still trying to hold their mother back.

"More worryingly, what if she decides to throw a tantrum this time if she's told she can't afford something? Can you imagine how embarrassing it would be, having to explain to the shop keeper that she's not well?" added Jamie, remembering the scolding frown she had already dealt him in the tea room.

"I only want to see," begged Matilda, still tugging to free herself from Ruby's grip, making the children feel suddenly very guilty.

Ruby sighed, resigning herself to the fact that however they felt about their mother's behaviour, she was still their mother, rather than the child she was becoming.

"Come on, let's have a quick look then," she huffed against her better judgement leading a very animated Matilda into the shop. A little brass bell tinkled above their heads as the door was pushed open and Matilda looked up in delight.

"Look at that," she giggled with glee, pointing at the funny little trinket that had amused her so easily. "It sounds like Santa's sleigh at Christmas."

Scarlet caught ruby's eye as the girls held back a snigger. She must have sounded terribly silly to the shop assistant, but he remained professional and pretended he didn't hear as he continued wrapping a gift for a customer.

The shop was full of hand-crafted gifts, fragrant-smelling pomanders, hand-made soft toys and children's clothes. On the back wall, a row of pretty little pocket handkerchiefs sat in stacked piles, all neatly arranged to show off their designs.

Matilda was instantly drawn to them like a moth to a flame; she couldn't help but pick a few up, examining each one in her hand, turning them as if trying to find a fault. The handkerchiefs had been embroidered with small flowers stitched immaculately with precise detail around the edges.

"I like these!" she said, holding them up to the shop assistant to see. "They're very soft. Are they silk?"

"No ma'am they're cotton, but they are lovely aren't they!" he answered, walking swiftly towards her.

"Not again!" hissed Jamie under his breath.

"Well I'd still like them please!" replied Matilda adamantly; shoving them directly into the shop assistant's hand.

"Certainly! Would you like them wrapped up ma'am?"

"Mum! Are you sure 'bout this? You do realise that you have to buy these, don't you?" asked Scarlet cautiously.

"Yes of course I know that. I'm not silly you know," Matilda snapped in answer, her voice sounding a little offended that Scarlet had presumed she was too stupid to not understand this.

"There's three here ma'am, is that correct?" asked the shop assistant, talking as he wrapped each of them in pretty tissue paper before placing them neatly in an expensive looking paper bag.

"Unless you have something nice for a boy too?" Matilda answered back hopefully.

"Actually, we do have some rather nice ones just on the other side with letters sewn onto them. Or there are some with embroidered names!" He pointed across to the other side of the shop. "Just next to the window."

Matilda hadn't seen these and hurried over to the other side where he had pointed. Neat piles of masculine looking handkerchiefs were arranged in straight lines, all in different colours and in alphabetical order. It didn't take long for her to see one there with Jamie's name on. She made a grab for it as though she thought it might be snatched away from under her nose before she could purchase it herself.

"I'll take this one too," she said, placing it down on the counter next to the paper bag.

Her face beamed with pride outside the shop as she handed the children each one of the handkerchiefs, and although no one knew it at the time, this would be the last thing she would ever buy them.

Chapter Ten
She's Fine

The days went by, but Matilda's state of mind did not get better. Her mind became ever more vacant, but still she refused to understand there was any problem at all.

The children came home from school one day to find their mother in the garden with the vacuum cleaner, hoovering the lawn. A long extension from the house trailed across the lawn like a malnourished snake as she busied herself, sucking up great lumps of soil and chasing bumble bees with the hose in an attempt to suck them to their deaths.

In fairness, it was quite comical watching her chase these buzzing insects around, her frustration obviously pumped to hysteria as she tried in vain to eradicate them.

However, the humour was short lived when eventually her actions were serious enough to put an end to any denial that there was anything wrong and it could not be ignored or dismissed any longer.

Upon entering the back gate, the children caught a glimpse of something peculiar in the fishpond. The surface was covered with a blanket of thick, green bubbles, and a head bobbed on the top like a football surrounded with soap. Realising something was terribly wrong, the children ran across the lawn to discover that their fears were well founded. Matilda really *was* taking a bath in the fish pond.

The beautiful, fully grown Koi which the children had bought with their mother from the nursery when they were still tiny fingerlings lay floating on their sides at the top of the water gasping for air. Mounds of frothy bubbles surrounded them as though they were lying on fluffy, green beads of polystyrene.

"Mum! What are you doing?" gasped Scarlet in horror when they saw her shivering away in the dirty pond. The cold water lapped around her shoulders leaving an edge of slime on her skin like it had been painted onto her. Green algae filled bubbles covered her hair and popped sporadically, splashing particles of the pond water into her face.

Matilda's sad, weary eyes met Scarlet's. She appeared to be in a terribly confused state, like a small child full of uncertainty.

"The water's gone cold," she complained. "Can I come out now?" She sobbed pitifully.

The children stared at each other in dismay; she couldn't possibly think they had instructed her to get into the pond to bathe.

"Let me get you a towel first Mum. Just wait a second."

Scarlet rushed into the house, reappearing hastily with a large bath sheet. "Come on, get out and I'll wrap you up – Ruby, will ya go inside and run Mum a warm bath while I help her out?"

Ruby didn't answer; she had already understood the urgency and had headed indoors to prepare the water.

Keeping her anger locked inside for the time being, Scarlet helped Matilda out of the pond and wrapped her tightly in the fluffy warm towel.

"Let's get inside and warm up properly," said Scarlet helping her mother upstairs and into the bathroom. "Look! Ruby's run you a nice warm bath."

Matilda stood expressionless as she stared at the bath full of warm water. "Come on Mum, step inside," encouraged Scarlet eagerly.

The girls helped her into the bath, gently washing her skin, splashing her with the warm water, cleaning her from the decomposing matter which clung to her from the pond's sediment.

"What made ya think the pond would be a good place to bath?" asked Scarlet curiously after a few minutes of silence, while removing another leech from her mother's back. She wasn't even sure if her mother remembered the incident despite it only just happening.

"What was tha' dear?" she answered. Her vacant eyes now replaced with a look of fear and confusion.

"You were in the garden pond Mum, just a few minutes ago! You do remember, don't you?" replied Scarlet, trying not to sound too concerned about it.

Matilda stared vaguely into space and the eerie tune slipped from her lips again, reverberating off the bathroom walls.

"Mum!" called Scarlet, with a firmer tone now as she desperately tried to get her mother to understand the severity of the situation. "Why did you go in the pond?"

Matilda jumped in fright at her sudden raised voice, immediately breaking the spell binding trance.

"Was I dear?" said Matilda in a surprised tone.

Scarlet sighed despondently.

"Do you know who I am? Do you even know *your* name?"

Matilda's gaze met Scarlet's as she eased her mother's chin, lifting her face to meet her own. Her eyes were warm with a distant, shadowy look as if she were trying to remember something important, the ghost of a woman betrayed, desperately attempting to unlock her puzzled mind. And then in a split second, Matilda's concentration disappeared again, resuming the look of insanity.

"That's nice dear," she answered. Her soft smile returned to her face as though her answer was satisfactory to the question asked.

A silence fell over them now, uncertain as to what they should say next, but they didn't have need to worry as Matilda quite unexpectedly broke the awkward silence.

"You know, you're very kind letting me take a bath in your house. Your mother must be so proud," she spoke softly, her eyes remaining lost in her glazed over absence. "I'm not sure I know your mother, do I?"

"She doesn't even know who she is anymore," mumbled Scarlet in dismay. "What we goin' to do Ruby?"

"We can't do anythin' unless Dennis gives his permission, but he insists there's nothin' wrong with her."

"Can I go home now?" interrupted Matilda suddenly, who was still sitting with bewilderment in the bath.

The girls' vacant expressions matched those of Matilda's. They didn't know how to respond to this.

"Can I go home now?" she asked again, the small child in her becoming more prevalent in her puzzled state of mind.

"You are home Mum," Scarlet replied, not knowing how else to react to such an upsetting question. "Come on, let's get you dried and in some warm bed clothes."

Matilda took Scarlet's outstretched hand and stepped out of the bath while Ruby dried her down, slipping a soft pink, brushed cotton nightie over her head.

"Here, put your arms through the sleeves," encouraged Ruby, holding a fluffy dressing gown around her shoulders. "Now your slippers. Just pop these on your feet," said Ruby helping her slide her bare feet into the spongey, soft, inners. "There you go; that's better isn't it?" Ruby continued softly, realising with every word, her tone sounded more and more like the kind spoken to comfort a child. She took her mother's hand and paraded her back into the safety of her bedroom. "See if you can get some rest now!"

Once the girls were out of the bedroom and had pulled her door too, Scarlet's anger appeared for the first time that day. Her eyes narrowed and the forced smile she had worn for her mother's benefit slipped off her face like water on wax.

"It's about time Dennis started answering some questions; this can't keep goin' on forever. Mum was lucky we came home when we did today. I don't get why Dennis isn't watchin' her anyway."

"Be my guest!" said Jamie sarcastically. "Dad's hardly goin' to answer anythin' though is he? You're more likely to get blood out of a stone than get 'im to discuss owt with you."

"So what would you have me do then? We can't just keep ignoring what's goin' on," snapped Scarlet in frustration.

"Don't ask – just let him know Mum's safe, and go from there. If he asks anythin', you can draw him into conversation on his terms," suggested Jamie.

"Are you comin' then? Or should me an' Ruby just go down on our own?"

"It'll look like I put ya up to it if I go too. Nah, I'll wait 'ere till ya ge' back."

"Fine! I jus' thought with Dennis being *your* dad, it might be better comin' from you was all."

"Dad's no better with me than he is with you, you know that. Anyway, it's your mum you want answers for, it's probably better if you girls go on your own."

With that agreed, Scarlet and Ruby nervously made their way downstairs with a plan in mind of how they hoped the conversation would go. They knew Dennis would be in the front room with the company of the television, soothing his tired overworked body with his usual glass of whiskey. They weren't disillusioned; the television could be heard before they even got to the bottom of the stairs.

Ruby tentatively raised her hand to knock on the door, her nerves growing in strength, her hand poised ready, but then it froze as if it suddenly had a mind of its own. All the children knew that Dennis didn't like being disturbed. Disrupting him could result in a punishment, not just for one, but for them all.

Scarlet nudged her sister,

"Go on, knock," she whispered encouragingly.

Ruby's frozen arm melted with Scarlet's incitement, allowing her to finish the knock she had attempted to make moments earlier.

"Wha' d'ya want?" came a muffled voice from the other side of the door. It sounded like Dennis had been disturbed from taking a sip of his all-important liquor.

Scarlet plucked up the courage to open the door, carefully pushing down the lever and letting the door swing open. He was slumped exactly how the girls thought he would be with his fat backside attached to his usual comfy chair with heavy duty stitching, his eyes glued firmly on the television. He didn't even blink; his eyes seemed incapable of moving in their direction.

Scarlet's heart removed itself from her chest as if it had somehow grown legs and lodged itself in her throat. The sheer audacity he displayed at a time when his wife was in such a deluded state of mind sickened her to the stomach.

He just sat there, seemingly detached from anything which was going on, unaffected and motionless.

Gulping hard, swallowing back her emotions, momentarily disregarding the frustration she felt, Scarlet stood purposefully in the doorway with her arms folded tightly together, desperately trying to appear confident as she stood by her sister's side. She cleared her throat as she remembered the rehearsed lines from the back of her mind.

"Dennis! Mum is in her room now. She's been bathed and cleaned, hopefully she will get some sleep."

Dennis didn't move; his eyes remained stuck fast to the screen like it was the most important thing in the world. Then almost as if he had a perfect answer, his brow furled suddenly into tight concentration as he forced out a loud fart.

"Why ya tellin' me that for? I couldn't give a damn wha' she does. Wha' d'ya wan' me to do abou' it?"

"Well, we just thought you should know she's okay now," retorted Scarlet angrily. "She is your wife after all."

He didn't answer. The girls weren't really sure if he had heard them, but there was no way he couldn't have.

"We were thinking Dennis," she tried again – perhaps something more tactful. "D'ya think it's about time Mum saw a doctor? She doesn't seem to know who she is, she doesn't even know where home is anymore and she…"

Without warning, Dennis abruptly snapped, miraculously leaping to his feet without the surgery Scarlet feared he may have so badly needed in order to detach himself from the seat *and* peeled his eyes off the television all in one go. His face turned a vibrant shade of purple as he slammed his glass of whiskey down onto the table.

"ARE YOU DARING TO TELL ME HOW TO TAKE CARE OF YOUR MOTHER? DO YOU REALLY THINK I NEED TELLING BY CHILDREN HOW TO BEHAVE? I THINK NOT – SO I WILL THANK YOU TO MIND YOUR OWN BUSINESS, STOP BEING SO MELODRAMATIC, AND LEAVE ME TO MINE," he shouted.

Bits of phlegm sprayed from his mouth in his rage showering them with light droplets of his putrid, alcoholic saliva.

They weren't going to get any help from Dennis, although they already knew this before they had tried. He wasn't about to help anyone, least of all someone he had cursed himself.

The girls felt helpless, the realisation finally sinking in as they saw the disappointment in each other's faces. If they were going to get any help for their mother it would have to be of their own accord, without his approval.

Turning away deterred, the girls climbed back upstairs to tell Jamie and Rose what had happened, leaving Dennis alone to continue staring at the all-important television screen and sipping his whiskey.

"How do we even get Mum help? Where do we go?" asked Rose when her sisters reappeared.

"I think we just call the doctor. Mums got the number in her little phone book, it's in her handbag. I'll get it," replied Ruby with enthusiasm, hurrying away to retrieve it.

Moments later, Ruby returned holding the little black book.

"I got it," she said, waving it in the air before handing it over to Jamie.

"Who's going to make the call?" asked Scarlet, shaking with nerves while Jamie flicked through the pages.

None of them really felt courageous enough to sneak downstairs to pick up the phone. If they were caught using the phone without permission, Dennis would go crazy, particularly after he'd already given his final, ridiculous, decision.

"I'll go," said Jamie bravely glancing up from the pages fleetingly. "I think it's probably my turn to risk a good hidin' this time anyway."

"Be careful then," said Scarlet as he tiptoed quietly away.

The stairs creaked in agonised pain as his foot gently pressed down on their surface. Dennis practically flew out the front room as though his chair had electrocuted him, catapulting him to the foot of the stairs where Jamie hovered on the wounded step like a statue, clutching the little black book, knowing full well that he was in trouble.

"Wha' d'ya think ya doin'?" he hissed. His eyes flicked over him quickly before settling on the book in his hand. "Aahh – I see. Ya thought you'd defy me did ya?" He grabbed the book from Jamie's hand and ripped it in half, tearing at the pages until tiny shreds of the book's pages lay in tatters all over the floor.

His calm tone dissolved; his temper exploded to another level.

"IF I SAY THAT WOMAN DOESN'T NEED HELP, THEN THAT'S WHAT I MEAN."

His words were precise as he emphasised every letter in his wrath as it flared inside him like a rocket. He flung his hand out towards Jamie, smacking him hard in the face and knocking him to the floor before grabbing his ear and dragging him back upstairs to his room. "GET IN YOUR ROOM AND STAY IN THERE BOY."

The door slammed behind him as Jamie was thrown stumbling into a heap. The clink of metal told the girls that Dennis had locked Jamie in his room, the bolt had been slid across and that was where Dennis intended Jamie to stay for the rest of the day.

Dennis's ugly face then appeared around the girls' door.

"Don't bother tryin' anything clever either, yer mother's fine. If any of ya try to go aroun' me, ya can expect to be punished too."

He slammed the door shut, leaving the girls alone to themselves, their thoughts in tatters as they realised that there was nothing they could do to help – unless Dennis permitted it.

Several hours passed, and at last the girls heard Dennis plod out to his shed dragging his broken-down shoes across the ground. There was no mistaking that sound; a scuffing drag over the concrete in the backyard had become the noise the children associated with Dennis and his shed over the years.

The girls seized their chance. The coast was clear to let Jamie out for a few minutes to use the bathroom and get a drink. Slipping across the landing to his room, the girls pushed the bolt back across the door. Jamie's face popped round as it opened, his cheek looked a bit bruised, but he still grinned with a wryly contagiousness at the girls on the other side.

"Are you okay Jamie?" asked Scarlet.

"Yeah, don't worry, I'm fine," he said, dismissing the obvious pain he must have been in, "I do need to use the loo though."

He pushed by quickly, knowing that time was limited; Dennis could come back in at any time without warning. But while the coast was clear and with only a few chances available, Ruby grabbed the opportunity, hurrying downstairs and snatched the biscuit jar from the cupboard. She slipped her hand inside pulling out four digestive biscuits then pushed them underneath the folds of her cardigan before hurrying back upstairs to Jamie, almost bumping into him as he reappeared from the bathroom.

"Here take these in case you get hungry," she said, shoving three of them into his hand, before practically throwing him back into his room.

Jamie gave a look of concern. "I can't take these Ruby! Dad knows how many are in the jar, he'll kill us if he finds out some are missin'."

"Don't worry, I've got it covered. Really, take them! Go now – you better get back, I have to lock you in."

The door closed gently and Ruby pushed the bolt back into place so that Dennis would be none the wiser.

As soon as the door was locked, Ruby turned towards her mother's room, tiptoeing in silence so as to not wake her, surreptitiously placing the fourth biscuit by her bedside table. It would look as though Matilda had eaten a few biscuits and there was just the one remaining. Hopefully Dennis wouldn't ask questions if he could see that Matilda had eaten them, it wouldn't occur to him that it wasn't as it seemed, besides, even if Dennis did ask about them, Ruby knew her mother wouldn't recall what it was doing there anyway.

Matilda looked so peaceful as she lay in bed, oblivious to what Ruby had planted by her side. Bending over her mother, Ruby gently laid a kiss on her forehead and slipped out of the room leaving her to sleep.

The next morning, as expected, Matilda woke up with no recollection of the day before. She felt particularly tired even though she had slept for so long.

Her eyes kept dropping whenever she sat down, but when she tipped a cup of coffee over herself as her eyes drifted off into yet another sleep; Ruby demanded that she return to bed.

Matilda didn't argue. Taking her by the hand, she followed her daughter to her room where Ruby tucked her comfortably back into her bed.

"Stay in here Mum. Sleep for as long as ya need."

Matilda's dreary eyes tried to smile, but couldn't quite manage to masquerade her weariness. She didn't resist, but instead allowed her eyes to close shut.

That was the last time the children saw their mother.

Chapter Eleven
Missing

It was the Sunday morning; two days after Matilda had taken a bath in the garden pond. The children went downstairs half expecting to see their mother feeling a bit better now and less exhausted, after all, she had slept most of the day before. Perhaps she would be busy making some strange concoction in the kitchen. It was quite normal nowadays to see her behaving unusually, but she wasn't downstairs, or outside mopping the yard, or anywhere else visible.

They hunted for her for a good part of the morning before they finally resigned themselves to asking Dennis if he knew where she was. He was sitting in his shed when the children found him, the door slightly ajar with his head hung down, muttering to himself under his breath.

His care free attitude was less than welcome and his unwillingness to help find her seemed even more callous.

"D'ya know where Mum is Dennis?" asked Ruby curiously.

Dennis glanced up, cold and expressionless,

"She'll be back," was all he could offer as an answer.

"Don't you even care where she is? She could be hurt, in a ditch somewhere, or lost and not know how to get home again. What's wrong with you? Why won't you help?" asked Scarlet in disgust, realising her whereabouts was no concern of his.

Dennis shrugged his shoulders and carried on studying a piece of circuit board, tugging at a few of the transmitters which appeared to be a little on the loose side.

Scarlet huffed angrily and glared at him, but he didn't seem to notice how frustrated any of the children were getting. At last, knowing that their pleas for help were falling on stupid ears, the children stomped away in outrage.

Dennis had assumed that Matilda would come home at some point, but she didn't, not that day, nor the next – not ever.

The children wondered if Dennis had even been bothered enough to file a missing person's report. He seemed to disregard her disappearance with such ease that the children began to think he had somehow hatched a plan to have got rid of her for good. All kinds of scenarios played out in their heads. They didn't know if their mother was even alive, and his vile attitude suggested that he couldn't care less.

"Did you at least file a report with the police?" asked Jamie boldly over dinner one evening, a few weeks after Matilda had mysteriously disappeared.

Dennis managed to glance up from his plate and tutted in exasperation. "Wha' ya talkin' abou'?" he muffled drearily.

"You know, with Mum. Did you file a missing person's report for her? She would have been considered vulnerable at the time she went missing, wouldn't she? We were jus' wonderin' if you at least managed to do that for her?"

"Oh right, I see. As it 'appens I did, yes," he coughed unconvincingly as though he were trying to clear his throat.

"And, what did they say?" Jamie bravely delved a little deeper, prompting him to give a satisfactory explanation.

Dennis sighed with disdain. "What does it matter wha' they said? She's gone, that's all ya need to know."

"It matters to us!" Scarlet snapped scornfully, just about holding herself back from leaping at him from across the table.

"If it's of any consequence to ya, they said she'd more than likely jus' gone on a road trip or run away from you kids, and I wouldn't 'ave blamed 'er if she 'ad either. Does that answer your tiresome questioning now?" he spat in contempt, slamming his knife and fork down irritably hard on the table sending them into a little dance.

The children weren't convinced that he had actually informed the police, but arguing with him was futile. Dennis had no interest in his wife's safety and hadn't cared for some considerable time.

The children didn't question him any further; the rest of mealtime was completed in an awkward silence. His pathetic explanation would have to do for the time being they decided, and perhaps in time the truth would come out.

The children pushed the food around on their plates in an attempt to make it look as though they had eaten enough. Since their mother had absconded, the quality of the meals had taken a downward plummet; Dennis had never been a cook, that side of things had always been done by Matilda, and the children could see why this was the case. His efforts to prepare anything remotely edible were nothing short of pathetic. However, the quality of his handy work when it came down to discipline was just as good as it had always been, that was an area in which he had always excelled.

"Can we leave the table?" asked Scarlet, unable to stomach any more of Dennis's dreadful cooking.

Dennis peered up from his plate, quickly scanned the contents of her plate and nodded. Neither she nor any or the other children wanted to sit with Dennis a moment longer, they were quick to respond, swiftly excusing themselves after Scarlet had left.

After the children had completed their daily chores, they went upstairs to bed, which was a time Scarlet in particular looked forward to. She had a secret which had made life more bearable for her; a secret she believed belonged entirely to her, because bedtime was the time when she could escape. In her dreams, Scarlet was free and happy, her mind offered her solace and safety and in Dreamworld Scarlet was powerful.

Chapter Twelve
Smoke and Ashes

For many years Scarlet had used her imagination as an escape, she had built a new world where she controlled what happened. Dreamworld was her world which she believed had been shaped to suit her.

But apart from finding solitude from the misery of the waking world, Scarlet's dreams gave her special gifts where unimaginable things could happen, things that were impossible to achieve when she was awake. While other children her age saw going to bed as a punishment, she saw it as an adventure. But tonight when she went to Dreamworld, she hardly recognised where she was.

In Dreamworld Scarlet was accustomed to seeing verdant surroundings, rivers flowing with clear, sparking water and animals both strange and indigenous inhabiting the lands. Tonight though, as she stood transfixed to the ground, a dose of chilling uneasiness swept over her so that she could barely breathe. Her chest hurt, it felt crushed like she had breathed in the air she remembered from the fire all those years ago.

Scarlet coughed, desperate to clear her lungs of the ash, her eyes stung as she tried to focus on the land in front of her, it was as though she had stepped into another world filled with unfamiliar and troubling scenes.

Her heart raced in her chest, pounding against her ribs like an animal caught in a cage. She didn't like where this dream was going and she didn't like it even more so that she was unable to stop what she feared might happen. Normally, Scarlet's dreams were lucid enough so that she was able to re-shape them to fit her own desires, but tonight her dream was not hers to control.

Scarlet rubbed her eyes, desperate to see what was going on, but fearful at the same time. She feared that she would see the smoke bellowing from her house, licking the sides of the building as the monster inside consumed the home she loved, she feared hearing the windows explode and the walls fall down, but most of all she feared seeing her father being brought out of the house like a rag doll again.

Scarlet wished she could shut her eyes or turn away, but this dream would not afford her such mercy, she was forced to watch as the smoke died down, until at last she was able to see through the dark cloud.

There was no house fire as she had suspected, no fiery monster from hell, but there had been a fire.

The land was not how she remembered it to be.

Huge plumes of smoke rose high into the air, dispersing into the sky and creating a thick smog over the land like a dark shadow. Ash fell thickly from the cloud like snow, coating the land below in a layer of powdery death. Bodies of tall trees had collapsed like fallen soldiers leaving their stumps to crackle and slowly burn to the ground.

This had to be Armageddon, and if it wasn't, she didn't want to imagine how much worse Armageddon was going to look.

Everything that had once been green and beautiful now lay dead. The terrain gaped open with the deep scars of a deadly disease which had spread through its veins as it searched like a cancer, consuming anything green, anything which may have had a future.

The aftermath now lay in disarray, spread out across the land as far as the eye could see in the form of a thick, silvery blanket of powder.

The land was dry and barren, prickly heat still permeated the ground where the fires had burned, purging every drop of moisture from the surface. Where there had once been flowing rivers, dried, cracked, riverbeds of dirt and dust replaced them.

The creatures which had lived there seemed to have disappeared, rendering the land completely lifeless. Scarlet couldn't understand what had happened, this was certainly not the way she had remembered it.

The breeze lifted a little, whipping up a dust storm, sending funnels of upward spiralling columns into the air. Her hair blew in her face, and automatically her hand retrieved it, holding it back behind her ears while shielding her eyes from the dust.

Scarlet squinted through the disturbance now fogging her sight, straining as she scanned the wilderness for an answer.

There was something that made her feel particularly uneasy, but the distressing scene made it impossible to understand the confusion raging in her head. She knew it had something to do with the white picket fence behind her. Its posts had been burnt back to the ground like cigarette stubs, the small, twirling, spirals of smoke twisted into the air like the tails on a kite, holding her hostage in a trance while she tried to focus… and then like a whisper in the wind she heard the faintest of sounds.

Her heart jumped from her chest as a vibrating rhythm pounded through her body from the ground, travelling through her and waking her from the blindness which clouded her vision.

Horses' hooves – Scarlet felt suddenly nauseous and dizzy as she realised what had troubled her.

Through the dust she could just about make out a handful of the wild horses which had grazed in the meadow on the other side of that white fence before it had burned. There weren't nearly as many as she remembered though, a huge part of the herd was missing.

Her heart picked up a notch again as the adrenalin poured into her veins for a second time, suddenly releasing her feet from the ground, allowing her to sprint towards the herd. Perhaps she mistook how many there were, she hoped as she ran. But as she approached, the full extent of her fear was revealed.

All over the dusty ground lay the bodies of the beautiful animals, all of them bearing the signs of scorch marks and dehydration. The ones still standing didn't look much better, their bones protruded, turning them into walking skeletons, their dull, lifeless eyes sunk deep inside their skulls, but at least they were still alive.

Scarlet dropped to her knees and sobbed; it was too much for her to take. The pain mirrored too closely the suffering she had witnessed watching her home burn to the ground and losing her father, causing her heart to ache and weep bitterly.

Scarlet woke with a start, almost throwing herself out of bed in confusion, leaving her thoughts in a state of shock and complete horror.
Her brow was beaded with sweat and tears prickled her eyes. Her mind raced with questions, why hadn't she been able to stop such an awful dream, and why on earth would she have dreamed up something so dreadful to begin with?

Perhaps it was her sub-conscious thoughts reliving the fire, she thought. But this idea didn't really make much sense to her; if that had been the case, then surely she would have dreamed about the house fire as it happened. Dreamworld had always been her escape; why would her mind destroy it so wickedly?

It had been a comfort to know that in her world, everything had been moulded to her liking, particularly because in the waking world nothing was within her control. Now it was beginning to look like even her own thoughts might not be within her control.

Scarlet puzzled over her worries, and then a thought even more troubling suddenly occurred to her. She remembered how her mother's mind had been taken away from her, how she eventually forgot who she was; maybe she was going crazy, or perhaps her mind was being taken from her?

Scarlet was particularly quiet that day in school, spending most of her time trying to fathom what could possibly have happened. Nothing came to mind, and that just left her feeling more and more frustrated and vulnerable.

"Hello Scarlet. Are you still with us?"

A distant voice invaded her thoughts, snapping Scarlet out of yet another daydream.

"Sorry miss," answered Scarlet sheepishly.

"Try to keep your thoughts in class please. You're not focused today and I would like you to at least pretend to be paying attention," said Mrs Saxby dryly, encouraging Scarlet to hear her words for a short while, before she once again returned to her deep thoughts.

The school day finished at last, and Scarlet dragged her feet lethargically behind her as she walked home with her sisters and Jamie. The children could see the top of Dennis's silver car as they came around the corner of the cul-de-sac in which they lived. It was always parked on the drive if Dennis was at home, and unless he was in his shed, he would be waiting to quiz them about the day's events.

He had an over active mind which made him very paranoid. He believed that the children were leaving school during the hours that they were supposed to be there learning, going off somewhere – wherever somewhere was.

It was a guessing game on the children's part, as his questions would be open ended. They had to determine what he was getting at, and then try to answer them correctly without getting themselves into more trouble.

It was nauseating for the children, their stomachs twisted into sickening knots, mostly because they had no idea what Dennis would ask or what kind of mood he would be in when they got through the front door.

Today, Scarlet could have done without any added complications; her mood was already agitated, and her inability to straighten her mind had left her stressed enough without having to deal with these extra guessing games.

The children opened the front door and peered around into the house to see what kind of evening they could expect. They were still desperately hoping Dennis would be in his shed, if he were, then that would present a quiet night for them all, but to their disappointment, he was waiting in the front room.

The recognisable stench of his overpowering aftershave and cigarettes had filled the entire room with his pungent whiff. He sat there like the lord of the manor, sipping his usual whiskey on ice from a crystal tumbler, drumming his finger nails impatiently against the side of the glass implying he had been waiting for quite some time for them to return.

He looked up when he heard them come through the door. He put his glass down on the coffee table making a little clink as it touched the wooden surface. "Ah, there you are." He grunted at them, glancing at his watch in an overly exaggerated manner so as to make it very obvious he thought that the children were later than normal, and that somehow, he had been unnecessarily inconvenienced.

He stood up from his arm chair, leaving the impression of his behind on the worn cushion, and walked purposefully to the door where the children stood paralysed to the spot.

His eyes stared hard at their faces for a while, inspecting, scanning them up and down, as if searching for tell-tale signs that might give him a clue as to all the wicked and deceitful deeds they might have been getting up to.

"Sooo," he said slowly, breathing his offensive, stale breath over the children. "What *have* you been doin' today? Who's going to be the first one to tell me what you've all been up to? I know you're hiding something. You see, children are never as innocent as they would have you believe. They're always scheming, always cheating or lying, doing things they know they shouldn't be. But I'm not stupid. Bad children always get caught out in the end. So, let's see – who can tell me what I already know."

His words were slow, emphasised and meaningful. His deliberate, precise language gave the entire speech an added feeling of threat and intuition. He could make these accusations so forthright that the children actually doubted their innocence.

Maybe he was suggesting they had done something terrible earlier in the day, or perhaps he was driving towards an incident which happened weeks ago, something they had forgotten about? The children knew this was a normal question in his quiz list though, whether they had done something or not, it didn't make any difference in the long run, because Dennis's ultimate goal was to find any reason at all as to why he should punish them.

The aim of the game was to get the children to overthink things, so that there would be plenty of reasons to be punished. The thing was, the children didn't dare do anything wrong, so to think about something, often meant recalling things that were perfectly normal, everyday things to anyone else.

The children's mind now raced through scenarios, reliving the day, hoping to find anything that they could find fault with. I say hoping, in the fullest sense of the word, because not finding anything had its own implications.

"Well I'm not sure I made my bed as well as I should have done this morning," said Rose, scrambling around in her head as though she were looking for a lost toy in an Aladdin's cave in the hope that this was a good enough answer. "I think I may have left a corner unfolded."

Dennis's eyes moved down the line to the next child.

"I didn't concentrate very well on my school work today, I was a bit tired, I'm sorry," added Scarlet.

Ruby was thinking hard, turning over as many stories as she could muster in such a short space of time, none of them sounding believable enough though. She simply could not think of anything that she may or may not have done wrong. But now her time for thinking was up.

Dennis's hardened eyes settled on her, boring a hole into her head as though he were trying to read her thoughts.

"Well, wha' about you?" he snarled, glaring at her like a lunatic ready to rip her to shreds.

"I don't think I did anythin' wrong," trembled Ruby at last, after a long pause.

"Ah, I see. You're perfect then, are you?" rasped Dennis with delight, jumping on her words the second they were released from her lips. "Either you're perfect, or you're a LIAR!"

This was the exact sort of conversation Dennis had been working towards. No matter what the children said or didn't say, the cards were always stacked against them, setting them up for a no-win situation. He had hoped for at least one of them to say this, and his nasty little trick had paid off.

"No, I'm not p – perfect, I'm s-s-sorry," stammered Ruby, wishing with every breath in her body that she had managed to find a fault in her day.

"And you! Are you perfect too?" jeered Dennis, now turning his vicious attention to Jamie, his eyes resting scornfully on him.

"No Dad. I made a mark on the towel this mornin'. I didn't wash away all the toothpaste from my mouth, and I think I may 'ave accidently got some on the towel."

Jamie of course, was only guessing. He couldn't be sure he had done that at all, but he knew he had to come up with something off the top of his head as quickly as possible, just to appease his father.

Dennis was extremely pleased with the children's confessions. He would deal with Ruby in a moment, after he had found a punishment fitting for the others.

Turning his back on the children he paced back and forth up the regimental line until he had carefully considered the inappropriate penalties due.

Dennis's top lip curled into a triumphant smirk, satisfied that he had decided the price they should pay.

"Well, ya can all stand in the corner until tea time. It'll give ya time to dwell on yer many sins. Ya will pray, an' ask the Lord for forgiveness, an' don't bother comin' out until you're told to – all of ya, except our perfect little angel… *Ruby*. You can wait here fer me. I've got a special job fer ya tha' can only be done by someone who's perfect."

All the children, with the exception of Ruby, traipsed upstairs to the bedroom with Dennis following closely behind. The children took their normal positions in the bedroom corners to begin their tedious standing punishment for hours to come which would inevitably go through the night.

The bolt rasped against the frame leaving the children locked in from the outside.

Ruby was already really regretting her inability to come up with a convincing story. She had followed Dennis outside to see what he expected from her before she would be allowed to return to the locked bedroom to fulfil the rest of the assigned punishment.

"These windows are lookin' rather dir'y, don't ya think Ruby?" he snorted, talking down to her as though she were something he had stepped in on the bottom of his shoe. "I wan' them sparklin' within the hour, otherwise you'll be wishing you were more than jus' perfect."

Dennis left her to get on with the job, smirking as he turned to leave.

Ruby sighed deeply, resigning herself to the job that needed doing. An old wooden ladder stood against the house, it wasn't the safest by any means; the rubber stops from the bottom had been lost a long time ago, but it was all there was.

She struggled as she propped it up against the wall just under the sill of the top bedroom window, then trudged back to fill the bucket with water from the hose. It wasn't meant to be an easy job carrying the weight of water across the garden. Its icy contents slopped over her feet as she shuffled along, back to the waiting ladder.

"*For goodness sake,*" she sighed. She hated it when that happened, not only would she get cold due to the nip in the air, but now her feet were sopping wet too, squelching with every step she made.

Ruby plunged her hands into the water, submerging her cloth into the bucket, wringing it half dry before carefully sidling her way up the precariously balanced ladder, clinging fearfully to the sides as she climbed.

The cold water trickled its way like rivulets down her arms, dispersing into the fabric of her sleeves and sending cold shivers coursing through her body as she went about her work. With every submersion, her hands re-emerged that little bit colder, the ice biting into her fingers, permeating deeper and deeper into her flesh, searching out and freezing the tiny bones in her hands and wrists.

Having cold hands would have never been a good enough reason to stop a job half way through though. If Dennis had requested something should be done, then it had to be done – period. The only way she could take her mind off the sharp jabbing sensation was if she were to mentally distance herself from the job.

She didn't think about which windows had to be done, she just went about it in a daze on auto-pilot, cleaning and scrubbing at the panes until at last they had all been cleaned.

Ruby wiped her feet on the doormat and opened the back door, just enough so that she could call to Dennis for her work to be inspected.

He waddled through from the sitting room, his usual glass of whiskey in hand, and slipped his misshapen, worn down, old leather shoes onto his feet. "You'd better 'ave done it properly girl. If you've called me ou' 'ere for nothin', you'll wish you hadn't bin born. I'm warnin' ya!" he spat, pushing past her as though she were invisible.

Although Ruby was pretty sure she hadn't missed anything, this kind of talk always made the children feel very nervous. It was a gesture which indicated he *would* find something even if it were a microscopic speck. If he couldn't find a fault, he was the kind of person who would plant a foreign particle smack in the middle of the said window anyway.

Ruby watched nervously as Dennis wondered from window to window with obvious desperation in his inspection, hoping to discover a mishap. His eyes scanned the surfaces like a mad man in search of some kind of unknown entity. Ruby considered asking if a magnifying glass might be of some assistance to him, but thought better of it in case he took her up on her ludicrous, sarcastic offer.

Satisfied at last that the job was done well enough, he grunted,

"Looks like ya were the right one fer the job today after all. Ya can go now."

Ruby was amazed that Dennis let her get away so easily. Normally he would have loved nothing more than to drag this torment on for as long as possible, but right now, she didn't care. She was just glad to be able to return to the bedroom to see out the remainder of the punishment standing in the corner with her brother and sisters.

Scarlet didn't really care about being stood in the corner. She needed time to think about Dreamworld. It had bothered her all day. She hardly noticed the rasping sound of the bolt being drawn back across the door to let Ruby in, and hardly noticed the satisfied smirk on Dennis's face when he saw all the children stood obediently facing the walls.

She was just beginning to resign herself to the fact that she must have had a nightmare, when Jamie whispered across the room to her.

"What's bin the matter with you today?"

Scarlet didn't answer, she was still lost in thought and completely oblivious to anything going on around her.

"Oy, Scarlet," Jamie tried again, this time prodding her in the back to get her attention.

Scarlet jumped and turned around to face Jamie. "What!" she snapped.

"I said, what's the matter with you today? You're not quite yourself."

"Ya mean apart from standin' here like a bunch of lemons?" whispered Scarlet keeping to a quiet mumble.

"Huh, yeah, I know," he giggled at her likening. "It's totally unfair isn't it, but yeah, other than being stood 'ere. You've been a bit quiet is all. You were in a strange mood this mornin' and you're still actin' weird now."

Scarlet was a little surprised that anyone had noticed her apparent distance at all, but decided it couldn't hurt to tell the others what had bothered her.

"Your dad makes me so cross Jamie," she replied.

She hesitated for a moment, unsure how she might bring up what was really troubling her. Dreamworld was a figment of her imagination, so to try and drop it into the conversation like it was a real place just didn't seem fitting. Nonetheless, it had bothered her enough to make it obvious that there was a problem, and he *was* asking her after all. It couldn't hurt to at least try and make the others understand.

She began slowly, thoughtfully picking her words as she started to tell her tale.

"I had a bad dream last night is all! It was like someone had invaded my personal space, nothing in my dream was how it was meant to be. I just don't understand. I'm so confused; it doesn't even make sense to me." She sighed in resignation.

It had sounded worse than she had thought it would when she rehearsed this in her head. It sounded like nothing but a load of stupid, meaningless words that had just spewed from her mouth, and she was left feeling really rather simple.

"It doesn't matter. Forget I said anything. I can't really explain," she whispered, now in complete embarrassment. Her cheeks flushed a bright shade of crimson as she reminisced the words she had spoken, in her head. "I'm talking nonsense – I don't know what I was tryin' to say."

Jamie's attention unexpectedly perked up. He hadn't given it much thought up until this point. He believed a dream was just that, and it didn't have any direct meaning to their lives, but now he was curious.

"Ya know, it's strange ya should say that actually Scarlet. I hadn't let it bother me too much, but now ya mention it, I had an odd kind of dream too."

He paused as he thought of the right way to address his speech. It was indeed a tricky subject, and he began to understand why Scarlet had such a difficult time trying to express herself, he had just heard how ridiculous it had sounded when she had tried.

"Somethin' similar happened to me last night actually. You will all probably think I'm completely insane, but when I sleep, I have a place I go to. Don't laugh - but I call it Dreamworld."

Jamie paused in anticipation of the giggling he expected to hear from the girls, but oddly enough, nobody so much as sniggered, so Jamie continued cautiously.

"When I slept last night, it was totally demolished. It felt like someone else had been there before me and destroyed my world, my memories."

With this statement, Rose, Scarlet and Ruby gasped and looked at each other in amazement, stunned at what Jamie had just revealed.

"You *know* about Dreamworld Jamie… All of you know?" asked Scarlet in astonishment.

The children turned from facing the walls and were now staring in disbelief at each other.

"I 'ad the exact same dream too," said Rose, still remaining as quiet as she could. Dennis was well known for listening outside the room to what the children might be saying to each other. "Dreamworld is a place where I go when I sleep too," she continued. "It feels real though, I play there and anythin' I want to do just happens like magic. But I had the same horrible dream las' night, only everythin' was burnt."

Her face dropped a little with worry. She was talking as though she thought this Dreamworld was a real place where she could physically go to if she wanted.

"I can't believe we're all dreamin' of the same place," butted in Jamie thoughtfully. "That would mean that Dreamworld isn't just a creation in our minds. It's not possible".

Jamie paused in thought. "Unless everyone sees different parts, think about it. If everyone dreams of the same place, perhaps everyone is unknowingly creating different parts, making it absolutely massive. Maybe that's why things which seem terrible to one person, might be trivial to others," explained Jamie in excitement, now that he believed he had worked out what was going on.

"So that would mean that we are sharing a world created in our thoughts with the entire population of the globe. Maybe cos we're so close, we dream abou' the same areas of Dreamworld?" he continued guessing. "Basically wha' we thought was our unique an' personal dream space is actually in part at least, bein' shared between us all. How weird is that?"

"That sounds really creepy," whispered Scarlet. "I wonder if it's only in our heads though – I mean like, d' ya think it's a real place? Only if it is – that would mean everythin' *really* has bin burnt. What' do ya think might 'ave 'appened?" asked Scarlet pensively.

Nobody spoke, the silence indicating that nobody had an answer. Just the idea that their Dreamworld might in fact be real enough to look for in the waking world was strange enough without the added complexity that they might all be able to visit it together.

Their deep thoughts were suddenly interrupted by Dennis. They heard him for once, as he walked over the landing. There were a few floorboards that creaked, giving away anyone who happened to step on them. The children had spent hours in the past memorising which ones made a noise in order to cross it to use the bathroom without being punished for getting out of bed. They had quite physically drawn an invisible map in their heads like a pattern, defining the quietest route across the landing so as to not be heard.

The children were suddenly very glad they were silent in thought and no longer talking in whispered voices. If Dennis had heard them, they would most certainly have been punished again for this despicable crime.

Dennis slid back the bolt and opened the door. He stuck his ugly face around into the room.

"Right! It's time for dinner," he said, standing to one side to allow the children out for their evening meal, smirking in his usual, despicable manner. "When ya finished, don't forge' there's a meetin' tonigh', so don't flounder."

Chapter Thirteen
Earwigs and Asthma

The children didn't expect anything exciting for dinner, they could smell nothing special had been prepared, but there was a distinct, burnt smell in the air as they emerged from their bedroom.

Dennis rarely did cook anything, so they weren't disappointed, but tonight he excelled in both his arrogance and incompetence.

A slice of burnt toast had been slapped onto the children's plates, giving off a strong, charred smell which seemed to purposefully seek out the children's nostrils, eagerly insulting their senses.

On the side of their plates, Dennis had ironically appeared to have made a slight effort, presenting perfectly formed balls of cheap margarine using a melon balling tool, neatly around the edge. It made absolutely no sense at all to the children as to why he would bother decorating such a poor and feeble excuse of a meal, other than perhaps to add insult to injury as some kind of sarcastic humour.

A jar of thin, runny jam, had been plonked in the centre of the table, undoubtedly meant to represent a special treat.

The children sat down in their places around the table and sulked. The smell alone had been enough to put them off venturing into the kitchen, but the comically attempts to try and make the incinerated bread look like a serious offer of a feast was nothing short of evil.

"Tuck in then," mocked Dennis sneering cruelly.

The children stared in dismay at each other from across the table. They weren't really sure they could muster up the courage to actually engage their hands into picking up the cremated bread, least of all actually put it into their mouths. But they knew only too well that if they didn't eat it now, it would taste even worse the next morning after it had been left out in the open all night.

At last, perhaps in silent agreement, they all picked up the toast together, slowly introducing its gruesome flavour on their tongues, nibbling carefully so as to not get too much of the ashy taste in one foul hit.

Scarlet instantaneously screwed up her face in disgust. Her immediate thought was to spit it out as fast as she could, but she knew from past experience, it would taste worse the second time.

Apart from it being completely unpalatable; like eating gritty cardboard rescued from a fire, it was also cold and dreadfully hard. As they chewed, it broke into sandy lumps which crunched between their teeth; in fact, they were quite certain that chewing coal would have actually tasted better.

Swallowing it was the hardest part though. It was so dry that their saliva couldn't penetrate the congealed mass, but thankfully they had been given enough water to help wash the indigestible lumps down their throats, otherwise they might have just ended up choking to death. The sloppy jam didn't help much, but at least it covered up some of the course, incinerated flavour and texture.

After meal times the chores had to be done, washing the dishes, drying them, sweeping, and washing the kitchen floor. Sweeping up was probably the worst job to do, one which all the children despised doing above any other.

The floors were laid with wiry, floor carpet tiles which perfectly hung onto bits of fluff, gripping it like Velcro. Sweeping them with a brush seldomly collected the bits properly; they could spend hours brushing over and over without the tiles ever giving up the dust.

It was easier for them to pick each bit up with their fingers until it was clear. Dennis would then inspect the job. If it wasn't completed sufficiently, the dustpans contents would be sprinkled all over the floor, emptying everything it contained back onto the carpet tiles to be cleaned up again.

Having said that though, washing and drying the dishes wasn't much easier. If so much as a soap-sud was still visible on the dishes, they too would all be swept back into the sink to be washed again.

"Remember cleanliness is next to godliness," Dennis would spit with his self-righteous, pious attitude.

This evening however, Dennis decided that the chores were all satisfactorily done, this being the second time in one day that Dennis had been content with the children's efforts. Whatever the reason for his gratification, the children didn't really care, they just wanted to get away from him as soon as possible; even if it was to another dull, dreary meeting.

The children rode to the meetings on dilapidated old bicycles which Dennis had so thoughtfully retrieved from the scrap-yard before they were melted down and recycled into something that was actually fit for purpose.

Almost every inch of the metal had been peppered in rust, eaten away by years of cold, wet weather making the chains and cogs look like something designed specifically for a medieval torture chamber, particularly with the excruciating screech which screamed from the mechanism with each turn of the crank.

It was nothing short of miraculous that the wheels themselves were still able to support the frame, the spokes barely clung to the hub, and those that did were probably only hanging on with solidified rust. As for the tyres, the rubber was so badly eroded, they would have been better used for the soft strings in a fly curtain. The girls had tried several times to pump air into the tyres for what seemed like hours with a hand pump, in the hope of inflating them just a little more. But every time the pump was removed, it seemed like more air escaped through the valve than they had fought to put in, leaving them soft and useless.

A huge amount of effort was needed to make these bicycles move, in fact, Scarlet was quite sure walking would have been quicker.

With every strained push on the pedals, the bike responded with a high-pitched squeak. The ear-splitting sound of metal grinding against metal rasped out, sending shudders up and down the children's spines.

You can only imagine the noise they all made as they trundled along the road on these heaps of corroded metal; it was terribly embarrassing. People would come out from their houses just to see what the racket was all about, crowds gathered in the streets to watch, their jaws gaping open in bemusement as they watched the circus go by.

It was easy for the children to understand how people deemed as freaks in years gone by must have felt when they were put on display in traveling circuses for paying visitors to be gawked at.

This was the children's very own freak show where the entertainment came to the doorstep of the audience, announcing their forthcoming presence with their distinguishable raucous sirens. Only this freak show was free, free to be enjoyed by anyone who happened to be on the streets for the ten minutes it took to pass through each neighbourhood.

SSSQQQUUUUUEEEEEKKKK, CLONK,
SSSSSSSSSQQQQQUUUUUEEEEEEKKKKKKK, CLONK,
SSSSSSSSSSQQQQUUUUUEEEEEEKKKKKKKKKKKK, CLONK,
SSSSSSSQQQQQQQUUUUUUUEEEEEEEEEKK.

A drop of oil would have helped of course, but that would have made the children's lives far too easy. Besides, making a spectacle of the children was part of the fun for Dennis, allowing them to simply blend into the background as most people prefer to do, would have been too compassionate.

Dennis didn't care about humiliating them though, it didn't affect him. Dennis didn't even feel the need to attend a meeting, let alone ride a broken-down bicycle to one. He insisted that religion was for people who needed guidance, and he clearly did not need anyone teaching or instructing him how to live. He believed with every inch of himself, that he was far too godly already.

The children pulled their bicycles out of the old lean to shed which was really a wooden frame, covered over in polythene plastic which had been stapled in place.

The bikes were packed away in such a manner that meant due to a lack of space, they were all crammed together in organised chaos. The larger bike was the support for the smaller ones to be propped up against. This meant the smallest bike had to be removed first.

This duty fell on Rose, since she was the youngest, and her bike was the smallest.

Dennis took his front row position and stood back with big, open eyes, (which is saying something, as his natural appearance made his eyes very small and squinty) and watched for the drama to begin.

Scarlet didn't know why Dennis didn't just build himself a permanent seating area where he could watch in comfortable, luxurious surroundings. This was after all an occurrence which generally happened every other day. He knew as well as the children the events which were about to unfurl as each bike was removed.

Part of the entertainment entailed the children being unable, or more to the point, not being allowed to help each other in the process. Rose, without a doubt would struggle to lift the heavy bike over the door frame, she always did, but first she would have to fight her way through the doorway.

The door often swelled inside the frame when it got wet in bad weather. In order to budge the door, Rose was made to push as hard as she could against it, battling with all her might to unstick it from the frame. And then it would swing open all of a sudden with a harsh jolt, sending vibrations through the entire shed causing a great cascade of earwig beetles and centipedes to drop down from the folds of the plastic above the door, directly into her hair, and down her back.

It was obvious Dennis got huge satisfaction watching this performance with Rose's distress. He had a hearty laugh as he watched and listened to her screams while she danced around desperately trying to brush the bugs away.

Still, nobody was allowed to help her, which meant that this show would be played out, keeping Dennis amused for at least a few minutes before Rose calmed herself enough, feeling sure that she had cleared away all the creepy crawlies.

When at last the children had finally retrieved their chunks of rotting metal from the lean to, they began their tiring journey through town, pushing hard to keep themselves going, puffing and panting in their efforts.

Quite unusually though, the journey for Scarlet this evening, seemed to be particularly tiresome. As she rode her chest began to feel excruciatingly tight and the normally simple task of breathing became exceptionally difficult. She ignored the pain and pushed through, deciding she just needed to keep going. It was by no means easy, but if Rose was managing, then she had no excuse not to keep up.

However, despite drawing on every ounce of energy she could pull on, Scarlet became increasingly weary, her head started to pound and a strange dizzy sensation began to take over her mind. The shapes of her siblings in front twisted into hazy silhouettes which seemed to turn grey as they slowly disappeared into the distance. Her palms became sweaty as she clung on to her handlebars and at last she wobbled to a stop, wheezing anxiously in an attempt to draw in enough air.

The others cycled on, oblivious to the well-being of their sister. She hadn't had enough strength to breathe let alone call for help, but at that moment in time, Scarlet didn't care that they had gone; breathing seemed more important.

Scarlet weakly pulled her heavy bike off the road and leant it up against a wall at the side of the footpath, then panting, she scrunched down next to it while she fought to control her breathing. It felt as though her airways had been hijacked and that she'd been given a straw to breathe through. Her heart raced anxiously as she fought to understand what was happening, but her mind was foggy and a loud humming noise rung in her ears, drowning out her thoughts.

It wasn't until the other children needed to turn right in the road that Scarlet's disappearance was final noticed. Jamie swung out his arm to make the manoeuvre, glancing briefly behind him to check the way was clear before turning. At first, Jamie didn't notice that Scarlet was missing, but as he led the way to the centre of the road it suddenly occurred to him that he hadn't seen her in tow.

Jamie swung his head round again hoping he had just misread the situation, but to his horror Scarlet was nowhere to be seen.

"Where's Scarlet gone?" he called over his shoulder to his sisters.

The girls looked behind them expecting to see her tagging along, but they couldn't see her either.

"For *goodness* sake where she is? We don't 'ave time for this," said Jamie drearily. "We'll have to go back for her, follow me you lot," he instructed, taking the intended turn right, before swinging into a U-Turn on the other side of the road, returning back in the opposite direction.

Scarlet had eventually managed to get up and was walking slowly along the footpath pushing her bike and dragging her feet laboriously behind her as though they had been tied down with lead weights.

"Scarlet, wha' *are* you doin'? Why are you walkin'?" shouted Jamie with annoyance at her. "You *know* we'll be in trouble if we're late, and now thanks to you we will be," said Jamie.

The frustration was rather obvious in his voice when he saw her dawdling along; ambling as though she had all the time in the world.

"I can't breathe." She gasped through laboured efforts.

"Of course ya can breathe," he snapped without understanding what she meant. "We're all tired but we carried on. None of us got off and started walking, did we?"

"She does look really clammy. Look at her face!" said Ruby, noticing how unwell she appeared.

"Just try and breathe then Scarlet, like this," encouraged Rose as she casually inhaled and exhaled with long, deep breaths in and out to illustrate how easy the whole thing was.

"I can't. Why can't you see – how difficult it is – for me," she gasped between strained breaths as she tried to explain the problem to her bewildered siblings.

The children had no idea what they were witnessing. They'd not heard of asthma before and didn't recognise it as a medical emergency, but in all fairness, Scarlet had no idea what was wrong either; all she knew was that she felt absolutely exhausted.

Not wanting to get everyone in trouble, Scarlet tried again, and with some unknown powers, willed herself to get back on her antique bicycle and finish the journey, wheezing all the way. It was a huge relief when they finally arrived at the meeting hall, only a little bit later than they should have done.

Still struggling to breathe, but glad to be resting, Scarlet forced herself to listen to the speaker. As a general rule the children thought these meetings to be really very dull, but tonight the speaker spectacularly excelled the normal monotony.

He was so boring, laboriously dragging on in the same humdrum tone, and the worst thing was that they had only just begun – there was still another 90 minutes of this crap to endure.

BLAH, BLAH, BLAHHHH, BLAH, BLAH, BLAHHHH, BLAH, BLAH, BLAH, BLAHHHH.

He seemed to go on and on. Scarlet hadn't realised just how dull this all was until now, she thought her ears might bleed if she were forced to withstand any more of this dismal garbage.

Once the meeting was over, Scarlet felt a little better. Riding back at least would be downhill, so it was less daunting for her to think about the return journey.

By the time the children got home, Scarlet's wheeze had grown from a rattle to a rasp as she gasped in the air. Her lips had taken on a bluish tint and her skin had drained of any colour replacing her normal peachy tone with a pale clammy appearance.

"What's the matter with you Scarlet?" growled Dennis maliciously, noticing that she was suffering.

"I can't seem to catch my breath tonight," wheezed Scarlet faintly. "It's probably just the warmer air."

"You can't... breathe? Wha' d'ya mean, ya can't, breathe?" he ridiculed, repeating what she had just said in a patronising manner. Spittle flew out from the corners of his mouth like droplets of rain, splashing her in the face as he spoke.

"I mean, I err – I just can't breathe very well – it's difficult. I don't know why!" stammered Scarlet, who couldn't understand the situation any better than anyone else in the house.

Dennis knew only too well what was happening. Asthma is not uncommon, but by playing the fool, he could seize this occasion to dish out more punishments if he refused to see or tell what was very evidently happening in front of him.

"Well, maybe ya need some time in the corner then while you learn *'ow to breathe properly,"* he said, mocking her anxiety.

Scarlet just stood staring at him, unsure of what to say or do and too frail to argue.

"Well go on then. Don't just stand there gawping at me, and don't move until I tell ya."

Chapter Fourteen
The Key

Scarlet took her usual place in the corner. She was too exhausted to cry and besides, crying just wasn't worth wasting energy on, if nothing else, the children had learnt that it was a pointless emotion that didn't make any difference to life. She didn't feel well or strong enough to stand. Her legs still burned from exerting her muscles earlier, they felt weakened and wobbly, threatening to collapse under her weight at any given minute.

Hours passed by, and eventually Scarlet heard Dennis move downstairs. The definite slopping of his feet padding down hard on the stairs as he made his way up, gave her a sudden, unusual sense of relief which passed through her drained body.

At last, she would be sent to bed, now that he was going himself. Normally the sound of his footsteps approaching didn't incur any thoughts of joy, but tonight they brought good tidings – or so she thought.

Scarlet remained perfectly still, even managing to stand straight with her head held high, defying her need to just collapse where she stood.

His heavy feet scuffed the carpet as he dragged them over the floor behind her and… walked right by and into his own room, completely ignoring that she was even stood there.

What the hell? Scarlet couldn't quite believe what he had done. Perhaps he was too tired to notice her still stood there she thought.

Scarlet strained her ears for any sign that he might suddenly remember. A small voice perhaps, or even the scuff of his feet returning to where she was stood, but there was nothing. The only sound was that of the mattress springs coiling down under his weight as Dennis eased himself comfortably into his bed, leaving Scarlet exactly where she was.

Scarlet's heart sank as it dawned on her she was here for the night. She sighed wearily, stretching her hands above her head as far as she could, before slowly sliding them back down the cold, smooth wall in search of a comfortable position to fold into a head rest.

Surprisingly, she discovered that by binding her arms together against the wall, she could easily and comfortably support her head into them like a pillow. She didn't dare risk sitting down or lying out on the floor, and the idea to sneak into bed wasn't worth contemplating. If Dennis were to come out in the night to check on her and find she wasn't there, or if he discovered she had made an attempt to make herself even remotely comfortable, (and him checking on her was a great possibility,) she knew the price would be too costly.

Scarlet's eyes grew heavy as the night ticked by. Knowing there was little choice but to make the best of a bad situation, she nestled her head into her arms as best as she could, then rested her eyes, propping her body into a slouched position against the wall. She did spectacularly well, managing the entire night through without once melting into a heap.

The sound of Dennis pulling open his bedroom door the next morning alerted her from her light sleep. It brushed over the deep pile, sweeping the fibres beneath as it caressed the surface. It occurred to Scarlet how soft and luxurious it sounded at that moment, as if teasing her with its thickness. It was then that Scarlet realised how numb her body had become.

A throbbing pain pulsed from her hips down the length of her legs and into her ankles, and her neck had seized into a downward position so that she was certain her bones would crack and break if she tried to move.

"You're still there then!" jibed Dennis as he came out of his bedroom, wearing a comfy looking, cotton dressing gown.

Scarlet exerted herself, painfully lifting her head to reply.

"Yes. Ya told me to stay here."

"So I did," he chuckled with glee. "I trust ya slept well?" he continued, snorting like a pig almost as though he were one. "Ya best ge' yerself ready fer school then, unless you'd prefer to stay here."

Dennis turned his back, still grinning, then farted loudly as he passed her by.

Scarlet instinctively screwed up her nose in disgust and slumped away lethargically. She wondered how on earth she was going to get through the school day feeling so exhausted.

As expected, school dragged by particularly slowly. The minutes ticked by like hours, and the hours like days, she could barely stay awake. Her elbows kept slipping off the side of the table sending her head into a vertical dive towards the desk. The sudden drop was thankfully enough to wake her with a jolt just before she had a chance of smashing her face into the hard surface. This behaviour didn't go unnoticed by her teacher Mrs Saxby though.

"Am I boring you Miss Hartman? That's the fifth time I've seen your head almost collide with the desk in the last hour."

"I'm sorry miss. I'm not feelin' well," answered Scarlet pitifully.

Mrs Saxby frowned. "Yesterday you weren't much better either. If this continues, I shall have no choice but to contact your parents and put you in detention. Is that clear?"

"Yes, sorry miss," said Scarlet apologetically.

"Perhaps you need to pay more attention to the time you're going to bed at night I dare say. If you're falling asleep in school as often as you seem to be doing, I can only assume that you're quite simply spending too much time watching TV instead of getting the sleep you should be doing at your age."

If only her lack of sleep was because of something so nice thought Scarlet to herself, wishing she could answer Mrs Saxby's remark with her own honest opinion. All Scarlet wanted was for the day to end so that she could go home to bed.

"I will make sure I get enough sleep tonight miss," answered Scarlet obligingly, deciding that it wasn't worth the back fire she would get from Dennis by being honest.

Scarlet rested her head in her hand, propped up on the desk with her elbow and for a few moments her mind focused on Mrs Saxby. She walked round the class while she talked about King Henry V111 and his poor health without noticing Scarlet's eyes momentarily betray her again. That was, until the school bell rung expectantly frightening her half to death.

Scarlet's reflexes thrust her automatically from her chair like a Jack-in-the-box, sending her scampering across the classroom floor like a deranged, petrified mouse. The class fell into fits of uncontrolled laughter, leaving Scarlet red faced and shaking with nerves.

"Let that be a lesson to you Miss Hartman. Tomorrow I expect better from you," said Mrs Saxby glaring over the top of her glasses in a bid to appear unamused, but her hand purposefully laid across her mouth did well to avoid a sneaky grin from escaping.

It was a wonderful sight to see their house appear as the children walked down the road, and better still, Dennis was not waiting in the house to question them that day.

Scarlet plodded her heavy, tired feet upstairs, ecstatic to think she could now rest, but as she walked past her window, she thought she saw someone standing in the garden.

She jumped back, taking a double look. The lady in white was standing in the garden again. She looked just as she remembered her from years ago. What on earth was going on? First Dreamworld, now the white lady had returned.

She just stood there, unanimated, shining like some kind of angel. Her long, silvery hair was neatly tucked under her hooded robe and her finger stretched outwards, pointing to something in the garden. It was shiny and small, but she couldn't work out what it was. It gleamed in the sunlight like a beacon, almost asking to be found.

Forgetting her exhaustion for just a while longer, Scarlet slipped quietly back down the stairs, and out into the garden.

The white lady was no longer there, but she could see exactly where the object was hidden as it still gleamed brightly.

Checking the coast was clear; Scarlet made a quick dash, running into the garden to retrieve the object. It was half buried in the soil, covered in wet sticky mud as if it had been there for years. Whatever it was, it looked rather intricate. She could make out a rough shape, but there was so much soil clinging firmly to it, she couldn't be sure.

There was no time to play with it now though; there was a good chance Dennis might catch her out here and quiz her about something. Pushing it inside her cardigan pocket, she slipped unseen back into the house.

The bathroom was conveniently vacant at the top of the stairs; it was the perfect place to uncover what she had found. Scarlet entered the room and slammed the door unintentionally hard, her small fingers fumbled against the lock as she nervously slid it in place, securing herself inside so that she wouldn't be disturbed.

Once she had caught her breath, Scarlet slipped her hand inside her cardigan pocket to retrieve the metal object she had discovered. It felt and looked smaller than she first thought it to be, but a strange warmth also seemed to radiate from it which she hadn't noticed in the garden either. Perhaps it had absorbed some heat from the sun she told herself, it had reflected the sun after all, that's why it had been so easy to spot.

Scarlet turned it in her hand with complete fascination. The earth still clung heavily to it obscuring its shape, but by picking it away with her fingers, she was able to define its now apparent shape.

It was a key, but there seemed to be something more. The tab appeared to be cut or engraved with something; the soil clung into this part as though it had been compressed into the fitting. It would need some attention if she wanted to see what secrets it was hiding.

Pushing the plug into the sink, Scarlet filled the basin with warm soapy water and carefully scrubbed away the dirt with a nail brush. A beautiful brass key re-emerged, quite different from how it looked before. The bow, now pristine and clean, revealed a marbled, turquoise gem set in its centre. An elegant, swirly, entwined, leaf pattern adorned the side of its shank finishing at the bit which itself had been fashioned into a neat square with an unusual tree shape cut into its centre.

The elaborate detail signified something of importance to Scarlet. Nobody would have gone to so much trouble crafting such an exquisite key for nothing of relevance. But despite her best efforts searching, there was nothing engraved onto it which indicated what it might unlock, no message from the white lady and no maker's name.

A surge of disappointment clouded her mind; she dropped the key back into her pocket and threw herself onto her bed.

By now, the idea of sleeping had well and truly been vanquished. The mystery surrounding the key had taken presidency in her thoughts raising more questions than answers.

It had to mean something, she just knew it. Why else would the white lady have brought it to her attention? What was the meaning of the tree cut into its bit, and why did it feel so warm? She mulled over these thoughts oblivious to anything else around her, almost flying into the air with fright when Ruby came through the door unexpectedly.

"Wha' ya doin'?" she asked curiously.

"What d'ya mean? I'm not doing anything. I'm just lying down," she answered nervously, feeling herself justifying her unnecessary guilt.

"What's in ya hand then?" Ruby quizzed in frustration, knowing that Scarlet's denial made her anything but innocent of doing nothing as she so purportedly claimed.

"Where's Rose and Jamie?" asked Scarlet, answering her sister's question with a question.

"Downstairs. Why?"

"Ask them to come up. I've got somethin' I want to show you all."

Ruby looked suspiciously at Scarlet. "What is it? Show me!"

"No. I'll show you when we're all together," repeated Scarlet crossly. "Just see if they'll come up will ya."

"Fine, be like that then," she snapped irritably as she turned away.

Moments later the three returned.

"Ruby says you want to tell us somethin'," said Jamie inquisitively.

"Yes, I do," said Scarlet with a mix of excitement and disappointment. "You remember when we first moved here, there was a white lady in the back garden?"

"Black you mean!" said Ruby severely, at the memory of it.

"No. White," corrected Scarlet in the same stern tone. "Anyway, regardless of what colour she was, she reappeared today in the garden to me…"

"Really?" said Ruby, cutting Scarlet short.

"Yes really. And oddly enough, for your information she appeared to me as a *white lady,* again." She gave Ruby a hard stare before carrying on. "As I was saying. She was stood in the garden pointing at somethin' so I snuck out to see what it was."

Scarlet rummaged in her pocket and produced the key. "Look at this. It was half buried in the ground but I washed it and it came up like this." She held the key flat in her hand, pushing it under her sibling's noses. "What d'ya think it could be?"

"Gosh," said Jamie. "I've never seen anythin' like that before – Or have I? Wait a minute – but I do believe it looks suspiciously like a key," grinned Jamie, mocking his sister sarcastically. "At least it looks like a key to me. What do you two think it could be?" he jibed, encouraging them to play along.

"Well if you're not goin' to take this seriously, I don't know why I'm bothering to even show it to you," said Scarlet bitterly, snatching her hand away in disgust as her siblings responded to Jamie's sarcasm with fits of giggles.

"I'm sorry Scarlet. I couldn't resist. Let me see again." He held his hand out apologetically waiting for her to forgive him and show it again.

Cautiously, Scarlet dug the key from her pocket again and wryly opened her hand for them to see, half expecting them to start laughing again. This time they didn't though. Instead a look of concentration spread over their faces as they examined the key in her outstretched hand.

"Can I hold it?" asked Jamie eagerly.

Scarlet dropped the key expectantly into Jamie's open hand, waiting in anticipation for him to notice how warm it felt.

"Blimey, this is warm Scarlet," he said almost immediately. "How long 'ave you bin holding it in yer hand?"

"I haven't. It felt this warm when I found it in the garden," she responded enthusiastically, hoping that it was of vital importance.

"Perhaps the sun had been on it then!" replied Jamie with a sniff, almost disregarding what she believed to be important.

Scarlet grunted with irritation. She had believed this to be the case earlier also, but the temperature hadn't cooled, not even after she had washed it. There had to be something more, she was certain of it.

Jamie continued to study it, squinting his eyes as he tried to focus on the minute detail.

"There's a tree cut into its bit," he said as his concentration intensified. "Have a look Ruby, see if you can find anythin' on it tha' I might 'ave missed. It just looks like a small key to me though, if I'm bein' honest with ya Scarlet. It's probably from an old clockwork toy or something," he said, passing it to Ruby to inspect.

Scarlet huffed angrily. She knew where this was going. They'd all think she was making the white lady up, then they'd imply that the key was just a toy.

"I can't think what it might fit. I've not seen anythin' in the house with a lock that small," said Ruby, examining the key with the same strained eyes that Jamie wore before her. "What d' ya think Rose?" she asked, passing it along to her.

Rose took the key in her hand and stared at it. "I think it's pretty. Can I keep it Scarlet?"

"No!" snapped Scarlet, snatching it from Rose's hand. "I knew it was a waste of time showin' it to ya all. I know wha' I saw, an' I don't care if ya don't believe me."

She turned her back disapprovingly on the others and opened her drawer. The handkerchief their mother had given her lay neatly folded on the top, still as new as the day it was bought. Opening its fold, she carefully laid the small brass key inside and placed it back in to the drawer. There was a moment of solace in doing that, as if it was now a secret only she and her mother shared.

She sighed as she pushed the drawer closed. She could feel the others staring at her from behind as if they pitied her.

"It is somethin' special. You'll see," she said quietly, before turning round to face them.

Bedtime couldn't come quick enough for Scarlet that night, her sleep deprivation the night before had made her excessively tired, and she was desperately in need of sleep. Her mind whirred with the events of the day and the confusion remained fresh in her mind of the nightmare she had dreamed of a few nights ago. She didn't think she would sleep with so much going on, but after tossing and turning for an hour or so she finally slipped into a deep sleep…

Chapter Fifteen
The White Lady

Scarlet wondered over to the window. The white lady had appeared again in the garden; it suddenly occurred to her how angelic she looked. Her iridescent robes blew gently around her in the night breeze, fluttering elegantly, giving the impression she had wings. The white lady pushed her hood down, sensing that Scarlet was watching her from the window and turned to face her.

Scarlet held her breath in anticipation. The white lady was looking right at her, beckoning her to join her outside.

"I can't," she mimed, desperate to relay her inability to follow. "I can't fly."

The white lady's smile broadened with amusement before motioning again, only now, Scarlet could hear the faintest of whispers echoing in her head.

"Open the window Scarlet. Trust your instincts and follow me."

Without being completely convinced the whispers weren't just in her imagination, Scarlet nonetheless did as she was told, pushing the window open wide in hope that whatever was about to unfold might take control of her inabilities and perhaps somehow empower her with special gifts of levitation.

She wasn't disappointed, in an instance Scarlet's feet left the floor as she slowly began to rise into the air while the bedroom ceiling rapidly seemed to meet her head. Automatically, Scarlet lifted her hand above her head, protecting the inevitable collision which ultimately followed.

For a few moments, Scarlet bounced off the walls and ceiling while her body became accustomed to such a strange, weightless sensation. Her heart pounded out an unsteady rhythm as her adrenaline rich blood raced uncontrollably through her anxious body, sending tremors of excitement and panic coursing round her veins in a spellbinding cocktail of euphoria.

In her ecstasy, Scarlet momentarily forgot about the white lady waiting in the garden until the familiar whispers filled her head again.

"Scarlet, I'm waiting!"

Scarlet glided back towards the window. The white lady stood patiently waiting for scarlet to float out of the open window and join her outside. It felt daunting suddenly to take such a leap of faith into the unknown; after all, she didn't know this lady, and on top of that, the darkness outside seemed to taint the air with a feeling of uneasiness.

Scarlet sighed anxiously and with a bit of willpower, eventually allowed herself to drift through the opening, into the night sky with the white lady by her side.

Although Scarlet had questions to ask, she felt a little weary. She had only just met this lady, but somehow, her intuition told her she was wise to trust her. There was just something about her that calmed any worries or reservations she might have had. It felt as though she had known her a very long time, but there was no reason to believe this statement at all.

Scarlet tried to keep her thoughts quiet for a moment, choosing instead to appreciate the spectacular views below as she flew overhead.

From the air, Scarlet had a perfect bird's eye view of the streets below. Red tiled roofs, and pretty gardens adorned the world below like a picture from a child's book. Smoke rose from chimneys, cars stood still parked up on drives for the evening, and lights in the windows of the houses gave off a warm, welcoming glow.

The night air didn't feel cold despite the breeze moving through the trees like a mischievous, invisible force. The fact she was scantily clad in only her night dress bore no relevance on her; instead the air felt soothing, refreshing even as it passed through her spirit without altering her state of mind.

Scarlet's attention was abruptly woken by the bark of a small beige and white dog. The world seemed to instantly come alive with its call, echoing in the stillness as it stood patiently outside in one of the neighbouring yards. A warm glow suddenly lit up the windows of the house, spilling its welcoming contents outside like burst pockets of gold. Moments later an elderly lady staggered to open the back door allowing the animal to share in her comforts. He didn't hesitate; with a youthful bounce, he bounded back indoors, pushing his cooled body against her unstable legs as he swept by.

Scarlet couldn't help wondering if the lady was being looked after; she seemed so frail and far too fragile to be alone despite the content smile radiating from her face.

The white lady nudged Scarlet from her thoughts, gesturing onwards. It was difficult to turn her attention away from the older lady, almost as though she were somehow neglecting her duties.

"Will she be okay?" Scarlet trembled quietly, hoping for some kind of reassurance from her guide.

The white lady answered with one single, simple word, "Soon," then smiled sympathetically.

Scarlet didn't quite understand what that meant, but her voice had a calming effect which instantly reassured her anxiety, resetting her troubled mind back to their journey.

After a little while, the pair reached a familiar looking wood. It was known locally as the Whispering Wood, purely for the reason that the trees seemed to sing a magical tune when the wind rustled their leaves. If you listened hard enough it almost sounded like a gentle humming, overlaid with a kind of crackling; like the trees were growing.

Scarlet's toes caught the tops of the trees canopies, tickling them slightly with the new, soft, spring leaves that grew, indicating she needed to fly up a little higher.

Down below, a small river ran through the woods, cutting a deep gorge through the middle, creating a steep bank on either side. It was here where the white lady gestured, pointing with her finger to Scarlet that they would descend.

The soft, damp moss felt comforting on Scarlet's feet as it pushed its way between her toes like a moist sponge, massaging the soles of her feet as she moved them gently from side to side over the top of it.

Scarlet's gaze lifted from her feet as she now scanned the landscape, taking in her surroundings, filling her mind as though she were plotting down everything around her in order to create a map.

They were stood in front of a willow tree. There weren't many willows here in this wood, maybe only two or three, but this one had long sweeping branches which seemed to caress the ground. Its leaves were a soft, silvery green colour making it appear majestic and more enchanting than any other willow tree she had ever seen.

The white lady lifted and pushed back its branches making a path for Scarlet to follow her through, right to the centre of the tree's trunk.

Its main root pushed through the ground like a strong animal which had dug itself an underground den. The base of the trunk had to be at least five foot in diameter, stretching its majestic height up tall over their heads, spreading its branches around them like a huge umbrella.

Scarlet sighed deeply. It was without a doubt a beautiful tree, even more captivating than any other tree she thought she had seen in her entire life, but when push came to shove, this was still only a tree, and in her humble opinion Scarlet still couldn't quite understand the significance of being here.

With a sense of bemused uncertainty, Scarlet turned to the white lady for an answer.

The white lady wore the same calming signature smile; her green eyes sparkled adventurously, but said nothing. It was obvious Scarlet was missing something, and the white lady wasn't really helping. Just standing there expectantly, glowing in the way that she did, wasn't offering her any assistance to what it was she was meant to be seeing.

"What?" huffed Scarlet in frustration after a short while. "What is it I'm supposed to be seeing? I don't get it."

The air seemed to shift in a foreboding way that made Scarlet think the white lady's mood had changed, but her smile remained fixed to her face. She knew the white lady would have preferred that Scarlet find the *Something* on her own.

"You have to learn to see past the obvious Scarlet," said the white lady in a gentle but firm way. "Look harder. Look past the things you've learned to be factual, and open your mind to things less so. Most of the problems people face in the world are not as literal as they would believe; these *problems* exist only in their minds because they can't see a way past what is apparent. It's why humans fail to accomplish so much, they use so little of their minds, they refuse to accept anything unless it's been scientifically proven, and that is mankind's biggest shortfall. It's such a waste – such a shame."

"Are you telling me I need to look for something in my *head?* Or that I have to believe there's something there which I'm simply not allowing myself to see?" asked Scarlet in a baffled tone.

"Both Scarlet! Every thought you allow to grow, makes you stronger psychologically. By exploring the possibility that life isn't as straight forward as you'd believe, is the start to unlocking the willow."

Scarlet smiled. The white lady's words sounded simple enough, but to her, they seemed jumbled, a bit mixed where she had to now redefine what was real. She said, "Unlocking the willow." What did that mean? The willow couldn't be unlocked, trees are not things you'd attempt to unlock and walk through – or were they?

Scarlet's mind suddenly leapt into thought. She had found a key. That's what the white lady must have meant. In feverish excitement, believing she completely understood the white lady's statement, Scarlet dropped to her knees. There had to be a door – why else had she been brought here?

Scarlet scanned the tree trunk searching for any signs that a door might be hidden among its cleverly patterned bark. It would have to end near the main root and its height would have to be at least five feet tall in order to allow any access inside.

What could be waiting on the other side? Was there another side anyway? Perhaps more to the point, what might be waiting *inside*? Oh, for goodness' sake, where was the door? It couldn't be this difficult to find. It really ought to be big enough to see, she heard herself reasoning in her mind, and then as she scrambled in the mossy earth, a tiny indentation appeared to her frantically wondering eyes – a miniature hole, no larger than a few millimetres in size.

Scarlet arched her back as she knelt close to the ground, enabling her to get nearer to the discovery. Its shape suggested it was a lock – the intended area that would host a key. It looked roughly the same size as the one which she had safely hidden in the folds of her handkerchief – *at home.*

Scarlet leapt to her feet in a flurry of excitement as she realised the importance of her find.

"I need the key. It's at home – I need it. I can't get in without it," she barked in desperation in a way that suggested the white lady might have brought it along. Her words mimicked the anguish which rushed through her veins as she pleaded for it to somehow appear.

The white lady looked amused. "Why do you need a key Scarlet?"

Scarlet felt a rush of frustration and anger replace her previous excitement. Was she mocking her now? Only a few moments ago this *woman* had told her to open her mind to new possibilities, ignore science, now she seemed to be laughing at the very notion of walking into a tree.

Scarlet was too angered to speak. She wasn't good with being made the obstacle of a bad joke.

"What do you think you'd find inside the willow if you could gain entry anyway?" said the white lady in a more serious tone.

Scarlet didn't know what to think. How could she know what secrets it held? She *knew* if she had the key, she would have been able to find out, that was for sure.

"Have a little think about it Scarlet. What would be in there?"

The white lady's voice seemed to peter away as Scarlet's own thoughts of wonderment pushed her aside.

"You know what I find most peculiar about you Scarlet?" boomed the white lady, suddenly sounding like a bass drum in her delicate ears.

Scarlet jumped in alarm. "What? What did you say?" she answered automatically.

"You've come with me tonight, you've crossed barriers which even in your own mind know to be impossible, and yet you've not thought any of it unusual. You don't question where you are, you didn't question how you got here and you haven't even questioned who I am, but you preoccupy yourself with unnecessary worries of keys and entry into an area you should be able to easily access, it's your mind after all."

Scarlet opened her mouth to speak, but the truth of the white lady's words seemed unanswerable. She shut her mouth in exasperation and sighed.

"Well," she said after thinking about her reply for a moment, "I'm dreaming, I can do anything in a dream. Everybody can do things they wouldn't be able to if they were awake." Scarlet smiled to herself. That told her.

"So why can't you open the door Scarlet?" she said quickly, as though she had already prepared her response beforehand. The white lady clapped her hands hard suddenly, sending a shock wave through the woods. "Who am I?" she demanded. "Why did you follow me here without question? Why can't you shake the feeling that you've always known me? Think Scarlet, it's time you remembered."

Stunned at her sudden mood change, Scarlet froze in shock as the white lady's questions shook her memories like the shaking of dust from an old cloth – as scales falling from the eyes of a blind man. Memories she had forgotten about played in her head like recordings from years gone by and she saw the white lady touch her cheek as she lay in a cradle on the day she was born.

She sang a sweet song of soothing calm when she had cried, reassuring her that her fear was unwarranted; she would be loved. Then the familiar scene she remembered so well appeared; the day she saw the white lady in the garden, the excitement she felt as she saw the face she somehow knew so well.

"You're my guardian angel," she said slowly as the realisation dawned on her for the first time what was going on.

"There she is! Hello Scarlet," whispered the white lady, gently laying her hand on her shoulder as her beautiful smile returned. "My name is Esperanza, and yes, I am your guardian angel. We've been given many names over the years; earth angels, guardian angels, time travellers even. You've been through so much already in such a short space of time, but things are going to get so much harder for you all, which is why I'm here tonight.

"Your life is building towards something that you will have a hard time accepting, but I hope that with my help, and if you are willing to adjust your mind, over time, you'll learn to grow in strength and take back the confidence that's been stolen from you by your stepfather."

Scarlet's mouth gaped open in astonishment. Where she had not known what to say seconds earlier, she was now having the opposite problem as questions seemed to be pouring in, flooding her mind uncontrollably.

"There's more than one of you? You said we!" said Scarlet in surprise. "Does that mean you've seen and know of everything that's happened in my life? D'ya know where my mother is...?"

"Wait. Slow down," said Esperanza cutting Scarlet's questions short. "You have a lot to ask, and that's quite understandable, but we need to take one thing at a time. Your questions will all be answered in good time, okay!" She held Scarlet at arm's length as she gazed at the confounded child. Scarlet nodded with understanding and took a deep breath in anticipation. "Good! Now going back to your first question. Yes, there are many of us; everybody ever born into this world has a guardian angel assigned to them, sometimes two, but that angel stays with her Nexus through life and after...."

"Nexus? What's a Nexus?" asked Scarlet dryly.

"I'm your Nexus. It's a word which describes the link, the bond holding us together," Esperanza replied. "But right now, there are more important things to discuss. Things which will make you see the world differently to the one you knew, things which are so dark you'll question everything you every think of or see again."

Chapter Sixteen
The Jinn

Scarlet stared blankly at Esperanza. What on earth could she say that would change the way she saw the world, including everything she had ever believed?

"I'm truly sorry for you and your family's loss Scarlet," continued Esperanza cautiously. "But the things I have to tell you about are not the kind of things anybody should have to be made aware of, particularly a child. But I'm afraid that your ignorance will be the reason your family continues to suffer if nothing changes."

Esperanza's voice was calming, but Scarlet felt that what she was about to told would not leave her feeling that way.

"Is this about Mum?" asked Scarlet fearfully; unsure now if she really wanted to know what Esperanza might reveal.

"In a way, yes, but your mother is merely a pawn in this story. It's your stepfather who has taken the lead role and his actions which have brought us to where we are now."

"Dennis? What's Dennis got to do with anythin'?" asked Scarlet in repulsion as though just the sound of his name disgusted her.

"Do you like him?" probed Esperanza.

"Like 'im! What's there to like? He's a horrid man! You should know if you've been with me for as long as ya say ya 'ave."

"Well I'm glad we both think the same of him, otherwise it would make my job so much harder."

"What d'ya mean? Look – just tell me won't you," snapped Scarlet, becoming increasingly frustrated.

"It's rather difficult to explain Scarlet in terms that you will understand, but I will do my best." Esperanza took a deep breath in, then cautiously began to tell her tale. "Dennis used to be like any other person once, caring, loving, considerate – *human*. He had friends, a family, a job, but then like many people, he suffered a loss. His first wife divorced him, which left him feeling angry, betrayed, unloved and particularly needy.

"In order to fill that void, he latched on to a couple, your mum and dad, and from there the pain in his heart seemed to ease; at least for a little while. But eventually the emptiness consumed the friendship like light being sucked into a black hole, causing his need to be loved to resurface, only now that desire had become too big for him to ignore. Friendship wasn't enough, he could see how much your parents loved each other and he yearned to be a part of that, however, he knew he'd never have what they shared while your dad was around.

"The jealousy grew, his heart led him down a path which he found he couldn't turn away from, he didn't want to – all he could feel was an unquenchable thirst for lust which grew stronger, taking over his mind and body, until at last his selfish longings took control. The passion burned so fiercely that he eventually succumbed to his infatuation, turning him into the monster he is today."

"What are you talking about Esperanza, what did he do that turned him into a monster? I don't think I understand."

But even as the words left her mouth, she realised exactly what she meant. Scarlet pulled her hands away from Esperanza in sheer horror.

"He caused the fire?" she whispered. "He killed my dad. He *murdered* my dad just so that he could be with my mum." And then her horror turned to rage so that she shook uncontrollably.

"My mother married that – that *THING*. How could she marry such an evil man knowing what he had done? I think I'm going to be sick."

"Honey, calm yourself. Your mother didn't know. I doubt she would have ever got involved if she had any idea. About a year ago however, your mother did become suspicious which provoked them into having so many fights. When she confronted him, you'll remember that your mother mysteriously lost her mind – and vanished."

Scarlet dropped to the ground as Esperanza's words sunk in.

"How could he have been so evil? He could 'ave killed us all, he didn't know we would get out..." Scarlet stopped in mid thought as it suddenly hit home just how much Dennis had planned this.

"Do you want me to stop? I can explain another time if it's better for you. I understand this is very difficult for you to hear."

116

"No! No, carry on," she said, drying her face on her sleeve. "I need to know what he did. I knew there was somethin' I didn't like about him, but I didn't think he was capable of all that."

"Dennis made sure you would get out. He left the door open that night when he left, leaving your dad trapped and badly injured in the basement. He made sure he wasn't going to get out alive and that's all he cared about." Esperanza spoke gently to her, calming her as she explained.

"When someone commits this kind of violent act, he becomes open to possession. In Dreamworld there are evil creatures known as the Jinn. They are normally locked down; they can't leave unless they find someone to latch on to in the waking world. By committing murder, Dennis became an empty vessel, the humanity is pushed out, thus allowing the Jinn to take over. The one living inside Dennis is called Abaddon.

"Once inside a human body, the Jinn can then move freely between worlds causing as much mayhem and misery as they see fit. The victims care for no one, as they rapidly lose any feelings of humanity they may have once had, replacing those emotions with hate and anger. These carcases then feed on the energy of others around them, normally their loved ones who try to help.

"In turn, this causes the people who were trying to stay strong for the possessed individual to eventually fall into depression as their own lives are drained a bit more every day like cattle to the slaughter. Over time these innocent individuals fall into a life of misery and despair, unable to find any joy in their once happy lives.

"The more lives the Jinn destroy, the stronger he becomes, systematically sapping up the person's life like a parasite.

"People who have no hope or no dreams are easy to control. They have less and less to live for as they're drawn deeper into the pits of destruction. They have no hope, no future, these people wonder around aimlessly like blind men unaware of the dangerous positions they are now in, and so the perpetual cycle continues.

"In order to keep the next person weak, the Jinn attacks the only thing left which restores some strength – their mind, their dreams.

"This is why Abaddon has caused the destruction you all witnessed in Dreamworld. He knows that this is where people in general go to replenish their souls. In Dreamworld people visit their loved ones, they find peace, something to cling onto which strengthens their spirit, allowing them to continue in life and fight back the evils that can easily destroy a person's hopes. But if their dreams are destroyed, it makes the person weaker, more vulnerable and in essence, easier prey to target and torment.

"If Abaddon can manipulate the soul in its waking *and* sleeping periods, the more likely he is to succeed in his demise, all while feeding off his diminishing strength."

Scarlet's emotions were all over the place now; she didn't quite know how to feel. From firstly discovering the most exciting thing in the world that she had a guardian angel protecting her; to now finding out the disturbing and shocking truth that her stepfather was some kind of demon who had murdered her father and was ultimately trying to destroy her life. It seemed so far-fetched she couldn't really believe this was true.

Of course she knew Dennis was an unpleasant man, everyone knew that. She knew perfectly well that he got a kick out of making other people's lives miserable, but she hadn't guessed in all her wildest dreams that he was a murderer who was hosting a Jinn.

On the other hand, it made perfect sense. He was perpetually dragging the children's spirits down, trying to break them, always looking for new ways to make his punishments more severe, and he relished in their agony.

"You said everyone has a guardian," Scarlet sniffed back her tears. "So where is Dennis's guardian? Why didn't his guardian intervene when she had a chance to stop him? Does he still even have one?"

"Yes, well it's not always that simple. You see – guardians can only help a person on the right path if they want to go that way themselves. A person's will is a lot stronger than anything we can offer. No child is born wicked; it's the temptations in life which interfere with their mind set. If they feed the wrong wolf, allowing it to take a presidency in their lives, they are effectively permitting the Jinn to lock onto them.

"In Dennis's case he allowed the wrong wolf to get stronger, more aggressive to a point where it took control of him. Most people put bad thoughts out of their head because they're too vile to contemplate, but as you saw, not everyone dismisses these evil thoughts. When that happens, we are pushed out and away. We still have a connection to that person, but if we are unwanted, we have no choice but to stand back until the time that we might be needed again. We can't force someone to listen to our advice if they choose not to."

Scarlet nodded with understanding. It made sense that some people are just that way inclined, the same way others prefer a path of kindness and love.

"It's not all doom and gloom Scarlet. There is hope. I'm here to help you open your mind; by taking control of your own special gifts and learning how to use them, you and your siblings can fight back.

"You will discover that your mind is a very powerful thing, so long as you harness your abilities to your own advantage. Allow yourself to believe in more than what you believe, search for answers beyond this world and you will create a new world of security and peace where you will find solace and tranquillity in places you never dreamed of. In time, these powers can be manipulated in the waking world so that your normal lives will be enriched in ways you wouldn't imagine possible."

"Powers? I don't understand, I don't have any special powers. I'm just me," sniffed Scarlet.

"You only think that because you haven't discovered them yet. Everybody has a special gift Scarlet; it's just that people don't normally stumble across these powers by accident. They have to need them in order to unlock them. Once they're found, they can be strengthened with use and practice, like anything." Esperanza smiled knowingly, "You know – Jamie has a gift, but he will be very afraid to use it, his father made sure of that a long time ago."

Scarlet's mind buzzed. She was too tired to ask about Jamie. Her mind fluttered and hummed with all this strange new information. It was completely bizarre to hear this lady speak with such rationality about her life, one which seemed to be sounding less and less like it could possibly be hers, and more with every passing word that she was listening in on somebody else's life story.

Esperanza's voice turned into a collection of words, the soft sound turned into a mellow song, soothing her mind. Her words washed over her as they faded into nothing. The sense that any of this was even remotely real rippled away, leaving Scarlet feeling sleepy as she drifted into a relaxed state of mind. And then it fell silent.

Chapter Seventeen
Jamie's Secret

The morning sun shone through into the girls' bedroom, waking them from their sleep. They yawned, stretched, and climbed out of their beds.

"What a strange dream," said Ruby quietly under her breath, as she slipped from the top bunk, landing on the floor with a little thump.

Scarlet looked at her, uncertain how to respond. Ruby was obviously fishing for a reaction, but she believed she already knew just what she was talking about.

It was absurd and unrealistic to think Ruby may have had the same dream as her again, but also unsettling to think that perhaps this may be the case. Their discovery a few days earlier was strange enough without thinking they would always be tied into having the same dreams.

She was determined not to ask or look interested; having had such an unnerving dream as it was, complicated how she felt without mixing anything else into the equation.

Pretending it hadn't fazed her at all, Scarlet yawned casually as she pulled on her socks while secretively listening in to anything else Ruby might say to add extra weight to her suspicions.

Rose's attention though had been captured. With her jaw open, she sat perched on the edge of her bed with a sock held loosely in her hand above her bare foot, her gaze rooted on her sister.

Scarlet couldn't help herself now. Her earlier determination to appear disinterested was suddenly blown away like dust in the wind as she was forced to comprehend that this was more than just coincidence.

"Come on, I mean really? There's no way we all had the same dream again!" said Scarlet sounding unintentionally enthusiastic.

Ruby and Rose stared in astonishment at Scarlet.

"D'ya think Jamie had the same dream too?" asked Ruby inquisitively.

They didn't have to wait long to find out. Within minutes of the girls getting dressed there was a soft knock on their bedroom door. It was Jamie.

"Come in," said Rose, anticipating what he was going to say. Her lips pursed tightly together as she waited ominously for him to say something.

"You're not going to believe me, but I had the weirdest dream las' night..." began Jamie.

"Did you dream about the willow?" asked Rose almost in a giggle, cutting him short.

It was Jamie's turn to look surprised this time.

"How did you know that?" he asked with a perplexed frown on his face, looking at each of his sisters in turn for an answer.

"How d'ya think we know?" replied Ruby, a little more sarcastically than she intended.

Jamie rubbed his head in thought. "So, does that mean that for some strange reason we're all going to have the same dreams as each other from now on then? This is getting really weird."

"I think it's probably more than that," said Rose sounding a little worried. "I think we need to consider the thought that our dreams are probably real."

"It's certainly beginning to look that way isn't it!" said Scarlet, suddenly remembering there was something more important than them all having similar dreams. "Out of interest, if we all had the same dream again though, I'm guessing that you were all told about Abaddon!"

The others turned sickly pale hearing this name. It was as if they didn't want to believe it had been said at all, let alone contemplating that it could possibly be true. There was an awkward silence briefly and then...

"Actually, yes. Breanna did tell me abou' him and what he is supposed to have done to Dad. I don't think I wanted to hear or believe it though if I'm honest," said Jamie quietly. "I hoped that part might've bin just a dream, but the more I think abou' it – well, I guess it would make sense." Jamie's eyes dropped to the floor shamefully.

"And Breanna is who exactly?" asked Scarlet, releasing Jamie from his sticky position.

"She's my guardian. She said we all have a guardian. You do – don't ya?" answered Jamie curiously.

"Yeh, I presume so. I do anyway," said Scarlet in a matter of fact way, glancing over her sisters for conformation of her implications.

The other two girls nodded in agreement, but it was clear that none of them felt comfortable talking about either Abaddon or Dennis just yet. It was as if by not talking about what they had been told, it somehow it made it less real.

Seeing that the other children weren't prepared to talk or entertain the idea of what was going on in their house, Scarlet decided not to push the subject any further. In her opinion she thought it should have been discussed more freely, but since now wasn't a good time, she would just have to wait until they were ready.

Scarlet had lots more to talk about anyway, there was the small matter Esperanza had told her about, regarding a special gift that Jamie had. Maybe he would be happier to talk about that instead.

"Okay. We don't have to talk about Abaddon now I s'pose, but Esperanza said you had a power you might be aware of Jamie. D'ya know what she's talkin' about?"

"Esperanza's your guardian, right?" asked Jamie, wrinkling his brow curiously without answering her question.

"Yes, she is. Didn't we just agree that though?" she asked dubiously. "She's the white lady I keep seeing Ruby," she continued acrimoniously, directing her comment at Ruby.

"The lady in *black* came to me," Ruby said smugly. "You know – the one I told *you* about. She said her name was Rhomelda." Ruby fell silent for a moment in thought allowing her mind to wonder off, and then quite suddenly snapped free of her trance. "Did your guardian visit you too Rose?"

Rose nodded. She could see Jamie wanted to share something with them, his face had gone pale and he looked panicked. She gestured with a slight sideways nod to get the others attention.

"What is it Jamie? What's the matter?" coaxed Ruby softly.

Jamie slowly raised his head, propping his brow in his hands, while his eyes remained fixed to the floor.

"Breanna told me somethin' else. Something I'm not comfortable talking about. Somethin' I shut off from years ago," Jamie spoke slowly and carefully, he had an edge of uncertainty about him. "She told me I shouldn't be afraid to use my power. She called it telekinesis."

Jamie glanced up to see how his sisters reacted to this news. They were poised at the edge of the bed, sitting perfectly still waiting for him to tell them more.

"It's a gift where I can move things with me mind," Jamie explained, his head remained low in his hands; obviously troubled by this thought.

"Whoa, really? You can do that?" chirped Scarlet in excitement. "That's amazin'."

Jamie didn't look pleased about this in the slightest; his eyes couldn't make contact with the girls, his shame disallowed him to even lift his head as he reminisced his past.

"What's the matter Jamie?" asked Scarlet with concern. "You look really upset. I would be thrilled if I thought I had a gift like yours!" She put her arm around his shoulders to try and comfort him, hoping it might help him divulge his secret.

Jamie lifted his head slightly, catching Ruby's eye. He had to tell now, he could see the girls were waiting for him to tell his story and he understood there was no way they'd let him back out now.

He huffed, taking in a lungful of air as if he were about to swim underwater for a while, but his nerves prevailed and his mouth locked shut. He squeezed his hands, locking them together into hard fists. Perhaps talking about it might help him feel better, he told himself. Maybe someone else could judge the situation better if they knew what he had kept secret for so long.

"It's really hard for me to talk about this. It makes me feel scared just remembering it, like it all 'appened yesterday." He paused again as if trying to find the strength to continue with his story.

The girls said nothing this time; they instead sat quietly, waiting for him to find the courage to speak. Jamie inhaled deeply again and then as if by some miracle he found the strength to talk.

"Something used to happen on a regular basis before my Dad and me came here to live with you lot. It terrifies me every time I think about it, so to 'ave it confirmed by Breanna, well – now it's made me even more afraid."

The girls looked on in anticipation, the suspense was killing them. They leaned forward on their bed to hear what Jamie was about to tell them.

"Go on, don't stop there," encouraged Rose, edging ever more forward.

Jamie glanced up at the girls and continued.

"Well, as I was sayin', before we moved in with you an' yer Mum, we lived just a few doors up from where you were.

"The 'ouse had two bedrooms, I gave mine up for you girls the nigh' of the fire and shared with Dad. The mornin' you left, I was playin' on my own in my room with the Lego. Do you remember – we were building a house?" He smiled as he remembered that particular moment in time. "Anyway, that's when I 'eard some really bizarre sounds comin' from Dad's bedroom. It was like 'e was whisperin' to someone, but I knew there was no one else in the 'ouse cos you girls 'ad left already.

"I was curious so I tiptoed across the landin'. I don't know why I felt compelled to go quietly, bu' I just knew I had to.

"Dad's bedroom door was slightly open an' I could still see enough through the crack – that's when I saw it…" He stopped again, almost unable to carry on.

"You saw what?" prompted Ruby.

"I saw Dad," he said sharply. "I saw Dad – only it didn't look like Dad anymore. He was hunched down on his toes, you know, like in a squatting position. His arms were outstretched and his hands were resting on the floor in front of him. He was – sort of shaking – like he had been given an electric shock or somethin'."

Jamie shuddered suddenly as though he had been locked into a state of fear; his eyes squinted as his mind re-played the horrific moment.

"He had these bright-yellow, neon eyes, and he was mutterin' somethin' in a different language. It really scared me, so I went back as fast as I could to my room. I didn't say anything to him when I finally saw him later in the day. I didn't want to go down at first when I 'eard him leave his bedroom; I was still too scared. He didn't say anything either, he looked normal again, and so I just hoped it was my imagination.

"That night when Dad sent me to bed, I was just about to fall asleep when I 'eard a tapping at the window. Then a soft voice called to me, it was a lady's voice – she was asking me to come away with 'er."

"Did you go and see who it was Jamie?" asked Scarlet, her eyes glistened with feverish anticipation as she listened to Jamie's story.

"I was going to," continued Jamie. "But then just as I was about to get ou' of bed, the flipping thing started to lift up from the floor dint it. It was only a little bit at first, but it scared the life outta me. Then I thought it was just my imagination, so I swung my leg out again, my toe almost touched the floor when it moved again, much higher this time.

"I quickly pulled my leg back in and hid under the covers. I thought that whatever was moving it migh' go away, bu' it dint, it just got worse, bouncin' about – making a huge racket. Dad must have 'eard it, but he dint come and investigate the noise. I was screamin' fer 'im to help, but he jus' dint come.

"When it stopped, I jumped outta bed and ran to Dad in the front room. I told 'im what 'ad 'appened, but he just laughed at me and told me I had an overactive imagination. I tried to tell 'im again – that's when he got angry with me, he demanded that I go back to bed. I was absolutely petrified – I mean really scared."

He stopped again. His eyes glazed over with the emotions he held back in his throat as he relived those terrifying moments.

"Then what 'appened?" asked Rose.

She was trying not to sound too excited by his story, but it was so difficult to sound sympathetic when his story was so creepy.

Jamie swallowed the lump in his throat. "I went back to the bedroom like he told me to. I go' back into bed and tried to sleep. I just couldn't settle though. I still wasn't sure if it had bin real, but the whole thing just kept replaying in me 'ead like a bad dream I was unable to wake from. When Dad came to bed, I was sort of relieved that I wasn't on my own anymore. His room was only across the landin' and I thought I'd be safe."

"Thank goodness you had your Dad then!" said Scarlet.

"No actually," continued Jamie. "I dint feel safe for long, 'cos shortly after he went to bed, my bed started shakin' again, levitatin' quite high and shiftin' from side to side like it was tryin' to throw me out. And then the covers were ripped off me bed with one sharp jerk, suddenly it came crashing down onto the floor again. I was more than petrified, I've never bin that scared since then.

"I ran as fast as I could to Dad's room and jumped in bed with 'im. I dint want to be on my own anymore that nigh'."

"So did he believe ya now?" asked Scarlet sympathetically.

"No. He just said I was makin' it up for attention – that was until it 'appened again. I was actually quite pleased it 'appened in his room this time. He couldn't say it was in me 'ed if he saw it for 'imself."

"It's just as well he saw it then. He had to believe you now," said Ruby feeling slightly relieved for him.

"Yeah, he believed me. But now he decided it was me who had been movin' the bed, and ordered me to stop it. I tried to tell 'im it wasn't me, but he just kept insisting tha' it was. He said, "Beds don't move on their own.""

"He made me get outta the bed and stand in the corner for lying and causin' trouble. I couldn't believe he was blaming me for this; most dads would be gettin' out the bed themselves to investigate what migh' have been goin' on, but he wasn't even worried, he dint even sound nervous. He just pushed the blame on me, then when it started again, he started shoutin' at me, telling me to stop otherwise he would throw me out into the street. I tried to explain – I tried, but all I could do was watch from the corner of the room while it continued bouncin' about.

"Anyway, after a while it calmed down and stopped. You've no idea how terrified I was. Nobody knows about it apart from Dad, but he dunt say anythin'. I was only 8; honestly, I can't tell you all how petrified I was.

"After that nigh', it happened again on several occasions, with me getting the blame every time. It all stopped when we moved 'ere, with you girls and yer mum."

The girls were visibly shaken up at this terrifying story. Jamie's head hung low while the girls wondered how they could make him feel less traumatised.

"Oh Jamie, that's really bad. I can't believe wha' you must have gone through," said Scarlet at last, finding a few words which she thought might help. She actually felt a bit guilty for feeling so excited about hearing his tale.

"That's why I'm so afraid to use my mind to move things now," continued Jamie with a fresh breath and a new found strength. "If that *was* me, I have no idea how I did it. Why would I want to relive my past? I obviously 'ave no control over it, you girls weren't there, you dint see or experience what I did, you've no idea how frightened I was. An' I don't want to be scared anymore."

The girls looked compassionately at him. It was very understandable why he didn't want to have this, so-called 'gift'.

"What about the lady's voice, did Breanna explain that to you?" asked Scarlet, changing the conversation slightly to take the edge off what they had just been discussing.

"Yes, she told me it was her. She said she was tryin' to protect me. Apparently, she had wanted me to go to a safe house in Dreamworld with 'er," answered Jamie in cold frustration.

"That makes no sense. Why would she want to protect *you* from yourself Jamie?" asked Scarlet.

"Well I don't know do I?" snapped Jamie sharply.

After a few minutes of complete silence, and deep thought, Scarlet interrupted with another question.

"You said Breanna wanted to take you to Dreamworld. That must mean Dreamworld really is a place we can get to from here. Wouldn't it be fantastic if the willow *was* the entrance into a magical new world?"

"It couldn't be an entrance to Dreamworld Scarlet, we all saw 'ow small that door was. The only thing even small enough to pass through there would be some kinda fairy. Besides, we already know how we enter Dreamworld, it's through our thoughts and dreams," explained Jamie factually.

"Small?" queried Scarlet in surprise. "You found a door? I couldn't work out where the door actually was. All I could see was where the key fitted."

"Really?" said Jamie in bemusement. "I saw the edge of the door almost instantly."

Scarlet felt suddenly annoyed. How on earth could she have not seen it if the others had no problems identifying it so easily? Esperanza had told her to see past what seemed impossible, perhaps she hadn't been able to visualise a small door simply because she had expected it to be big enough for her to enter through.

"The key in Scarlet's drawer *does* look like the one. It might fit!" continued Jamie ignoring Scarlet's obvious confusion.

"The tree *was* a dream wasn't it?" said Scarlet with uncertainty.

"Perhaps not! What *if* the key fits into it? The key is real – why wouldn't the tree also be real?" said Ruby hopefully.

The children by now were ready for school, and together they left the house, talking as they went.

"I think I'd like to know how much of the dream was real, and how much was just in our minds?" said Jamie. "I mean, we can't all go flyin' around like we did in our dreams, can we? But there has to be some aspects that are real!"

"We could go to the Whisperin' Wood after school and find out," suggested Scarlet. "We might get some answers, we migh' even be able to find the willow – if it really exists. We'll have to go home first to collect the key though."

"Sounds good to me!" said Rose, probably more enthusiastically than she had intended to.

Chapter Eighteen
The Willow

"We'll need to take extra food from the school canteen at lunch time; Dennis will go spare if we take food from home. You know how cross he got at us when he thought we had taken a spoonful of sugar from the sugar bowl."

Scarlet was referring to the time that Dennis had seen sugar grains on the tea tray. He had insinuated that the children had been greedily gobbling it up and had punished them all for not owning up to it. The fact remained that the only person allowed to consume sugar in the house was him. He used it in his tea, piling spoonful's of the sweet, sticky stuff into his drinks and often spilled some from the over heaped spoons onto the little silver tray.

There was no wonder his teeth were so rotten, alongside his smoking habit, the cards were heavily stacked up against his gingivitis gums to ever make any comeback, but then, he didn't deserve nice teeth anyway; it served him right for being so selfish.

"You know that's a good point," said Jamie. "We migh' get hungry on the way."

School dragged by again that day. Just lately, it seemed as though extra hours had been added onto the ends of the days just to make them more tedious. When eventually the school bell rang announcing the end of day, the children hurried home, anxious to meet back there in order to make a start on their adventure.

Scarlet rushed up the stairs to her room, grabbed the small package from her drawer and pushed it into her coat pocket.

Dennis was nowhere to be found again. He was more than likely hiding away in his shed, but that was always good for the children as it meant there would be no head games. The children got changed out of their school clothes, scribbled a quick note to Dennis then hurried back outside.

Their excitement was heightened beyond any feeling they had felt before. They weren't sure what they would or wouldn't find once they reached the willow; if there really was such a magical tree to begin with, but they hoped they hadn't been tricked into believing something so miraculous could exist, only to find they really had been just dreaming.

There was a huge amount of chatter among the children, and great excitement as they walked to the wood. It took a little while to get there, but as soon as they came in sight of the trees, the children found a sudden urgency to reach them sooner.

"Come on, where almost there," shouted Jamie, encouraging the girls to follow him as he miraculously unleashed some pent-up energy from goodness only knows where, injecting it into his tiring legs, working them into a gentle jog.

Without arguing, the girls raced after him despite feeling tired, so that all four children set foot in the Whispering Wood together.

The Whispering Wood was an ancient forest full of oaks and pine trees, all of which appeared to resemble old folk, each with a pair of reading glasses perched on the ends of their noses. Scarlet imagined the tales they would tell if they could speak; the things they would have seen and heard spanning over hundreds of years, full of wisdom and knowledge.

Each tree grew a different way in shape, but always strong. Their branches grew out majestically like arms reaching upwards, firm and solid with roots which drove deep into the ground.

The children nervously headed into the wood. The beautiful tree canopies above covered their heads with new spring leaves that had formed as they pushed their way out into the light, hiding the sky from view. Little twigs crackled under foot as they walked, and the soft peaty soil squashed down like sponge.

The smell from the leaves gave off a fresh, potent aroma; so distinct that it was like a magic potion, coaxing unsuspecting hikers into a long perilous walk which would go on forever. The songbirds called to one another in chorus, perhaps watching the children as they sat in the branches above, wondering what these two-legged creatures were doing in their vicinity.

The children had no idea in which direction to go, but they guessed they needed to be heading towards the centre of the woods, so following their intuition; they travelled onwards in that general direction – walking deeper, and deeper, and deeper.

By now the children had been walking continually for over two hours and they were becoming weary. Nothing had looked familiar from their dreams, no river, no gorge and certainly no willow, and if they were honest, they were all beginning to wonder if their trip was going to be a fruitless one. None of the children had wanted to be the first to sound defeated, but the numb, pained expression on Rose's face was enough for Jamie to save the downward spiralling mood. He sat down on the forest floor.

"I don't know about you three, but I'm hungry," he said, allowing the girls to take a break without feeling beaten. "We'll have somethin' to eat, then once we've had time to rest our legs, we can carry on a bit further."

The girls flopped down next to him, relieved that he had suggested the break while Ruby took charge of the picnic, handing everyone a sandwich from the packet.

"Does anyone think we'll find the willow?" asked Rose through a mouthful of food, daring to ask what everyone else had been thinking.

"We all had the same dream Rose. There has to be some truth in it. I can't believe that we'd all be here if we didn't at least feel that it was real," answered Scarlet thoughtfully.

She was right of course. Now that the children had taken a moment to rest and reflect over their doubts, the urgency to venture into the wood had been enough to entice them all in – it had to be for a reason.

When the children had had ample time to eat and rest, they got back to their feet feeling refreshed and ready to continue. They had to keep going, none of them wanted to give up and admit defeat particularly now that they had re-evaluated their belief, and besides, it had taken a long time to get to where they were.

The trees seemed to get thicker the deeper they walked, very little sunlight penetrated the dense foliage so that the children weren't sure if the daylight still gleamed above the canopies. It made them feel uneasy knowing that they could easily get lost in such heavily growing surroundings, in fact there was nothing to say they weren't already, apart from the fact they hadn't tried to get out yet.

Dennis would question them for sure if they did get lost. He'd want to know why they had gone to the wood to begin with and what they were looking for, they'd be in huge trouble. The children were starting to feel the stress involved if they weren't back home soon, finding the willow couldn't be worth the amount of trouble they'd certainly be in.

"Jamie!" called Scarlet weakly, feeling the need to set them all home. "I think we ought to head back now. We're not going to find anything I don't think, perhaps we can try again another day; maybe the weekend would give us more time."

"We have to be close now. We can't turn back yet Scarlet, we'll be there soon, I know it," Jamie replied, spurring the girls on, probably as much for his own benefit as for theirs. "See, look over there. Wha' did I tell ya?" he pointed to a clearing in the distance; a steep, dark bank obscured the horizon preventing them from seeing what was on the other side.

He was right. It did look vaguely familiar, like an image from a dream, which is precisely where they had seen it before.

"LAST ONE THERE'S A ROTTEN EGG!" shouted Jamie in excitement as he took off as fast as he could, racing towards the bank.

The children, although weary, played the game and began running. If it was the bank they hoped it was, then getting there suddenly felt like the most important thing in the world.

They came to a sudden halt stopping short in front of the bank. It appeared steeper from this angle than it had done originally.

"Are you going to be okay Scarlet, it looks quite steep to climb?" said Rose as she glanced quickly from Scarlet and then back to the bank with perturbation.

"I'll be fine, don't worry," replied Scarlet. A little wheeze had surfaced again from the exertion she had made while running. "I'll take it slowly and I will rest if I need to, as long as you guys don't mind waitin' for a few moments if I need to stop!"

"Okay, take it easy then and don't rush. We don't want you 'alf dead when we get to the top. It would be such a waste of time if we 'ad to turn back just as we arrived because of your lungs," said Jamie.

A cheeky smile had made its way onto his face hiding the real worry they all shared for Scarlet's health.

The children carefully began their ascent, climbing slowly, taking care not to slip on the tree roots or fall into small animal holes which had made their homes there.

It was a struggle for Scarlet. The steep climb took more energy than she thought it would, but she didn't want to slow anyone down on her behalf. It had taken ages to get this far already and she was just as eager as the others to know if this was the final leg of the journey.

As they finally reached the peak, the children were relieved to see not just the river, but also the willow. It was just as they had seen this vision in their dreams – absolutely breath-taking.

Their hearts leapt with joy, skipping a few beats out of turn at this extraordinary sight set out before them. To think they had started this journey on just a whim, to now behold a vision from a dream seemed surreal. They had even doubted its existence as they had walked knowing they were just as likely to find nothing.

"COME ON!" Jamie shouted to the girls suddenly as he began his descent into what would turn out to be the most undignified, humiliating event to ever make a mark in his life.

Unfortunately, any logic that had been in his head previously, now seemed to vanish, rendering him brainless. Without taking the steepness of the bank into consideration, or the fact that gravity would also have a huge part to play in his next move, he began to run.

Initially, he maintained his stature of grace, but before long the inevitable happened. The obstacle course that they had all been so careful to avoid becoming ensnared in as they had climbed, now appeared to be sprouting new protrusions from every direction on the way down.

One minute he was in control of the descent, and the next, his foot became tangled in one of the many tree roots, tripping his pace into a full blown, downhill sprint. Faster and faster he went. He looked like a boy possessed, having no control over his body as his legs raced down the bank until he became nothing more than a fuzzy blur heading straight for the river flowing at the bottom.

The girls stared on in bemusement. They could see exactly what he was about to do and had now started to laugh at how ridiculous he appeared and at the obvious outcome of his new found, sporting, athletic abilities.

Jamie's speed took him swiftly to a ledge near the bottom before forcing him to make his most spectacular, Herculean movement yet.

Initially the girls thought he was going to try and leap from this ledge, catapulting himself across the river to the other side – which in itself might not have been a bad idea, but this didn't go to plan if indeed these were his thoughts.

Instead, his ungainly descent had one final twist to play. His foot sank deep in a rabbit hole, sending him hurtling into the air, his legs sprawling as though he believed he might gain some magical ability to suddenly walk through the air, while his arms flayed wildly around like a crazy person.

Within a fraction of a second his humiliation had etched its place permanently in his life concluding with the biggest splash, sending huge droplets of water high into the air. Jamie's ultimate mortification eventually ended with him sitting on his backside in the river with water cascading off his face before trickling down his back, completely soaked and feeling extremely sorry for himself.

The girls fell onto their knees, laughing until they ached. Their minds replaying over and over again the frenzied strides he had taken in order to stay upright as he plummeted towards the river at such phenomenal speed. It didn't help that he remained glued in his final position dripping like a drowned rat, looking ludicrously pitiful.

The girls carefully picked their way down the bank and reached the bottom, safe and dry. They were still laughing when they approached, just as Jamie was getting to his feet.

"Are you hurt?" asked Scarlet through broken laughter, desperately trying to stop laughing at him.

"Only my pride," he answered timidly. "I'm just wet. I feel like a right prune."

He waded out of the river and climbed up the river's edge, still managing to add a few extra slips on the wet, green pebbles for good measure as he scrambled out.

When he was firmly back on dry ground, and after the girls' had recomposed themselves from their hysterics, they made their way to the willow. You couldn't miss it with its beautiful, long swishing branches. They reminded Scarlet of animal tails the way they swayed from side to side brushing the forest floor.

The children gulped as they carefully pushed aside the branches, unsure of what they'd find in its centre. In the middle, the big old trunk they expected to see, stood strong and thick. It was easy to imagine there might actually be a secret door hiding in its bark. The children glanced over it, looking for the little door that they desperately hoped would be there.

"It's there. Look!" gasped Rose in surprise, pointing to the little door obscurely and cleverly hidden within the pattern of the tree bark.

The children bent down to see – sure enough there it was. A small hole where the key fitted was showing. It looked tiny and so easy to miss if someone had stumbled upon this doorway by chance.

"The key Scarlet!" said Ruby almost bubbling over with excitement. "See if it fits."

Scarlet was so fixated on the size of the door; she had almost forgotten she was carrying the key.

She swallowed hard, shoving her hand into her pocket. Her fingers trembled over the soft fabric of the handkerchief and she squeezed it gently. The hard lump had vanished.

Fumbling in blind panic, her fingers searched the entire pocket feeling for the tiny metal object before finding it tucked neatly embedded in the corner. Gripping it firmly between her finger and thumb she pulled it out, relieved she hadn't lost it after all.

Her hand shook with nerves as she carefully placed the key inside the lock. It fitted perfectly – and then she stopped.

"What's the matter? Why you stopped?" asked Jamie with a puzzled look on his face.

"We have no idea what's behind this door. We could be walking straight into a trap, or be letting something out that shouldn't be. Esperanza told me Abaddon had come into our world, how do we know that something else won't escape if I open this door?"

The children looked a little concerned for a moment. It was a valid point; they didn't want even more horrid things coming through that door.

"Our guardians wouldn't have brought us to this place if we were going to be in any danger or if we run the risk of letting something evil out. By the sounds of it, the evil already came through anyway. We're goin' to just have to trust that our guardians are here to help," reassured Ruby.

"I suppose so," said Scarlet thoughtfully, her mind now at ease. "Okay – here goes."

Chapter Nineteen
The Tree House

Scarlet turned the key. The moment it clicked into place unlocking the mechanism, a cloud of golden dust enveloped them, magically shrinking all four children to a size no larger than a mouse.

The door swung open and the children cautiously entered. They were amazed at what had just happened and even more stunned at what met their eyes.

As the children crossed over the threshold, they instantly returned to their normal sizes.

The tree they had entered now opened out into a huge treehouse. A fire crackled in an open fireplace across the other side of the room and a copper kettle hung over its flames.

"Blimey," croaked Jamie with a dry, hollow voice. "Who d'ya reckon lives 'ere?"

Nobody answered him. As though he hadn't said anything, the girls cautiously broke away from the group tentatively stepping away from the doorway to inspect the enchanted tree they had magically entered. Four wooden doors led off from the left of the main entrance, each with a room for the children to explore.

Although being completely stunned by what had just happened, not only to their bodies, but to what now lay before them, the children couldn't contain their excitement. Their adventurous side compelled them to investigate what might be behind each of these doors, and for some strange reason they felt an invisible force draw them each to a particular door, as if what was behind was intended solely for that child.

There was a sudden squeal from one of the rooms.

"COME QUICK. SEE WHAT'S IN HERE!" shouted Rose before the others had even managed a glance into their rooms.

The children rushed into the room where Rose stood waiting, expecting to be confronted with a problem, but then they realised why she had made such a commotion.

Rose was in a room which looked like it had been made especially for her. Everything in it was designed to suit her perfectly; it was even decorated in her favourite colour of tranquil shades of green, giving a very calming effect. A large feather bed adorned one end of the room and big, soft, fluffy pillows were scattered over it giving the finishing touches. It was absolutely stunning.

A little fireplace in the corner of the room had been neatly piled up with firewood ready to be lit for when the weather changed, a wardrobe stood tall next to an open window opposite her bed.

Rose couldn't resist a peek; their own clothes at home had taken a dive in regularity and style since their mother had apparently taken a long holiday somewhere.

She hardly dared open it just in case they didn't meet her approval, but she needn't have worried. Rows of clothes hung on hangers, separated into their own category of garment and colour. Rose squealed in excitement again, pushing the clothes and parting them down the middle only to discover there was more. On a shelf below, rows and rows of shoes sat neatly in pairs waiting to be used, and more incredibly, they were all in her size.

As if this delight wasn't enough, on the far side of her bedroom stood another door. Rose could hardly breathe with anticipation. Slowly she grasped the knob, twisting it in her hand and pushed it open.

A bathroom fit for a queen lay out before her. Its splendour so intriguing Rose hardly dared to believe it was real. The room opened up to the outside with glass sliding doors which ran all the way around the far wall, and in its centre, an elegant bath took precedence.

Candles glowed warmly, casting a soft light which silhouetting the branches from the tree outside like ghostly patterns against the wall as they swayed gracefully. A balcony from the bathroom extended outside, surrounding the entire perimeter of the treehouse.

The children couldn't quite believe what they were seeing. This type of thing was only something they could muster up in their own imaginations; they had never physically seen anything like this before.

Having seen what lay behind Rose's door, the children felt an irresistible urge to explore their own rooms. They had only managed the slightest glimpse earlier before being distracted, immediately running to Rose's side. If hers was anything to go by, then they too would have a room just as enchanting as the one they'd seen.

They skipped off at once in different directions, leaving Rose to enjoy her room alone. She flopped onto the bed like a starfish, sinking into its luxurious softness the moment the others left.

From every direction of the treehouse, little squeals of joy filled the air. Even Jamie managed a "Whoa" when he saw his room.

Scarlet's room was decorated in a soft lilac and cream colour. Again, a supersized, feather bed took priority in the room, scattered with its own finishing details. A large wardrobe just like Rose's adorned her room, again fitted out with the most elaborate clothes, dresses and outfits for pretty much anything, as did both Ruby's and Jamie's.

Through an adjoining door, another room spread out into her very own magical bathroom. As the door opened, Scarlet thought she was prepared for what she might see. But this was a bathroom unlike anything she could have ever dreamt up.

It looked like a rainforest. Everything about it suggested it really was just that, but then the only way it could be, was if this room was a portal of some sort allowing her to step right into another world.

It was too much to take in. Slamming the door shut, she stood in shock as she tried to register what she thought she had seen.

It was impossible; there was no way this could be happening. In fact, the whole experience was too much to believe. Perhaps if she opened the door again a more realistic bathroom might present itself to her.

With her pulse racing and with a shaking hand, Scarlet nervously pushed the door open again.

The same sight greeted her, only this time a few colourful birds which had been disturbed from the trees flew right in front of her. She jumped back in alarm letting out a high-pitched squeal.

A humid, warm, air filled her lungs as she breathed deeply, smelling the perfume from the flora, and for the first time she allowed herself to believe this really could be as it seemed.

A pool bubbled with blue water a little way ahead; she watched as it trickled over the top and soaked into the ground.

A waterfall could be heard splashing down onto what sounded like rocks and she found herself scanning the room to see where the sound was coming from. It didn't take long to discover the source. Through a network of vines, Scarlet could just about make out what appeared to be a waterfall spilling down from a mountain into a small pool below. She had been just about to explore a little deeper, when a sudden shout interrupted her again.

"SOMEONE MUST'VE BEEN EXPECTING ME. I'VE GOT A BATH MADE UP AND SOME DRY CLOTHES 'AVE BIN LAID OUT," Jamie shouted through a half shocked, half amused giggle. "COME AND LOOK!"

Distracted once again Scarlet pulled herself away from the enchanted room to see what had excited Jamie so much. Her own bathroom would have to wait a little while longer.

Poking her nose around Jamie's bathroom door Scarlet could see what had astounded and excited him so much. There was a warm bath full of bubbles and a set of fluffy white towels had been set out on his bed, and hanging neatly on the back of a bedroom chair, were some dry, fresh clothes.

"It's like someone was expectin' us," said Jamie again, with a smug smirk on his puzzled face. "This is so weird."

"It does seem that way!" agreed Ruby slightly annoyed. "If ya don't mind though, I think it would be rude of us not to enjoy what's so obviously been put out for our use. So if it's okay with you – can I get back to what I was doin'?"

"Oh yeah, sorry, of course. I'm goin' to 'ave a soak in the bath anyway – that's wha' I was abou' to do," said Jamie who was now feeling a bit silly about a bath of bubbles. "I smell of the river."

Scarlet grinned behind her hand and returned to her bathroom. She thought hers was more unique than Jamie's, but then he probably wouldn't have appreciated hers as much anyway.

Cautiously opening the door again, she stepped out into the forest.

The ground was familiarly spongey under her feet as she made her way over to the pool. It bubbled enticingly as if inviting her to step in, while small plumes of steam spiralled into the air like transparent ribbons of smoke.

She dipped her toe into the water's edge. A strange shiver ran through her as if something from the pool had magically attached itself to her, its warmth permeated her body bewitching her desire to step into the enchanting water.

Pulling her clothes over her head, Scarlet threw them into a pile as she stepped further in. Any worries she previously had, washed away until she completely surrendered to its magic, totally relaxed.

It was easy to forget where they were, and why they were there. Time didn't seem to have any relevance.

When the children eventually pulled themselves away from their baths, they felt sleepy. The feather beds were practically begging the children to try them out for comfort. And as they lay down, giving in to their luxurious surroundings, they unwittingly drifted off into a peaceful slumber.

Chapter Twenty
Tobias

The children woke to a delicious foody smell percolating from somewhere in the treehouse. They rubbed their eyes and followed their noses as their senses pushed them to investigate the smell.

Scarlet was startled to see a peculiar little man – or was it a boy busying himself in the kitchen?

He had a boyish smile with big, silver, sparkling eyes and copper hair styled immaculately on his head. He wore a blue and white striped apron over a pair of grey and purple pinstripe trousers, with a grey shirt buttoned to his neck which was hidden under a little purple waistcoat. His feet looked quite large in relation to the rest of his body, dressed in black, shiny shoes with a cowbell decorating the fronts.

He was hopping up and down from the work surfaces, collecting spices and herbs from little plants that were growing in hanging baskets and terracotta pots above the work tops.

His hand worked at super speed chopping the ingredients into tiny pieces with a large kitchen knife, which he then added to a large pot hanging on a hook over the open fire.

In the centre of the kitchen, a large, rustic table was laid up for dinner with cutlery, and sparkling water glasses were set to the left of every placing. It looked beautiful, and the smell of the food made them realise how hungry they had become.

The little man looked up from his work when the children came in view.

"Ahh, so sorry, I didn't notice you there children. Come on through then and take a seat. I trust you all slept well?"

He spoke as though he knew the children well and that they ought to know who he was also.

"Yes, thank you," answered Scarlet, a little lost for words. "I'm s-sorry, but do we know you?" she asked with a slight stammer in her voice, hoping she hadn't offended him.

"I'm Tobias of course. Who else would I be?" he chuckled in amusement. "I think you preferred to call me Toby though."

"I do? I mean, I did?" said Scarlet in bemusement not entirely certain he was talking to her.

Toby's smile disappeared. "You don't remember me, do you?"

Scarlet felt her cheeks flush crimson. Why would she know who he was? Why did he pick her out from the group anyway? She puzzled over him for a moment, studying his face. Had she known a Tobias?

"I'm really sorry, I erm…"

Toby laughed, "Its ok Scarlet. You created me in your imagination once while you were in school, you told me you were feeling lonely and…"

"I needed a friend," continued Scarlet, cutting him short as her memory jumped into action. "Oh my," she said in surprise, "I didn't expect you to be real – I mean you were real to me, but I thought you were just a figment of my imagination."

Scarlet was starting to feel a bit silly now; she was talking to an elf that she had made up in her head years ago. She wasn't entirely sure she wasn't dreaming, she thought she might wake up at any moment and realise she was talking to herself in her sleep.

"Yes, and no," said Toby. "You can create anything you want in your imagination, some of the things you dream up are wanted or needed so badly that they are created to stay if you like. Other things are just a whim, a fancy – they can disappear as easily as they were thought up, particularly when they're forgotten about. They turn into a mist and evaporate. I suppose I should be thankful that didn't happen to me really considering you forgot about me."

Tobias glanced up at Scarlet making her feel suddenly more guilty than she did already.

"Anyway, I figured this was the best place for me until I was needed again, so here I am. I think we will be seeing a lot more of each other from now on, don't you?"

"I'm so sorry," murmured Scarlet shamefully as she tried to work out how she could have possibly forgotten about him.

"Don't worry about it. If you'd forgotten completely about me, I couldn't be here now living in the back of your memory."

He smiled sweetly as he showed the stunned children to their seats, pulling them out from under the table where they were neatly placed.

The children sat down at the table in complete silence. They couldn't believe what was happening, this was all so surreal.

Toby hurried around the table oblivious to the shock the children were feeling, serving up the hot vegetable stew he had been busy cooking up. It smelled divine; despite feeling overwhelmed the children were famished and couldn't wait to taste it.

They eagerly picked up their spoons, ready to plunge them into the stew to eat, when suddenly Tobias shouted out in alarm.

"NO, NO, NO, NOT YET – I'VE MADE BREAD, WAIT!"

The children dropped their spoons in fright, clunking them hard on the table as they fell.

The children, already nervous from the strange situation they had found themselves in, hadn't expected Tobias to start shouting at them.

Unaware of the commotion he had caused, Toby hurried over to the oven, bringing out his fresh rolls of bread. He cut each of them open, spreading them thickly with butter before offering them to the children from a silver serving plate.

The children gingerly took one and thanked him, they weren't sure now whether they should begin, or wait for Toby to invite them to eat – so out of caution, they waited.

"You can eat it you know. It's not poisonous," said Tobias obviously now offended – not entirely sure why the children hadn't started.

The children scrambled to pick up their spoons and began eating. It didn't take long for their nerves to calm. The food seemed to ease their tensions, relaxing them enough to forget their earlier worries and compliment Tobias on his cooking skills.

"This is amazing!" said Ruby through a mouthful of bread and stew.

Of course, compared to what the children were being fed at home, there was little wonder why they enjoyed it so much.

The children were actually very glad they had waited for the bread to come out. It really was the most delicious bread they had ever eaten, soft and still warm from the oven, complementing the stew perfectly.

Resting his head in cupped hands under his chin, Toby watched as every loaded spoonful was hungrily eaten, his own mouth acting in unison with theirs in anticipation of what they were eating.

Although he obviously took great satisfaction seeing the children enjoy his cooking, it was actually quite off-putting. Scarlet supposed it might be likened to having a skinny, undernourished street kid pressing his face up against a fancy restaurant window. Worse still having to pretend she didn't mind being gawped at.

"Tha' was wonderful, thank you so much," said Scarlet at last, trying her best to remain polite.

"I'm glad you enjoyed it," said Tobias, now turning his gawking attention to the others who were still mopping up the last scraps from their bowls with their remaining bread.

When the children had cleaned their plates, Scarlet decided the time was right to ask a few more questions.

"Toby," she began gently. "I don't really know where to start, but there are so many things we need to know. Life hasn't bin exactly straight forward for us recently. Even this place is out of the ordinary. What's goin' on? I mean I don't mean to sound rude, but is there someone we can talk to, one of our guardians perhaps?"

Toby listened carefully, smiling in his usual sweet way. "They're here if you want to talk to them, you just decide who you need to speak to and call for her. They're all telepathic you know," he said in a stunned way, realising that they didn't already know this.

Scarlet didn't quite know how to react to what seemed a ridiculous statement. She knew only too well that the guardians were not in the treehouse, certainly not visible anyway, but she did know who they needed to talk with.

Scarlet felt uncomfortable calling to someone who was very clearly not there, but she had been told by her own guardian to start believing in more than what met the eye.

Scarlet rolled her eyes nervously, deciding that it couldn't hurt to try.

"Are you there Breanna?" she called quietly, not wanting to sound too silly if there was no reply. "We need to talk with you."

A sudden shrill voice pierced the air.

"You called for me!"

The children stood up from the dining table to see a lady sitting in one of the comfy chairs in the sitting room.

A pair of big brown eyes sparkled under a cascade of beautiful, fiery orange hair which hung around her shoulders. Her mouth was shaped like a dainty, pink love heart perfectly setting off her elegant face.

She wore a beautiful, lime green dress which reached down to her feet and trailed over the floor. It was made with a stunning, super fine material, like some kind of silk.

"Wow! I love your dress," said Scarlet enthusiastically, completely distracted from what she had called her in for. "What is it made from?"

Breanna laughed, "Well thank you Scarlet, its spider silk actually. It's a finer silk than the threads from the silk worm and also a lot stronger."

"Breanna, how did you get here so quick?" asked Jamie, when Scarlet's awe had died down long enough to give him a chance to speak.

She laughed for the second time it seemed in as many seconds. "We can all get from one place to another instantly if we need to. We are tied to our Nexus when we're assigned the task of watching over you, and since you are all together, I can appear to you all."

"Nexus? What the hell's a Nexus?"

Scarlet stared in amazement for a moment, surprised that this time Jamie hadn't realised their connection. She had felt left out when everybody else had seen the tiny door cut into the willow's bark, now she felt a bit better that she knew something that he had only just discovered.

"You are my Nexus Jamie. It's just a name to describe our connection."

Jamie thought about it for a few seconds, "So you hear everything I think then?"

"Not quite, only when you talk directly to me." She laughed again at the concern on his face that suggested he thought she may be hearing his most intimate thoughts.

"I know what you're thinking Jamie – it's not like that at all. Anyway, your sister didn't call me to discuss how we are telepathically linked I'm sure, and I don't think she called me here for her benefit either."

"No, I know that." His eyes dropped to the floor in embarrassment. "I think she called you here to talk about my gift."

"Yes, you have a very rare and remarkable gift," she answered.

"I don't think I want it," he said suddenly, almost rushing his words before he had a chance to think better of it. "And I don't want to use it any more either. I can't control it."

He sounded a bit ungrateful for his powers, and realising this, decided he should try to explain himself.

"I used it a long time ago, it got me into a lot of trouble and frightened the hell outta me. I can't use it – please don't ask me to practice."

He was practically pleading with her now. He sincerely hoped she would understand and tell him he wouldn't need to work on his skills if he didn't want to.

For a moment, there was an awkward silence.

Breanna stood up from where she had been sitting and walked purposefully to where Jamie stood.

"You poor, poor boy. I thought I made it clear to you when we spoke about your father and Abaddon a few nights ago. It wasn't you who caused all that commotion; it was your father – or more accurately, it was Abaddon using your father.

"Your father had been made aware of your special gift through the presence of Abaddon. When you saw him talking in the bedroom that day, when you were a small boy, it was then he opened himself up to the Jinn – making a pact with him. That was the day Abaddon told your father of your gifts, he knew if he didn't try to stop you from ever using them, you might learn to overpower him later in life.

"If you master it, you will grow in confidence – if you become confident and strong – you could be a real threat to Abaddon, and that would mean he has no power over you anymore. So, to ensure you never discovered your precious gift or want to use it, if indeed you somehow understood your potential, he caused those awful things to happen to you.

"All of the supernatural activity you witnessed, like your bed moving apparently by itself was nothing more than a ploy to frighten you severely. His plan worked didn't it? I wanted to protect you that night Jamie, I tried, but I was too late. Abaddon got to you first, frightening you enough so that you wouldn't come away with me. You were too frightened to even get out of your bed to look for me.

"As it happens, you have never used telekinesis Jamie, despite your father blaming you for the unnatural events. You didn't even know you had the gift, because you've always been too afraid to open your mind to the possibilities. It's time to start taking your life back. Practice Jamie, keep practicing and in time you will be free and grow strong again."

The children listened closely to Breanna. It was an extraordinarily, incredible story.

"You must've great powers if he went to such extreme measures to make sure ya didn't want to use them Jamie," said Ruby with amazement.

"You all have powers that he doesn't want you to use," replied Breanna, looking around at all the children in surprise. "Keeping you all submissive makes you easy to control, but that's precisely why you have to practice."

Breanna walked over to one of the windows in the tree house.

"Come and look at the turmoil he's caused already."

The children gathered around the windows and gazed out. They knew what to expect because they had seen the ashy waste land in their dreams, but it still didn't prepare them for what they saw outside.

They gasped; it looked tragic and so much worse in real life. The trees had been burnt to ashy stumps, river beds had dried up and cracked through severe drought, everything looked completely desolate.

They were so mesmerised by the ruination they almost missed how high up in the tree they actually were.

"This is an oak tree?" said Jamie in astonishment. "We came through a willow, not an oak. Did we miss somethin'?"

The children looked at Breanna expectantly, waiting for an explanation.

"It's complicated really, but the best way to try and understand it is if you think of the willow as a kind of portal. You step through the willow on one side, and come through to Dreamworld on the other – in an oak. The treehouse is open to you children only since this place was created in your imaginations; most other people enter Dreamworld through their dreams, and only their dreams, while a few others have special portals of their own that they use in the waking world."

Like my bathroom! realised Scarlet to herself quietly.

The children looked out again. The boughs were almost bare apart from the odd few bunches of acorns that were stubbornly clinging together in tight clumps against a scattering of remaining curled up brown leaves.

As the children gazed up the tree, they saw exactly how high the tree actually grew. Its uppermost branches were stretching right up into the clouds so that they were almost invisible.

"What happened here exactly?" asked Ruby quietly, turning her gaze from outside and back onto Breanna. "I mean we all know that Abaddon destroyed these lands, but why? Who is he really?"

Now that was the real question. None of the children had any understanding of what made him so evil, or where he was from. Simply being told that a Jinn did this, didn't answer anything really.

"Okay, let me try to explain," said Breanna gently, "Sit down all of you. This could take a long time."

Chapter Twenty-One
Abaddon and Choronzon

"Dreamworld is split into three main areas," began Breanna. "Three land areas that is, but a fourth part is of a different mass, it's like the atmosphere of Dreamworld, which cloaks it, but I'll get to that in a moment."

"So not land at all then?" said Scarlet with intrigue.

"Exactly," replied Breanna with a smile. "Firstly, there is a part of Dreamworld where everything is at peace. There are no troubles, no worries, it's all very tranquil. This area is known as Elysium and it's from this division where Esperanza and I are from. On a completely different end of the scale is another part of the land known as the Harrowlands which is where beings like Abaddon wait for their calling. Then between these two lands, sits the Shadowlands. Together these three regions make up Dreamworld.

"Now just to make it a bit more complicated, it's not called Dreamworld for any old reason. Its name suggests exactly what it is. You see as well as having the land part, it also has a fourth dimension which encapsulates the world. This layer not only envelopes Dreamworld, but it also fills the world with a gas like composition, allowing any number of creations to temporarily cling onto the land surface." She paused to make sure the information was being retained.

"This layer is known as the Ephemeral Layer," she continued. "In this region, things are only ever temporary, so whatever is created, normally disappears after a short while. When the person wakes, the creation automatically disperses, like a cloud, thus becoming completely erased from the Ephemeral Layer and therefore from the dreamer's mind, which is why if you ask most people what they dreamt of only moments earlier, they will tell you they don't remember. They don't remember for the simple reason that the creation wasn't designed to stay forever. These creations are what we call Transient Magic.

"Now some creatures prefer the darker lands to live in, while others prefer the light, or the land in between. Every creature has a preference, but be careful not to fall into the trap of believing that everything that thrives in the Harrowlands must be bad and vice versa. Not every creature living in Elysium is peaceful, but as a general rule the land in which the creature lives depicts how the being thinks and behaves. The majority of creatures that seek out the dark do so because they have an essence of wickedness about them, but others do so purely because that is how they best adapt.

"The Harrowlands are a place many of us would struggle to survive in; it's harsh and rocky. There are caves and mountains; the soil is infertile, dusty and inhospitable. Fire spurts up like fountains through the dry ground; only the hardiest of plants or vegetation grows there. You have to be very strong and determined, or very powerful to live or survive on that side.

"This is where Abaddon fits in. He was created in the mind of another human who became possessed by the original Jinn, Choronzon. When the entity is complete, the Jinn enters Dreamworld through the hosts mind when he sleeps, and there he waits for his own calling.

"You see when humans open themselves to the Jinn, they find an irresistible urge, compelling them to create another Jinn, thus enhancing the strength of their army. The first and original Jinn, as I just stated, was named Choronzon. He didn't materialise from somebody's imagination though, he actually started off as a guardian.

"He realised that he had power to influence his Nexus and that power got him thinking. Instead of serving, he realised that by manipulating his Nexus, he could in fact take control, and with enough time, have power over mankind.

"The more he was able to influence his Nexus to act on his behalf, the more he was able to take over the human mind, basically poaching the body like a parasite, thereby claiming the life of the very person he was supposed to protect.

"After he had complete possession of his Nexus, he began building his army of Jinn. The Harrowlands were the perfect place to house them, a place where nightmares are naturally born.

"Choronzon saw first-hand how he was able to sway a person's mind. He had watched over his Nexus for many years and knew exactly what made a person vulnerable. He understood that throughout the day, people become tired and mentally fatigued, but when they sleep, they rejuvenate their energy making them able to fight on with another day and the problems that day might bring.

However, by causing a person to have unsettled sleep, it eventually breaks the mind and therefore the persons' spirit, making them an easy target. The weaker the mind, the easier it is to cause torment until eventually, the human is driven to insanity through continual haunting nightmares.

"Thankfully, a human doesn't normally just fall under the influence of a Jinn by losing sleep though. For this to happen, the person has to have committed a horrific crime first. The Jinn is then able to lock onto its human host, and from then on, the person slowly loses himself to the demon possessing him.

"Now, when Dennis committed arson and murder, he attracted Abaddon who locked onto him, making him his host, and from that day on, he was able to make your lives miserable."

"What happened to Mum then? Where is she and why did he get rid of her? We all know that he did something. You don't jus' forget who you are overnight. It doesn't make any sense why she just went away," asked Scarlet, her tone mixed with both intrigue and anger.

"The moment he married your mother, his main objective was to destroy and humiliate the family. Any love he thought he had towards your mother previously, died the second Abaddon entered his body. When your mother started asking questions about the night of the fire, she became suspicious of him and threatened to go to the police. Since she was no longer any use to him, and because his initial feelings for her were erased, he discarded her, focussing his attention on making your lives difficult instead.

"Abaddon's goal is to primarily destroy and disrupt as many lives as possible. Since people live in family groups it would be logical to get in the middle of these and start picking away at its foundations until cracks appear.

"If you imagine a wall, the more you thrust a hammer into those perfect, beautiful walls, the more the wall will crumble, until it eventually falls down, collapsing and turning to dust. The mission is complete; a family is destroyed and the Jinn along with his host is free to move on to the next unfortunate family.

"Of course, there is the real possibility that a family could fight back, so long as they hold on to their hopes and dreams of rebuilding that once harmonious bond. And this is where the destruction of Dreamworld fits into the puzzle.

"If the dreams of mankind have been erased, if their minds are no longer able to focus on anything good through sheer exhaustion and torment, the hopes and dreams of humanity will be lost forever. The Jinn wins, and wins and wins again. The more loss of hope there is in the world, the more destruction he can leave in his trail, getting stronger while preying and feeding on the despair and depression of those he leaves behind to suffer."

She stopped for a moment, there was so much to tell the children and she realised it might be too much to take on board straight away. "Are you keeping up?"

"Yeah, kind of," nodded Scarlet and the other children automatically.

"Okay, this brings us to where you children come into the story. Before you and your dad moved into the house you all live in now, your father began behaving in an unnatural manner, didn't he Jamie?

"You remember the day you saw him acting strange, talking in an unusual language. You watched in fear through the crack in the door."

Jamie shuddered as he relived those moments again, managing only to nod his head.

"Well the language he spoke in is known as Dremathian. It's the tongue that is spoken most in the Harrowlands. That was the day it all happened Jamie. That was the day that your dad invited Abaddon into his body allowing him to move freely in and out as he desired, becoming the vessel Abaddon needed.

"From that day on, Dennis has been nothing more than a serving capsule for Abaddon. If I'm not mistaken, he's doing a pretty good job of ruining what you all once had. Hasn't your mother already been driven away – amnesia wasn't it?"

"Do you know where she went?" asked Scarlet hopefully.

"I know Abaddon caused her to have a lot of nightmares, and I know she lost her mind through the persistence of them, but where she went is anyone's guess I'm afraid. I'm sorry Scarlet. Maybe in time you will find her again. You have to stay strong though, that's the most important thing. Abaddon will try to separate you children next, you can't let him win though, you have to fight back.

"With the gifts you have all been given, you have to find a way to stop him, otherwise his destructive regime will just continue."

"Wha' gifts?" snapped Ruby with frustration. "Okay, we know Jamie has a gift now, but we don't have anythin' to fight the Jinn with. You tell us that firstly, Dennis is not quite a man, he is basically a human shell for a demon to hide in, and then, if that's not enough, we've somehow been thrown into battle with him. It sounds to me like we'd be better off falling at his feet and begging him to do us over as quickly as possible. There's no way we can defeat him, we're jus' kids, we don't have magic powers or anythin'. At least the las' time I looked at myself in a mirror, I didn't spot anythin' superhuman!" she spat crossly out of pure irritation.

"Trust me when I say you do, all of you do! It might be best if you all speak to your guardians. They will visit you all tonight in your sleep. You've all had a long day, and if you're not home soon you may get into trouble. Abaddon isn't aware that you have discovered this place yet. He knows you can enter Dreamworld through your dreams, but entering through the waking world is very different.

"Everybody has a spirit force, it's the part that leaves you when you die, and when you sleep, your spirit temporarily leaves your fleshly body to go to Dreamworld. We don't want him to discover that you have found a secret way through to here. It must remain secret for as long as possible.

"When you speak to your guardians later you will fully understand the implications of your presence here in the flesh. It is your trump card. Keep it hidden!"

The children nodded, there was so much information to take in, and it was starting to sound quite scary. Breanna was talking about fighting and using some kind of undiscovered magic and destroying things; it wasn't what they were used to hearing, and they weren't sure they were strong enough to take on the task.

"One last thing before you all leave," continued Breanna.

Opening the window, she cast her hand over the land as if she were scattering seeds, but instead of something being discarded, quite the opposite happened. Four dusty, brown pebbles floated in from the outside and dropped into her expectant, open palm.

Breanna smiled at the look of shock on the children's faces, but pretending she hadn't noticed, continued with her spell. Closing her fingers around them, she rolled the stones, turning them together in an incantation. The stones made a soothing tapping sound as they scraped against each other.

"Hold out your hands!" she ordered when at last the rolling stopped.

With their palms open, Breanna placed a pebble in each of the children's hands, only now, they were not just common pebbles, but had turned turquoise in colour, marbled and shiny, matching the one set in the centre of the key. They felt strangely warm and smooth to the touch.

"These are Transportation Stones. They will move you from one place to another just by thought. Simply hold it in your hand and turn it while you think of where you need to be. You will arrive instantly. I suggest you use them today to get home. DO NOT, under any circumstances let Dennis know you have these Stones. If he finds them, he will take them from you leaving you all very vulnerable."

"Thank you. We'll keep them safe," promised Jamie gazing down at his pebble in amazement.

"And one last thing before you go. Leave the key here. It will be safely hidden outside the door under some turf. That's where it will always be, that's where you will always find it – again, if Dennis finds the key and discovers what it is, he will take it from you so that you can't enter Dreamworld this way."

The children knew keeping this a secret would be difficult; Dennis loved nothing more than to quiz them. Perhaps this was the reason why; perhaps he was trying to learn of any secrets they might unwittingly tell.

"Go now, be safe, and remember what I've told you."

Chapter Twenty-Two
Eat Pie

The children turned the pebbles in their hands and thought of home.

A haze of cloud enveloped them like morning mist, while the world around them faded.

They appeared in the girls' room, everything slowly became sharper and bolder, until they had completely materialised.

"That was amazing!" said Jamie in disbelief.

"The whole thing was amazing!" corrected Scarlet in a hushed voice, just in case Dennis was eavesdropping at their door. "Can you believe what Breanna told us? It all seems so surreal. And the treehouse – how fabulous was that?"

"Erm, changing the subject slightly – does anyone else think there's something wrong with the time showing on the clock?" said Ruby, seemingly captivated by what she was seeing.

The clock showed 6.30 pm. They knew it had been about a two hour walk to find the willow, they knew school finished at 3.30, and they knew they had slept and eaten in Dreamworld, not to mention the lengthy discussion they had had with Breanna. Yet only three hours had supposedly passed by.

"It doesn't make any sense!" said Scarlet incredulously.

Jamie who had been quiet up until this point, suddenly spoke out in horror and shuddered.

"What if we've been there longer than we think and time has actually overlapped into another day?"

That was a troubling thought, one that would be hard to explain to Dennis if he were to enquire of their whereabouts.

"What will we tell him if he asks?" mumbled Rose in a panicked tremble.

"We could just say we wen' for a walk and got a bit lost in the Whispering Wood," suggested Scarlet preposterously.

"What! For an entire day? Don't be stupid, he's not likely to buy that is he? We need to 'ave somethin' more believable than a flimsy, story like tha'!" exclaimed Jamie, biting his lip and twiddling his fingers which he often did when he was worried.

"Well it's all I can think of right now Jamie, unless you've got a better idea," Scarlet snapped back defensively.

"Well let's hope it's not as bad as all tha' then. But if it turns out that we have been gone ages, then I guess it's the only option we have. It's true in part anyway, we were in the wood, an' I s'pose Dreamworld essentially falls into that category too."

Scarlet rolled her eyes to the heaven. It would have been too much to ask for Jamie to apologise after belittling her so badly.

The children tried not to think about the length of time they may, or may not have been away; instead deciding the only way to take their minds off the extraordinary trip would be if they got on with some of their homework.

At seven o clock, Dennis came upstairs to investigate why the children hadn't come down for the evening meal.

"Aren't you lot hungry tonigh'?" he asked. His voice was worryingly calm, no sign of anger or his usual contempt for them showing at all.

"Sorry Dennis." Scarlet looked up. "We were getting our homework done and hadn't noticed the time."

"Actually, I was late gettin' dinner on today anyway; I 'ad *things* I needed to do. Anyway, it'll be ready in a moment. I'm jus' goin' to serve it up."

He was acting suspiciously pleasant. He never spoke to them in a friendly tone, and he wouldn't normally go to any real trouble when, or if he did cook anything. Something felt very wrong, but it was best not to antagonise him, especially if he was just being nice.

"Thanks Dennis, what have you made?" asked Scarlet, trying to sound genuinely hungry and thankful, without sounding sceptical.

"It's only liver an' onion pie. I was thinkin', ya migh' be hungry tonigh'. You've bin at school most the day – school makes ya hungry."

The children didn't know how to respond to this statement. What they would have loved to say was, *Actually we have eaten already thanks,* but since he seemed to be in a good mood it was better to at least appear appreciative.

The children smiled gratefully, which was very difficult to do since this was a meal that none of them particularly enjoyed. In their opinion, liver tasted like hard, bitter leather, especially if it was over cooked – and Dennis was certainly no cook.

"Sounds lovely!" said Scarlet, trying to sound genuinely thankful.

Dennis smiled back; his yellow teeth gaped through his grin making his gesture look dubious.

As soon as Dennis left, the children breathed a sigh of relief.

"We 'aven't been gone as long as we thought," announced Scarlet. "I don't think he even realised we'd been away at all."

"Tha' means time goes faster in Dreamworld then, roughly twice the speed of the time here. We could spend several hours there and it would only equate to an hour here, meaning no one would suspect we'd even left. And now that we have the Transportation Stones, we don't even need to worry abou' the time it would normally take us to ge' there and home again. This is really going to make our lives easier," said Jamie thoughtfully, who was now very excited at the prospect of being able to get about so much quicker, and unnoticed.

The children dragged themselves unenthusiastically down the stairs for tea. They knew this was going to be difficult, but it couldn't be as vile as the incinerated toast they had been forced to eat before.

It actually didn't smell that bad. At least they could make out the aroma of cooking pastry and the odd hint of something meaty which they presumed to be the liver.

The children sat down in their normal seats, none of them prepared for what Dennis had in store for them.

They could hear the repulsive 'SLOP', as the portions were dished up onto the plates, putting them off before they had even seen what was on offer. It sounded like slimy mud with a bad tummy, farting as it hit the plates, and now that the pie had been opened, the smell was really offensive. It reminded the children of something that had started to decompose.

The children instinctively clasped their hands over their mouths in an attempt to stop the stomach-churning odour reaching their nostrils, as each plate landed in front of them.

"What did you say it was?" asked Jamie cautiously without taking his eyes off the slop.

"Liver and onion pie," replied Dennis. "It took me ages to prepare, so don't waste it."

It didn't look at all appetising, and the smell was enough to make them feel nauseated, let alone allowing any of it to touch their lips.

They looked at each other apprehensively, hoping to derive some courage. It was transparently clear no one wanted to be the first to try the latest of Dennis's culinary delights, so courageously Ruby took one for the team, slowly cutting a small piece away from the pie and reluctantly dropped it into her mouth.

"How does it taste?" asked Scarlet in the quietest whisper she could produce.

Ruby's twisted face spoke volumes. The fact that she was gagging didn't instil much confidence for the others to sample theirs, making it harder thereafter for them to begin.

There would be no escape from this. They all knew they would have to eat at some point, delaying it would only make it worse.

One by one, they all eventually plucked up the courage to make a start, pushing their forks into the hard pastry; they warily introduced the offending matter to their unwilling mouths.

The gravy seemed okay, and the onions were not too bad either, a little soggy perhaps but at least they tasted oniony. The liver however, had a unique taste all of its own, not in the way liver would normally taste with its usual bitter, drier tang – maybe even a bit leathery if it was overdone – but in a way that was unrecognisable as food.

It had the same texture as kidney, crumbling into a powdery concoction the moment it touched their tongues.

The revolting smell that had emanated from it earlier now seemed to entwine with the flavour, the rot obviously having a firm grip on the matter it had engulfed. Even so, the children knew they had to eat enough to ensure Dennis remained happy; they needed him to believe that they hadn't eaten today, and they didn't want to give him reason to erupt into one of his well-known volatile moods.

Forcing every bite into their mouths they managed to keep up the charade that they were hungry, all while frantically trying to keep their stomachs from erupting projectile vomit.

Over an agonisingly slow time, the pie slowly disappeared from their plates. They were very thankful when they were finally permitted to leave the table and get on with their normal chores.

The children made sure these were done especially well this evening. They didn't want to give any excuse for Dennis to quiz them about the day's events, preferring to just let the day slip into another without disruption.

"Did ya'll enjoy your dinner tonigh'?" jeered Dennis, after they had finished clearing up and putting everything away.

"Yes, thank you," answered the children in a synchronised performance, now becoming even more untrusting of him than they had been previously.

Dennis broke into the most disturbing roar of laughter, holding his stomach as he tried to catch his breath between his exhausting wheezes of delight.

His eyes watered as his face turned a bright shade of red, making it appear that a great big, oversized beetroot had been plonked on his shoulders in place of where his head should have been.

The children felt suddenly paranoid. It made them extremely uncomfortable watching him laugh so hard that he was having trouble catching his breath.

It took a few minutes for him to stop laughing and explain his mass hysteria. He wiped the tears away from his ugly red face using the back of his hands, then proceeded to inform the children of what he had found so entertaining.

"Dogs – HAHAHAHAHAHAHAHAHAHHAHA – dogs – that's wha' ya'll are."

But before he was able to string his sentence together, he erupted into another bout of uncontrolled laughter.

It wasn't making any sense to the children what he was trying to tell them, so they waited patiently for him to regain his calm, and try again.

"Dogs," he blurted out again. "The dogs wouldn't even eat it. I found some discarded dog food in the neighbour's dustbin this mornin' an' I couldn't help but think how you'd all like it. Seemed a shame to let it go to waste, so I pulled it out jus' before the bin men took it away. There were maggots in there, and it 'ad gone a bit green, but once it was cooked up and mixed with gravy, you'd never know would ya!"

He licked his lips, smacking them together with his vile tongue, mocking them with yummy noises, adding to his snide remark, before bursting into a heartily laugh again, not caring whether the children stuck around to take in the spectacle he was making of himself or not.

The children felt suddenly very sick.

"Dirty filthy pig," Jamie cursed under his breath when they had left the room, leaving Dennis to fully embrace his delightful prank.

Rose had already run ahead of the others, her hand clasped tightly around her mouth as she raced to the bathroom gagging, while Scarlet raced in after her.

"What's wrong with tha' man? Why does he always have to be so cruel?" Rose sobbed through her tears.

Chapter Twenty-Three
The Gifts

Bed time came, but funnily enough the children were not able to settle. Apart from the fact they weren't as tired as they should have been, if they hadn't already slept in the tree house, it was proving impossible to shut off from the monstrous prank Dennis had played on them earlier at dinner time.

Rose was still slipping in and out of short spells of anguished tears while trying to sleep, and the others were writhing in so much anger and hatred, that they had great difficulty to even entertain the idea of sleep.

The children remained awake several hours after Rose eventually drifted off to sleep, and Scarlet still lay awake after the others had fallen asleep. She just couldn't shut off after what they had learned from Breanna, and on top of Dennis's disgusting behaviour, it made her rest impossible.

She wondered how everyone else had managed to actually nod off; her thoughts were so malevolent and full of schadenfreude that hearing her sisters quietly snore, seemed ridiculous, infuriating her even more.

In a final attempt to take her mind off the day's events Scarlet quietly slipped out of bed and went to the window.

The moon shone brightly in the black sky like a beautiful piece of art. It was as though it had been placed there just for her, like some kind of beacon promising hope even when everything else around her seemed so dark and bleak.

She found it absolutely amazing that its craters were so visible from Earth, even without the use of a telescope, despite it being over 380,000 km away.

It seemed unbelievable that regardless of its distance, its light gleamed through pushing aside the darkness that got in its way and still illuminated the night's sky, and this thought gave her hope.

With these encouraging thoughts fresh in her mind she at last drew her eyes away. Her mind now relaxed and her anger calmed, she turned quietly on her toes believing that at last she might get some sleep.

It took a few seconds to register she had seen something strange in her peripheral vision when she had turned. Her heart instantly beat faster warning her that whatever it was she'd seen wasn't normal, but her curiosity forced her back nonetheless.

Being sure to hide herself behind the curtains, Scarlet's eyes fixed onto an area in the garden just in front of Dennis's shed. A strange creature was perched on its toes hopping around in a way which implied it was snatching moths from the night sky.

She rubbed her eyes, straining harder as it became evident that this was in fact Dennis.

"Wha' the bleeding hell…?" she whispered in horror.

Rearranging her position slightly, Scarlet watched as she kept herself hidden. It was one of those times where fear would normally take over and force a person to flee, to run as fast as possible. But her body refused to move and her eyes remained glued to the deformed shape below.

He was squatting down on his toes, the same way Jamie had described him once. She could see his eyes were shining bright, neon yellow, like an animal whose eyes had caught the reflection of a torch.

And then even more strangely, and quite suddenly without warning, he leapt up in one movement, landing perfectly on the shed roof. He automatically repositioned himself back onto his toes, balancing precariously at the edge.

He continued with this abnormal behaviour, spontaneously leaping back and forth from the shed roof for several minutes snatching moths out of the air before hungrily crunching them between his teeth and gulping them down hard.

It was completely inhuman, verifying what Breanna had told them and confirmed what Jamie had seen many years ago when he had spied on his father through the crack in the bedroom door.

Somehow, Scarlet found herself completely fascinated with Dennis's gruesome performance, despite it being so disturbing, and although very unsettling to watch, she couldn't take her eyes from him.

At last, as if she had seen enough, she turned on her toes again, creeping as silently and as humanly possible back to bed, hoping with all her might that he hadn't seen her watching.

She lay down with her nerves in tatters. How could he behave like this, and in the open no less? He didn't even care that someone might have seen him. How audacious and conceited could he be? To her, it showed he lacked humanity; there was definitely something wrong with him, something which made him anything but human.

Enraged, but still very anxious, Scarlet contemplated going outside to confront him, but something told her to bide her time. Tonight was not the night to pick a fight. He was unpredictable and dangerous; she was better off staying where she was for now.

She lay motionless, listening for a while, just to make sure that Dennis wasn't up to anything more perverted or sadistic.

After a few more hours of tossing and turning, Scarlet finally fell asleep.

She found herself standing at her bedroom window just like she had done in many dreams before. Pushing it open wide, her feet left the carpeted floor, gracefully floating up and out into the night sky. She knew where she wanted to go tonight, and surprisingly enough it wasn't to the Whispering Wood, or the willow.

Tonight, Scarlet yearned to be in a place where she could relax, a place where her thoughts could be heard and answered, where she could be herself to mull over the things she had both seen and heard.

There was a place she remembered that her parents had taken her and her sisters before her life had been turned upside-down. It was a stunning, ragged coastal town in Cornwall called Porthcurno where the sea lashed against the cliffs and the spray left an unmistakable taste of salt on the skin. Here she could completely relax; it was the perfect place to talk to Esperanza.

Scarlet's night dress flapped around her legs, and her hair blew in her face as she flew. It was an odd feeling as the gentle breeze passed through her, momentarily becoming a part of her, before escaping through the other side.

On she flew, passing over the Whispering Wood, the trees still giving off the same earthy freshness as she went. She felt a bit regretful that she was only passing over today and not visiting, but the anticipation of being by the sea spurred her on.

Before long, a line of beautiful hazy blue appeared on the horizon. The promising smell of salt and seaweed swept in on the currents, encouraging Scarlet to reach her destination.

At last she found herself flying above the wild blueness, the surface swirled turbulently reflecting the unsettling thoughts in her mind while the waves crashed relentlessly on the shore, smoothing and clearing anything in its path. Down below she spotted an area where some jagged rocks protruded out from the sea, showing their peaks through the churning surface like a small island.

Gently, Scarlet's toes touched the cold, grey, rocks, probing the surface before gracefully setting herself down.

The sea air was exactly how she hoped it would be. There was enough salt concentrated in it from the sea, that a fine layer of the mineral essence coated her skin, tantalising her lips with its flavour.

The sea crashed against the rocks she sat on, sending particles of salty spray into the air which gently rained back down over her like a fine misty cloak.

In the distance high up on the cliffs, a bright light flashed across the sea at regular intervals from a lighthouse, setting the sea on fire with its white glow.

Feeling ready to have her questions answered, Scarlet called out to Esperanza to appear.

"You're getting the hang of this," said Esperanza quietly taking a seat on the rocks by her side.

"I knew you were there all along," said Scarlet, watching another wave form in the distance before rolling in towards them.

"It's very beautiful here. But I'm sure you didn't ask me here just to watch the sea – did you?" said Esperanza knowingly.

Scarlet smiled to herself uncomfortably. "There were a few things I needed to know really, but I'm not sure I know how to ask. I feel silly even wondering about them if I'm honest."

"Just ask Scarlet. It can't be all that bad!"

Scarlet cleared her throat. "Breanna told us we all have inner powers," she huffed with disbelief.

"That's right," answered Esperanza.

Scarlet turned to face Esperanza. "I'm sorry, but I just find it hard to believe that there's anythin' special hidden away in me. I can't imagine having a gift like Jamie has, but she insisted we all have something. I don't mean to sound so doubtful, but I'm curious – well, we're all curious actually to know what our gifts are. That's if she's right of course – do ya know?"

Scarlet's look grew apprehensive as she gazed at Esperanza. She suspected that she would hear something which might dampen her enthusiasm, like her gift

163

was the ability to turn herself into a caterpillar, or something just as disappointing, like having extra smelly feet.

"Really Scarlet! I thought it might have been obvious to you. You met Toby, didn't you?"

"Yes." She smiled as she remembered how his shoes tinkled with every step he took. "I don't understand though. What's he got to do with any special powers I might have?"

"You brought your imagination to life. Toby is a real, living being, because you wanted him to be so. You have the ability to restore Dreamworld to how it was before Abaddon destroyed the majority of it. Not only restore, but make it better than it ever was. You can create a land that is filled with magic, everything within its borders will have the capacity to contain magic because your imagination is more beautiful than most people could ever dream of; you have a natural, artistic talent. As I told you before when we first spoke, you have the ability to create things, both living and inanimate in Dreamworld.

"If you learn how to channel your powers properly in Dreamworld, in time there'll be nothing to stop you from bringing your gifts into the waking world.

"When Jamie and Rose sleep, they use Transient Magic which needs to be Overlaid if they intend the creation to remain in place after they wake up – unless the magic they're using is of their own special gifts. If they do use the magic within their own gift spectrum, then they can expect that to stay as a permanent fixture whether they're in Dreamworld in spirit or there in the flesh.

"Most people wouldn't see the difference, but to the trained eye, to beings such as Abaddon and myself; we can see the difference quite easily as haze sits around Transient Magic.

"What's Overlaying mean?" asked Scarlet thoughtfully.

"If you can imagine a pencil sketching," said Esperanza pensively, "You begin by using soft lines to gain shape of what you're drawing, then as you become happy with how it takes form, extra, more solid lines go over the first markings, building the picture into a more permanent solid piece, does that explain it better?" she asked.

Scarlet nodded, "Could take a bit of time then!" she answered, understanding that this type of magic wasn't straight forward at all. There was no wonder people often forgot their dreams.

Now, unlike Jamie and Rose, whose magic is dependable on when or how it is made as to whether it stays or not, your gift is one that is permanent regardless

164

of whether you're asleep in Dreamworld or there in the flesh, it's called Physicorum Magic. There are no boundaries to what you can create, which is why you have something extra special. That is your gift.

"Really? Anything I want, no limits at all?"

"Yes really!" laughed Esperanza.

"What about Ruby? You didn't mention her gift."

"Ahh! Hers is a bit different, Scarlet. It's probably best if you let her fill you in tomorrow. I'm sure the pair of you will have lots to talk about."

"But how could I have a gift like this without ever knowing about it?" asked Scarlet, wrinkling her nose in confusion.

"Why would you know about it Scarlet? Until recently, you didn't realise that Dreamworld even existed, other than in your mind."

Scarlet thought about it for a moment before another question surfaced. "What happened with Toby? You said I would need a lot of practice before making anything happen in the waking world."

"That's a very good question Scarlet. But to answer quite simply, you made Toby slightly different. Do you remember what happened?"

"What d'ya mean, *Do I remember what happened?* I created him, didn't I? You even said so yourself."

"Yes, you did, but you didn't believe he was ever going to be anything more than a figment of your imagination – did you? He was dreamt up in your head as an imaginary friend. The more you spoke to him and relied on him for friendship, the stronger he became, until he had been built on so much, he became the real person he is now. He was no longer just an idea, but a full living being.

"When that happened, he couldn't remain in your head anymore without blocking your thoughts, one being is enough in any one body, so he had to leave. When he left, you forgot about him, the memory was pushed to the back of your thoughts until recently – knowing that the waking world was no place for him, he chose to take advantage of the situation when you slept, materialising himself into Dreamworld."

"There's no wonder I couldn't remember him then. I mean when he told me who he was I remembered, but it's odd that it took Toby to help me remember a person I created.

"I can't believe I can actually do this. Me – creating life! I could have so many friends if I wanted, I'd never get lonely again," she said, getting carried away in the moment. "You know, I always wanted a horse of my own, one with wings and coloured a beautiful shade – now *that* would be amazing."

Her eyes glazed over in excitement as her mind raced with all the possibilities available.

"Be careful what you create Scarlet. Making mythical creatures in the real world could get you into a bit of trouble. Toby coming to live here in Dreamworld was a good thing, he could have got away with staying in the waking world, but anything too different will look completely out of place. Save it for Dreamworld!"

"I suppose you're right. I might get some funny looks if I were to fly around on a winged horse here." She laughed at the thought. "It would be interesting seeing some people's faces though wouldn't it?"

"Wouldn't it just? But one step at a time Scarlet," laughed Esperanza.

"Esperanza!" Scarlet asked after they had stopped laughing. "Do ya think we really have a chance fighting Abaddon, or Dennis, whoever he is? He scares me. He scares us all. How can we fight someone who has so much power over us already? Ya said fear feeds him, won't our fear of him just make him stronger?"

"No more than he has already become. The fear you have now, isn't greater than it was before, is it?"

"I don't think so," answered Scarlet timidly.

"Well then, he's already fed on your fear, he can't take what he's already had. As you and your siblings' powers grow in strength, you will all become more confident. There will come a time when you feel that you can stand up to him. I promise." She smiled, reassuringly draping her arm around Scarlet's shoulders.

"Besides that," she went on, "Dennis will age like any human, and Abaddon won't want to stay in an old man's body forever. Eventually he will search for another evil entity, one he can relate to and someone who like Dennis is only out to get satisfaction from making other peoples' lives miserable.

"As you grow up, you will find your own powers will exceed Dennis's. Trapping Abaddon in Dreamworld is the best option so that he can't just keep jumping from body to body. As for Dennis; well let's just say he will get what's coming to him. You can't dabble with evil like that and face no consequences."

Scarlet remained silent, it was so much to take in. She hadn't wanted to fight evil spirits or her stepfather, she and her sisters had only wanted a happy childhood like any other normal child.

"I wish Mum had never met and married Dennis. Things would have been so much easier and nicer. Dad would probably still be here if she had never known Dennis."

A few tears rolled down Scarlet's cheek and she wiped them away as quickly as they had appeared. Scarlet didn't like to cry; it was something Dennis enjoyed making her do.

"Things don't always turn out the way we want them to Scarlet, but you will be okay, you all will be. Just stay strong." She pulled Scarlet into a comforting embrace; it felt good to have a cuddle, motherly even. "It's a lovely place here, even if it is a bit wild. I can see why you chose to come," said Esperanza gently.

"Yes, it is," replied Scarlet, sniffing back her tears. "I love the sea, even when it's stormy. It helps me think; it's like it understands how I'm feeling."

Esperanza nodded in agreement. "And that lighthouse over there," said Esperanza pointing towards the gleaming light, "That beacon of light stands as a reminder that no matter how crazy and turbulent our lives may get, the light of hope will always shine through. Come on Scarlet, its best we got you back."

Esperanza helped Scarlet to her feet, and the two flew home, hand in hand until Scarlet stepped safely back inside her sleeping self.

"Don't forget Scarlet, I'm always here with you, you only need to ask," Esperanza spoke in a soft whisper leaving Scarlet to sleep the remainder of the night in peace.

The children woke refreshed in the morning, all of them with stories to tell, but they remained calm and quiet until they were out of the house and on their way to school.

It was a Friday morning, the day they had all looked forward to, as it meant they could visit Dreamworld over the weekend.

As they walked, they spoke of what they were told by their guardians in the night. They bubbled over with excitement, each desperate to tell of the things they had learned.

Ruby spoke first, she was a bit anxious to begin with. In fairness she had been a bit taken back by what she had learned herself, but since it had been explained to her, she felt confident she could help her siblings understand too.

"Don't freak out okay!" she began, looking particularly at Scarlet as though she believed that out of everyone, she would be the one to have the biggest problem dealing with what she was about to reveal.

"There is a reason my guardian appears to me in black. She's from the Shadowlands, the land between the light and dark. She has an appreciation for things from both sides of Dreamworld – the mysterious and the more beautiful. She says sometimes the things from Elysium can get a bit boring for her; she thinks too much goodness can leave a person longing for a bit of an adventure, a bit of mystery.

"She performs black magic, but she only uses it for good. Rhomelda told me that I possess a natural talent for black magic. If I wanted, I could summon up dark forces to work for me; I can even dream up and create weird or dark creatures, even if I'm awake.

"She warned me not to let my hatred for Abaddon or Dennis consume me though, otherwise the magic could take hold, and I could be the one who falls under its control rather than the other way around. It would mean I risk being filled with a black emptiness just like Dennis has."

The children stared at her unable to say a word and in complete shock.

"Say something. Don't look at me like that. I'm not evil and neither is Rhomelda," she snapped, feeling everyone's eyes glaring at her in a judging kind of way.

"I'm sorry Ruby, but that sounds really scary, aren't you worried? Even a bit?" queried Scarlet.

Jamie and Scarlet looked alarmed. They weren't sure how to react to this.

"You have dark magic! Aren't you afraid that could actually be a bad thing Ruby?" asked Jamie, now finding his tongue to express his own concerns.
"Black magic is called black magic for a reason and a good reason at that."

Ruby hadn't expected this kind of prejudice; she had hoped they would understand her properly. After all, she was happy with this now that she fully understood the significance.

"Why would I worry?" she spat with frustration. They were implying that her powers were evil and were looking at her as if she was about to curse them with a wicked spell.

"Sometimes life isn't all rosy, you should all know that. Evil spirits can't always be stopped with just goodness and light. Sometimes you need a monster to fight a monster. Just trust that if I have to use any black magic, it will be against Abaddon or Dennis, nobody else – so you don't need to stare at me like that. You think that because you're all goodness and light that you're somehow superior to me, don't you?"

"That's not what we meant Ruby. It's just hard to hear that you could potentially be gettin' caught up in the very thing we're fighting, that's all," Scarlet said calmly, in an attempt to defuse the situation.

"Well, you don't need to worry. I can take care of myself. Besides you all seem to have forgotten I won't be alone. Rhomelda will always be by my side."

"Since you put it like that, I guess it makes sense," said Jamie. "So long as you're careful then." He rested his hand on her shoulder. "We just don't want you to get mixed up in bad things Ruby. Remember, I saw what happened to my Dad when he started to meddle with things he didn't understand."

His attempts to calm her were suddenly thrown back into chaos, her anger flared up again.

"Didn't you hear a word I just said? I already told you I'm not meddling with evil spirits. I'm not siding with them and I'm not an open door for evil to possess me either okay? And for your information, I completely understand what's happening."

"It's okay Ruby, we trust you. Relax, breathe before you explode," said Scarlet anxiously. "It actually sounds rather interesting. You're going to have fun creating some new mythical creatures anyway. They will prefer to stay in the Shadowlands though, won't they?"

"Of course they will, that'll be where they live. They'll only come out of the shadows if I ask them to, to help us imprison Abaddon. Then, when we have done that, they'll go home," replied Ruby flatly.

The children's fears alleviated a little. They really hadn't expected to hear that Ruby had powers which they had considered to be dark, but now somehow their fears were mitigated.

"What about you anyway Rose?" asked Ruby. "Did you speak to your guardian?"

"Yes, I did. I don't think I've ever mentioned her before have I?" she replied nervously.

"Now you come to mention it, no I don't recall ever hearing about her Rose."

The children felt suddenly very ashamed of themselves for being so wrapped up with what had been going on that they hadn't even asked about her.

"Rose, we're so sorry. You must tell us about 'er," said Ruby, it felt terrible to realise that this had gone unnoticed for so long.

Rose didn't seem too phased by it, she seemed more than happy to tell everyone about her guardian.

"Well, her name is Emberleigh. She's very beautiful, she has reddish, pink hair down to her bum, and her eyes are like a chestnut brown with an edge of flame orange." Rose paused in thought, "You know I think she's a bit different to the other guardians."

"How do you mean, different, Rose?" enquired Scarlet, a sense of curiosity engulfed her so that she yearned to know more.

What Rose would have liked to share with the others was that her guardian was also from the Shadowlands, but after seeing how they had just reacted to Ruby, she felt it would be better if she kept that bit to herself. Even so, she had suggested that Emberleigh was indeed a little different to the other guardians and that comment now demanded a suitable answer.

"Well she doesn't wear a dress or cloak like the others, she wears a red outfit – you know, like a matching top and trousers made out of soft leather. Her face is quite angular and defined and her eyes sort of shape upwards at the sides, a bit like a cat.

"Anyway, Emberleigh told me I can shape shift and morph into any animal or person I wanted. I can even become invisible if I chose to be. Isn't that brilliant? I can only do it in Dreamworld for the moment though, but she said if I got strong enough, I should be able to use my powers in the real world too jus' like the rest of you."

"Really! You can do that?" said Scarlet stunned by such a remarkable gift.

Rose felt very proud of herself; her brother and sisters looked flabbergasted; she hoped that her siblings wouldn't ask too much more about Emberleigh now, but just to make sure of it, she needed to seal the conversation down with a touch of teasing.

"And, I can fly in the waking world if I wanted to," she continued mischievously, watching her sibling's reactions rise with envy. "Right now in fact!"

"No way! None of us can just fly around in the waking world, not without practicing in our dreams first at least," complained Scarlet feeling that this was so unfair.

Rose burst into laughter. "I'm only joking, I can't really do that yet, but your faces were so funny I couldn't resist. Ya should have seen yourselves. I *can* do the other things though."

"Yes, very good, well done," smirked Scarlet, now feeling a tad silly that she had been roped into Rose's trick.

Rose rolled her eyes furtively to the heavens and let out a quiet sigh of relief, glad that none of her siblings had picked up on her nerves.

"Anyway, speaking of unusual things, last night I couldn't sleep well," continued Scarlet now changing the subject. "So, I looked out of the window – I often do when I have trouble sleeping, and I saw your dad Jamie. He was behaving just the way you had told us he had done once when you were younger. He was jumpin' up and down from his shed roof, and his eyes were bright yellow. Don't you think that's odd? He didn't seem to care at all if anyone saw him. I'm not really sure how much of him was actually operating in that body if I'm honest!"

"Maybe he lets Abaddon come through fully in the night. Perhaps he thinks he is safer in the dark. He does come from the dark side of Dreamworld after all, remember," said Jamie tentatively.

"This is very true. It was still strange seeing it though. There's no wonder you were scared as a small boy watching that happen," said Scarlet, "It made me feel quite ill watching too."

"You know its Saturday tomorrow," said Ruby sounding suddenly excited. "We could visit the willow and spend most the day there, couldn't we?"

"Exactly what I was thinkin'," said Jamie enthusiastically.

Chapter Twenty-Four
Horsehawks

Dennis hadn't shown himself by the time they got downstairs, so the children scribbled a note to say they'd gone for a walk in the Whispering Wood and that they'd be back soon.

With the room clear they linked arms and turned their Stones. The space around them faded as it had done before, and they reappeared by the side of the willow.

The children pushed the tree branches aside and collected the tiny key which had been hidden under a piece of turf just beside the little door, exactly where Breanna had promised it would be.

"Do ya think I could turn the key today?" asked Jamie. "I know it sounds a bit silly, but I really would like a go – if no one minds that is?"

"Yeah, of course," said Ruby holding it out in her flattened palm.

"Thanks," he said. A silly grin spread over his face as he slipped the key into the door and turned it.

The children didn't think they would ever get used to the transformation, or the feeling they got when they passed through into the magical tree. It was the strangest, but most enchanting feeling imaginable.

It was just as magnificent as they had remembered it from the last time they had been there. The fire crackled away under a heavy cooking pot and the same smell of something cooking filled the treehouse.

"Hello children!" squeaked a high voice from somewhere in the house.

The children recognised the voice instantly as Toby's and automatically stood on their tiptoes to see where he was hiding.

He appeared from behind one of the comfy chairs he had been sitting in. He slid down and made his way over to the children who were still standing in the door way.

"Hello Toby," said the children together.

Their faces beamed with joy at the sight of their lovely friend. The girls gave him a big hug, while Jamie just placed his hand gingerly on Toby's shoulder in a casual, friendly manner; he didn't like the idea of pecking him on the cheek like the girls had done.

"I presume you understand things clearer now? You *have* spoken to your guardians, haven't you?" said Toby, checking the reactions on the children's faces to confirm this.

"Yes, we have thank you Toby," said Jamie.

"We can't wait to start reshaping Dreamworld," said Rose in an elevated tone of excitement.

"Well that's all very well, but you can't go running into Dreamworld on an empty stomach now, can you?" he said, knocking their enthusiasm down a little in order to feed them. "I picked some lovely fruit this morning, I can mix it into a salad if you would like some?"

"No, I think we will be okay today Toby," said Scarlet trying to be as polite as she could without wanting to hurt his feelings. "Maybe later though. We're pretty keen to get out – you know; to get a feel for the place. We haven't been into Dreamworld yet; not in the flesh anyway. We were hoping to start making a few improvements as soon as possible," she smiled at Toby.

"Yes, yes, I understand. Maybe later then!" He gestured at them with his hands indicating they were excused. "Go on then, go and play."

The children strolled over to the door which stood between two windows on the far side of the sitting room, but Scarlet was still studying Toby's face, hoping to convince herself that he wasn't too upset at having his fruit salad turned down. Walking casually backwards towards the balcony on the outside of the treehouse, the ground beneath her foot suddenly vanished, throwing her into an irresistible, ungainly wobble.

Her arms flayed in a swinging motion, her back thrust over into a human bridge, while she desperately fought every conceivable aspect of the fall which awaited her.

Somehow at last, she managed to pull herself from the brink of overbalancing, back into an upright, stable shape.

"There are no steps!" she gasped in shock. "I might have fallen to my death. Who would build such a dangerous balcony?"

Toby laughed at the horror in her face, his nonchalant manner openly expressed.

"I don't see what's so funny! I thought you actually cared about us. I don't think you'd have found it so amusing if I'd fallen, would you?" Scarlet spat contentiously.

"Scarlet, stop being so melodramatic! With an imagination like yours, it would be quite difficult to die here. It's possible of course, but your imagination is very creative. You fall from the tree house, you grow a pair of wings, find yourself drowning, I don't know – grow some gills or something. And to answer your question, you all built the treehouse, don't you remember?"

Scarlet was so shocked at nearly falling, she had forgotten where she was – forgotten anything was possible and that actually, Toby was very correct. They had all dreamed up what might have been on the other side of the willow.

Scarlet brushed herself down with her hand in an effort to divert her embarrassment while giving herself a moment to get over her initial fright. Her mind replayed what Toby had said, sparking her imagination – and then she had it.

It was an idea that in reality didn't need that much thought. For a long time, she had known exactly what she would like to see materialise in Dreamworld. But to get them right, not to rush the creation through without taking every detail into consideration was of vital importance to her.

Her mind notched into overdrive, images raced through her head as she grabbed at certain aspects, building her creations to perfection.

A gentle swishing sound caught the children's attention as Scarlet's magnificent dream materialised in the distance, the sound growing in volume the nearer they came.

Daring to edge forwards of the balcony, the children were now able to see what approached. Gasping in awe, the most enchanting, winged horses drew near, their magnificent feathered wings spread in flight as they hovered to a standstill by the side of the treehouse.

These horses were beyond anything the children had ever seen before. These could have only been created in a dream, their elegance and beauty unmatched, unlike anything ever seen.

Scarlet had created more than just a few in number. A good hundred or so pastel coloured winged horses had come within touching distance of the children.

Their giant wings beat in rhythm, holding their positions while the children looked over them.

Each animal had its own unique colour combination, their tails and manes perfectly contrasting against their coats bringing out the individual colours they bore. The sun's reflection gleamed brilliantly off their backs adding to their beauty.

"Everyone. Meet my Horsehawks!" Scarlet announced proudly. "If you all think of one that appeals to you in both looks and temperament, then that Horsehawk will come forward and present itself to you as your match. You and your chosen Horsehawk will share an unbreakable bond which will last a lifetime."

The children were obviously captivated by their presence, their splendour unrivalled, but to actually own one of these Horsehawks seemed incomprehensible.

"Really Scarlet? Will that really happen?" asked Rose with a hint of uncertainty, remembering how she had tricked Scarlet into believing she had been gifted with flight at any given time.

"Try it Rose, see for yourself," said Scarlet full of elation, eager to see which one Rose would choose.

Apprehensively, Rose churned this concept over in her head. Of course, she knew the colour which suited her best, but the manner of the Horsehawk wasn't really something she had thought about. But within minutes of riddling through her dilemma, the very one she needed pushed its way through the herd to her side.

A soft green coloured Horsehawk presented itself. Her deeper, apple green tail flicked impatiently while her co-ordinating mane blew gently in the breeze like grass dancing in the wind.

"Offer your hand to her Rose; she needs to know you'll accept her."

Cautiously, Rose held out her hand to touch her soft muzzle. The Horsehawk responded, lowering her head to gently meet Rose's fingers.

A strange, prickling sensation leapt from the Horsehawks skin the moment she made contact, causing Rose to pull away in shock as though she had just been electrocuted. She stepped away from the Horsehawk, staring in trepidation at Scarlet for an answer.

"What was that?" she growled, feeling a part of her had been too trusting. Perhaps Scarlet was trying to get even after all.

"Your Horsehawk was only tryin' to make a connection with you Rose, it's how they speak. It's a bit like telepathy; you know, where you communicate through your mind to each other. She didn't mean to scare ya. Just touch her again and she'll tell you about herself."

"Well I wish you'd told me that before, it would've saved the shock," she said, nervously offering her hand back to her Horsehawk and laying it over her muzzle, aware now of the sensation she would receive.

The prickling sensation passed through her fingers again, although this time it felt less severe, perhaps because she was expecting it. Spreading from her fingertips and down her arm, the message she had tried to convey earlier now reached Rose's mind.

The look of uncertainty vanished from Rose's face and a smile replaced her surprise as the telepathic link connected, enabling the pair to speak; their words remaining a secret; unheard by anyone else. After a few minutes of conversation Rose slowly removed her hand, allowing it to drop back to her side.

"Well, what did she tell you?" asked Scarlet who had now become enthralled with what the two had exchanged.

"She asked me to name her, which I did. She's called Applerose, after me. Then she told me about her characteristics. She's strong willed and brave but also cautious at the same time, she felt a pull towards me and our personalities engaged when she came near – and the rest is secret." She smiled knowingly at the others as their anticipation grew.

The atmosphere suddenly grew heavy with excited commotion as the other children began sending their thoughts out into the herd as they too searched for their Horsehawk.

A stunning silvery lilac Horsehawk with a co-ordinated purple tail and mane broke through towards Scarlet. His immensely polished coat gleamed in the sun like chrome.

The rest happened so quickly as a rush of silent messages from the other two children reached the Horsehawks. Each chosen Horsehawk broke through the herd as the specifics were relayed telepathically to the relevant animal.

"I think we should have our first ride now, don't you?" said Scarlet after everyone had been introduced to their Horsehawks.

Swinging their legs cautiously over the animal's backs, with their knees cradled in the crease of their wings, they carefully edged away from the treehouse balcony.

The Horsehawks sensed the initial uneasiness in the children.

With every sweep of their wings, the children's balance shifted precariously on their backs, while their grasps tightened firmly around the animal's manes.

The Horsehawks flew as smoothly as possible, easing the children into the ride, gliding on the current like kites until the children felt more relaxed. Then as their nerves calmed, the Horsehawks flew higher, introducing the land below in all its ruination.

Long, thin ribbons of smoke spiralled in twisted columns high into the air, the remnants of what used to be a river, laid scorched in the aftermath of the hellfire.

The sight of Dreamworld's complete desolation touched Scarlet more than she imagined. From this perspective, everything the fire had touched seemed to call out in agonised pain compelling her to do something about it.

A lump appeared in her throat, one she recognised instantly to be the something which happened before the tears flowed. She gulped hard forcing the emotional tears to return to the pit of her stomach, instead allowing her anger to take their place.

"Come on," Scarlet called to the others. "We're going to land – right down there."

She was pointing at a part of the old river which bent sharply to the right.

The Horsehawks landed on its bank and the children slipped off the animals' backs.

Chapter Twenty-Five
Reversing the Damage

Bending low to the ground, Scarlet picked up a handful of the cremated soil and crumbled it into a powdery dust before letting it slip between her fingers, allowing it to blow away on the wind.

She scanned the wilderness which covered the entire landscape and her anger grew. Anything that had managed to escape the furnace would surely be suffering under the conditions thrust upon them. Without water or vegetation, it had to be unbearable.

Scarlet closed her eyes, filling her mind with what she longed to see, then with a sharp flick of the wrist, cast her hand in the direction of where the river used to flow.

At first, there didn't appear to be any change, but as she waited, the ground darkened as if there had been a recent shower of rain.

The land sizzled under the permeating heat, cooling as the water seeped up from the grounds belly, as if some huge creature deep beneath the surface had been forced to regurgitate what it had stolen.

The children stared in amazement at what they were seeing. As quickly as the water surfaced, it dispersed back into the parched ground, drinking it as fast as it was given up, quenching its thirst and replenishing its cracked wounds.

As the cycle persisted, the fight slowed, until the ground's thirst was satisfied. At last, the water now built in volume and eventually began to flow, slowly at first, but then a huge torrent of water cascaded through the scarred river bed, flowing downstream for many miles.

Scarlet had no idea how far it travelled, neither did she care, just so long as its life saving water had been restored to the land.

"There. That's better don't ya think," she said with satisfaction to the others as she turned back to face them. "I think we should call it the 'Long River'."

"It's amazing Scarlet. I wish I could make things the way you do," said Ruby with a hint of envy. "First the Horsehawks, now this beautiful river."

"You can though Ruby, remember. Just not this kind, but that doesn't make it any less impressive. You could easily summon up creatures none of us could even begin to imagine, like dragons or somethin'. Just remember to save them for the Shadowlands though!"

"It's a good job ya reminded me of that. I was just startin' to think how brilliant it would be to 'ave them flyin' around breathin' fire. Not that it would've mattered much at the moment though – the land couldn't look much worse than it is already could it? I can't wait to try. I hope I'm just as good and as powerful as you."

"I'm sure you'll be wonderful Ruby. Anyway, there's nothin' to stop any of us from havin' a go now. From what I gathered, the guardians said we could all create things here. Unless the things you create are within your powers though, they'll have the typical haze over them that Transient Magic has, so they might need to be Overlaid if you want them to last," reminded Scarlet.

Neither Jamie nor Rose needed any further encouragement; they grinned at each other like Cheshire Cats as they wondered away, chatting in excitement as they shared their ideas.

Scarlet and Ruby just caught a glimpse of Rose turning into some winged, bird like creature before taking to the air, leaving Jamie to walk on alone. Ruby let out a deep sigh as Jamie's head disappeared from view.

"What's bothering you Ruby?" asked Scarlet sensing that her sister had waited back with her for a reason.

Ruby's mouth was pursed tightly with apprehension. "We're goin' to need more than just the rivers to flow you know. It's all well and good havin' the waters return, but we need the trees and grassy meadows to regrow too if we expect normality to ever be restored."

Scarlet glanced quickly at Ruby. "Yes, and what's your point?"

"If it's right what the guardians told us, the moment we start restoring Dreamworld with life, Abaddon will know we're here."

"He will know *someone* is here, not necessarily us. But that's what we're here for. The guardians have brought us here to challenge him remember. If we leave Dreamworld as it is, Abaddon will win the fight and life won't be worth living. Can you imagine living in a world where everyone we love ends up losing their mind, like Mum?"

Ruby didn't answer, she didn't need to. Scarlet gave her sister a friendly nudge in the arm, "We have work to do," she smiled bravely with a look that suggested she had already started.

The ground beneath them began to tremble unexpectedly.

Ruby stared down at the ground in alarm, but nothing broke the surface where they stood. Small particles of sand and stone rolled towards the girls as the ground vibrated, causing Ruby to let out a high-pitched squeal of fright.

"It's okay," said Scarlet with a grin as she reached out to grasp her sister's hand. "Look".

In the distance, the arid soil had quite literally come alive. A fresh green carpet of growth now covered the area and seemed to be dancing chaotically as it grew.

"Are they small trees?" asked Ruby in utter shock as she stared in amazement.

"Yep, well seedlings at the moment, but keep watching," replied Scarlet proudly.

Thousands of seedlings continued to push their way through the dusty soil, spreading their tiny leaves into the suns light and wriggled up like enchanted vines. Higher and higher they grew, strong and tall replacing their predecessors on either side of the Long River for miles around.

"I think they'd benefit from a good watering now, don't you Ruby?" said Scarlet with a slight tone of naughtiness in her voice and smirking with delight. "Brace yourself; it's going to get a bit wet. I wonder how long it'll take before Jamie and Rose come running back like drowned rats."

Both Ruby and Scarlet sniggered at the mischief she was about to cause; the look of sheer amusement on Ruby's face did nothing to discourage her.

The sky turned suddenly grey with doughy clouds, forming a heavy blanket of unfallen rain over the land – and then it started. Small drops fell at first, then larger drops formed as the clouds emptied their loads over the parched land, drenching both the trees and the children alike.

"Look, look. Here they come," giggled Ruby as they watched the pair speed towards them, shrieking with a mixture of delight and confusion at the newly formed forest and the torrential rain which had come from nowhere.

"Did you do that Scarlet?" demanded Jamie, panting out of breath as he approached, still unsure if he found this amusing or just downright annoying.

"Yes, she did," answered Ruby, still giggling. "It's wonderful isn't it?"

"Oh yes, absolutely. It's fantastic Scarlet; we owe you a huge thank you, we'll be forever in your debt," jibed Jamie sarcastically.

A deep frown had set on his forehead, beads of water trickled down his face, and his clothes had stuck to his wet skin making him look remarkably like a straggly old man.

"I'm starting to think that gettin' myself dry is a waste of time; this seems to be my new look just lately." He snarled, as he tried to wring his trousers dry as they clung to his legs.

"Well the trees needed the water. I'm sure they appreciated it even if you didn't," Scarlet teased. The trees did look better for it and somehow greener too. "We'll all dry off soon enough anyway, once the rain stops," she continued. "You just need to quit the moaning."

"Moaning?" Jamie snapped back. "You think I should be pleased abou' this?"

"Hey, if you hadn't noticed, we're all wet. Stop getting so upset abou' nothing." replied Scarlet crossly.

She turned her back on Jamie before waving her arm across the sky, as if wiping away chalk from a chalkboard, revealing a blue sky again.

"There. Is that better? Or is it too hot for you now?" continued Scarlet, still trying to provoke him a little.

"If you're trying to say sorry, you're not doin' a very good job of it. But yeah, that's better," he answered, still showing his displeasure in his screwed-up face.

The children walked to the edge of the wood, taking a seat under the bough of one of the larger trees. A few drops of water splashed down onto Jamie's head almost in defiance. He shot a look of disapproval at the offending tree and tutted loudly.

"Did you *really* have to make it rain so heavy? I hate gettin' this wet," complained Jamie, now pulling his shirt crossly over his head and wringing it out in condemnation.

"You're not still whining about a bit of rain, are you? I thought you would have given up on that by now!" Scarlet teased again, trying desperately to stay straight faced.

"It's lovely though, now that some life has been restored," cut in Ruby, staring across to the other side of the Long River. A small natural pool had accumulated in the shallows along the water's edge.

"It would be more lovely if my backside wasn't soakin' wet. My pants are stuck to my butt, it's disgustin'. I don't know how you can all be so relaxed being as wet as you are, unless of course you've magically dried yourselves off!" grumbled Jamie again, in an accusing manner.

He stood up, desperately yanking at his underwear in an attempt to pull them free from the crevice in his bottom, his face expressing every inch of his discomfort for the girls to see.

"Oh look!" exclaimed Scarlet suddenly, ignoring his attention seeking behaviour as she pointed to the slow flowing part of the river.

The embarrassment momentarily left Jamie's mind as he and the girl's turned to see what had caught Scarlet's eye.

They were in the perfect place to witness the herd of wild horses appearing unexpectedly from between the trees, before cautiously trotting into the river. They still looked a bit on the thin side and a bit dusty, but other than that they seemed in good spirit. A moment later, as if they were suddenly at ease with their new surroundings, they began to bend at the knee, welcoming the water as they wallowed in its cool freshness, cleansing their coats from the ash still deeply ingrained.

The children stared on, feeling suddenly very proud that they were able to save some of the animals just by restoring a flowing river.

"Can you see how they're enjoying the water Jamie?" said Scarlet seizing. yet another opportunity to callously tease her brother. A mischievous grin spread across her face before she continued.

"They're not complaining about bein' wet, but that's probably because they aren't doin' it right. Perhaps you could show them how *you* do it. This is your field of expertise after all, you've had loads of experience jumpin' into rivers and soaking yourself to the bone recently haven't you?"

"Oh, shut up Scarlet!" sulked Jamie angrily without so much as a disdainful glance. She'd only use that to poke more fun at him he decided.

The girls burst into a fit of giggles again, much to his disgust.

Chapter Twenty-Six
Abaddon's Dragon

The sky above thickened, rapidly plunging a part of Elysium into darkness as the heavy, black clouds raced in. Jamie noticed immediately and shot a hard glare at Scarlet.

"Don't bother Scarlet. I think once was enough, don't you?" he scolded. "You're really not funny you know!"

The girls stopped laughing in an instant sensing something was wrong.

"It's not me. Not this time," Scarlet answered quietly with a shudder.

Her eyes glanced from the darkened sky back to Jamie in complete confusion.

"Somethings wrong, we need to move out of view. Get behind the tree quick!"

"What's goin' on Scarlet?" asked Rose in alarm, sensing the panic in her sister's voice.

"I'm not sure, but at a guess I'd say it has somethin' to do with the note we left for Dennis. If it's right what the guardians told us, then I wouldn't mind bettin' he and Abaddon are working together to try and find us, and if either of them manages, well I'd rather not think about the consequences," whispered Scarlet. "Quick, we need to hide – and fast," she continued, grasping hold of Rose's shirt in an attempt to draw her nearer before conjuring up the first thing that popped into her imagination.

A tree root burst from the ground, spreading and dividing itself quickly around the children like a network of veins, while the ground beneath them dropped a few feet. Large, leafy foliage and tall grasses camouflaged the gaps between so that within a matter of moments, the children were completely hidden from view.

The children hardly dared to breathe as they huddled together in silence for whatever darkened the skies to pass over.

The leaves rustled in the trees above signalling the imminent danger, and then an ear-splitting shriek tore the sky in two. The children thrust their hands over their ears, watching and waiting in horror to see what creature was capable of making such a blood chilling shriek.

A dark shadow raced across the ground, almost as though it were running in fright from the thing which cast it. Like black fluid, it filled holes and crept into crevices, seemingly hunting the children down like a phantom blood hound with infra-red technology.

Scarlet hoped that wasn't the case otherwise her hideout might prove insufficient in keeping them safe.

The shadow was now right over them, but the dark tide showed no sign of slowing as it continued to trickle over the ground like inky water, seeping through the foliage and into their hideout.

The children squeezed themselves tightly against the earthy walls, desperate to keep the shadow from touching them, while its owner suddenly paused briefly overhead.

The children froze, gripped with fear for what felt like an eternity as Abaddon scanned the land below, unaware that the prize he sought, was hidden directly below him.

At last, out of curiosity, Scarlet dared to move forward slightly, tilting her head so that she was able to catch a glimpse of what hovered above them – and gasped.

Through the undergrowth, she managed to make out what appeared to be a dragon beating its gigantic wings so that it seemed to stay glued to the spot without moving an inch.

Within seconds of casting her eyes over the beast though, something strange happened. Instead of the fear which held the children captive only minutes earlier, a feeling of tranquillity and ease washed over her, so that she could have now easily been under a hypnotic spell, captivated by its sheer size and elegance. The fact that such a creature could hold its position so precisely, somehow mitigated its presence so that Scarlet forgot the danger it posed. With her eyes wide open in amazement, Scarlet found herself leaning forward a little more hoping to get a better look, almost allowing herself to come in contact with the dark shadow still lurking in the hideout.

Luckily, Jamie realised Scarlet had let her guard down. He quickly grabbed her shoulder stopping her in her track before she gave the game away, yanking her mind back to the situation.

Scarlet glanced at her brother, shocked that she was so easily distracted. He put his finger to his lips, gesturing a hush before pointing up above her head. There was a gap big enough for them all to see the dragon without any risk of being seen themselves.

It was beautiful, with scales that pulsed various shades of iridescent greens like a cuttlefish, and a collar of horns which encircled its neck. It lowered its head briefly allowing the children to see its bright yellow eyes and it's sharp, beak-like snout.

A harness was attached firmly under and around the beast's belly holding a saddle in place, and sitting upon its back - the rider, whom the children presumed to be Abaddon.

He sat tall and straight as he held tightly to the reigns securing the beast's flight path. He was dressed in dragon-hide, or at least that's what the children assumed it to be. The sheen which radiated from it glinted in the same majestic way that the dragon did, only this time the colours were of chainmail greys and flint blues.

Abaddon's face was completely hidden beneath his helmet and his strong hands were clad in gloves, matching his outfit. It seemed wrong that a monster such as Abaddon should be adorned in such majestic clothes, and then the full horror of the situation struck Scarlet which ultimately made sense – he was wearing a dragon like a trophy, he really was a monster!

The children stared on, mesmerised by such a powerful and oddly beautiful sight. Then completely out of the blue, the dragon's tail whipped through the top of the trees breaking the spellbinding enchantment.

A huge cracking sound reverberated around them followed by a torrent of branches and leaves which came crashing down. The sounds were deafening as the upper most boughs hurtled towards the ground so that the children began to fear the trees might not be strong enough to stay upright. If they were to tumble over now, they would surely be discovered.

The leaves continued to tumble to the forest floor, but to Abaddon's annoyance, he could not see where the children were, despite his attempts at breaking their cover.

The dragon's wings beat hard above them, driving a downward force over the ground's surface – and then in defeated agitation, Abaddon pulled hard on the reins, moving the dragon and its dark shadow away from the children's hideout, taking his search elsewhere.

"Bloody hell! That was a bit too close for comfort. I can only imagine what might 'ave 'appened if we had been caught," said Jamie. "I think we ought to get back to the treehouse before he decides to come back."

"Okay, but I don't think we should use the Horsehawks; they will cause too much attention. We'll have to fly back on our own," said Scarlet tentatively.

"Oh really! You know how to fly then do ya?" said Jamie sarcastically, who still hadn't quite gotten over the soaking from earlier and the ridicule he'd been forced to endure.

"How hard can it be? We've all flown before in our dreams; it can't be that different can it?" answered Scarlet coolly, ignoring his attempts to get even.

"Go on then. Show us how it's done clever clogs," Jeered Jamie smugly, folding his arms tightly around his puffed-up chest.

"All I know is that when I fly in my dreams, I sort of bend my knees to push off from the ground and direct myself with my arms, like this."

Scarlet pushed herself from the ground with a leap – and fell on the floor in a heap.

Jamie was the first to burst out laughing. It was ironic to see Scarlet make a fool of herself this time for a change.

"That was brilliant Scarlet, show us again!" He hissed, through over exerted laughter, relishing in the spectacle she was making of herself.

Scarlet didn't find it very funny. "Why don't you show us then Jamie, *if you know any better*," she retaliated defiantly.

"I didn't say I did. It's only *you* that thinks you know everythin'." He laughed as he continued to mock her, dramatically falling onto the floor in a comical manner, thrashing his arms and kicking his legs simultaneously.

In her disgust Scarlet tried again, more to prove her point that it couldn't be that hard than anything. With her knees bent in position she launched herself again, only this time her arms flapped wildly, bent at the elbow with her hands tucked tightly into her arm pits.

Again, nothing happened, apart from losing a little more dignity.

Jamie was now rolling on the floor, holding his tummy in uncontrolled hysterics.

"You look like a chicken trying to fly!" laughed Rose.

This likeness sent the entire group into fits of giggles as they imagined this scenario. They were so caught up in laughter they didn't notice Emberleigh had appeared right by their side.

"Believe you can do it children. If you don't believe you can do it, you'll never succeed."

These guardians had a knack of just turning up when the children least expected them to.

"Emberleigh! We didn't see you there," gasped Scarlet in surprise, while still trying to catch her breath.

"Obviously! But if you're going to make this work, you'll need to have faith in your own abilities. Now try again, this time believe it's possible." Her glare firmly stuck on Scarlet, since she had been the one who'd turned this exercise into a laughing matter.

"Yes, believe you're the chicken," giggled Rose again, setting the group off for the second time.

"Stop laughing, all of you!" snapped Emberleigh crossly. "This is not a game. Now, put your mind onto the job in hand. This is important and something you all need to learn. Now, have faith! Feel it! Believe it!"

The children stopped giggling; Emberleigh had a stern look about her, one that demanded respect.

"Good. Now try again," she demanded with the same hard stare, set like stone on her face.

The children did as they were told, their attention was now focussed as they stretched out their arms, and with a little push from the ground they found themselves rising into the air.

"Good. Now, have the confidence to continue. Turn your bodies in the direction you wish to go and use your thoughts to guide you," Emberleigh called to them, as she hovered a small distance away before disappearing again.

Armed with the confidence they needed, the children put into practice Emberleigh's words of encouragement, twisting their bodies in the direction they wanted to go as they became accustomed to this very odd feeling.

The thought that they were suspended in nothing but thin air caused their stomachs to twist anxiously. There was nothing solid under their feet and the realisation that they were totally reliant on their own abilities unnerved them.

After a few minutes of practicing their new skills and hovering short distances from the ground, it suddenly occurred to Scarlet that Abaddon hadn't long left the area. Abaddon was undoubtedly still within the vicinity and their safety was possibly still in danger. With this thought in mind, Scarlet dared herself to fly higher, quickly scanning the horizon for a glimpse of the dragon. Sure enough, a small dot in the distance could still be seen flying away from them.

For a moment her heart almost stopped. There they were, pretty much fooling around under his very nose without having given the matter much thought. Scarlet was just about to warn the others when a stupidly bright idea entered her mind.

Without saying a word to the others, Scarlet flicked her wrist in the direction of Abaddon, sending a spell hurtling after him at full pelt before calling to her siblings urgently.

"Quick, back to the treehouse before he comes after us."

"What 'ave you done?" asked Jamie sternly, spinning around in mid-air to face her.

Scarlet couldn't answer for giggling, but he knew just by her reactions that she had done something blatantly foolish. Without waiting for an answer, Jamie called to Ruby and Rose to follow, his face full of frustration knowing that they were all suddenly in danger. The children shot up high above the tree tops and raced back towards the treehouse as fast as they were able.

They practically tumbled into the treehouse just as the magic caught up with and made itself visible to Abaddon.

A mighty roar echoed through the air sending shock waves through the land, rattling the treehouse as if there had been an earthquake.

"Scarlet! What did you do?" demanded Jamie again.

"Nothin' much," she smiled nervously. "I only turned his dragon into a fluffy pink one. It's a pity really cos its original colour was really quite stunning."

"You idiot!" he retorted angrily. "There's no wonder he sounded livid then, I can't believe you'd do somethin' so stupid. It's bound to 'ave repercussions on us at some point. Ya can't just go around making a mockery of him like tha' and get away with it. Abaddon isn't going to take that lying down."

Toby had just walked into the living area to see the children come bounding in like a human beach ball. "What's going on?" he asked in surprise at their sudden appearance, turning to Jamie for an answer since he was the only one who wasn't laughing.

Jamie had flopped himself down in one of the comfy chairs, completely disconcerted, his fingers combed through his hair while his face winced with worry.

"Don't ask," he spat with fury, now shaking his head incredulously at Scarlet's thoughtless prank.

"Well someone needs to tell me what's going on!" answered Toby, who had picked up on Jamie's utter frustration.

"Do you want to tell 'im how stupid you've bin, or do I 'ave to?" asked Jamie sternly, staring angrily at Scarlet.

Scarlet didn't answer; she was still too busy smirking into her hand.

"Fine, I will then," said Jamie. "Scarlet only turned Abaddon's dragon into a lovable, cuddly, pink teddy. We ran into him on our trip out, he didn't see us thankfully, but he's goin' to know we were there now thanks to Scarlet's thoughtless stupidity."

"Oh, take a chill pill Jamie. He won't know we were there, I bet there are loads more creatures in Dreamworld that could have just as easily have done that," replied Scarlet trying to make her actions sound less severe, after managing to stay straight faced long enough to respond.

"Actually, there aren't that many creatures that have that kind of power Scarlet. The majority of creatures that live in Dreamworld would be far too afraid to anger Abaddon let alone confront him. I'm afraid Jamie might be right. You may have blown your cover!" Toby spoke with concern; his eyes fixed pensively to one spot on the wall as though he were in a trance.

"Abaddon didn't see us," Scarlet pleaded innocently again as though nobody was hearing her. "He can only guess what might have happened, but he can't know for sure. He's hardly going to believe we had anythin' to do with it is he? He doesn't even know we have any powers."

As it happened, Scarlet was beginning to feel a bit worried now.

"Well, just be prepared for the fact that if Abaddon re-enters your step-father's body by the time you get back, he's very likely to be a tad annoyed and somewhat humiliated," replied Toby thoughtfully. "You're going to have to play dumb if he questions you about it or of your whereabouts when you return. If he suspects that you were involved, it could get very unpleasant. Just be careful."

"Toby, he won't know it was me. Besides, he knows that the guardians could just as easily have done it. What's he going to do even if he suspects it was us anyway?" said Scarlet, her arrogance returning slightly in her defence.

Scarlet was suddenly interrupted when a roaring noise filled the treehouse for a second time, vibrating through the air and causing a tremor to run through the ground.

"Did you hear that Scarlet?" retorted Jamie, "You still think that he's 'cool' about being made a fool of?"

Scarlet, although a bit worried continued with her defiant attitude, refusing to allow Abaddon to frighten her.

"Well, maybe he preferred his dragon the way it was after all – I know I did! Perhaps a different colour next time will sit better with him," Scarlet replied pretentiously. "I only wish I'd seen his face when he realised what had happened. Personally, I think he should 'ave bin delighted and full of gratitude when he saw his dragon had had a makeover."

A slight smile lifted the corners of Toby's mouth as he visualised the picture Scarlet had painted.

"Okay, so maybe it was a bit funny then, but remember that you still have to go home tonight," said Toby. His mouth straightened into a more serious look again. "I'm still convinced that your stepfather is going to be furious. You'll have to expect some trouble and be prepared for how he might react. I'm not saying Abaddon didn't deserve to be made a fool of, but you have disgraced him rather severely…" Toby paused.

"Anyway, while you were gone, I prepared you all something to eat. You've probably guessed by now that I like to cook, especially when there's someone worth cooking for."

As it happened, they were feeling hungry. They hadn't thought about food while they were out, but now Toby mentioned it, it dawned on them how hungry they were actually feeling. As soon as they sat down to eat, their mouths salivated in anticipation.

Toby always looked peculiar as he wobbled around completely unbalanced carrying pots and dishes. They looked far too heavy for him, but it never hindered him.

In and out of the kitchen he hurried, bringing in what seemed to be the entire contents of the kitchen cupboards. Pots, pans and plates, then cutlery all slowly made their way through onto the dining room table.

He placed the pots neatly in the centre on slate mats then climbed up onto a chair to remove the lids. It was like watching a magician slowly opening pots of potion, exposing the secrets inside.

A whirl of deliciousness swirled out into the air enticing the children to peer through the steam.

As the vapours cleared, they could see what Toby had been busy preparing that day while they were out. Half a dozen grilled Parrot Fish with fresh, green, coriander lay at the bottom of one dish. In another there looked to be a kind of vegetable bake with stewed tomatoes and sweet peppers, another was filled with buttered baby potatoes with chopped herbs, and in the final dish, a duo of young samphire seaweed filled one half while baby sweetcorn occupied the other.

"Would you all mind passing me your plates? It's easier for me to dish up," said Toby now concentrating fully on the one thing he loved best.

It looked delicious; the smell permeated their nostrils as the aroma tantalisingly crept its way into their noses. The fishes still had their heads on which made Rose feel a bit uncomfortable; she was sure they were watching as the children greedily eyed up their dinner.

Their skins were still beautifully coloured in delicate pearlescent shades. It seemed a shame to dish up and eat such intricately patterned fish, but the pity was soon forgotten when the children tucked into their meals.

"Where did ya get all the food from?" asked Jamie curiously, still with his mouth full of food. "I didn't think anythin' survived Abaddon's rampage."

"Not everything was destroyed. There are still plenty of small pockets in Dreamworld that haven't been decimated. Take my garden for instance," he pointed to a window in the kitchen. "Outside that window I have a secret garden, not too dissimilar to a few other places in the treehouse." He grinned knowingly at Scarlet. "I grow lots of my own food there, and of course I grow some herbs in my hanging gardens." He pointed to the pots hanging off hooks from the kitchen shelving as he continued serving up the meal.

Toby seemed to be more knowledgeable than the children imagined, he seemed to have secrets hidden safely away, appearing to have more about him than he was prepared to divulge.

Without asking him anything more, the children left the table with their tummies full and sat down in the sitting room, aware that very soon they would have to return home to any consequences which may be waiting for them.

Chapter Twenty-Seven
The Punishment

Dennis by now would have his suspicions that the children were in Dreamworld, and they knew he would more than likely have questions, not that they needed answering because ironically, he already knew the answers himself.

Jamie finally pulled himself to his feet. "We'd better be headin' home you three, come on."

The children, polite as always, thanked Toby for his hard work, before turning the Stones in their hands.

They decided it would be better if they reappeared at the top of the street; just turning up at home would arouse suspicion that they might have some kind of device which aided their journey. At least if Dennis was waiting for them, he would see them walking home.

Apprehension began to nag at the children's stomachs as the house appeared around the corner. Of course, Scarlet's trick had been hilarious if not just plain insolent, but the anticipation of meeting Dennis was becoming more daunting with every step they took. A punishment seemed more and more likely with every passing thought. How could there not be?

"We may as well get it over and done with," said Ruby with a dry, croaky voice.

"So long as he never finds out about the key or our Stones, I think we can deal with most things," replied Scarlet boldly.

"We mustn't laugh at him if by any chance he actually admits he was in Dreamworld riding a pink, fluffy dragon though," sniggered Rose, setting off a contagious attack of uncontrolled giggles among the others again.

It took a few minutes for them to calm down as they entered the house still trying to catch their breath.

"Something funny is there?" Dennis snarled from the front room the second the children came through the front door.

He was sat in his normal position, moulded like wax into his favourite armchair and sipping whiskey from his glass. He looked agitated and somehow flustered. His normally stuck down, heavily lacquered hair was sticking up in every direction as though he had been dragged through a hedge backwards. There was a wild, crazy, bewildered look about him that made the children feel both humoured and uncomfortable.

"Where have you all been?" he continued without waiting for an answer. His tone was silky smooth, controlled and dangerously unemotional.

The fact that he was so calm took the children by surprise. They were expecting thunderous, volatile aggression from him. They glanced quickly at each other in bemusement.

"We left you a note! Didn't you see it?" asked Scarlet in confusion.

"Ahh yes. The note. Yes, I got the note – but you see, the problem I have, is that I find it hard to believe tha' you all went to the woods for – wha' did you say…" he opened the letter scanning the words quickly. "Aahh yes, that's right, here it is – just a walk. It's a bit odd don't ya think, that none of ya thought to pack some essentials. Ya go out all day and don't bother to even take a coat, or any food."

"Were we allowed to take a picnic?" asked Jamie quickly, answering his dad's question with another.

Dennis turned his head violently towards Jamie, snorting like an angered bull. There was no come back to that question for he knew as well as the children that the answer would have been a certain - 'No.'

"You like the outdoors then I presume, since ya spent most the day out there?" His mouth curled into a nasty snarl. "Now let me see, you must have been outside for at least, oohh, five hours wouldn't ya say? Let's work it out shall we? - What time did you leave? I'm guessing around 10 this morning – would that be about right?"

"It's true," protested Scarlet quickly. "We were only in the wood, honest!" Scarlet began to feel her pulse speed up in response to his unsettled array of questions. They were all perfectly aware that Dennis was trying to unnerve them enough to trip them up.

"I see. And what else did you do – besides walk in the wood I mean?" Dennis continued; his eyes stared from one child to another in a bid to break their silence.

Scarlet felt suddenly angry and unable to hold back an overwhelming urge to play him at his own game. Resigning herself to the fact that Dennis seemed to want to play games, she shrugged her shoulders and took a deep breath, before defiantly looking him straight in the eye.

"Okay," she said. "If you really want to know what we did, I'll tell you." The others glanced sharply at her with disapproval. "We did nothing wrong. It's true what Jamie says. We jus' wanted to get out for a while; it was a nice day for it, so this mornin' that's wha' we decided to do. As Jamie said, we didn't take food because we knew you wouldn't be happy abou it, so we ate berries we found as we walked. We did think abou' you on the way though!" Scarlet smiled contentiously, waiting for Dennis to take the bait.

"You did?" he asked curiously, hoping that Scarlet would divulge their secrets.

"Yes, we found some really pretty pink flowers, didn't we?" she looked to the others for approval, but Jamie who knew where she was going with this, shot her a stern warning look.

"Yes, they were very unusual," agreed Ruby, who was stuck for the right thing to say.

"They had the softest, prettiest, pink petals I've ever seen," continued Scarlet rebelliously. "I think they were some kind of Antirrhinums, Mum used to call them Snapdragons though." She paused briefly to absorb the anger Dennis fought to retain; it oozed from him despite his exerted efforts to keep it hidden.

"Do you remember the ones I mean Dennis?" she continued, stirring him into a state of exasperation and anger. "Mum used to grow them in the garden! If you squeezed the petals together in the right place, they looked a bit like dragon heads trying to bite."

It took the children everything they had to stop themselves from sniggering at Scarlet's insolence. They were so busy trying to keep themselves from laughing they hadn't noticed just how angry Dennis was becoming.

His eyes squinted into slits of resentment while his hands clenched tightly into fists. Abruptly, the mood in the room thickened as his temper bubbled over. Slamming his fists onto the coffee table, he threw himself from his chair and marched briskly to where Scarlet stood, each step powered by pure, unadulterated rage. He almost walked into her, fuelled with such anger, but stopped short just in front of her face.

"YOU DID, DID YOU? SO WHERE ARE THESE – THESE FLOWERS NOW, HEY? WHERE?" he screamed venomously so that Scarlet couldn't escape the powerful whiff of whiskey emanating from his breath.

"We – we left them there," stumbled Scarlet, her voice shaking a little as she desperately fought to take control of her nerves, determined that his explosive outburst would not scare her into submission. Scarlet continued with her story knowing that she had the upper hand. If Dennis was becoming riled, she knew they must have hit a nerve earlier that day in Dreamworld.

Scarlet took a deep breath, determined to continue with her contentious explanation. At this rate, Dennis would be giving up his secrets before the children.

"They were too fragile to bring home unfortunately. They might 'ave made the journey if they weren't so straggly, but I suppose now I think about it, these ones were pathetic really, weedy even. Perhaps you wouldn't have liked them much after all, and pink probably isn't your favourite colour either. It's just as well that we left them where they were."

Her hands trembled nervously while she waited to see how he would respond; her eyes held his stare confrontationally, aware that at any moment she would frustrate him enough so that his involvement would be obvious. If they weren't in trouble before - they most definitely were now.

Dennis moved away from Scarlet, his stocky fingers rubbed his chin pensively. He seemed to be having trouble accepting what he thought they knew. The last thing he wanted to do was admit he was hosting a Jinn, never mind openly confessing to his involvement with what could essentially stop him in his tracks. The slightest emotion in the wrong direction could ruin both his own and Abaddon's power over the children if he allowed them to make a mockery of him.

He mulled over his options for a few minutes, and then as if coming to a decision, his tone calmed as he began to speak again.

"Well that really is too bad. I would have liked to have seen such, *unusual,* delicate flowers. Such a pity tha' yer mother isn't here to see them too, but I'm sure she's 'aving a ball where ever she is now." He sneered at her before continuing "You know – I don't think I ever did tell you why she left did I?"

The children's eyes nailed him to the spot demanding an explanation.

"No, I didn't think so," he snarled delightfully now that the tables had turned and the children were again compelled to hear out his vindictive story. "Well, I guess it's only fair I tell you wha' she told me, you're old enough to hear the truth." His tone changed to complete excitement, relishing in the delicious, juicy lies he was about to tell. "After your feckless father burned to death, she couldn't bear the sight of any of you. You reminded her of *him* ya see, and after the fire, the only rubbish left from that marriage was you girls. She said you were like a thorn in her side that she couldn't get rid of, and the only way to free herself of you all, was if she left. It was the best thing yer mother ever did; she hated you – all of you, and I can't say I blame her."

His words sunk in heavily, perhaps it was true. Matilda had never defended them from him, but on the same hand they couldn't be sure his words weren't malicious, vengeful, poisonous lies.

He smiled gleefully recognising his weapon of choice had beaten them back. The children fell back into submission, numb to his parting words.

"You mustn't feel too downhearted," he continued, now that he had the upper hand. "I've got just the thing to cheer you, a wonderful treat really considerin' how much you like the fresh air." He paced back and forth in exuberant victory smirking in the most ridiculous manner as he divulged his vengeful plan. "You can all sleep outside tonight, get lots more of that lovely air you all crave for so much. Off you go then, you won't need anythin' from indoors."

"It's getting dark, can we get a torch? We'll need some light while we pu' up the tent," protested Jamie.

"A TENT!" he mocked in an overly exaggerated, shocked tone. "I don't remember saying anythin' about a campin' trip ya fool. Why on earth would ya need a tent? Ya dint need one earlier!" He hissed spitefully; his piggy eyes stared scornfully at the children.

"Can't we at least get some bedding then? We'll get cold!" asked Jamie desperately, suddenly understanding the severity of their situation, the realisation dawning on him that his father did not intend to make this experience pleasant.

"No, no and no. You won't be needing anythin' tonight. NOW GET OUT." He pointed to the back door, opening it with force to indicate there would be no bargaining.

The children dragged their heels to the back door. It looked quite clear tonight, the sky was beginning to darken as the sun disappeared over the horizon, but at least it was dry; for the moment anyway.

"You must 'ave really humiliated Abaddon for Dennis to over-react so badly," whispered Ruby when they were sure they were out of ear shot.

The children looked helplessly at each other, not quite knowing what to do next. Dennis was sure to be watching for at least the next few hours to make sure they were in the garden – suffering. They could see already that he'd taken up a position by the kitchen window and was watching intently to make sure they weren't getting comfortable.

They decided to just sit on the lawn and wait it out. There was nowhere to go, and he wasn't going to allow them out of sight anyway. It didn't matter too much to begin with, the air wasn't cold, but as the night drew in, the temperature fell, forcing the children to huddle together in a protective, warmth conserving cluster. It worked for a while, but the colder air inevitably crept through as the night ticked by, until at last, the first shivers took hold.

Rose was the first to complain.

"I'm gettin' really cold. Is there nothin' we can do Scarlet?" she asked hopefully.

"I'm sorry Rose. It's entirely my fault. I don't know what came over me today. I s'pose it was just frustratin' seeing Abaddon trash my beautiful forest, I'd only just worked to restore it – I was angry. Then to top it off we had to listen to Dennis pretendin' he didn't know what was goin' on. I'm sick of his stupid games."

"It doesn't matter now," said Jamie gently. "At least we all know for certain that he and Abaddon are one now. Dad wouldn't be this angry for nothing, would he?" Jamie smiled dismissively, but the girls knew his smile was covering up the fact that everything the guardians had told them was undoubtedly true.

As the night progressed the temperature dropped further until at last, all the children were shivering violently. Downstairs in the kitchen, the lights were still burning bright, making the room inside appear spectacularly warm.

"I wonder what he's doin' inside," said Rose, dwelling on the comforts he was more than likely wallowing in. It didn't take much to figure he would be snug, sitting comfortably, his feet on a foot rest with a glass of his favourite liquor tucked securely in his hand.

"Speak of the Devil," said Jamie with a huff, gesturing with a flick of his head towards the house.

Dennis's smug face suddenly appeared at the kitchen window. He held up a hot drink, pointing at it with his other hand, and smirked.

"Well at least it's not whiskey! – I thought wrong about that," said Jamie bluntly.

"What I'd give for a cup of tea right now," grumbled Scarlet, eyeing up the cup in his hand. "If we were in Dreamworld, we could be enjoying the comforts of home." She sighed deeply. "Look at him standin' there thinking he's beaten us."

"He has beaten us. This time anyway," said Ruby pitifully.

A few moments later Dennis disappeared from sight and the scratching sound of the key in the back door announced his intentions of going to bed. The house was now locked for the night with the children unable to sneak in later.

Almost on cue, a few spots of rain began to fall which progressively grew fatter in size and faster in speed until what seemed to be the coldest downpour, fell densely from the dark sky.

"Fanbloodytastic! This is all we bloomin' need," complained Jamie, wrapping his cold, wet arms firmly around himself, as though he believed they might somehow keep him dry. "It's always bloody rain."

The girls scrunched up their knees, drawing them close to their chests, clutching them tightly with their arms. It didn't make them feel any warmer, but for a moment or two, it helped them forget how cold they were feeling. For Rose though, it was all becoming too much, tears welled up in her eyes as they silently fell.

"I just want to go to bed now, I'm so c-c-c-cold," she begged through her shivering voice. "Can't you just tell him you're sorry Scarlet?"

"I'm only sorry you're all being made to suffer Rose, but I'm not sorry for anything else," replied Scarlet, draping her sodden arms around her sister's shoulders and smearing the tears off her cheeks with her cold, wet hands.

The lights downstairs were finally turned off, but not before Dennis peered through the window for a final time, ensuring that the children hadn't moved. Satisfied they were there for the night, he chuckled heartily to himself before walking away, convinced that the children were going to have a very rough night, and made his way upstairs to his bed.

"Right, that's enough. He's had his fun, now we're going back to the treehouse. Use your Stones everyone," commanded Jamie, the moment he was sure Dennis wouldn't be coming back down again.

They didn't need any encouragement. Rose stopped sobbing instantly and delved into her pocket for her Transportation Stone. It was buried in the bottom, its warmth felt comforting in her cold hand.

"Ready?" said Jamie.

The girls nodded but said nothing, preferring instead to think of their destination as they all turned the pebbles in their hands – and they were gone.

Chapter Twenty-Eight
Hot Chocolate and Cookies

They arrived at the entrance of the willow looking very forlorn, and completely miserable.

"What on earth was your father thinking, inflicting such a cruel punishment on you all?" Toby hustled the children inside properly. "It's just as well I knew you were coming. There's a lot to be said about being telepathically linked, isn't there Scarlet?"

Scarlet just looked sadly at him with a half-hearted smile.

"Right, come on you lot, I've run the baths for you. The water should help you feel better; I've added some healing salts. When you're finished, put on your night clothes and come through into the sitting room, I've got something special for you all."

The children, too tired to ask questions or argue, willingly made their ways to their rooms.

Scarlet had a spectacular bathroom, but tonight even the thought of seeing it again didn't inspire her to run. Instead she dragged her feet wearily to her room where her beautifully comfortable bed stood almost in welcome homage. She glanced longingly over its deep pillows, its soft feather mattress, its fluffed duvet; but fighting back the urge to succumb to its promise of peaceful slumber, she passed it by reluctantly.

Pushing the bathroom door open unenthusiastically, Scarlet was almost knocked off her feet with the potent smell of leaf litter and young ferns unfurling in the evening night. Light dew carpeted the mossy ground making it appear softer than usual and an extra fragrance in the air wafted by her nostrils, enticing her to step out into the forest.

With the thoughts of falling into her bed left behind, Scarlet was now bewitched by what had captivated her senses. Her feet sunk instantly into the soft moss which moulded around her bare, cold feet, making every step she took feel as though she was walking on air.

The pool bubbled tantalisingly, releasing the sweet, earthy fragrance of Toby's healing salts which had lured her into the forest. Scarlet breathed them in deeply, permitting them to fill her lungs with their relaxing, magic aroma.

Peeling off her soaked clothes, she dipped her toes into the pool allowing the water to linger around her cold ankles. It felt strange, as though she was being brought back to life. The warmth permeated her skin, chasing away the coldness which clung menacingly to her flesh. Carefully and deliberately, she eased herself into the pool until the water lapped around her shoulders, wrapping her body in its cloak.

After her bath, Scarlet dressed herself in a thick dressing gown which hung from one of the branches, before making her way into the sitting room as Toby had asked.

Everyone else had already gathered, sitting in cosy chairs forming a semi-circle around a fire blazing fiercely in the hearth – there was one chair left for Scarlet.

"Right," said Toby when he saw the children had returned. "Well you all look better now anyway, that's a good start. I'm just finishing off my speciality. I'll be back shortly, make yourselves comfortable." Toby hurried off back into the kitchen.

He wobbled over to the open fire in the kitchen where his copper kettle hung directly above the flames. With a cotton cloth he pulled the swing bracket out, carefully releasing it from the hook before walking steadily to the work surface and pushed the hot kettle onto a wooden chopping board.

There was an ear-piercing screech as Toby dragged a stool across the floor before clambering onto it. It was rather comical watching as a pair of bright eyes appeared over the top of the work top, then a little nose, and then gradually his whole body materialised in front of them as he slowly stood up. The children wondered if they should offer assistance, but thought better of it when they saw how determined he was.

Four cream coloured mugs were perched on the work top and very cautiously, Toby tipped his kettle into each, releasing a hot liquid. The children couldn't make out what he was pouring, but it did look interesting. A thick, brown liquid slowly flowed into the cups and steamed upwards, releasing a wonderful chocolatey odour into the air, filling the treehouse with its delicious aroma.

Meticulously, Toby placed the cups on his silver tray taking care to line them up perfectly so that all the handles pointed the same way, then carried them through to where the children were waiting.

"Here we go! This is my specialty," he announced proudly. "Chocolat chaud à la crème avec orange'. I hope you all enjoy it."

"That's French for creamy hot chocolate with orange," said Jamie with smug enthusiasm glancing at his sisters proudly. "We learned that in school."

Toby didn't look too impressed, he grimaced at Jamie.

"You did, did you? Well this is *my* recipe. It took me years to perfect and you won't be finding another chocolate drink like mine anywhere else, not even in France," he snapped crossly.

Jamie felt a bit embarrassed now; he hadn't meant to offend Toby. He hung his head uncomfortably low, deciding it was probably best not to draw any further attention to himself.

Toby went back to his chocolate drinks, methodically handing them out to each child.

"One for you, and you, and you – and one for you too clever clogs," he said, handing them out making sure Jamie received his last. "Enjoy, ooohh, I made some cookies too. Let me get them for you," he said, suddenly remembering them as he hurried off again. He returned moments later with a glass cookie jar filled with his freshly baked confectionary.

Biting his tongue in concentration, Toby unscrewed the lid and dipped his hand systematically into the jar, producing a cookie for each of the children. They watched in astonishment as he quite purposefully handled each of them before placing them onto small tea plates. He seemed oblivious to what the children found so distracting, thinking they were just keen to sample his work.

Of course, his hands were clean enough, but it brought out the childish ignorance in him, making it obvious that he didn't fully comprehend the customary etiquette which came with age. He was created in the imagination of a child much younger than Scarlet was now. It was quite amusing to see how proud he was of his abilities, like a toddler looking for praise from his parents.

"Toby?" asked Scarlet casually. "I couldn't help noticing that my bath water was blue and fizzing when I was in it earlier, what did you put in it? I mean what exactly is in your healing salts?" The other children had noticed the blue water in their baths too and looked at him with curiosity.

"It's a magical formula I make myself with herbs that I grow, and minerals I collect from Dreamworld. There's a whole world of natural deposits here that you've never heard of. Anyway, I collect them up, purify and dry them, then mix and cook them together until they turn blue. It's a very useful formula you know. It can be used for lots of things, soothing tired bones, healing wounds or injuries…" Toby paused momentarily, almost as if deciding whether he should tell all of his secrets, "It can even cure terminal illnesses, among other things."

He smiled at Scarlet before turning to face Jamie again with a sneer. "I suppose *you* learned how to make my secret healing potion in school too didn't you, Mr know it all?"

The girls had to bite their lip. Toby was having a real problem letting Jamie's cleverness go so easily, seeing his behaviour as insolence. Maybe he was a tad over enthusiastic, but he didn't deserve a second telling off.

"Wow, this is delicious," said Rose desperate to ease Toby's frustration. She had already taken her first sip of the chocolate, managing to outline her top lip with its creamy residue.

"What's it like Rose?" asked Ruby.

"It's delicious. Try it yourself – go on," she coaxed, eager for the others to sample its richness also.

The others took a sip. The thick, creamy, cocoa coated the inside of the children's mouths, its flavour sticking to their pallets and throats even after they had swallowed. Then an orange twist filtered through, bringing a punch of warm cinnamon and an almost alcoholic citrusy kick at the end. It made the children feel sleepy, but with the cookies sitting untouched it felt impolite to leave them.

Ruby broke a piece off and popped it into her mouth. She didn't need to say anything, her face spoke volumes without a word being heard.

The other children took a bite too. Soft, chewy pieces dropped into their mouths and melted like warm butter, leaving them with huge chunks of chocolate and hazelnuts to chew.

"How are they?" asked Toby proudly.

"Heavenly," answered Scarlet through half a mouthful of cookie.

"Good, good. Any more to drink? – Anyone?" Toby asked as politely as he could.

"No thank you, I think we've had enough for tonight. We really should be gettin' some sleep, Rose is very tired," said Ruby, speaking on behalf of them all.

"Yes, of course. How silly of me. You should all get some rest now. Go on, I will clean up." Toby smiled gently as he hustled the children to their rooms.

By now the children were fighting to stay awake. The thought of having a comfortable bed to go to aided their dreary shuffle to their rooms before drowsily flopping into their beds for the night.

They slipped into serene sleep the minute their heads hit their pillows before making their way outside into Dreamworld.

Chapter Twenty-Nine
The Shadow People

The Shadowlands had been on the forefront of Jamie's mind since Breanna had spoken about the place. It sounded mysterious, exciting even, and to him, the timing to explore had finally come. The girls were too busy playing to notice his mind had wondered so far away, so taking advantage of the opportunity, Jamie quietly snuck away, undetected.

The land in the Shadowlands was very unlike Elysium. The trees seemed to be haunting and creepy, bending in ways that appeared excruciating, and the ground was dusty and barren, although some hardy plant life flourished, and yet it was all so strangely beautiful.

Long, dark shadows swept the ground, racing the gleaming light from the bright moon, casting mysterious silhouettes over the ones already made.

A noise in the leafless forest caught Jamie's attention suddenly, alarming him enough to make him jump in fright. A pair of green eyes shone through the darkness before taking flight and heading straight for him. He fell backwards just as it swooped low over his head revealing its identity. It was only an owl, or at least something which closely resembled one.

Patting himself down, he laughed nervously, before heading off into the wood in search of somewhere fitting for the vision he had in mind.

As he passed through, Jamie felt very aware of the strange creatures lurking in the shadows. He could feel hundreds of eyes staring at him through the dark, but nothing appeared.

At last the trees parted, giving way to a terrain of rocks and steep mountains where an array of deep caves lodged between the tight crevices. He smiled with satisfaction, having found the starting place he would use his powers for the first time.

Jamie squeezed his eyes shut, refreshing the vision in his mind. The image was strong. He concentrated all his efforts, seeing his desired idea in every detail, then slowly began shifting the scenery in front of him, cautiously dragging the enormous landscape to fit the picture in his head.

The ground shook violently as the mountains were forced across the ground to form the range he remembered, all of them near enough the same height. Jamie paused momentarily, opening his eyes to compare the scene to how he mentally imagined it to be. It was harder than he anticipated, but in fairness he hadn't started with an easy task.

His head hurt a little from the enormous strain he'd put into his efforts, but his vision still needed more work. Jamie wiped his brow with his arm, determined to refigure the land as he had envisioned it.

A long crack suddenly split the ground in half as Jamie's eyes closed for a second time. A smaller peak pushed up in front of the range, piercing the land as it took its position. It rose steadily from the trembling ground, forming a jagged, pyramidal, tooth like shape, steadily growing in height until it towered above its sisters behind. Capes of frosty white quickly settled over their peaks so that they appeared to be crowned in pearly opals, making them gleam in contrast with the rocky greys.

For the final time, Jamie squeezed his eyes shut, this time forcing the ground at the foot of the mountains to unexpectedly cave in. It was as if a huge plug had been pulled away sucking the ground down below to form an enormous pit.

Jamie's face strained with exertion, his mind grew heavy with weariness, but now wasn't the time to stop. With one last will of power the landscape took the shape he desired as the basin began to fill from the bottom up with dark, inky water. When at last the flow of water stopped and the moon glinted over the lake, filtering its silvery light from behind the mountains, Jamie couldn't help feeling just a bit proud of his work.

He sat and stared at his creation for a moment, lost in its beauty. He jumped in alarm when he heard someone from behind call his name.

"Jamie wha' ya doin' over here?" asked Ruby appearing behind him, quite out of breath. "We were worried about you. We didn't know where you'd gone…"

Ruby was suddenly aware of the spectacular scene laid out in front of her, stopping her in mid-sentence. The moon's glow reflected on the dark lake like something from another world.

"Blimey, did you do that?" Ruby asked in surprise.

"Uh-huh. I did indeed," he answered calmly without taking his eyes off the view to speak to her.

"We heard the ground tremble all the way in Elysium and guessed it migh' have had somethin' to do with you, but I'd never have guessed that this would've bin the reason behind it," she said in amazement, taking a position, sitting next to him. "It's incredible Jamie, where ever did you get an idea like this from?"

"School! We were looking at mountain ranges in geography. I remember in detail a picture we were shown of this range in Switzerland, the Matterhorn to be precise. I've not bin able to get it outta ma head since."

"Shame about that soft haze around them!" said Ruby pointing out the slight glare illuminating off the sides like it had been edged with misty glitter. "It's pretty, but if you intend for them to stay, remember what our guardians told us. You'll need to go over the outlines a few times, Overlaying, they called it, didn't they?"

"Yeah, but not now Ruby. I couldn't even if I wanted to anyway, I'm knackered."

"Well soon then. It would be a terrible shame if this were to disappear."

The two sat together staring at Jamie's creation in silence.

"Have you given this place a name yet?" asked Ruby quite suddenly with intrigue.

He thought for a moment quietly contemplating a few ideas. "The Ebony Lake and the Opal Mountains," he said, proudly.

"Yeah, I think I'd agree with tha'. They're both perfect names." Ruby smiled. "I don't s'pose you'd mind if I added a few details would ya?" she said, suddenly animated.

Jamie turned to face her, automatically assuming she wanted to change his work. "Like what? I thought you said ya liked it?" he said, sounding wounded.

Ruby laughed at his presumption. "Not that! What you've done is totally awesome. I meant in the lake. I've got a few ideas of my own, I think they'd fit in splendidly with the Ebony Lake."

Jamie frowned a little with uncertainty. "I guess it wouldn't hurt, just so long as ya keep to the water then."

Ruby jumped up in excitement, launching herself to her feet before Jamie changed his mind. "I promise," she agreed dancing on the spot, eager to move closer to the lake.

Jamie stood up next to her, his curiosity growing as Ruby's uncontrolled excitement became ever obvious. "What d'ya want to make?" he asked casually, trying not to sound too bothered.

"You'll see," she answered, not willing to divulge her secrets yet.

The pair walked out from the overhang of the forest and down towards the lake. Ruby's face beamed with intentional delight while Jamie nervously studied her.

"Did ya see those trees as ya walked through the forest? They looked as though they were covered in spider's web, don't you think?" he said at last in an effort to stop Ruby smirking like she was demented.

"Yes, oh my God did I! I thought they were covered in cotton candy until I saw all the insects caught in them. Did ya see the spiders they belonged to?"

"No thankfully. I'm glad I didn't either – why did you?" Jamie asked, full of disgust.

"No. But I bet they were huge," she said enthusiastically.

They abruptly stopped talking as they approached the lake, stopping a few metres short of the edge.

"I feel a bit under pressure now, what with the things Scarlet created and now with wha' you've done here. I hope I can live up to the expectations," sighed Ruby, feeling suddenly uneasy. "The standards 'ave bin set rather high, haven't they?"

"The trick is to not worry, just create what comes naturally – withou' forcing them," encouraged Jamie.

"They're goin' to be a bit strange, but I can see them clearly," she hesitated as she looked to Jamie for approval.

"Go on then Ruby, give it a go," he urged impatiently.

"I hope they won't end up lookin' half formed or anythin' because I missed something out or forgot an important part of them," she continued gabbling nervously, feeling the pressure mount.

"Stop your gassing, an' just do it," snapped Jamie at last reaching the end of his tether and getting rather exasperated at her procrastination.

"I know. Sorry. I'm just a bit nervous is all. Right, here goes."

Ruby's eyes dropped to the water's edge as she focussed hard on what she saw in her mind's eye. The water licked the shore in the gentle breeze as it slipped to and fro in rhythm and Ruby slowed her breathing, pacing her heart in time to match the ripples.

Jamie watched in anticipation for something to happen, but nothing seemed to emerge. A few coils erupted from the ground where lugworms had regurgitated their castings, but other than that there was nothing.

"Well? Are you going to start or not?" he asked irritably, tutting with frustration.

"Sshhh… just watch," she said calmly, pointing to the coils as if they were somehow really interesting.

Jamie looked in confusion. He'd seen loads of these at the beach and knew they were nothing special. "You made lugworms – really? I thought you said you had ideas?"

Ruby smiled sarcastically, "Yes Jamie, I made some lugworms."

But as he watched, the coils started to move, gently at first, but then they began falling in on themselves, collapsing, as though somehow, they were falling through the gap of an hourglass.

Jamie stepped back a pace suspecting that this phenomenon might actually be the start of sinking sand.

The circular sink holes grew larger as more of them appeared along the lakes edge. Automatically Jamie grabbed Ruby by her sleeve, pulling her away from the imminent danger.

"Wha' ya doin'?" she barked with annoyance, frowning at him crossly.

"Really? Are ya blind or somethin?" replied Jamie aghast. "Can't ya see the ground is sinking?"

"It's not sinkin' idiot! Just keep watchin'," she said knowingly.

Jamie grew suddenly nervous as he waited to see what would emerge from the hole. Judging by Ruby's calmness, it was probably nothing to be afraid of, but she certainly had a unique and unsettling way of creating suspense.

A grey, webbed hand abruptly shot through the surface, causing Jamie's nerves to turn to complete fear as he let out a girlish squeal. "Ruby!" he croaked in utter panic, his eyes widened into orbs of white as he glanced fearfully from one hole to another, shuffling backwards away from what was soon to appear.

"Don't panic," she said gently, realising how petrified he had become. She stepped a few paces backwards, offering Jamie her hand. "There's nothing to be afraid of Jamie. Here, come with me and watch."

Jamie took her hand cautiously, unable to decide if he was safer watching from afar. His body still trembled at the unexpected hand he had seen suddenly whip into the air like a zombie.

"What 'ave you made Ruby?" he trembled.

"You'll see in a minute. They won't hurt you, just try to stay calm, you might frighten them otherwise."

"Me, frighten them? Why the devil would ya think that?"

"SSHHH. Just watch," said Ruby, becoming irritated by her brother's pointless questioning.

Ruby squeezed Jamie's hand tightly with sheer excitement as they anxiously waited for the first creature to appear. They didn't have to wait for long; an arm pushed its way through while its clawed hand grabbed the outer ridge, clumsily dragging its body out and onto the dimly lit sand.

For a moment it lay lifeless while it regained its strength. Then slowly lifting up its head, it began scanning the land in a way that implied it was clueless as to what was going on.

"You sure ya know wha' ya doin' Ruby?" Jamie shuddered under his breath.

"I think so – she looks a bit lost though, don't you think?" answered Ruby nonchalantly, her eyes firmly fixed on the creature.

"What? You mean to tell me that you don't know if they actually feel safe now?"

She smiled. "It's fine, ignore what I said. They'll need to adjust to the light was all I meant," she replied, talking in a casual manner.

The two stood perfectly still until all the creatures had freed themselves; Jamie only following Ruby's lead of perfect stillness out of fear. Despite the dull light, Jamie could still see every detail of the creatures, which did nothing to ease his concerns.

When the last one had made its way into the Shadowlands, they all stood up in unison as though they shared one mind.

It struck Jamie how stone like they were in appearance, living statues of cold flesh with opaque blue eyes. Their skins were coloured in various shades of flint greys, scaly and armoured in texture, and their faces seemed to be fixed in one, unresponsive expression.

As Jamie studied them, he noticed the webbed skin not only between their fingers, but also between their extended, fin-like toes. Even more oddly were the dagger like claws which protruded from every finger by about twelve inches. Jamie could only assume they were for jousting fish, otherwise he didn't want to imagine what else they might be used for. Their feet were long and narrow, obviously designed for swimming, and then much to his embarrassment it dawned on him that they were all naked.

He turned away, slightly unsure where to look next.

"You could've covered them Ruby! They've all got their – their bits and boobs out!" he said, blushing a special shade of crimson. "They must have thought I was ogling them just now."

Ruby sniggered quietly. "They're hardly visible Jamie. Their skin is so scaly they're hardly even noticeable. Besides, I don't think they need clothes! – Do they?"

"I'd feel more comfortable if they did! Anything so that I don't have to see them naked. I don't know where to look for heaven's sake," he pleaded.

"If it makes you happy, but I don't think it's necessary," she replied, but accommodated his request nonetheless.

Flicking her hand in a quick movement, Ruby covered their nudity, dressing them in silver blue, fish-skin clothing. It actually suited them beautifully, more so than Ruby had believed it would.

Now the females were not only elegantly dressed, but their black, thick, curly hair cascaded down their spiny backs, giving them a look of unusual beauty.

The males on the other hand appeared to all have the same shade of silvery hair as though a thin layer of glitter had settled on their heads.

It struck Jamie that however strange and however much these creatures had at first startled him; they were mysteriously captivating. The dim moon light perfectly highlighted every part of their bodies as their skins sparkled sporadically, as though a fine layer of diamond dust had been sprinkled over them.

Jamie stood transfixed, unable to move or speak.

"See how they shade their eyes from the dim light!" whispered Ruby as quietly as possible. "Their eyes are very delicate; they're better adapted for the murky water. They don't see very well out of the water, everythin' is a bit cloudy for them, even this light is too much for them really."

Jamie hadn't actually noticed this at all, but now he observed, they all did in fact have what looked like a thin membrane covering their eyes like a second transparent eye lid.

"When they go back into their natural habitat; your lake – the second eye lid flicks back revealing their glassy eyes; a bit like having automatic contact lenses

I s'pose," explained Ruby, after Jamie had been given a moment to understand her clever ingenuity.

"They're amazing Ruby," he whispered in astonishment, a little louder than he intended, startling one of the creatures nearest to him.

Jamie hadn't realised how skittish they were. With one alarmed, it set off a chain reaction among the others as they all ran for cover, hiding behind some rather large boulders which had settled on the lake's shore when Jamie had shifted the mountains earlier.

They peered round from the stones, shifting their position as they tried to focus on the strange beings that had frightened them.

"It's okay," called Ruby softly. "We won't hurt you. You don't need to hide from us."

Silently the two children waited as the creatures edged wearily out of hiding and cautiously approached. They remained still, afraid to move too quickly in case they alarmed the creatures again, and in Jamie's case, afraid that they might take a bite out of his arm if he tried to show any gesture of friendship.

"Wha' do they want? Why they lookin' at us like that?" whispered Jamie anxiously.

"They're curious. Wouldn't you be?" replied Ruby, as she held out her hand to one of them in friendship.

One of the creatures nearest to Ruby copied her gesture, reaching its cold, wet fingers out to touch Ruby's. The sudden warmth from Ruby's fingers seemed to frighten her though, so that it yanked its grip away in confusion.

Ruby didn't flinch; she stood calmly with her hand held out waiting for the creature to come back. Within a few seconds, the creature's curiosity was rekindled, it stretched its fingers back into Ruby's grasp and the two were suddenly mentally connected.

"What's happening now?" whispered Jamie in amazement watching the way Ruby seemed to disappear into a trance like state.

For a moment Ruby didn't answer, but gradually, as she became aware of her surroundings again, she was able to translate what had been discussed.

"She wants to know who we are – and who they are," replied Ruby, sounding a little troubled.

"You mean they don't know yet? Well, don't you think you ought to explain it to them then?" he said in shock. "Why didn't you tell her already?"

"I'm gettin' there," she snapped. "I'm just tryin' to figure out the best way of doin' it. I don't want to frighten them, but I also have to think of a way of telling them so that they all know together."

"Well I wouldn't leave it too long. They hardly look happy," said Jamie, who was really getting worried they might become violent or suddenly very hungry if they got too frightened.

Ruby had already come up with an idea though and had taken her position back alongside the female creature who had just stepped away. Reaching out, alerting the creature to her intentions, Ruby gently placed her hands on either side of her head.

A warm, bluish glow radiated from Ruby's hands as she began to deliver a message directly into the girl's mind. Surprisingly though, the moment Ruby placed her hands over the girl, something more miraculous happened. The entire group were swept into an eerie calm as they tuned telepathically into the message being delivered.

Ruby focussed, carefully choosing her words before speaking.

"I know you're probably wondering who we are, so let me introduce ourselves. I'm Ruby and this is my brother Jamie. You don't need to worry, we're friends and I created you to live in this land. My brother created the Ebony Lake which is where you'll predominantly live; it's where you're best suited. As you'll have discovered already, your eyes won't easily adapt to the light, but once in the water you'll understand and realise your full potentials. For this reason, I've chosen to name you the Shadow People.

"There may come a time we might have to call on you for help, but in the meantime be free to enjoy your beautiful home."

Ruby dropped her grip from the girl, instantly releasing them all from her spell. The girl though remained entranced, her pearly eyes fixed upon Ruby as if waiting for further instruction.

"Wha' did ya tell them Ruby? Why she staring at you like that?" asked Jamie apprehensively.

"She's okay! She's just takin' in what she's been told. I put her in charge of the Shadow People and will talk to her from now on if I need to deliver any further information."

"Sorry? The who?" he asked in bewilderment. "I seem to have got lost somewhere between you doing that glowy thing with ya hands, and hearin' some new made up name for them. When did ya decide on a name for them anyway?"

"I sort of already had one actually. This lady is called Anwen."

"Well she's kinda freakin' me out the way she's staring at us. Is she hungry or somethin'? Does she know we're not food? Ya need to tell her to go away and find food somewhere else."

"She doesn't want to eat us, you lemon. She's had a lot to learn. If it makes you feel any better though, they can go to the water."

"Erm, yeah. I think I'd be happier with that ta," said Jamie grimacing nervously, preparing himself for the possibility he might have to run for his life.

Ruby tutted disapprovingly and sighed. "Fine!" before turning back to address the Shadow People.

"You can go now. Explore your new home," she said pointing in the direction of the open water.

Anwen's eyes dropped to the ground in an understanding way, then took her leave, guiding the Shadow People towards the Ebony Lake. The first sounds of wading feet broke the strangely silent mood as the splashes turned to what sounded like strange, captivated, nervous giggles.

The water rippled around their waists and for a moment, Jamie wondered if they were actually going to swim away. They seemed unsure for a while, then almost spontaneously, their instinct kicked in as though a button had been flicked, turning them all into proficient swimmers, plunging themselves down deep into the inky depths. A final flick of their long, flipper like feet told the children they were gone, as they disappeared beneath the surface of the Ebony Lake.

"Thank God for that. I thought they migh' change their minds and come back again," said Jamie sighing with relief. "I still think that girl looked hungry though."

Ruby giggled and shook her head in disbelief. "She'd have had to have been pretty desperate to be hungry for you," she teased.

"Ouch, that was harsh," replied Jamie, smiling.

Ruby continued through fits of giggles, "They're nothing more than fresh water lake mermaids Jamie, but without the tails. They don't eat people; they'll eat fish and water vegetation."

The two watched the steady ripples glinting under the moon light as they sat peacefully in thought.

"I wish life at home could be as peaceful as this is now," said Ruby, tuning into the stillness of the lake.

Jamie smiled to himself, he knew exactly what she meant, as he also felt the calmness washing over him like some kind of contagious, lunar magic.

"You can't let this place dissipate Jamie. You need to Overlap before its forgotten about," said Ruby, elbowing Jamie sharply in the arm so that he got on with it as a matter of urgency.

"Yeah, okay, okay. I'll do it now," agreed Jamie smirking proudly at his sister. "I think I've got some strength back now anyway."

It wasn't difficult to do; with several lines of Overlaying in his head, the image was re-enforced, ensuring his creation would not slip away into the night. Satisfied at last their work was done here, the children stood by the water's edge, staring thoughtfully across its glassy reflection and smiled.

"You know, I didn't realise how big the Ebony Lake was. But now that we're standing here though, it's dawned on me just how big you made it."

"It is misleading isn't it? It would take ages to walk all the way around. That's if you wanted to see all of it!" answered Jamie hopefully.

"Except we have the added advantage of bein' able to fly!" replied Ruby enthusiastically.

Grinning at each other without saying another word, they leapt into the air, leaving the ground below as they glided over the lake.

From above, the Ebony Lake looked even more beautiful. Its black inkiness secretly hid the mysteries it held beneath the surface, while the tall, rocky mountains disguised it to be as normal as any other place in the world.

The sky thickened as they ascended and the air thinned, numbing their minds as their senses drowned in deep drowsiness – a vision of misty white.

Chapter Thirty
Getting Stronger

The children were abruptly woken from their dreams with a sudden sharp jab to their sides.

"Wake up sleepy 'eads. I trust ya'll slept well?"

They bolted upright, wincing in pain to see Dennis hovering over them. His squinty eyes were scrunched with devilish delight and beaming with great satisfaction at their appearances which suggested that they had had a very traumatic night.

The children were astonished to see they were back where they needed to be for Dennis to see in the morning. They didn't mind feeling slightly wet or cold, as they knew this had only been a very recent occurrence and that their guardian angels had somehow transported them home in time.

He had in his opinion given out the most rewarding punishment conceivable, one which he found to be absolutely impeccable without having to do too much. Little did he know that the children had had a wonderful night, thank you very much.

"Sleep well did ya?" he jeered, nudging Jamie hard in the side with his foot again. "Get up and get dressed, all of ya. Ya gonna be busy today wha' with it bein' a Sunday. I can see ya all 'ad plenty of sleep, so you'll have no excuse to be feelin' sluggish today."

He stood back allowing them space to move, his glare following them as they walked indoors.

The children hardly dared to look at each other as they passed him by out of fear that their bemused facial expressions might arouse suspicions. It was hard enough trying to keep a straight face as it was. He had no idea that they hadn't even been outdoors, never mind enduring the elements he believed they had.

As soon as they had dried off, the children waited in the kitchen like regimental soldiers awaiting their orders for the day. Dennis's feet scuffed the floor from somewhere on the other side of the kitchen door, seconds before he appeared around it. The usual depraved looking face met them with the normal demented look about it, confirming his earlier suggestion of hard work was no threat.

"Right, we need logs to be collected and chopped into pieces for the fire," he barked, beginning his bucket list of chores that needed doing. "Ya can all go to the woods and bring enough back to see us through the next few weeks. Make sure ya collect some kindling; the wood shed is almost empty and needs refillin'. Jamie, you can 'ave the job of chopping the logs, then ya can all carry them 'ome in these." He handed the children a bundle of old, paper, potato sacks, and pushed an axe into Jamie's hand. "After the wood shed has been thoroughly cleaned out you'll find that the coal bunker needs sweepin' out too, and then the coals will need to be pu' back in tidily. It should take ya most of the day, so ya shouldn't get bored."

The children stared at him in disbelief, he couldn't be serious! Even the most uneducated person knew that paper sacks were of little use to carry heavy loads, let alone odd shaped, protruding logs that would only rip under the strain.

"Well, wha' ya waitin' for? Get on with it then," he demanded.

The children turned away. This was going to be a very long day, and they couldn't see how on earth they could get themselves out of this one. No magic stone was going to help this time, and no amount of dreaming would help either.

Sadly, there was not much they could do but to obey his ridiculous orders, setting off down the street to begin their long, tedious day.

"This is so unfair," complained Rose. "It's going to take ages to get everythin' done today. What are we going to do Scarlet?"

"Well, I don't know about you three, but I've got no interest in breakin' my back for him. I suggest we at least use our Stones to get us into the Whispering Wood, then we'll take it from there."

They all agreed that that was one part of the problem solved. They knew it would take at least an hour and a half to even reach the wood, and that was before they had done any work at all.

"Over there! – Come on! If we hide behind that hedge, we can use our Stones without being spotted," suggested Scarlet, dragging Rose by the arm to where she had been pointing.

Once out of sight the children reached into their pockets and turned the Stones in their hands, being sure to link their arms so as to not all end up in different parts of the wood. They reappeared together in a part of the wood that they didn't recognise. It was dense, the trees tall and dark, with very little sunlight penetrating the forest floor.

"We had best get to work; it's going to take ages to chop enough logs to keep Dad happy," Jamie groaned, pulling out the axe he had put inside one of the paper bags as he resigned himself to the inevitable task awaiting him.

The girls wondered off into different directions, collecting twigs and small branches which had littered the forest floor. The weight of the branches soon made a difference to how the girls were able to carry the bags. The sticks pushed through uncomfortably into their sides, while the weight quickly wore down the strength in their arms.

"I think it'd be easier if we just dragged the bags across the floor. They should move quite easily," moaned Ruby wearily, moping her brow with her sleeve.

"Do ya think we've got enough Ruby? Can we go back yet?" asked Rose almost in tears.

Ruby looked at Rose sympathetically. "Well let's see how Jamie's gettin' on first and we'll make a decision then. Come on, we can always come back and collect more if Jamie hasn't finished."

The girls made their way back to where they had left Jamie chopping logs. They could hear the hacking of the axe before reaching the clearing, making it apparent that Jamie was still busy, but seeing him exert himself so ferociously wasn't quite how they expected to see him on their return.

With his axe held high in the air above his head, he brought it down as hard as he could over the logs, time and time again as though it were the most important thing in the world. He looked like a boy possessed with the unsettling speed at which he worked. His small frame somehow appeared so fragile from where the girls stood, he looked unsteady and tired, his weakening arms shaking under the weight of the axe as he persevered relentlessly.

"Jamie, put the axe down and rest for a moment before ya seriously hurt yourself," begged Ruby, marching with authority to where Jamie worked.

Jamie looked up from his work; he had been so preoccupied he hadn't seen the girls' approach. He dropped the axe to the ground, collapsing in a heap beside it. His brow dripped with sweat, plastering his hair down solidly to his head.

The two other girls rushed to his side, dropping to their knees beside him.

"Are you okay, you look terrible Jamie?" asked Scarlet, moving in closer to his side. "You're shaking! What's wrong?"

"My hands hurt! They're burning! I'm okay though," he said, in an overly controlled voice, attempting to hide his pain before pushing them inside his pockets.

"No, you're not. Let me see yer hands," demanded Scarlet, grabbing his right hand free from his pocket. "Open your hand – let me see!"

Slowly Jamie uncurled his clenched fist. There was no use resisting, he knew Scarlet wouldn't give up pestering until she had seen them.

"Oh my god Jamie. Why didn't ya stop? You can't carry on." She gasped in horror, as she examined them, turning them this way and that in her own hands.

It was obvious to the girls why he had been in so much pain – now that they had been revealed. Huge, broken blisters covered his palms where he had gripped the wooden handle of the axe. The friction from the repetitive, strenuous work had caused abrasions and burns marking his skin in blood.

"They'll heal, I'm okay," he insisted, bravely forcing a smile.

"This is totally ridiculous," said Scarlet suddenly angered. "We can't keep on like this, we could be here for hours at this rate, and besides, how do you think you will go on using that stupid axe with torn hands?" She paused for a moment contemplating their options. "I think what we've cut and collected is enough for today anyway," she continued. "And if it's not, then Dennis will have to find another way to punish us, won't he? But we're not doin' anymore. In fact, I think we ought to go to the willow, and I don't care how long we're there or if Dennis finds out either. We'll take the wood home afterwards using our Stones." Her hands settled onto her hips defiantly. "Who's with me?"

Thankfully nobody argued with her, even if they wanted to, they wouldn't have dared with her looking so determined. Besides, they were secretly thinking the same thing, they wanting nothing more than to be in Dreamworld with Toby, and in a bath full of magic healing salts. That was all that was needed to prompt Toby into sorting out the willow for the children's imminent arrival.

"Right, let's go," said Scarlet impatiently, gesturing to her siblings to hurry.

Arriving at the willow always felt wonderful. It was one that made the children's lives seem completely normal, making them believe they didn't have a care in the world, and how they wished this was true. Even so, it didn't matter that home life was outrageously abnormal, what mattered most was that they had an escape where they felt safe – a place where their wildest dreams could come true.

Toby greeted the children as he always did with his big smile and twinkling eyes, and as normal knew exactly what the children needed.

It was over lunch that it suddenly occurred to Scarlet that their actions had gone deliberately against Dennis's orders. She had been sipping some herbal potion that Toby had made for them to help heal their sores, when she gasped in shock at this observation.

"Oh my gosh," she said, setting her cup down hard on the table. The other children, alarmed by her sudden response, jumped with surprise.

"What? What's the matter?" asked Jamie, who couldn't see what the problem was.

"Don't you see?" she asked when she saw everyone was oblivious to her sudden epiphany. "We have quite literally stopped workin' the way Dennis wanted us to, decided that we've all had enough, and used our time instead to take a break and relax. Can you imagine how fuming he'd be if he knew we were here instead of slaving away for him? I think we might finally be gaining the confidence we need if we have a chance of fighting back. We'd never have even considered doin' this just a few weeks ago, but now, I don't think any of us care about the consequences."

This revelation gave the children a welcome sense of achievement. To think that they would have ever gone against the requests of Dennis before would have been unthinkable, but here they were in the treehouse, drinking magic tea without giving him or the consequences a second thought. Even more amazing was that now they came to think of it, their fear of him was subsiding. In reality what could he do to them that he hadn't done already?

"What does it feel like knowing you're getting stronger?" asked Toby. "Does it feel how you thought it might?"

The children were still overcome with shock to have considered how they felt. It never even crossed their minds to disobey or deliberately put a foot wrong in the past. Dennis had never needed an excuse to punish them before, so looking for trouble had never been an option.

"I don't know, but I guess it feels quite surreal," said Ruby. "To know we finally have a chance to break free of Dennis's control without worryin' what he migh' do – it's just so weird – I like it."

A strange silence clouded the air while the understanding of what could never be reversed, sank into the children's heads. There was no going back to being the submissive, compliant individuals they had once been.

"Well, since we've started, we may as well carry on," said Scarlet leaping to her feet in a wave of energy. Then quite unexpectedly, she sprinted towards the balcony and leapt from its side, unconcerned by its height as she fell freely through the air. The sudden explosion of exhilaration coursed through her, giving a feeling of complete invincibility, ready to take on whatever Dennis might throw her way.

Falling like a stone she plummeted fast towards the ground before exerting herself from the fall at the last moment, pulling herself back into an upward thrust, soaring higher than ever back into the clouds.

The sun shone brilliantly up here, it was a different world with the bright rays glowing steadily, penetrating the fluffy clouds so that they glistened on the Long River below.

In its warmth she lay suspended in thin air, breathing deeply and calmly for a moment while she allowed herself to absorb the fact that she hadn't begun to even get near to her full potentials.

At last, and in a state of meditation Scarlet dropped from the heavens with her arms outstretched like a swallow, scanning the arid landscape below. Her mind slipped into an oracular state as she fell, her visions never clearer than they were now.

The others had landed by the Long River, not too far away. They were already chatting about the things they hoped to perfect or change, when Scarlet gently landed beside them.

"Did I miss something?" Scarlet asked. "It sounds as though I just caught the end of a conversation."

"Only that Rose and myself can only use Transient Magic while we are physically in Dreamworld so unless we are using magic within our powers, we need to remember not to create potentially important structures or beings which could ultimately disappear after we leave," said Jamie.

"I was goin' to remind you of the same thing actually," said Scarlet. "Of course, you could always Overlay if you become particularly fond of something I suppose. I think that since we're here to make a point we really ought to make it well. I want Dennis to know we mean business and I want Abaddon to know we've been here," she said boldly. "That means we don't want anything to disappear after we leave. Be safe all of you. Shall we meet back in the treehouse afterwards?"

"I think that's probably best, particularly if you intend to antagonise Abaddon. Jus' be careful alright," said Jamie wryly. "We're not dreaming; if somethin' bad happens here it could be disastrous, so no pink dragons today."

Scarlet turned away with a look of purpose in her eye. Jamie knew that look all too well, it was one of belligerence and determination, one that was dangerous in the hands of someone like Scarlet.

With her mind overflowing with spectacular ideas just waiting to spring into existence, Scarlet left her siblings, shooting high into the air knowing exactly what her intentions were.

Chapter Thirty-One
Restoring Dreamworld

As far away as she could see over the horizon, Scarlet set to work, thrusting her hand out into the distance and allowing her vision to unfold. A beautiful vast sea of crystal-clear turquoise waters appeared, seemingly attached to the sky.

The cool, briny water soaked deep into the sea bed, soothing the parched ground while restoring the basin with its life-giving medicine.

It was so transparently clear that in places, the ocean floor was visible despite it being so deep. Scarlet had made light work of the Sapphire Sea, it hadn't taken much imagination to create, but her next vision needed more insight.

Scarlet sat on a rock at the edge of the shore pensively watching the waves gently ripple in, flicking particles of white coral sand around her feet as each grain built steadily around her to form the long, pale, sandy beaches of the sea.

A small clump of brown seaweed floated in, settling itself on the shore by her feet and Scarlet found herself gazing at it in wonderment. It had a unique shape which made it look surprisingly like a small person resting on the beach. It was just the something Scarlet needed, she had been quietly mulling it over in her mind, and now like magic, the something appeared, presenting itself to her as a starting point - it was perfect.

Scarlet immediately set to work. Using her finger as a wand, she pushed it into the clump, twirling it in circular motions while her imagination spilled from her mind. Instantly several hundred tiny lobster like creatures erupted from the centre and spilled across the shore, mimicking the way an ant's nest would react if it were disturbed. As they hurried away, they grew rapidly; filling out and taking the shape Scarlet had envisioned them to become – mermaids.

At first, they appeared to have been created without much thought. They were colourless, like a pencil sketching with only an outline to suggest what they actually were, but this was all part of Scarlet's plan. The mermaids seemed to understand the process though, they sat and waited patiently on the edge of the shore, awaiting the final stage of their evolution.

When at last all of the mermaids had escaped from the seaweed and had grown to the size intended, Scarlet set back to work, this time turning her mind into a paint pallet. She selected an array of pretty, pastel shades, painting their sleek, fishy tails in their chosen colour. Their golden-brown skin tones almost glowed against their elegant tails, while their long, feminine hair rippled down their backs.

They were beautiful creatures to behold, but Scarlet's exceptional imagination didn't stop there.

There was an unmistakable, special smell which Scarlet had remembered. A memory she clung onto from a time she and her sisters had visited Cornwall with their parents. She remembered how the smell had been so potent, that at times it was actually possible to taste the scent in the air. The aroma of the sea, a mix of seaweed and salt combined with the fresh air formulated the unique perfume of how she believed the mermaids should smell.

She painted as she reminisced over her happier days, her mind so enveloped in thought that she almost lost herself in the past.

The mermaids, who were obviously thrilled with their beauty jolted Scarlet from her deep concentration with squeals of excitement. Scarlet smiled to herself as she watched them, the vanity they possessed already immensely clear in their actions. They took great delight comparing the length and colour of their hair with each other, combing their fingers through their curls and relishing in their beauty. Then giggling with exuberance, they slipped into the Sapphire Sea, splashing between the waves before finally disappearing beneath its smooth, silky surface without giving Scarlet a second glance.

For a while, Scarlet watched the sea glistening in the suns light, completely hiding the creatures that lived beneath. The only disturbance was the smooth ripples on the surface as the breeze brushed its cool fingers over the top, pushing it up into small waves so that each of them glided gently to the edge of the shore. It appeared so romantic, almost as if the ripples were actually kissing the sand.

It was in that peaceful, serene moment it suddenly occurred to Scarlet, she had only created females. The very notion of 'kissing' abruptly wakened her short sightedness and inconsideration, compelling her to immediately afford proper attention to some mermen.

Plunging her wand finger into the seaweed once again, she whirled it around cleaning her mind of the remaining feminine paint, and started again.

The seaweed erupted spontaneously with life for a second time, as several hundred or so of the same lobster like creatures emerged from the weed, each following the same formation pattern as the females. Just as the ladies had done, the males now waited patiently for their turn when a colour would be chosen for them.

They were handsome creatures even before a specific shade had been allocated, with their chiselled features and rippling muscles. They sat on the shore with grace and stature as the waves washed enticingly around them.

A pallet of flinty, earth-greys and blues were chosen as Scarlet carefully filled between the blank sketch marks of their strong sleek tails, paying specific attention to their scales. Each and every one was edged with a corresponding pearlescent paint specifically aimed at catching the light from the sun's warm glow.

The mood was calm, the Sapphire Sea sparkled brilliantly, and then as if an epiphany of realisation washed over them that they were now complete, the mermen slunk into the sea. For a short while, they stayed at the surface, athletically competing with each other in boisterous play and frolicking in the waves, and then, almost as if something caught their attention, they glanced back at Scarlet momentarily before diving down deep, and then they were gone. The sea returned to its natural soothing rhythm.

Scarlet's imagination was on a roll, it was as though she had been keeping her creative thoughts locked away especially for this day; they seemed to be coming from nowhere, so thick and fast she thought they might never stop. Everywhere she looked, ideas of creativity danced out their existence as if persuading her to make them a reality. Whispers in the breeze mingled with sounds she thought were familiar to her, a cacophony of gentle voices, but none loud enough for her to hear properly.

With strained ears, Scarlet fought to understand what was being said. She knew the whispers from somewhere, but the memory seemed to be drowning in a pit of forgotten dreams. The harder Scarlet tried to fish out the memory, the more it seemed to elude her – and then just as she was beginning to think she'd never regain the knowledge, it came to her, as if the outstretched hand of a phantom helped her from the shadows.

The whispering now turned into a harmonious, peaceful melody as the voice became one united sound. It was that of the Whispering Wood.

She wasn't sure if the whispers were real or if they were an echo from her subconscious self, luring her into recreating a replica of itself. All she knew was that Dreamworld had ben cruelly robbed of so much woodland, so in her opinion, replenishing some of it couldn't be wrong.

Leaping to her feet, Scarlet sprung from the sandy beach hurtling herself high into the air, taking the seed of understanding with her. From this height the land looked so lonely. The recent creations stood out boldly against the otherwise barren land. It's humiliating degradation so apparent that it looked naked against the fine garments of sporadic foliage, contrasting against its weary, dry, infertile terrain.

With one swift, confident movement, Scarlet flicked open her clenched hand sending a scattering of fine silver dust to rain down like mist. Some of the grains were carried in the wind as they fell, casting the magic further still.

As the last of the dusty seeds settled, the familiar sound of crackling could be heard. Scarlet knew that sound all too well; - she had made forests grow in Dreamworld before.

Small seedlings sprung from the arid land as it fought the lifeless clutches which held it captive. The saplings grew fast, thrusting their strong roots into the ground, spreading their branches and flaunting their fine new garments of green. Matured oak trees now covered a huge area of land bringing with them the promise of restored life within their khaki coloured canopies.

Scarlet breathed deeply with satisfaction taking in the beauty which now clothed another part of Dreamworld. The air smelled fresher, the combined fragrance of new leaves entwined with the delicate perfume of the salty sea, emitting its scent up from the land, and into the atmosphere.

The whispers fell silent now, the voices appeased and calm, and for a brief few minutes Scarlet felt proud of her work. She had been just about to turn away, when the whispers returned.

Scarlet froze in mid-air. The calls were desperate and anguished, making Scarlet feel terribly sad just hearing them. The low, mournful tone echoed from the forest in a wave of despair.

The grinding chatter intensified, but no matter how hard Scarlet listened, she could not make out what the sea of voices were saying. The feeling of pride that she previously felt disappeared as if it had never been; a candle puffed out in an instance with one swift blow, leaving her lost and unable to respond.

The trees olive leaves began to wilt, the tops of the canopies drooped and then like a disease, a soft brown colour slowly spread through the branches, administering its fatal concoction to the newly formed forest.

The tortured whispers fell silent, a silence so deadly it amplified over the quietest murmur sending Scarlet into an impulsive, panicked dive, forcing her into the thick of the tortured forest.

She landed hard on the forest floor, her heart pounded heavily in her chest making far too much noise for her to concentrate. But she didn't need to worry; it was instantly apparent what had called her. Scarlet rubbed her eyes in disbelief and gasped.

Under every tree sat a scrunched up giant male figure, all of them old and shabby in appearance. Each sat with their backs resting against a tree trunk – no, not resting; attached to the tree as though they were a part of it. Their skin had a wood like effect, brown with a green moss which crept over the tops of their heads like hair then slunk down the sides of their faces, joining under their chins to form long green beards.

They looked down at Scarlet as she stood in their midst, their sorrowful eyes pleading for help while they scanned her from head to toe, but they did not speak a word.

Scarlet had heard about these creatures before, but doubted their existence – until now. They were known as the Leshy or the Green Men, spirits of the trees, protectors of the forests. She also knew that they were capable of shape shifting, naturally appearing as human if they wanted to be seen, while still holding a strong connection with its tree.

If their own tree dies or is destroyed, the Leshy is forced to leave, where it wonders around pitifully, until it can persuade or encourage a new sapling to grow in its place. It's the punishment for failing to protect the tree it's bound to.

As a general rule, the Leshy are not friendly beings, the story Scarlet had heard was one that made her very weary of them. For centuries humans have cut down and destroyed thousands upon thousands of trees, forcing the Leshy to retaliate. If a human was to find himself lost, the Leshy are well known to hinder any progress he might make, luring him instead in the opposite direction deeper into their realms with calls of comfort until he becomes so weary and disorientated, he's never seen again. For all Scarlet knew, this might be a ploy to trap her here as well.

Slowly Scarlet backed away; being in plain sight of the Leshy was not something she thought to be a good idea.

The renewal of the forest had given the Leshy a second chance to protect it, but being in their vicinity or getting caught up in their games was not a part of her plan. But as she moved away, she noticed a look of despair spread across their faces, and she stopped.

Almost in synchronisation, the Leshy cupped their woody fingers together before bringing their clasped hands to their lips, replicating the act of drinking.

"You want water!" she mumbled under her breath, realising at last what was wrong. The Leshy had deliberately caused the trees to wilt in order to get her attention. Their cries for help had been ignored due to her inability to translate their language; it was all they could do to make Scarlet understand that the trees needed proper replenishment and water.

Understanding the urgency, Scarlet pushed off from the forest floor, soaring above the wilting canopy. The Long River hadn't branched off in this direction and it was situated too far from where this wood had grown. The only way to bring relief to the forest's heart was if another body of water was made to pass through.

By now Scarlet had no trouble re-forming the land, it was like plasticine between her fingers. Scarlet worked quickly, drawing up the land at the edge of the forest into a rocky terrain, sending a few mountainous sky scrapers soaring up in front. A deep gorge scarred the land between the mountain range and the forest making it an ideal basin for another river to flow.

Now with her finger, Scarlet carved a network of smaller river beds through the forest, carefully tracing each to run at spacious intervals between the trees like blood veins.

Scarlet's attention turned back to the mountains as she now focussed her energy on the life line, immediately causing a flow of water to bubble up through the rocks. Torrents of fresh water rushed down the side, flooding the ravine at the bottom, before steadily trickling through the freshly etched network in the forest and finally filtering away into the Sapphire Sea.

The trees wasted no time replenishing their thirst, within minutes the wilting brown lifted and the original oak greens were restored.

With a sigh of relief, Scarlet turned away at last, satisfied that this time, all was well. All she wanted to do now was rest.

In the distance she could still see the Sapphire Sea, sparkling in the sun. The forest boundary had grown close to the beach pushing some of the smaller shrub like trees onto the shore, but the forest was the last place she wanted to be right now. To think that something which should have been so straight forward, could have turned into something quite extraordinary unnerved her.

The soft sand welcomed her back, pushing between her toes upon landing.

Scarlet flopped onto the sand, deliberately pacing her breathing into a relaxed state. The surprise of what she had seen had panicked her, only now realising just how much.

Goodness only knows what else lives in Dreamworld, she thought. There was so much she had yet to discover, things which were still to make themselves known to her, creatures that were still hidden away just like the Leshy.

She lay in thought, dragging her fingers through the soft white sand, scooping it in her palm and letting the grains slip between her fingers. She had no intention at this point of creating anything else, especially after her encounter with the Leshy, so it came as a surprise to her when another idea crept into her head without even consciously giving it a thought.

She had been thinking about the animals that were indigenous to these lands, she was beginning to feel better that there was now enough water to support them, when suddenly her mind switched from water to food.

New grasses now carpeted vast areas of Dreamworld for grazing animals, but other than that, nothing was available – nothing that she was aware of anyway.

It must have been a thought in the making, at least subconsciously, because quite surprisingly and for no real reason at all she had already given a name to the uncreated root shrub. She knew exactly how this plant would look, how and what it would grow, and its purpose.

Since this was Dreamworld and because it would develop underground on a root system, the name Somnroot had come to the forefront of her mind. It was abundantly clear that first and foremost, the plant's natural objective would be to grow food for the animals, but how wonderful would it be if they also grew a spectacular kind of fruit for human consumption purely just by thinking of it.

It was too brilliant for her thought to be left another second.

Pushing her wand finger into the sand like a probe, Scarlet's thoughts radiated from her mind. The magic flowed in an electrified strand, spreading on a network resembling the tunnels of a long ant's nest. The ground rumbled in a way she had become accustomed to hearing, just before the first plants pricked the surface on its thread like root.

Pink heart shaped leaves sprouted first, uncurling in the sun like tea plates before turning a brighter burgundy red. At the base of each leaf, a small shoot burst from its stem which developed into beige, acorn sized clusters sitting heavily on the top of the leaves like grapes, ripening in the mid-day heat.

After witnessing the successful growth of the berries, Scarlet couldn't resist imagining a fruit for the Somnroot to grow. It wasn't out of hunger, rather a case of curiosity which enticed her actions.

There was a huge range of possibilities to choose from, but at last she settled on a tantalising mix, consisting of a pineapple and a pear. Initially it was actually quite difficult to imagine how this might look as it grew; its shape and texture, all of which required her attention, she only hoped that its taste would be taken care of naturally.

Starting with the basic details, Scarlet pieced together the fruits in mind, combining the traditional characteristics of a pear with the yellowish, scaly skin similar to a pineapple. Then hanging onto that image briefly, she allowed it to slip from her mind and develop on the Somnroot.

To her surprise, small, pink knobbly protrusions pushed their way out from under the heart shaped leaves, lifting the grape like berries up into the air as they grew. They were peculiar fruits, reminding Scarlet of dragon fruit as they ripened from pink to yellow in the warm sun.

It felt remarkably smooth in her hand despite its skin suggesting the opposite. The scales, although defined, were actually rather silky. She brought it up to her nose and breathed in its smell. It had an unmistakable fragrance of something sweet like honey blended with a faint, fruity aroma stimulating her taste buds to salivate in anticipation of its essence.

Biting into its soft flesh, the juices were released en masse, flowing out and down her chin as her mouth bounded into an overdrive of exquisite deliciousness. Its flesh had the same texture as that of a mango, but the fruit itself was compact with small, succulent, nodule like pods, bursting open like caviar when she bit into them.

Wiping the juice from her chin with the back of her hand, she dropped the last bite into her mouth before taking leave, flying on towards the Long River where another creation waited to materialise.

She hardly dared to look down over the forest as she passed over, for fear of hearing the Leshy again, but this time thankfully, there was a peaceful silence implying all was well.

The Long River glistened in the distance, flowing quicker as it turned into a bend. The grassy banks were higher at this point where the water cut through the steeper land.

Scarlet set herself down in amongst the soft grass, her gaze fell across to the other side of the river. She would get a spectacular view from this point when her creations emerged.

There was a flower Scarlet had seen many times before in the waking world, called a Fuchsia. Her mother used to plant them out in hanging baskets or in tubs which bushed into healthy vibrant shrubs with an abundance of flower buds. The flowers grew in an array of dazzling colours, all resembling what she thought looked like tiny fairies.

She remembered how the stamen hung from the centre of the flower longer than its petals, which looked remarkably like little legs poking through a frilly tutu. At the top of the flower, where the petals joined at the stem, a bobble held everything in place mimicking a pin-sized head in relation to the size of the flower.

Perhaps it was the fact that she knew only too well how these plants grew, but almost instantaneously, the plants shot out from the ground like fireworks bursting with colour.

Every plant had its own variation of small flower buds, or baby flower fairies, which in an actual fact is what they were. They looked like infants swaddled within their own skirts, hugging them warmly, waiting for them to grow big enough before the petals loosened their grip, exposing the newly developed fairy to the sun's warmth.

As they grew, the petals unfurled into frilly skirts revealing their tiny legs underneath, then stretching into consciousness their tiny heads lifted, waking them from their sleep.

The final transition was the most exciting though. Two delicate, lacy wings burst out the back of the flower, then just like a butterfly, pulsed open as they dried in the air.

When at last this stage was complete, the fairies stretched their arms, opened their wings then pulled away from the mother plant, taking to the air as the now matured flower fairy.

The sky came alive with a loud humming sound as hundreds of flower fairies hovered like hummingbirds across the river, dancing as though they were skating on ice for a while before venturing across the water to where Scarlet sat.

Chapter Thirty-Two
The Ebony Army

Ruby had gone off on her own leaving the others to do what they did best while she revisiting the Shadowlands. Her thoughts seemed to come alive the strongest in these parts and if she were to create life within her powers, this was the best place for her to be.

Ruby drifted into a hypnotic state as she stared across the Ebony Lake. Her heart paced in a steady rhythm to the ripples of water caressing the bank, her mind concentrated on the calmness in the air, she breathed the mist as it hovered like a cloak over the lake, tuning herself in to the surroundings of the Shadowlands as she became one with nature.

Her eyes rolled back into her head as she fell into a trance.

Within her mind, Ruby was able to see the bottom of the lake. It was thick with clay and silt, perfect for what she had in mind.

Ruby's hands reached out in front of her, her fingers outstretched as she began to draw up huge piles from the bottom. Her fingers and hands moved chaotically over the surface of the water, while her mind replicated what she created on the lake bed. Over and over Ruby's hands seemed to go through the same format, shaping and twisting, collecting and moulding as her mind and body worked tirelessly like a machine. And then abruptly – she stopped.

She froze for a moment, her palms turned down over the lake as if she were now keeping an invisible force back.

The previously still waters erupted sporadically with large bubbles, floating up like glass domes, breaking as they surfaced, and all the while Ruby remained in a trance holding the creatures in the abyss. Now at last she turned her palms to face the heavens and the lake seemed to boil with ecstasy.

An enormous, gloopy mass oozed onto the shore, sliding over the sand like liquid mercury as the water drained slowly from the residual matter before dividing into thousands of smaller individual blobs. Each nodule dragged itself into its own space, congealing enough to rise from the ground and grow in mass, developing into their programmed shape.

Globules of sediment fell as each creature shifted from a slumping stand, dragging their heavy weight upright from the shore. Muddy water trickled from their porous bodies and ran out through their feet as they slowly took their positions in regimental lines.

Ruby slipped out of her trance just in time to see the last of these swamp creatures take his place. Her jaw dropped aghast at what she had summoned up from the depths as she stared blankly with shock at her own creations.

It was quite unsettling to think she was in control of such a ghastly army, much more horrific in reality than she had envisioned in her mind's eye.

Their faces sagged with the weight of the wet, slimy mud, dragging down the folds of skin around their eyes. Their bodies were undoubtedly built for battle, standing strong and tall like some kind of extinct dinosaur, with faces that lacked emotion as though their minds had been cleared, empty carcases ready to be summoned, knowing only how to fight, with little, or perhaps no conception of compassion. All they were capable of was the ability to accept, and willingness to obey any commands Ruby asked of them without hesitation.

Ruby couldn't help feeling a bit guilty; a pang of overwhelming sadness for them washed over her. They looked so forlorn and miserable, which made her remember how they themselves had felt not so long ago when Dennis had made them sleep outside in the rain.

She almost regretted her actions; she didn't think she had ever seen any creature so wretched or down cast as these. Their heads hung low, dripping with dirty water as it trickled off their black stringy hair and down their faces, cutting deep tracks into their pliable flesh as the water filtered away. The wet flesh reformed just as quickly as it eroded, filling in, and smoothing itself back out. This process continued until the excess water had drained away from their bodies leaving large puddles on the ground where they stood.

Still they waited in silence as Ruby contemplated what she ought to do, her thoughts conflicting and crashing into each other while her mind battled with itself.

Being made from the silt and decomposing matter which lay rotting at the bottom of a lake was hardly the most respectable material to be constructed from.

If they were to have feelings, this may have negative repercussions on themselves as soldiers, particularly if their own pride were to be under scrutiny.

The guilt built inside her as she studied the shameful creatures, desperate to see a sign from them – anything that suggested they were content with how they were created, but nothing emerged – how could it? All that stood before her was a compliant, walking dead army, thoughtless, without any understanding of self-pride or vanity.

Scarlet's eyes fell from one soldier to another, eventually catching a glimpse of one who had momentarily glanced up at her. It felt as though he was asking what she commanded of them. They wanted to be instructed and they were happy to be under her rule.

The look of emptiness in his big brown, wet eyes bothered her though. She really didn't like that they were so hollow, they may as well have been zombies.

At last, her overwhelming compassion and guilt consumed her, over riding any conflicting thoughts in her head. She knew what to do. These creatures were alive, and life deserved to understand empathy, capable of feeling love and the warmth that came with it. Being a soldier didn't mean being void of thought or feeling otherwise they may as well have been a creation of Abaddon.

With her mind made up, Scarlet swept her hand over the army, instantly releasing an orange dust over them, warming their souls, and allowing them to feel for the first time.

The army responded, systematically lifting their heads high and proud, their eyes twinkled as they felt an odd warming sensation build inside.

Ruby felt alleviated and so much prouder of her creations now that they stood fulfilled, rather than the sadness that had enveloped them to begin with.

A slight smile warmed their faces in gratification as they waited to be dismissed.

"Go on now," she ordered, wiping a tear from her eye.

The Ebony Army marched back into the waters from which they came, still proud and tall, slowly letting the lake re-take and dissolve their bodies so that they slid silently back down into the murky depths.

The children met back up in the treehouse when they had finished for the day. Toby had once again met the children's expectations, preparing a delicious supper of fresh, crisp green salad. He had prepared the leaves in a lemon and olive oil dressing with a sprinkling of limey zest. A citrusy smell percolated around the treehouse with its fresh clean fragrance and penetrated the air outside, welcoming the children home.

The table was set up with the usual glasses of freshly squeezed orange juice and warm bread. In the centre of the table, a few small bowls of grated parmesan cheese were laid up for the children to compliment the salad.

Automatically they seated themselves as though this was their normal place of residence, while exciting talk surrounded the table from all sides as they chatted about the things they had been doing during the day.

"Toby, I met the Leshy today when I recreated one of the forests. I didn't realise they were real beings though. I mean I've heard stories abou' them before, but I thought they were only stories," said Scarlet in an innocent, nonchalant voice.

Toby stopped cleaning to deliberately shoot her an unimpressed glare.

"Well where did you think the stories came from Ruby? Dreamworld is where all these weird and wonderful beings emerge from. People dream them up. You will find more creatures here than you dare to believe exist – and not all of them are ones you'd want to run into. You should consider yourself very lucky they weren't in a playful mood."

"What kind of creatures Toby?" Scarlet probed.

Toby collected his thoughts together before answering. Scarlet's question wasn't difficult to answer, but it did mean he had to be careful how he answered. If he made these creatures sound exciting, there was a chance she and her siblings might go looking for them.

"There are things living in Dreamworld you would never want to meet Scarlet, things so awful they can change a person's mind, you'd never be the same again. Just hope you never come face to face with them. The fact that you have Abaddon on your case would be enough to frighten most people, you don't need more trouble." Toby smiled in satisfaction. That answer would suffice for the moment.

Scarlet sighed with disappointment. "Do you not think we should at least have an idea of wha' we might meet? At least then we would be more prepared," she insisted.

Toby frowned, uncertain if he should divulge the information. "Okay," he sighed reluctantly. "But just promise that if I tell you, you won't start looking for adventures. Not every creature here would entertain the minds of children's curiosity, they stay out of sight for a reason, so deliberately looking for them can't end well."

Scarlet grinned victoriously. "We promise," she said, pursing her lips mischievously.

Toby seated himself as comfortably as he could get, his fingers entwined as he fidgeted nervously, and then in a constrained, hollow voice he began.

"There are strange things that live in Dreamworld; most of them keep to the Shadowlands or the Harrowlands. There are some very odd creatures that live briefly in the Ephemeral Layer, but they won't give you much of a problem since they don't normally hang around for long.

"The ones I know of though, the ones you really don't want to get mixed up with are the Sand Demons. They lurk in both the Shadowlands and the Harrowlands. They roam the deserts where they lead the dreamer or traveller into a false sense of security. The desert may look normal for example, like there's nothing remotely dangerous there, but once you start to cross, you'll notice that the goal posts seem to move further away.

"Common sense is quickly forgotten about. Any magic the person might possess evades the memory, so that imagining a way out of the danger doesn't even surface, and all the while the traveller moves on in the hope that they will cross the desert soon. Sometimes the Sand Demons will encourage the traveller on with promises of water on the other side, cruelly turning the pools into nothing but a mirage the closer they get."

Toby shuffled uncomfortably in his chair, edging himself nearer to the children as though he were afraid to disclose too much. He picked up his glass of grape juice, wetting his lips with the sweet flavour before continuing.

"You know the feeling of falling, dehydration or overheating you can sometimes get when you're asleep?" The children nodded with understanding. "Well, these feelings are known as Nudgers. They're the body's natural defences which keep you safe; alerting the sleeper to when something isn't right and forcing her to wake from the imminent danger. That's why they're called Nudgers. But if the Sand Demons find you, they stop the Nudgers reacting to the danger they themselves pose. Normally their hideous presence would alert the Nudger instantly, dragging you away from their threat, but with the defence down, the traveller walks on and on until he disappears into the jaws of the Demon itself."

"You mean they eat people?" gasped Rose in alarm.

"Yes, they eat people, but they do other things too depending on their mood I'm afraid."

"Like what?" asked Rose nervously, unsure if she really wanted to know.

Toby's attention crept away for a moment as he deliberated briefly, his short stocky fingers twiddled pensively under his chin and he sighed decisively. He'd already told them this much, he might as well continue.

"Well, if you met one on a normal day, you know, like if they didn't care much for playing, you can expect them to behave much worse. They're monsters – they torment the mind, preying on the victim's energy, absorbing their strength in the day while feeding on their restlessness at night without the victim ever knowing what's happening.

"When that person falls asleep at night, exhausted from the arduous day, the Demon picks up from where it left off the night before, perniciously digging away, gnawing into their minds, cruelly tormenting a bit at a time until the victim becomes so fatigued that his mind can no longer take the beating. The life force is virtually sucked from the person while he sleeps leaving a jibbering carcase in the waking world.

"These souls are incarcerated within the body of the Sand Demon for the rest of the persons' time on earth, only freeing them when the body in the waking world dies".

"Do you suppose that's what happened to Mum, Toby? Do you think she might have been hounded by a Sand Demon? She was always tired - it didn't matter how much sleep she got; she just couldn't get her energy back!" asked Scarlet with an edge of worry in her voice.

"It's possible Scarlet, but there are so many creatures that could potentially have caused her illness, it's difficult to say for sure what happened," replied Toby apologetically. "Should I stop for today?" he asked, sensing that the children were beginning to fear the worst.

"No, tell us more," begged Scarlet quickly. "I just couldn't help but wonder if Mum might be in trouble and needed our help."

Toby looked concerned suddenly. "You can't start worrying yourselves about the possibilities of what might be. You will get yourselves into all kinds of problems if you go hunting for all the different possibilities that could have befallen your mother. I'm not sure we should carry on with this conversation, I can see it's stirring your imaginations."

"Please don't stop Toby, we need to know a bit more, just a little?" Scarlet pleaded.

"Okay, but only a little more then," agreed Toby against his better judgement.

"Right, where was I? There's another creature that you Jamie should be especially aware of," started Toby again, making Jamie sit bolt upright in dread at hearing his name mentioned. "Dream Sirens are the most beautiful spirits to have ever graced the planet, capable of capturing the heart of their male victims with just one look. Their appearance overwhelms the dreamer giving them the feeling of infatuation, making them believe they are in love. The unwary dreamer becomes so bewitched that they allow the Sirens access to their minds, allowing them to extract any information they want at any time. Once in, the Siren can manipulate the victim, preying on their deepest desires so that eventually he gives in to the Siren handing full control over along with his thoughts.

"Now completely besotted, the dreamer never wants to leave, never wants to wake and actually chooses to stay in the clutches of the Siren forever. The body left back in the waking world vegetates, slowly degrading until again it can no longer operate. The mind maintains the body, and in both cases without it functioning, the body can't live."

Toby stopped to see if he had made any impact on the children. They sat with their mouths gaping; the horror of what Toby had told them sinking in more severely than he had imagined.

"Anyway, I think that's definitely enough for today," he said in a bid to stop the children asking anymore questions. "Did you all manage to gather enough fire wood in the Whispering Wood?"

They almost forgot that they still had to carry heavy logs home for Dennis. It came crashing down around them rather abruptly, rudely awakening them from the horror stories Toby had been telling them.

"Yes. Yes, we did Toby, thank you. We just 'ave to get them home now," answered Jamie in a flat, distant voice.

"Well so long as you don't hurt yourselves anymore. I can't help you, unless you're here. Anyway, you had best be getting back now. Be careful and remember you always have a place to stay, you're always welcome, and you're always safe here."

Jamie turned his hands over examining his palms, the herbal teas they had been given had worked miraculously on his open blisters, there was no sign that only a few hours ago he had been injured.

"We had best be going I suppose," Jamie said, getting to his feet. "Come on you three, back to work."

Chapter Thirty-Three
The Nightmare

The children appeared back in the wood where their heavily laden paper bags stood waiting to be carried home.

"I think we ought to transport ourselves most of the way home, and then carry the bags the last stretch down the street. We don't want to arouse suspicion," suggested Jamie thoughtfully.

"It's still going to be quite difficult dragging them down the road even that short a distance, but it's better than nothing." said Scarlet rummaging through her pocket to retrieve her Stone so that she wouldn't get left behind.

The group re-appeared on the small stretch of road just before the turning of the cul-de-sac in which they lived. It became very clear within seconds that the arduous walk home was going to be the easier bit.

Huge splashes of rain fell over them as they materialised, rapidly soaking both the children to the bone and destroying any strength the sacks might have had left.

"Chocolate teapot springs to mind," sniped Jamie incredulously as he glared in disdain first at the paper bags and then at the sky, still heavy with thick, doughy clouds of unfallen rain. "There's no point dilly-dallying around here though," he huffed. "The longer we're out in this, the more difficult it's gonna be to bring these sacks back in one piece."

The children understood immediately the implications of being out in the rain and hurried along as best they could, dragging the sacks behind on the wet footpath. It didn't take long though before the inevitable happened; the bags disintegrated from the bottom, allowing the logs to tumble out across the pavement.

"Just great," tutted Jamie with agitation, as the children desperately fought to reload the logs, piling them on top of the wood still inside the flimsy remains.

Their efforts were futile. The moment the children heaved on the paper sacks, the logs fell back through the bottom, scattering like marbles in the deep puddles flooding the street.

After much failed perseverance the children finally gave in to defeat.

"If I run home, I can come back with the wheelbarrow," suggested Jamie wearily. "Stay here with the wood and I'll be back in a second," he ordered, turning quickly on his heel, disappearing with speed down the remainder of the street. He returned moments later as he had promised wheeling the barrow as fast as he were able back to where he had left the girls.

It took two trips to collect the scattered wood off the footpath and the children were completely drenched by the time they all returned home, but they were glad to have finally made it back – which in itself was saying something.

"Ahh, you're back I see." Dennis grimaced at the group of sorry looking children, dripping with water from the torrential weather. "Ya can load the wood shed now and clean the coal bunker, and make sure it's done properly. Afterwards yer can all go to bed. There's nothin' fer tea, I've bin really busy today."

It was his slitted eyes that Scarlet hated the most. They seemed to ooze with hatred; his contempt for them was clearly visible without him having to say a word. His eyes had a language all of their own which translated his haughty, conceited mannerisms, they could sneer without trying and were full of pure unadulterated venom. A look of cold loathing had completely killed the part of him which had once made him human. It was hard to believe that he used to have a mother who adored him, who would have once upon a time gazed into her baby boy's eyes and loved him.

Regardless of the animosity they felt towards him, the children were still obedient, and neatly piled the freshly chopped logs into the wood shed after sweeping it clean. It was a horrid job while being wet and cold. Their clothes stuck to their skin exacerbating the sensation, but they had been in worse conditions. It didn't take too long with everyone lending a hand; the silence broke as the last log was neatly placed back in the shed.

"I think we can safely say we're done now. Come on, let's get back indoors and dry off," said Jamie with relief, his face brightening up at the thought of being liberated.

The children, all eagerly wishing to get indoors rushed out of the wood shed. They barely noticed Dennis as they blundered their way through the rain, almost running into him.

"Goin' somewhere are ya?" he said coldly in an overly calm way, sending shivers colder than the weather through their bodies.

"Sorry Dennis, we didn't see you there. We've finished outside and were just trying to get out of the rain," apologised Scarlet timidly.

"You're only finished when a say you 'ave," he spat, his eyes narrowed spitefully. "Ya know, your mother was right to leave. The problem with that though, among others, is that I got landed with her rejects. Who in their righ' mind would want to be saddled with scum? No! That's too good. You're the scum off the scum. You're the filth left over in the gutter after the putridity has festered, leaving behind the stuff that isn't worthy of rot. But not for much longer, soon you won't be my problem anymore."

He pulled up his shirt sleeves, folding them neatly to reveal his tattoos. Scarlet wasn't sure why he decided to behave so strangely in the rain, but his actions did capture her attention. Her eyes fell onto the beasts inked on his arms and for a second, she was certain they twitched under his skin and even more certain that their eyes moved.

It couldn't have been real she convinced herself at last, it must have been her overactive imagination. After all he had just come out with a vile statement, her nerves were just on edge.

"Do ya like my *pets?"* he hissed when he realised she had seen them move. A few droplets of saliva splattered her face.

Scarlet hastily looked away ignoring his jibe, she didn't want him to see the disgust in her face. It unnerved her considerably, but she held her composure and remained silent.

"Goodnight children!" he growled, standing to one side. A sickening snarl twisted his mouth, spreading like rot across his face.

The children sidled by him feeling his eyes burning as they passed and hurried out of his way.

"Wha' on earth 'as he got planned now?" whispered Scarlet, feeling suddenly very sick. "He never wishes us a good night, and nothin' in his actions suggests he meant it either."

Jamie shrugged his shoulders in confusion. "We'll just 'ave to watch our backs I think."

"Wha' did he mean though?" asked Rose trembling.

"I've no idea, but I don't think it's gonna be anythin' pretty. At a guess though, I'd think he's got somethin' planned for us when we fall asleep tonight," said Jamie, mulling his thoughts over in his head for a brief moment. "All of ya be alert when ya drift off. We'll meet in Dreamworld later, I've got a bad feelin' somethin' dreadful is gonna happen, I'd better get to bed now, otherwise I'll only ge' into more trouble with Dad when he sees I'm not in my room. Nigh' girls."

It was very difficult to sleep that night; the children tossed and turned for hours. The words from Dennis echoing in their heads, but eventually their eyes shut as they fell into an uneasy sleep.

Scarlet being the last to doze off had to find where the others were waiting. They were all sat under the boughs of the oak tree. Rose was huddled into a tight ball hardly daring to move, she had been more afraid than the others and on edge before she had even fallen asleep.

"We didn't think you were ever going to get here Scarlet, we've waited ages," said Ruby impatiently.

"I couldn't settle – sorry. I'm here now though."

Jamie's eyes moved towards the skies above gesturing his concerns, they were a strange shade of grey and green as though they were being swirled together in a blender.

"The sky's wrong tonight, it's got Rose worried. She doesn't need to be any more upset than she is already," said Jamie, offering his hand to Rose in order to help her to her feet. "We need to stay together and find some shelter, just in case the sky makes good its threat; it doesn't look very friendly. The forest looks safer and we'll stay relatively dry if a storm is on its way. Come on!"

"Why can't we just stay in the treehouse?" protested Rose, gazing longingly at the cosy looking house tucked neatly in the oak's strong boughs.

"We could, but we won't find ou' what's goin' on if we keep running away. Besides, we can always come back if we get into trouble. There's something here that Dad wants us to discover, whether we like the idea or not. We'll be fine, I promise," he grinned reassuringly.

The children took each other's hands as they cautiously walked towards the forest. It looked surprisingly welcoming; the freshness offered a familiar smell, and the bird's song gave off a somewhat tranquil atmosphere.

"See, there's nothin' here to be afraid of. It's just as it's always bin," encouraged Jamie with a bright smile.

"What do you s'pose Dennis meant about us not bein' his problem anymore then?" Rose argued, still unconvinced things weren't as they appeared.

"I don't know Rose," Jamie answered. "He migh' have bin just tryin' to scare us, but y'all 'ave to remember this is only a dream. We can wake from a dream, we just *give* ourselves a Nudger. We just 'ave to fall or somethin', and we will wake up straight away."

"That sounds logical, so long as ya promise we'll turn round an' go back if things get tricky. We don't have to play Dennis's game just because he wants us to," said Scarlet in a final sort of way.

"Fair enough, I promise," agreed Jamie.

Scarlet smiled wryly. "I'm sort of curious too if I'm honest," she admitted.

"What we gonna do if we actually come across Abaddon? I don't s'pose anyone stopped to think abou' tha' did they? It's not normal here tonight, there's definitely somethin' going on, and I'm not sure I want to find out what it is," said Ruby sharply. "Abaddon doesn't play games, he's destructive. Or have you all forgotten wha' he did here not so long ago?"

"So what d'ya propose we do? Maybe ya think we should all run back and hide? Better still, perhaps you think life at home will miraculously ge' better if we pretend it's all hunky-dory do ya?" Jamie snapped contentiously.

"That's not what I meant and you know it," retorted Ruby defensively. "I'm just not sure we should go runnin' off into Dreamworld when firstly, Dennis pretty much threatened us, and then when we arrive here, the sky even looks like it wants to kill us."

Jamie twisted his face in irritation, goading her on to speak her mind.

"Oh, I get it," she continued. "You didn't notice. Perhaps your ego is so big you've suddenly lost the ability to see when things are dangerous?" mocked Ruby acrimoniously.

Jamie folded his arms haughtily before retaliating, allowing ruby to have her final say.

"If you'd actually listened to me, I'd already agreed that we should go back if it got ugly, but you're so stubborn you don't know when you're beaten," Jamie bit back. "Everyone apart from you understands that if we don't face up to this now, we'll be permanently worried abou' goin' to bed at night, an' I for one am not prepared for tha'. Stay here if ya want, but I know where I'm goin."

"Fine, but just so ya know, I'm not happy with this at all and neither's Rose," retorted Ruby angrily.

"Understood," answered Jamie assertively without trying to aggravate the issue any further.

The children paced through the forest, keeping their wits about them as they went. They'd already been warned of some of the more distasteful characters they could meet, but they were also assured that these creatures lived in the Shadowlands. Even so, there was nothing to say Abaddon could still turn up uninvited.

The oak forest Scarlet had encouraged to grow was thinner on the outskirts, but towards the centre, the trees grew denser, and that was Scarlet's main concern. Unlike her siblings, she had already met the Leshy and knew that in that instance she had been lucky. A second meeting might not be so favourable and the longer they walked, the more unlikely they were to evade them.

The sky was no longer visible, the trees canopies completely covered their way, shading the path and giving an eerie, unnatural atmosphere. The former serenity had somehow managed to escape unnoticed, leaving all of the children feeling apprehensive.

"Are we ready to turn back yet? Or did ya want to carry on lookin' fer somethin' that's not visible?" asked Ruby sarcastically.

"No. I don't think this is servin' any real purpose anymore," agreed Jamie, much to Ruby's surprise. "I think it's probably time to go back, I'm not comfortable with this if I'm honest. If Abaddon meant for us to see somethin', or if Dennis had something planned, I think it would've 'appened by now."

"Good, I'm glad you're in agreement now, and not too soon either," said Ruby, taking Rose by the hand with an air of authority about her.

Defeated and slightly embarrassed, Scarlet and Jamie silently led the way. They were sure there was something they were supposed to have seen and most definitely a reason they were here under these strange circumstances tonight. It still felt odd that nothing had made itself apparent.

Ruby and Rose walked a few paces behind with a spring in their step. Getting back to where they had started was of paramount importance after feeling as nervous as they had done.

"I don't mean to cause alarm," said Scarlet after a little while. "But does this path look familiar to anyone. I don't think it's the way we came, is it?"

"It's fine. If we carry on walking this way we'll get back," said Ruby pushing past her sister to take the lead with Rose. "The sooner we ge' back, the better we'll all feel."

"Well as long as *you* recognise it, I'm happy too," answered Scarlet still unconvinced.

A loud, sudden crack from above brought the children to an abrupt standstill. The looming storm which up until now had held off, finally broken through with an almighty crash of thunder, followed by its customary flash of light which seemed to rip the entire sky in half. Torrential rain poured from the heavens as though someone had split the sides of a water container, almost instantly turning the soft, peaty, forest floor into a watery marsh.

"And there it is. I was beginning to miss it!" said Jamie sarcastically.

"Miss what?" asked Ruby curiously with a furled brow.

"The rain of course," he replied with a huff. "It seems to follow us around where ever we go."

"Can't you make it stop like ya did before Scarlet?" grumbled Rose. "It's not nice here, I just wanna go home."

Scarlet didn't answer though, she had a troubled look of confusion pinned to her face.

"Wha's the matter Scarlet?" asked Jamie, as Scarlet continued to stare into space.

"Why haven't we woken up? I don't understand why we're still here. The clash of thunder should've bin enough of a Nudger to wake us," said Scarlet with bewilderment. "I know I jumped, and I'm sure you all probably did too."

"That's a good question," said Ruby who sounded just as perplexed at being enlightened of the now obvious revelation.

"Wait a minute," said Scarlet. "I just want to take a look from above the trees to see if the oak is near. At least then I can be sure we're on the right track."

Scarlet sailed high into the air above the tree canopies, turning a full 360 degrees in the hope of seeing the giant oak, but it had completely vanished from view.

Rose stared at Ruby the minute Scarlet disappeared with a puzzled look on her face. "The oak? What she talkin' about? There are oaks everywhere!"

Ruby shrugged her shoulders. "I don't know, she's probably just tryin' to sound important."

Normally the treehouse could be seen for miles around; there was no way it could just disappear. Slowly with more deliberation, Scarlet carefully turned again being sure in her own mind that it hadn't escaped her attention, but still there was nothing, only the tree tops and the heavy sideway streaks of linear rain.

It was a bit unsettling, but Scarlet was determined that it would not fluster her. The last thing Rose needed was to see her normally strong sister panicking. The least she could do was to try and stop the storm if it made Rose feel more comfortable.

Concentrating hard in a bid to gain control of the downpour, Scarlet poured every ounce of effort she could muster into stopping it – but nothing happened. She couldn't make it stop. It was as if Dreamworld had suddenly developed a mind of its own, or as if it were being controlled by someone or something more powerful just like it had done before when the land had been turned to smoke and ashes.

Worry started to creep over her. Nothing that they had experienced so far resembled the normality of the Dreamworld she knew; it was normally obliging. Now it was being deliberately belligerent. Something was very wrong.

Chapter Thirty-Four
The Abstract Forest

Gliding back down to the ground, Scarlet kept her composure about her, landing in the same spot she had left a few moments earlier. She didn't want Rose to pick up on her anxiety; she knew she had to play this calmly if Rose were to remain unaffected. Ignorance can be a blessing she reminded herself.

"How strange," she said casually.

"What's strange Scarlet?" asked Rose.

"Oh, nothing really," she began in her most nonchalant expression. "It's probably just the bad weather cloudin' the oak tree. I couldn't see it through all the rain. Don't worry though." She smiled at Rose in an attempt to ease her mind as well as her own.

Rose frowned; she didn't know how to answer Scarlet. As far as the eye could see, there were oak trees in every direction.

Scarlet kept quiet in her thoughts after that, thinking it better to try and figure what was going on without broadcasting her concerns. She was trying to visualise the treehouse, but her mind was persistently being blocked. Although that was a cause for concern, the real problem was that without having a clear vision of the treehouse, there was no possible way to return or even materialise back there like they had done so many times before.

The very beauty about being in a dream is having the ability to just flick from one place to another based purely on thought. That thought can only become a reality if the apparition is clear, it's imperative the vision is whole, undisturbed and transparent, without that, Scarlet knew it was futile trying.

Scarlet puzzled it over in her head as they walked. She was sure the others would figure out what was baffling her soon enough. How could they not realise that they could get back to the treehouse if they put their minds to it?

At last, because it seemed to escape her sibling's thoughts, and after careful consideration, Scarlet decided to jog their memories a little.

"I wish we hadn't left the oak. We could still be safe and warm if we'd listened to you Rose."

"Scarlet, we ignored you the first few times when you said you couldn't see the oak. We don't know what you're talking abou', there are oaks everywhere if you care to open your eyes properly," snapped Jamie with frustration as he continued marching onwards.

"Okay, since you're being picky with words, I meant the treehouse. Maybe I should have been more direct, but I didn't want to alarm anyone. What I meant to say was that I don't remember the treehouse very well - well not clearly enough to get us all back anyway. If any of you three can visualise it clearly we could save ourselves the trouble of tramping aimlessly through the rain."

The very notion of the treehouse had somehow mysteriously escaped their thoughts. It was only when Scarlet mentioned it, that they vaguely remembered there had even been one. It was as if it had been erased from their memories.

It suddenly dawned on them what Scarlet meant when she had referred to, 'not being able to see the oak.'

"How could we forget about the treehouse?" said Ruby in bemusement, coming to an abrupt standstill. "You didn't forget, but we did. How is that even possible?"

"All we were hoping for was to get back to where we started, the treehouse wasn't even in my thoughts," added Rose nervously, backing up Ruby's fears that perhaps Dreamworld could disintegrate if the children allowed parts of it to be forgotten.

"It appears there's more than the treehouse escaping our thoughts though. I couldn't stop the rain either," said Scarlet drearily with a twisted frown, looking up at the clouds still emptying their load over them. "I still don't think we're on the right path either if I'm being totally honest Ruby. The trees look an odd sort of shape – beautifully interesting, but not at all familiar to me. I'm certain I'd recognise these particular trees if we had walked past them once already. See how they bend; they look as if they're specialists in contortionism." She laughed weakly, knowing that in reality their world was changing around them and they were powerless to stop it.

Ruby didn't answer. As it happens, she had begun to doubt the way also, but hadn't wanted to admit her mistake for fear of being ridiculed. It was she who had been adamant that they were on the right path, and her alone that had taken the lead so competently.

"What if we try a different way round?" Scarlet suggested with a fresh mind, convinced that perhaps their dilemma just needed to be approached differently. "If we can't visualise the treehouse, maybe we could try goin' someplace else."

"Like where?" asked Ruby dryly, not wanting to sound too hopeful that Scarlet's idea might actually work, just in case it didn't.

"The Long River for example? Perhaps we'd 'ave a better chance makin' our way back from there?" said Scarlet feeling suddenly more positive.

"It might work," said Jamie, visually seeing the Long River in his mind's eye as clearly as if he were standing in front of it. "All of ya hold hands," he ordered excitedly. "That way we'll move together."

Without further ado the children grasped hold of each other's hands while holding onto the river's image. Their eyes flickered in deep concentration, meditating intensely on their destination.

The familiar sudden jolting sensation churned their stomachs as the land around them whirled, spinning their senses and making them feel giddy before abruptly dropping into place around them, suggesting their plan had worked. But when they opened their eyes, their hopes were instantly dashed when the Long River was nowhere to be seen. They were still in the forest – a different part, but still the forest.

"I don't understand. Where's the river?" asked Rose gloomily, rubbing her eyes in complete confusion. "I can hear it, I just can't see it."

"Up there!" answered Scarlet in shock, pointing up towards the trees where it was evidently clear to see why she looked so flabbergasted.

A part of the river was flowing upside down, falling into a waterfall which cascaded up as if an abstract of it had been cut from a glossy magazine, then randomly stuck into the strangest position onto another page, completely out of place.

"What the hell is goin' on?" said Jamie slowly, who was now just as flummoxed. "What's that all about?"

"I think someone's playin' games with us," said Scarlet, her voice trembling a little at what this could mean.

"Like who? You mean Abaddon?" said Jamie, hoping that's not what she had hinted at.

"Not necessarily. It could be the Leshy; they're known to play tricks like this on people too, aren't they?"

"And they give people amnesia as well, do they?" Jamie barked with contention.

"No, not that I'm aware of. But they could do, Toby didn't say they couldn't cloud a person's mind, did he?"

"Well regardless of who's playin' games with us, the question still remains of what we're s'posed to do abou' it?" said Jamie.

"I don't think we can do much about it, except to keep goin'. If it is the Leshy, then hopefully they'll get fed up soon. If we just stand still, we stand no chance of getting out at all, do we?" Scarlet bit back in a matter of fact way, hoping she might be making sense to at least one of her siblings. "We just need to keep reminding ourselves that this is only a dream. At some point we will have wake up, won't we?"

"I feel cold and wet Ruby!" grumbled Rose again. "I want to…"

"Did you lot just see tha'?" said Jamie aghast, cutting Rose short of her obvious statement. "Tell me someone else just saw the trees change shape! Just look at them! – They look all twisted and gangly."

His jaw had dropped in astonishment as he stared in disbelief that they actually had the audacity to move and shape shift right under their noses.

He was right. The trees had somehow contorted; twisting so much that some of the big boughs hung heavy like lifeless limbs threatening to drop off at any moment. On top of that, it appeared that the forest floor had miraculously contorted too, as if the children were seeing it through a reflection in a hall of mirrors, stretched like chewing gum into an odd, deformed shape.

"This is mental. If this wasn't so scary right now, I'd be quite impressed by what's going on, but this – this is just crazy," said Jamie, with a hint of excitement prevalent within his otherwise perplexed tone.

"Does anyone have any idea of wha' we ought to do? Seriously, I don't think just walking around aimlessly is goin' to solve anythin' after all, and if the forest *is* somehow moving, then we've got an even smaller chance of getting outta here," Scarlet said in frustration, changing her earlier opinion quickly.

"We've tried to imagine our way out. All that did was make things worse, the forest wasn't a mish mash of jumbled jigsaw pieces before. I don't personally see what else we can do," Ruby answered with the same frustration.

"I don't like this anymore," mumbled Rose again, as a tear sneaked out from the corner of her eye and rolled down her cheek. "I want to go home."

"I know ya do Rose. We're trying! It's not quite goin' to plan though," said Ruby gently, holding back her own exasperation as she tried to console her sister. "We'll get back soon I'm sure."

"Come on, we may as well just keep walkin'. Hopefully we migh' see a way through soon," said Jamie optimistically, seeing no other option available.

Silently, the children followed after Jamie as he now took the lead. Thoughts of elusion rushed through their minds, plans of escape seemed to build with possibility, but dissolved within seconds when the reality of every conceived idea all came back to the same final conclusion – they were lost, not just physically, but their minds also. They all knew they wanted to get back to the treehouse, but what was it? And where was it?

Jamie had been desperately lost in thought. The complete vexation of not being able to understand who was responsible for their dilemma added to his building anger so much that neither he nor the girls had noticed the forest change dramatically again. That was, until Jamie stumbled over a floating tree branch which sent him tumbling to the ground in an ungainly fashion.

He stayed on the ground, dumbfounded by what had just happened, hardly able to comprehend what was quite clearly the cause of his sudden fall.

"Since when did tree branches learn how to float in mid-air?" snapped Jamie crossly as he gazed up at the offending branch, hovering like an enchanted witch's broom in front of his face.

He was right. The trees had now taken on a new, strange form of floating, suspending themselves in mid-air without any support from the ground and with no other apparent footing to hold them there. What was even more peculiar was that the trees were not all fully formed. They reminded Scarlet of a piece of abstract artwork, drawn by an artist with a creatively, messed up mind.

Branches were conjoined with fragments from other trees, and small sharp twigs hung unsupported in the middle of the pathways, surreptitiously waiting to poke an unsuspecting traveller straight in the eye if they went unnoticed. It had somehow all become distorted in the same way you would see a pattern through a kaleidoscope, twisted into a new shape which is neither familiar nor unfamiliar.

It began to dawn on the older children that this is what Dennis had meant when he had told them, *"They wouldn't be his problem for much longer."* This was not a dream. This was a nightmare being forced upon them by Abaddon. He had found an intriguingly, elaborate way to break into their minds without their knowledge, blocking and twisting their memories so that they were incapable of finding safety.

"Fanbloodytastic. This is just perfect. Now wha' do we do?" snapped Jamie at last, his anger visibly oozing from every part of him. "We're stuck here. We're never goin' to get outta this place, are we?"

"KEEP CALM FOR A START," shouted Scarlet ironically. "Shouting is hardly the best way to keep the situation under control, think about Rose won't you! We can take whatever he throws at us; it's never stopped us before. We've all got powers to fight back, and since it appears that we're stuck in this dream and none of us seems able to remember our way back, I suggest we just get on with it and stand up to him. It's what our guardians wanted us to do eventually anyway."

"Why can't we just wake up then?" asked Rose. "When I've had bad dreams before, I just wake up."

The children hadn't really given this much thought. They had been too busy trying to find a way out, but Rose was right. They had all woken from nightmares before, especially from the ones which were particularly distressing. The severe weather hadn't woken them despite feeling the accompanying elements, and on top of that, the Nudger hadn't worked either. Everyone had jumped in alarm when the thunder had rattled, so they knew the Nudger hadn't been too weak. However, physically trying to wake up was something they hadn't tried to do yet.

"Well let's try it then. All of you wake up!" encouraged Ruby, not convinced such an easy option would work.

The older children glanced at each other, hopeful that Rose's idea could be so uncomplicated, but closed their eyes shut anyway, focusing their energy on waking their own minds.

It felt silly, ridiculous even. They could hear their own voices desperately trying to stir them from their sleep, but their bodies refused to obey the commands their minds gave. They had no control over their sleeping selves at all.

"It's not workin'. What's he done to us?" asked Rose in a panic when she finally understood the severity of their plight. "I couldn't even make my finger move."

"I dunno," whispered Jamie under his breath. "It felt like my mind had been completely separated from my body, but I could hear myself tellin' me to open my eyes, I just couldn't do it though."

"Well whatever he's done, we'll be okay. Somethin' will come through for us, even if we 'ave to work it all out on our own," said Scarlet defiantly, desperate to hide the fear she really felt. "There's no way Dennis can keep us trapped here forever. We just 'ave to stay alert, stay together and keep our eyes peeled, c'mon."

But Jamie had other ideas. A sudden rush of adrenalin pulsed through his body, giving him a burst of energy and exhilaration. Without waiting to hear anyone's opinion, he abruptly thrust himself up from the forest floor and was now soaring into a steep ascent, climbing high into the sky to see if he could make any sense of what was going on around them.

"I just wanna see if there's a way out yet," he yelled hastily, as he shot past his sisters at phenomenal speed.

Scarlet had already thoroughly scanned the area earlier, there was nothing then and it seemed unlikely there would be a land mark now, but it couldn't hurt to take another look.

Up he went, but as expected he saw nothing from over the tops of the tree canopies, they looked oddly familiar, but no different from how they appeared on ground level. The trees from above were all mixed in the same abstract fashion with no obvious way of returning to the treehouse.

Resigning himself to the fact that he wasn't able to help after all, Jamie gave up looking, slamming his feet hard into the ground as he landed.

"It's useless," he groaned. "There's nothin' there. It jus' goes on forever."

"We'd best keep movin' then," sighed Scarlet. "Its pointless stayin' still, especially since the land keeps turnin'. You never know, it might even be kinder on its next turn." she sniggered sarcastically, knowing in the back of her mind that such a possibility was as likely as them all waking up to a life before Dennis.

Dragging their feet, the children continued to walk. There was very little they could do but play the game Abaddon had set for them. All too soon it became evident that once again the scene was on the change. This time the children hardly blinked – dismissing it as a normal event – without any care. In reality they all knew Abaddon had no intention of making it easy for them, if anything, Dreamworld would be churned into a bigger mess than before.

It wasn't until the last piece of abstract dropped into place that the children actually took notice of this latest turn.

The land had now interlocked with the Shadowlands. Intangible pieces of twisted, dead wood filtered in among the live forest and fragmented boulders of rock hovered in mid-air.

This latest mix looked more eerie than what they had been accustomed to. It was strange enough seeing branches and tree roots hovering in their way, but now this additional variation made their journey more hazardous. Apart from the obvious visible change, the uneasiness of what stayed hidden away preyed heavily on the children's already anxious minds. They almost expected some amalgamated half formed beast that might have unfortunately got caught up in the twist, to come bounding out from one of the floating rock formations in a ferocious attack.

The children kept these unnerving thoughts to themselves though. It wasn't going to help if any of them dwelled too long on these scenarios. It was hard enough picking their way through this elusive jumble of forest and mountains without adding other distracting worries into the equation.

Now, the only light that crept between the trees was the last rays of sun breaking between thick clouds on the horizon. With so little light, their eyes were unable to maintain a definite visual guide, so with their arms outstretched, the children guided themselves through the obstacle course, feeling their way as an extra precaution.

Scarlet shivered, only now noticing how cold she was becoming. Her warm, exhaled breath poured from her mouth like steam from a hot bath, rising into the cooler air and evaporating as it melted into the atmosphere. She shivered again, this time realising her siblings were also experiencing the same strange phenomenon.

"It's just a dream," Scarlet whispered to herself. "We're not really here." Jamie turned to her, "Did you say somethin'?" he asked, still pushing forward through the terrain.

"I'm just reminding myself that I'm only dreamin'" she replied, still shaking with cold.

"It doesn't explain why we are all feelin' the same thing though does it?" he answered, desperately trying to keep himself from shuddering.

"I dunno. A dream manifests a vision and the body automatically responds, that's normal isn't it? I mean, it's got darker, it's natural that we'd feel colder."

"Yeah, but it's not just the cold is it!" he replied, sensing that there was more to it than she was letting on. "If you're feelin' anything like me, and I bet you are, then you are also feelin' weak and sleepy and giddy and your skin is prickled with goose-bumps. In fact, you don't even need to answer that, I know you are." Scarlet couldn't deny his intuition even if she wanted to. He was right, there was no point arguing.

"Certain things in dreams like temperature and the elements are completely irrelevant," continued Jamie. "They shouldn't have any effect, unless of course these things are filtered through into our dreams from the waking world."

Scarlet knew what he was implying, she already knew that certain things from the waking world could entwine with Dreamworld. It's how Dennis had been able to corrupt their minds for some time now.

"Can we stop for a while? I'm getting cold and tired," said Rose interrupting the conversation suddenly before dropping feebly to the ground.

Scarlet stopped walking. "Wait a minute Jamie," she called. "I think Rose has fallen."

She could just make out a faint outline of her sister through the dark, but little else.

"I don't feel particularly well if I'm honest either Rose, but I don't think it's a good place to stop, it's not safe." said Scarlet with concern. "Wha' do you two think?" she continued, passing the decision over to her siblings.

"I'm really tired too actually," admitted Jamie, allowing the girls to know he was also suffering.

"What about you Ruby? Can you go further?" said Scarlet straining her eyes to see around. "I just don't think this is the best place to stop!"

"And where is a good place to stop Scarlet?" snapped Jamie suddenly. "It's dark, we can't see, we're all cold, and if you ask me, it's damn obvious we can't win, especially while we're stuck in the bleedin' jungle."

"Ya think we ought to just sit down and wait to die then?" retorted Scarlet, at what seemed defeat in her opinion. Giving up was not in her vocabulary and neither was feeling sorry for herself.

"I just meant tha' it seems pointless wearin' ourselves down like this, we're all exhausted and cold. We've been walking for hours now, there doesn't seem to be an end in sight; it just keeps goin' on and on."

"Okay. How about we carry on a little further to see if some kind of shelter becomes available, we can rest…" Scarlet stopped as the realisation of her words registered in her mind.

"Rest what?" asked Jamie in bewilderment, not understanding why Scarlet sounded so stunned.

"A shelter… We've bin so preoccupied looking for an escape, I forgot I could've made a shelter. How stupid could I get?" answered Scarlet in complete frustration and annoyance.

"Looks like ya migh' have to now anyway if Rose has anythin' to say about it," said Jamie smugly, indicating a sideways nod towards a curled-up ball on the forest floor.

Rose had taken the opportunity to conveniently fall asleep while the others were debating their plan. Small cooing sounds of peaceful slumber came from Rose's direction which sealed the strategy; they would be resting here for at least a few hours.

Scarlet smiled to herself before lifting her wrist and flicking it into a dome like shape over the top of everybody. A tent slipped around them all, confining them in a space of relative safety for one night. Within minutes the children felt a slight relief from the torment they had been subjected to.

"Who knows, we might wake up back in our beds if we're lucky," said Scarlet hopefully, before her eye lids slammed shut for a few hours.

A loud creaking sound disturbed the children, alerting them to another turn of the kaleidoscope. The sky had finally broken through the trees' density, casting yet a different shade of light over the land.

The forest had thinned and the rocky boulders had cleared. The forest floor was scattered with dead twigs and leaf litter, but it appeared that the game was still not quite over. Even with the dark grey backdrop, there didn't appear to be a clear way out of the forest.

Crawling sluggishly from the folds of the tent, the children quickly scanned their new maize as they sat on the leafy floor in front of their shelter.

"Any new ideas… anyone?" asked Jamie hopefully, knowing full well this day would probably mimic the one before.

Nobody spoke. There was nothing they could do that they hadn't tried already. Everything they'd tried had fought back hard, resisting their efforts valiantly, and so in silence the children remained locked deep in thought with ideas of escape skipping in and out of their minds.

"What about you Scarlet? You normally have somethin' to say about most things. Not got any bright ideas, no big plans to walk around monotonously today then?" continued Jamie scornfully, more because he hoped she might have a new idea rather than not.

She knew Jamie didn't mean it. He was frustrated and tired and needed someone to blame. She gave him an unimpressed warning glare and then turned her back on him in protest.

In anger, Jamie slumped down against one of the trees. His slim fingers rummaged through the leaf litter, searching for small, dry twigs from the forest floor which sufficed as some kind of stress relief. He violently snapped each in turn, hurling the pieces in rage as they skimmed and bounced across the ground.

"This is stupid," he said at last, hurling yet another twig, this time in Scarlet's general direction. "Fine mess you've walked us all into this time!"

Scarlet whipped around in disbelief, her brow frowned as she scowled at him before biting back in fury, "ME? YOU ACCUSE *ME* OF WALKING US INTO THIS? I BELIEVE YOU WERE THE ONE WHO WANTED TO KEEP ON GOING. I DIDN'T FORCE YOU. IN FACT, YOU WERE VERY ADAMANT IF I REMEMBER CORRECTLY."

Jamie knew she was right and stared at the floor in shame, but Scarlet wasn't finished yet, she suddenly remembered there was someone else she was actually feeling bitterly betrayed by. "YOU KNOW WHAT?" she continued, "I THOUGHT THE WHOLE IDEA OF HAVIN' A GUARDIAN WAS TO KEEP US SAFE. WE'RE HARDLY SAFE ARE WE ESPERANZA?"

Esperanza appeared next to her in an instant, but her strange and sudden appearance took all the children by surprise. Her normal bright, solid figure appeared now as a blurred, weakened vision.

Scarlet's anger died away instantly, realising something was amiss. "Esperanza, what's wrong? Why do ya look so – so faded?" she trembled in horror at such a weakened version of the guardian who she knew to be excessively bright.

"You're all in a state of what is known as sleep paralysis," answered Esperanza. "You won't be able to wake up as you've already discovered, so for the foreseeable future, I'm afraid you're trapped here. Abaddon has found a way to stop myself and Breanna getting through properly into Dreamworld. There is a boundary he's put in place by twisting the lands together, it's fragmented everything. It's unnatural for Dreamworld to be contorted like this; it's a violation of everything that it stands for.

"Breanna and I don't have dark powers to fragment ourselves like that; it would quite literally mean us having to shred our bodies to match what Abaddon is doing here. He's stopped us from gaining entry and helping you in the way you need us to. You mustn't try to fly out of this either," she warned. "In the same way that we cannot travel by your sides, you also risk being caught in one of the turns, I don't think you need me to go into too much detail.

"I'm doing all I can in the waking world to keep you safe, but Dennis is making things difficult. Emberleigh and Rhomelda are trying to get through, but every time they make progress, the land twists again which throws them off course. Just hang in there for as long as you can, they'll be with you as soon as they can. I'm sorry, I have to go, I can't reflect my shadow much longer, but I can talk to you telepathically if you just listen for me Scarlet."

Esperanza faded and was gone again as quickly as she had arrived, leaving the children to wait it out alone in the cold, dim forest.

"I hope she's not gone long. I just knew there was somethin' wrong," snapped Jamie.

"You worked that out all by yerself did ya?" retorted Ruby, who'd had her fill of his angry outbursts.

Jamie stared hard at her, his thoughts now turning to retaliation as he prepared himself to strike back.

Sensing the pair were about to go head to head in a pointless verbal fight, Scarlet cut in quickly. "Don't bother! We've had the contact we needed; things will be back to normal before long, so just for the minute can we try to get along?"

Jamie turned to Scarlet with a look which suggested he might insist on a fight, but her look of disapproval seemed to be enough to make him think again before foolishly taking a swipe at her with what would have undoubtedly been a well thought up line.

Keeping their frustrations locked inside they sat in silence and waited for what seemed like an eternity. In reality it was little more than a few minutes, but sitting in such haunting, eerie surroundings amplified everything making it all seem so much worse. Bizarre noises from unseen entities seemed to notice this was their cue to begin making the atmosphere more unsettling – noises which were peculiar and disturbing.

"What's makin' those awful noises?" asked Rose nervously who was struggling to deal with the fact that something might be watching them, perhaps even stalking them.

Scarlet held Rose's hand and gave it a squeeze. "It's okay, try not to worry abou' them. It'll probably just be a bird or somethin," she said as convincingly as possible.

"Or somethin'," smirked Jamie under his breath. "At least ya got that bit right."

Scarlet tutted loudly, ignoring her brother in the only way she knew how. "You know what?" said Scarlet brightly. "I think I'm feelin' a bit warmer now. It doesn't feel nearly as cold as it did earlier."

"Me too," said Rose in surprise, who had suddenly stopped shivering and perked up a little, now that Scarlet had brought it to her attention.

A faint outline of Esperanza dimly glowed by Scarlet's side moments later. Her shadowed reflection wasn't even half as bright as it had been the first time, but it was still reassuring to see her again.

"You should all start to feel warmer now. Dennis wasn't playing fair, but then I guess he never did. He'd opened the windows where you slept and taken the bed clothes away which is why you were feeling so uncomfortable." A small smile curved her lips, but Scarlet wasn't sure Esperanza was telling them everything. "As you can see, I'm too weak to come through again so you're on your own until Breanna or Emberleigh breaks through. Trust your instincts; I'm sorry. It's all we can do for now."

Esperanza evaporated like mist on a hot day and was gone, leaving the children again to fend for themselves.

"C'mon you three, best not dawdle," said Jamie suddenly animated, feeling a new sense of purpose now that they had all begun to feel slightly better.

"Wha' is it with you? One minute you're the gloomiest person ever, and the next, you're almost dancin' with glee and enthusiasm. You're so unpredictable it's ridiculous," said Scarlet sharply. "I don't know whether to walk on eggshells around you or treat you as though you've gone completely insane."

"Yeah well, Sorry. I'm all over the place just recently. Anyway, I feel motivated again now. Ya best make the most of me before I turn into a monster again," he joked.

"Hormones more like," retorted Scarlet under her breath.

The kaleidoscope twisted again as they walked, disproportionately stretching the already contorted landscape into a fragmented unrecognisable shape. It was as if the entire land had been shredded into millions of tiny scraps to form an ill-fitting jigsaw puzzle, then nudged into position by something with the intelligence of a goldfish, giving a whole new meaning to the word 'puzzle'. Abaddon was without a doubt pushing the children further and further into the Harrowlands.

Scarlet stopped walking suddenly as a thought developed in her mind, her look must have appeared more concerned than normal because in the next instance, Ruby had grabbed hold of her sister's arm in a state of panic.

"What is it Scarlet?" she shrieked.

Scarlet wasn't entirely sure if this was a question, or if Ruby was merely looking for reassurance, but believing it was the latter she answered.

"He can't hurt us in a dream."

"Ya reckon? He seems to be makin' a pretty good job of it considerin' he can't hurt us," said Ruby. "He seems quite capable of makin' us feel exceptionally uncomfortable without really gettin' anywhere near us. I'm not feelin' as well as I normally do, and we've only just started warmin' up after the prank Dennis pulled. I don't even know who's responsible for the sleep paralysis, but if that's not hurtin' us, God only knows wha' is!".

"That's what I was just thinkin' abou' though. Why would Dennis and Abaddon want us in sleep paralysis? The only thing tha' comes to mind is if they don't intend for us to wake up. If we stay sleeping, it means our minds are permanently under mental attack and our bodies will suffer physically," Scarlet answered with a look of worry on her face.

"Wha' ya getting at, *not wake up*?" said Jamie in confusion. "Why would Abaddon even want us in Dreamworld? Wha' purpose would that fulfil? We're hardly makin' his life easy bein' here, reversin' everythin' he does. Why don't you just say what you mean instead of talkin' in riddles all the time?" Jamie's face had scrunched up with obvious irritation. His eye brow furled over the top of eyes as he glared hard at his sister.

"What I mean is, we can't be hurt in a dream, but our bodies can be. Perhaps they want us to *die* here. By keeping us busy here, tormenting us at every opportunity, perhaps they're hoping we forget about gettin' home long enough for our bodies to give up. Is that easy enough for you to understand you dummy?"

Scarlet spat, annoyed that she had to spell it out for him with Rose listening to the conversation.

Rose's face turned pale. "Die? Dennis wants us to die," repeated Rose in abject horror as this thought sank in, causing tears to well up at such a daunting prospect and making Scarlet's theory sound factual.

Scarlet felt suddenly very guilty for retaliating so ferociously at Jamie. In fairness, Scarlet had been churning her theory over in her mind the moment the treehouse had become obscured, but when the land persistently changed formation, it only strengthened her concerns.

"Don't cry Rose, I was only guessing." Scarlet backtracked desperate to comfort her sister. "I could be completely wrong, you heard Esperanza; our guardians are helping us too. I'm sure we'll all be okay." Scarlet put her arm around her shoulders, pulling her into a tight hug and smiled reassuringly. "Take no notice of me."

Chapter Thirty-Five
The Sand Demons

The children walked on in silence, no one dared to speak another word of supposed theology for fear of saying the wrong thing. There hadn't been a turn for some time, but as they passed through, the deformed, broken trees began to appear less distorted, straightening and re-forming until the forest thinned out, giving hope to the children that they were almost out.

"I think we've made it!" gasped Scarlet at last when she was sure that there was no chance of another turn. The trees were gnarled and contorted in strange ways, but they were whole and the ground on which they stood had become sandy.

Their relief was short lived though, as they emerged from the Abstract Forest, a desert landscape stretched out like a large, beige carpet before them, giving off an unsettling vibe which threatened an almost certain plight if there was any attempt to cross it. Sand whipped up in the wind forming several spiralled columns of dust, gathering speed as they churned up the surface, growing ever larger as more and more sand and debris collected in their funnels.

On the horizon, the children could see a range of mountains. They didn't know how far they were in relation to where they stood, but they knew instinctively that this was where they were supposed to go.

Huffs and sighs of disappointment slipped wearily through the children's lips, uncertain if they really wanted to enter this new territory. The forest, looking like the better option, compared to what lay ahead.

Rose looked back, affirming they were all thinking the same thing.

Scarlet took a deep breath and sighed reluctantly. "C'mon, we may as well make a move. Abaddon has brought us here for a reason. The least we can do is accept his invitation since we've come this far."

"Erm, aren't you forgetting what Toby told us Scarlet?" said Ruby in fright. "Sand Demons and deserts!"

As it happened, Scarlet hadn't thought too much about any of Toby's stories since becoming trapped in the forest. She was just glad to be out of it.

"What shall we do then Ruby? Should we go back, stay where we are, or attempt to cross the desert? Personally, I think that whatever we've been brought here for, doesn't end here!" said Scarlet firmly.

Ruby looked up. The skies above hadn't settled since they found themselves trapped in Dreamworld. The vibrant green and violet colours still churned together in a high-speed wind, spiralling and twisting in fury. They might have appeared actually very beautiful if it hadn't been for the fact that these skies indicated Abaddon's presence.

"Okay, we go across," replied Ruby boldly. "Maybe you're right. Perhaps there is something more on the other side, but can we at least remember that these are the grounds of Sand Demon's, I don't fancy meeting my end inside one of them."

The children gazed across at the mountains ahead. They didn't appear to be that far away, but they knew that looks could be deceiving. Even so, an overwhelming sense of urgency built within the older children to make a start on the journey. Without the safety of the tree's canopy over their heads, the children felt exposed and particularly vulnerable to any further attacks Abaddon might inflict upon them.

With luck, the mountains would offer shelter for the night and if they were really fortunate, they might be able to stay there until the guardians found a way through to help.

"Are we really going to cross the desert Scarlet?" asked Rose in a wobbly voice.

"Unless you want to go back into the forest Rose, I don't see what choice we have," replied Scarlet, desperate to sound contained and ready for whatever lay ahead.

"It looks better to me," she mumbled. "We don't know what to expect in the desert."

A glance over Jamie's and Ruby's face though outnumbered Rose's preference to stay where they were, and Scarlet believed they should cross also, adding extra weight to their final decision.

Cautiously and begrudgingly the children set foot onto the sandy ground, its density softer than they had expected, instantly buckled under their weight giving the feeling they were far too heavy to be walking on this fragile, hungry surface.

With each careful step, the children were maliciously grabbed by the unseen monster lurking beneath, sucking them into its porous mouth, consuming them up to their ankles before allowing them to pull free from its deadly grip - only for them to step right back into its clutches in their next step.

It took a huge amount of effort to drag their feet out of what felt like a vacuum sucking them down, making it too easy to lose concentration on where the twisters were dancing. It was only when Scarlet stopped briefly to catch her breath from her vigorous efforts that she noticed a change in the wind.

The menacing funnels which had been swaying over the desert on arrival, had now miraculously grouped together to form several larger windstorms. They wobbled carelessly around in disarray without any meaningful direction, but seemed to keep their distance. Like wolves watching their prey, they skipped back and forth waiting for the right moment to strike.

"Is it just me or did those funnels get suddenly a lot bigger?" asked Scarlet fearfully, drawing her siblings' attention to the imminent danger lurking ahead.

The children stopped yanking their ankles free to see what had worried Scarlet. Their faces suddenly drained of all colour leaving them pasty and sickly white as their widened eyes took in the terrifying sight swirling dangerously close to where they were fixed. They didn't have long to react, in the next instance a bright flash of light suddenly lit up the land, momentarily blinding the children.

Once they had adjusted to the phantom light still flashing in their eyes, a new terror swiftly overtook their confusion before they were able to process what was going on.

A vision of newly spawned columns had swooped down from the thick sky like vultures, sporadically appearing then disappearing indiscriminately across the land like apparitions playing some perverse game in which they were doomed to lose.

Huge boulders skipped across the land like pebbles, bouncing towards the children before being sucked in at the last minute into the whirling columns. With ease, they were whipped round at speed as if in a giant sling shot before being finally catapulted back out as enormous projectiles.

"He's tryin' to kill us!" shrieked Jamie in shock as a boulder bounded right past his head at speed, narrowly missing him by inches. "What else is he gonna add to his fun house before he finally manages to kill us?"

The mountains looked more inviting and safer by the minute despite their haunting, shadowed appearance as they loomed in the distance. Their magnificence cast a huge greyness around them as they stood firmly rooted, deep into the ground.

"We need to get to those mountains!" shouted Rose over the wind. "And we should be flying not walking!"

The children squinted through the dust. Flying would have been a better idea but they had been so used to walking through the Abstract Forest in case the kaleidoscopic turns had mangled their bodies, that flying hadn't entered their minds once they were free of it.

It was obviously clear what the children needed to do, they could see their target and getting there as quickly as possible was of vital importance. But their chatter hadn't gone unheard. Before the children had managed to release their feet from the ground, the funnels transformed, gravitating towards each other like a gigantic magnet reforming now into one, single, giant, whirling wind. The sandy grains evolved as a new shape formed within the storm.

It was difficult at first to determine what was happening, but as the grains fell it became evident what they were seeing. The children stood transfixed in horror as they realised this monstrosity could only be the Sand Demons they had been warned of.

The grains bound tightly together creating a compact figure as it grew taller from the ground, shadowing the children below. Huge black eyes fell into its face, standing out dramatically like pits in its bald, cracked head, before it came crashing down to the ground like a spitting cobra, propping its malnourished body up on two thin, bony arms.

The children stared in revulsion, completely traumatised by such a creature. Its body glided out across the sand like a long thin snake, its back end hidden beneath the sand, seemingly attached to something which hid below, but it was those eyes that tormented the children the most. Like black holes, they captured the children's senses, seemingly dragging their thoughts into an abyss of perpetual darkness, eating them from the inside out.

"Don't look into its eyes!"

A voice from somewhere inside Scarlet's head abruptly alerted her to the danger she and her siblings were in, imperatively waking her from the soul eating trance.

Realising the others hadn't heard their guardians, Scarlet shouted to them, yanking her feet desperately from the sand's firm grip in a bid to free herself, but her calls were futile as were her attempts to escape.

She could see even as she watched how her siblings had become entranced, their gaze steady and wide as they stared helplessly into its hungry eyes. Scarlet squinted through the storm, she could just about make out a dark claw-like hand stretching out from the Demon's eyes. It took Scarlet a few moments to understand what was happening, her fear confirmed when the claw reached purposefully into the children's eyes. The Demon really was slowly feeding on their souls, emptying their bodies where they stood.

Scarlet looked on; her mind blanked with fear while she desperately sifted through her mind for a way to help. There had to be something of use that her guardian or Toby might have told them. Then she remembered, there was something useful locked away after all. Toby had once told her that the only way she could die in Dreamworld was if her imagination failed. That was it, fright had stopped her siblings from imagining an escape, but not her.

It was harder than she expected due to the mounting pressure rapidly being placed upon her, but with as much concentration as she could afford, Scarlet imagined her feet to be dipped in the crystal-clear water of the Sapphire Sea. As soon as the faintest glimpse of transparency appeared around her feet, Scarlet ripped them free, sending her bounding into clumsy flight towards her siblings, yelling as she drew close.

"WAKE UP," she screamed, shaking Rose furiously from its grip as she hovered precariously in front of the Sand Demon. But it wasn't enough, she couldn't wake them all in one go, the other two were still being dragged from their bodies like water being sucked through a straw.

Scarlet's only hope of freeing them all was if she could temporarily blind her siblings so that their gaze was broken. Her hand shook nervously as she cast her wand finger in front of their eyes, immediately shielding them long enough to break the trance.

A screech echoed from the Sand Demon as its control over the children was severed. Angrier than ever, the Sand Demon launched itself forward on its forearms, crawling towards the terrified children at incredible speed, revealing its abhorrently disturbing body in all its grizzly detail.

Impressions of human hands pushed against its body from the inside, while the faces of the souls it had consumed imprinted their facial details against its thin membrane, giving the impression they were being asphyxiated in an unbreakable bubble.

There was no hope for these lost souls, shadows forgotten with time, spirits eaten alive by the Sand Demon, fated to become part of the monstrous beast, helping it to grow, all the while keeping it forever hungry.

Scarlet imagined the sea to be around her sibling's feet again, giving them the time they needed to rip themselves free from the sand's grip. They literally catapulted themselves into the air as they fled towards the mountains.

Jamie glanced back at his sisters ensuring they were all air borne – it was then he saw they were not alone. The Sand Demon had reformed into a whirling column giving chase after them. Its ghastly face still perfectly etched within the tunnel as it hungrily pursued the children like a starved hyena hunting its first meal in months.

"WE NEED TO HURRY – GO FASTER," shouted Jamie to the others as he tried to maintain a speed to keep them ahead, while leading the group to the relative safety of the mountains.

The Sand Demon kept up the chase, clawing every so often at Rose's heel with a swiping motion in a bid to unnerve her enough to bring her down. The sight at what they had seen trying to crawl free was enough to spur them into staying ahead, but with every added exertion, the Sand Demon responded with the same urgency, increasing its speed the nearer to the mountain the children got, so that they were now flying faster than they believed was possible.

They could feel the Demon closing in without looking back, they didn't dare to see how close it actually was, but they felt its presence so near, they were sure they might be sucked into its gaping mouth at any minute.

"WE'RE ALMOST THERE, KEEP GOING!" Jamie shouted to the girls, sneaking a quick glance behind him. He could see the Demon, its jaws open wide like a vortex, the lost souls still hopelessly grappling in its throat looking for an escape, serving as a reminder as to why they needed to stay ahead.

The mountains were almost touchable now; the last few metres saw them pretty much crash-land as their target was met. The girls blundered into Jamie hurtling themselves over him, then tumbled in an ungainly heap onto its ledge.

As if knowing it had lost, the Sand Demon instantaneously fell silent, dropping to the ground like a sandy rainstorm.

Chapter Thirty-Six
The Mountain

The children lay in a heap, piled on top of each other, panting for breath as they tried to comprehend the severity of their situation.

"He's not goin' to be happy until he's killed us, is he?" said Jamie when he finally caught his breath. "I don't think I shall ever be able to forget what we saw trying to escape from the insides of that Sand Demon. Can you imagine how terrifying it must be, knowing you're in the belly of something like that while being completely conscious that you'll never be free of it? I can only guess that that must be the meaning of hell."

The girls didn't answer; they were still in shock of what had chased them into the mountains and were staring into space.

"We may as well see if there's any shelter here since we've been so graciously invited. I dunno 'bout you three, but after that I could do with a rest, or at least my heart could. I'm surprised I didn't have a heart-attack," continued Jamie, trying to ease the tensions a little bit.

The girls automatically followed Jamie up the mountain, their steps blindly shadowing his as he took the lead, that was until Scarlets footing crumbled beneath, propelling her irresistibly forward onto her hands. It didn't hurt, but did frighten her enough to make her pay proper attention. She watched as a small landslide tumbled down the sharp ledge, smashing into smaller pieces as the rocks fell.

"Pay attention will ya?" sniffed Jamie crossly, staring back at the girls trailing behind.

"I don't understand why these Nudgers haven't woken us yet," complained Scarlet gloomily, wishing that the near slip over the ledge might have been sufficient.

Nobody answered; there didn't seem to be much left to discuss. The prospect of ever waking seemed to elude them at every opportunity, making it a foregone conclusion that they were going to be stuck in Dreamworld for the foreseeable future, regardless of how many Nudgers they encountered.

The air felt harder to breathe as they climbed, thinner as the oxygen levels plummeted the higher they went, casting a daze of giddiness over the children. It was only when Rose stopped for a moment after turning a corner to catch her breath, that she spotted the danger ahead.

"W-what's – that?" stuttered Rose in alarm, pointing to something obscured behind a boulder further up the path.

Coming to an abrupt standstill, the children scoured the land ahead where Rose was still pointing. It was rocky and difficult to see anything other than plain rocks – that was until the creature accidently sent a small pile of dust and grit from under foot tumbling down the path to meet them.

Now that the disguise had been lost, the children could see what they were facing, making it clear there was more than just the one creature spotted by Rose.

Several of these strange creatures stood blatantly visible, indifferent as to whether they were seen or not. The children knew there had to be a lot more of these creatures, but with their dark grey coloured coats it was difficult to pick all of them out against the mountains, perfectly, camouflaged backdrop.

Standing on their stubby hind legs, unmoving, they watched intently as the children stared back, gathering detailed information in order to figure out what was coming up their mountain.

Their bloated round bodies were sparsely covered with wiry hair, like that of a warthog, but their faces were so unnatural, they made Scarlet's stomach retch with repulsion. Extraordinarily large mouths exposing short, razor sharp teeth took priority in their scabby, warty faces, and their opal white eyes rolled back in their heads with each blink, returning in a vivid yellow colour.

The creatures were fully adapted to the mountain's steep, unstable sides. They clung onto the powdery rocks with long clawed feet, standing perfectly balanced on its edges.

"Do you think they're friendly?" asked Ruby. She couldn't be sure what their intentions were at this moment as all they seemed to be doing was observing them.

"I dunno," croaked Jamie. "Why don't ya ask them?"

Ruby gave him a harsh sneer and rolled her eyes in disgust. "Did anyone ever tell you how funny you are?" she asked sarcastically. "No? Strange that, don't you think?"

"We jus' gonna stand here like statues then, are we?" continued Jamie, coaxing the girls to make a decision just so that he didn't have to.

But he hadn't realised that the creatures had already made their next move. While the children had been discussing their plans, a few of the hidden creatures had gained higher ground and were now hovering over their heads ready to launch an attack.

A slimy, yellow trail of snotty drool glopped off Scarlet's head and slopped onto her shoulder, alerting her instantly to the creature's position. Scarlet spontaneously reacted, throwing her hands above her head and casting a protective shield over herself and her siblings who were still squabbling.

With nowhere to land, the creatures fell hard, bouncing off the shield and over the side of the mountain. This sent the others into a frenzied attack.

Slapping their eyelids back, the creatures descended at full speed down the mountain, leaping with precision towards the horrified children and squawking in the most ear-splitting, high pitched squeal the children had ever heard.

"Do somethin' Rose," Scarlet barked urgently. "I can't hold all of 'em back, ya have to shape shift, do it now, do somethin'– quickly."

Rose wasn't expecting to have to perform like this, but with no time to think or prepare for her next move she panicked, embracing the first thing that sprung to mind.

Her body responded like a machine, firstly notching up her heart rate allowing the fear to take over while it enlarged in size. Pounding hard in her ears, it pumped the rich cocktail of adrenalin fused blood around her expanding frame.

A sickening crack, crack, crack reverberated from her body as she began to morph. Her back dislocated and her neck stretched into a long, twisted bony structure, while the rest of her body contorted and spasmed, before settling into a hunched, agonising, crescent-like shape.

Scarlet stared in disbelief, dumbstruck to think Rose was capable of imagining such a grotesque thing in her sweet innocent head. Her hands dropped in unison with her jaw, forgetting about the shield she had been casting over them all as Rose continued to dramatically alter.

Blisters now erupted from Rose's skin, bubbling first before bursting open under the heat forming inside her new anatomically evolved body. The dislocating, nauseating, cracking sounds persisted during the entire transformation making the children feel quite unwell, but knowing that she was on their side was enough to prevent them from throwing up with disgust.

Her beautiful golden hair had long gone, leaving a thick bed of scaly bumps in its place, while her facial features had adjusted so dramatically, they were no longer recognisable as human. Her jaw had disengaged, dropping down to allow room for several large canine teeth along with several rows of teeth, and her once tiny button nose had disintegrated, leaving only a disfigured, enlarged, cartilage mass strewn in its place.

The children were so transfixed they didn't see the Mountain Goblins bounding towards them, but Rose was ready. Leaping forward in battle, Rose thrust out her clawed hand in quick reflex, warding off and batting the Mountain Goblins straight over the jagged, sharp sides.

With no hope of stopping, the leaders were effortlessly thwarted while the more fortunate others skidded to a desperate stop, almost turning in mid-air before fleeing back up into the safety of the mountains.

With the danger averted, Rose slumped to the floor. Her breathing slowed and gradually her disguise melted away.

"Where the hell did ya pull tha' monstrosity from?" croaked Jamie who was still visibly shaken at what he had seen.

"She's from my nightmares – she's called a Preta. I figured that since she's in the Harrowlands somewhere, it couldn't hurt to use her for our benefit for a change. She's of my makin' anyway and it was all I could think of to do."

"Well it worked," said Scarlet with relief. "I was afraid you might not 'ave bin able to think that quick. Don't do that again for a while though, it was bloody revolting. There's no *wonder* she's in ya nightmares."

Rose smiled to herself knowing she did have the courage needed if she had to use it again. Up until that point she had been dubious of her own abilities and lacked in confidence, but now she felt an overwhelming sense of strength, encouraging her to trust in herself that little bit more.

"Well done anyway," said Scarlet as an afterthought. She hadn't meant to sound disgusted, but realised she hadn't congratulated her either.

"What d'ya s'pose those things were anyway?" asked Rose changing the subject slightly.

"I presume they're Mountain Goblins. Well – if they're not, they should be anyway," said Scarlet thoughtfully while they continued to climb the mountain.

The air still felt heavy, thick with the evil that loomed over them. An overwhelming presence of Abaddon lurked in the atmosphere as though he were watching their every move. It was evident that he was near; the sky still threatened a storm if the children dared to make their way back down the mountain. But in all honesty, none of them had any desire to return to the desert tonight anyway.

Just ahead the children could see what they had been searching for. A cave was cut into the side of the mountain; it was obscured well, jutting in at a steep angle making it practically invisible from the outside.

Sidling their way in through the narrow opening, the children entered the cave. The sides were short and steep, joining together in a point at the top. The space wasn't huge but it was safer than being outside.

"We'll stay here for tonight, but tomorrow we'll have to go back down. There's a reason Abaddon wants us up here and I can't imagine it's because he simply wants to keep an eye on us," said Jamie calmly. His gaze had settled on the wilderness below as he peered from the caves entrance. "By mornin', I hope the sky will have calmed, otherwise we might be stuck up here longer than we want to be."

Rose had already curled up, her head resting comfortably on Ruby's lap and was snoring lightly.

"At least one of us is relaxed enough to sleep," said Ruby, running her fingers through Rose's long, silky hair.

"Well since we're staying here, I'd be more comfortable with a few home improvements," said Scarlet, brushing the powdered rock dust from her clothes and getting to her feet. "A few beds wouldn't hurt," she said talking quietly to herself as she began conjuring up several small beds around the cave. "We could use some light too," and even as she spoke the cave was warmly illuminated with a gentle light hanging in mid-air, casting a soft glow into every crevice.

"There, that's better isn't it!" she said confidently as she wondered over to the caves entrance. "One last thing now," she said raising her hand, sweeping it in a downward stroke over the narrow opening of the cave. A strange darkness fell over the entrance disguising the cave from the outside giving it an optical illusion of emptiness.

"What did ya do?" asked Jamie curiously, his face wrinkled in bemusement.

"I think they call it magic in the waking world," replied Scarlet. "Do you remember that cheap trick made with smoke screens and mirrors, supposedly making things disappear?"

Jamie nodded.

"Well, I've basically given us a smoke screen without the mirrors. I don't fancy sharing our bed with any of those strange creatures, so if anything else comes down the mountain now, hopefully we won't be spotted. From the outside the cave isn't visible, with luck, they'll just pass us by."

"Thought of everythin' haven't ya!" said Jamie with a wry smile as he lifted Rose onto a bed before settling onto one himself.

The light dimmed to a slight flicker in the cave and Scarlet lay down on the remaining bed. Her eyes probed the ceiling, analysing every nook and cranny as moments from the day played back in her mind.

It looked as though the ceiling was moving. Scarlet rubbed her eyes and blinked a few times, but the movement continued. It took her a few minutes to realise that the ceiling hadn't come alive at all; instead hundreds and hundreds of small centipede-like creatures were scuttling out of the rock face at speed.

Her attention turned solely onto them. Long tentacles protruded from the tops of their heads acting as feelers in the dark as they went about their business. She followed them, watching closely as they urgently scrambled across the ceiling, gathering in a mass around something black and slightly shiny.

Scarlet rubbed her eyes again adjusting herself to the dimly lit room; it was then that she fully comprehended what was happening. These things were hunting, and there, tangled up in a thick cotton like web, was a bat struggling to free itself, its time running out as the worms homed in on their prey.

Almost as though a signal had been given, the worms now suddenly lit up giving off an illuminous green light. Their tiny mouths opened and all at once they sank their microscopic teeth into the bats skin, leaching onto it like vampires, sucking hard, grinding, and burrowing into its writhing flesh, bleeding it dry from the inside out until all that remained was a shell of what it used to be. Its loose skin hung to its skeleton like a floppy lettuce leaf, pulsing with the carnivorous worms that still remained inside.

Satisfied at last that there was nothing left of the poor animal to devour, the worms crawled back through the holes they had made, sluggishly returning to the crevices.

Paralysed with fear, Scarlet hardly dared to breathe. She only hoped they had no appetite for human flesh and that their stomachs were satisfied for a while. Not wanting to see anything else that might unsettle her, she turned onto her side and closed her eyes; glad of the fact the others hadn't seen the carnage above their heads.

A strange noise woke the children the next morning. Scarlet sat up in bed and listened. It was a sound she had heard somewhere before, but she couldn't remember where or what. It was a strange humming sound, beating at a regular pace and definitely getting closer.

"Dragon's," whispered Ruby under her breath.

Scarlet's heart almost stopped beating as that word sunk into her head. Her face drained a pale, sickly white as she understood what that meant, her stomach knotted nervously, but even so, she mustered up enough courage and strength to shimmy to the caves entrance and peep around the shroud.

The sky had a crimson blush to it, bathing the horizon in fire, completely distracting Scarlet with its colourful paint. On top of that, the angle of the cave's entrance made it difficult to get a good view without coming out of hiding, but she knew they were out there. The tremendous sound coming from their wings beating in rhythm told her they were still very close.

"They won't find us, will they Scarlet?" trembled Rose with uncertainty in her tone.

"No, I don't think so. The shroud hides the cave making it look like the rest of the mountain," said Scarlet soothingly, as much for her own benefit as for Rose's.

A dark shadow fell over the mountain as the dragons now came into view. Six black ones, flying low and synchronised across the sky as they passed over for a second time.

"They're flying circuits over us. They're lookin' for us, aren't they?" said Jamie knowingly.

"I think so," said Scarlet. "They've obviously been sent on a mission to find us. That means Abaddon can't locate us – it *was* gettin' dark last night when we slipped in here. He probably didn't notice when we disappeared and now he's worried about where we could 'ave gone."

The dragons flew past again without discovering the cave, the sound of their wings fading as they left.

"D'ya think they'll give up soon?" asked Rose who was still worried they might be found.

"Eventually I guess, but they'll have to be sure we're not here first before they move on," said Scarlet with a croak, giving her real worries away.

"You're afraid they might find us, aren't you?" said Jamie accusingly, realising Scarlet was just as concerned as the rest of them. "You said the shroud would hide us – was you lying?"

Scarlet turned on him in fury. "Lying? You think I'm lying about keepin' us safe? If we were in danger don't ya think we'd 'ave bin spotted by now? The only reason those dragons are circlin' is because they can't see us. The last place Abaddon knew us to be was on this mountain. If anythin', Abaddon is angry that he's lost us so easily. Just keep quiet and they will move on soon."

Several hours passed by, with each lap the dragons became more and more agitated by the sudden disappearance of the children. Abaddon had insisted that the children had to be there somewhere, but due to the disobliging attitude of the children, they eventually gave up the search, flying away in frustration with nothing to show for their efforts.

The children breathed a sigh of relief, but knew they still had to come out of hiding at some point and escape, even though they weren't exactly sure what escape meant.

"We have to get outta here without being seen," said Scarlet still in a hushed tone.

"Why ya whisperin'? They're gone now," said Ruby with a smirk on her face which suggested she was as much relieved as she was puzzled that they were still so quiet.

"I dunno. I guess I'm still being careful in case Abaddon has sent other spies to scour the mountain for us," answered Scarlet with a shrug of her shoulders.

"I can make myself invisible," piped up Rose enthusiastically. "Maybe we could hide ourselves like that."

"Yes, but *we* can't do that Rose, that's your special gift." Scarlet paused in thought. "But that has given me an idea though. I could cover us all over with something similar to what I used last night to hide the cave's entrance – let me try."

Scarlet flicked her wrist over her siblings, a silky, black muslin sheet fell over them, hiding them from view which seemed to work until they started to walk.

"It's no good, we can't see through it and besides, I can see your feet Jamie!" she sighed in dismay, "And if I make it longer, we'll end up trippin' over it."

"There's no space either, Jamie kept steppin' on me!" complained Rose.

"I didn't think it would work if I'm honest, but I had to try. Just give me a minute while I think," said Scarlet feeling slightly agitated.

For a moment you could almost hear the sound of time passing – ticking as her thoughts went into overdrive.

"I've got it," she said abruptly jumping to her feet again and organising her siblings into a small group. "Stand still a minute while I do this and don't move, I don't want anyone cut through the middle."

"W-what d'ya mean, cut thought the middle?" asked Jamie nervously, tucking his arms protectively across his tummy and pulling his chest in tightly.

Scarlet tutted and pushed herself in among her siblings. "You'd better crane your neck in too Jamie," she teased unmercifully. "Unless you don't mind me taking your head off."

Jamie quickly bent his head low, making himself as small as he could while Scarlet flicked a circular movement around them all with a devious smile etched on her lips.

A large elastic, bubble like ball suddenly stretched around the children, enveloping them within its protective walls.

"This should keep us all together, it won't let you step outside of its boundaries," explained Scarlet, still smirking at Jamie's over-reaction. "The sides feel like a solid wall so you'll know if you accidentally get too near the edge, but it's flexible enough from the outside to mould around tight or sharp objects without breaking. Shall we see how it works gettin' through the caves openin'?"

The children walked slowly towards the cave entrance, unsure if Scarlet's contraption would actually work. Gently the ball rolled, and the children held their breath as it squeezed through the narrow gap.

It worked exactly how Scarlet hoped it would, effectively acting like a giant soap bubble without popping, allowing the children to pass through safely and unseen.

Carefully they headed back down the mountain, confident now that they were concealed safely inside. The terrain was hard going, but slowly they descended, sliding a little on the powdery formation, all the while remaining completely undetected until they reached the base of the mountain.

With their feet back on firm ground the children started their trek across the desert wasteland, knowing at some point they were meant to face Abaddon. They didn't really know what to expect let alone what he wanted with them, but they were sure their wait would be over very soon. They could sense the cold eeriness of his presence lurking in the air, but without their guardians they were reluctant to drop their protective bubble and confront him.

Chapter Thirty-Seven
The Hunt

On they walked undetected, inside their very own protective bubble, obscured from the dangers on the outside and from Abaddon's prying eyes, when it suddenly occurred to Scarlet that they were probably going about this hunt for Abaddon the wrong way.

"Wait a minute," she said sharply, coming to a stop as the stupidity of their actions suddenly dawned on her. "Why are we even playing Abaddon's game? This is exactly what he wants us to do – he sets up a game and, like idiots, we go after him, looking for whatever it is that he wants to find. In the meantime, we get weaker while he stays far enough away, so that he doesn't come under any direct attack from us. He's toying with us, messing with our heads and doing God only knows what to us while we sleep in the waking world.

"If we want to wake from this nightmare, we have to show ourselves to be unafraid, challenge him even. We'll be here forever otherwise, running frightened and looking for places to hide while he jus' sits back and watches us get weaker and weaker until we…"

She hesitated for a moment, not really wanting to say what she feared. She had already upset Rose the previous day by being insensitive to her thoughts.

"Until we what?" asked Rose curiously.

Scarlet glanced at the other two hoping they understood what she meant without having to spell it out in front of Rose.

"Yes, until we what?" goaded Jamie.

Scarlet tutted loudly, annoyed that she hadn't made her point clear enough. "I think we might end up dying here," she said cautiously. "Our bodies are back in the other world, sleeping, unnourished, unfed… if we don't get back soon, I think we migh' just die. We'll never make it home again, but if by some miracle we did, we can't enter a body that is no longer waitin' for our return, can we?" she explained as plainly as she could manage.

"Wha' the hell are you talkin' about Scarlet?" asked Jamie. He scowled at her for suggesting such a morbid idea, looking her up and down as if she had gone insane. "You want to put us all in jeopardy jus' so that ya can test out another one of your absurd theories? I think not! Besides, you've no idea if that theory's even accurate, you're guessing again and you're upsettin' Rose again. That's all you ever seem to do jus' lately."

"D'ya 'ave a better idea then? It's all okay criticising me, but I bet you have nothing better to offer up. Perhaps you like the thought of marching around aimlessly fer days d'ya? Maybe you think wastin' our time and energy lookin' for somebody who obviously revels in delight at our suffering is worth continuing to appease? Or maybe, ya just think hidin' away like this will benefit us in some other way? Please, do divulge your thoughts Jamie, I'm sure we would all love to hear your opinions on the matter," retorted Scarlet, her exasperation showing clearly both in her tone and on her frowning face.

"Fine! Drop the bubble then, but if it all goes wrong, don't forget it was all your idea and you can take all the credit," said Jamie in retaliation.

Rose wasn't entirely convinced Scarlet was right in this instance either; it sounded very risky, but hearing her siblings fight made her feel awkward. There wasn't any right or wrong way to go about getting home again. She wished that the guardians would hurry in getting to their sides, maybe then they'd have a better idea, but since they were still alone, Rose cut in, hoping to defuse the tension mounting between her siblings.

"D'ya think Emberleigh or Rhomelda might 'ave found a way through yet? Esperanza did say they were working on gettin' through to us."

It worked. Scarlet and Jamie's verbal exchanges stopped as her words echoed in their minds. It had been a few days since they saw Esperanza; surely, they would be there soon.

"I hope it won't take them much longer," said Scarlet feeling suddenly ashamed. She had been getting rather argumentative with Jamie since they had been trapped in Dreamworld, but fighting was not going to make it an easier. "But I don't think it's a simple as just gettin' through Rose. They have to locate us first and with the land swirled together the way it is, it can't be as easy as just gettin' somewhere in the way you're supposing it to be. I'm sure they haven't forgotten us though, but in the meantime, we need to stay alert." Scarlet rested her hand on Rose's shoulder. "I'm sorry Rose, I think we're all gettin' weary and hungry, it's making us all a bit snappy with each other. I'll try to keep calm."

"Listen to yourself Scarlet," butted in Jamie crossly. "You think you have all the answers don't ya? But ya know, I don't remember anyone puttin' you in charge. Ever since we've bin stuck 'ere you've bin callin' all the shots, dictated where we go, wha' we do, when we stop and so far, it's got us nowhere. We're not any closer to gettin out of 'ere than we were a few days ago. I think it's abou' time someone else did the leadin'," said Jamie in a patronising, haughty way.

Scarlet was too surprised to respond for a moment, unaware that she had been behaving in the accused manner.

"I was only trying to help," she muttered. "It's not been easy you know, I'm no wiser than any of you to know what's the best thing to do. But if you think you know better, then be my guest. In truth it'll be nice not to be under pressure all the time, finding answers isn't easy ya know. So, what do *you* propose we do then?" She hung her head low, propping her forehead with her hand in defeat while attempting to hide how upset she was.

"We do what we agreed to do before settin' off. We wait for the guardians to show up. We're safer stayin' hidden and better protected with their help," said Jamie with conviction.

"Fine, we'll do it your way," agreed Scarlet under duress.

"I'm gettin' hungry!" said Rose, still hoping to calm the animosity between Jamie and Scarlet by changing the subject and also because by now, she really was starting to feel the hunger pains setting in.

"We all are," said Scarlet trying to show as much disinterest in the matter as she could, afraid of being cut down if she had any other ideas.

"Can you make something to eat Scarlet? My tummy's making funny noises." Rose tried again in a bid to lift her sister's spirits.

"No, not really Rose, I don't think that'd be a good idea." She smiled in appreciation, understanding what Rose was trying to do. "We're in the desert, there are Sand Demons here remember. If I draw attention to us by making things grow I may as well jus' put a sign out the front of the dome inviting Abaddon to join us."

Rose sighed with frustration. "Can't we do anythin' then? Nothin' at all?"

"What d'ya want me to do Rose?" snapped Scarlet with exasperation, knowing that her sister wasn't really taking on board the fact that she had been demoted.

"Ask Jamie for heaven's sake, he's in charge, he's got all the answers, not me."

"I only meant that if we can't eat, maybe I could make some animals – I'm bored." replied Rose pitifully.

"Animals?" Scarlet repeated back in disbelief. "I dunno Rose. Not that my opinion matters, but I think that might give our position away still. Wha' do you think Jamie, you're the one in charge now?"

"We wait till the guardians show before we do anythin' else. Jus' sit tight," barked Jamie. "They'll come."

Without any new ideas or any clear way to break free from the nightmare, the children resigned themselves to the fact that there was little choice but to wait quietly in the hope they might hear a message from their guardians.

A dark cloak shrouded the sky for a second night taking the children's moods into the shadows with it, as their hopes faded of seeing their guardians vanished with the bleak light.

The morning broke, the sky was never bright over the Harrowlands, but the slight change of colour from jet black to a morbid grey indicated a new day had begun.

"Did any of ya manage to sleep?" asked Jamie miserably who obviously hadn't slept a wink. His eyes were puffed like airbags with a colour that rivalled the grey in the sky.

"Not a lot," answered Scarlet. "I don't think any of us did really."

"I had a little bit, but it was hard to sleep knowing Abaddon is still lookin' for us," added Ruby.

"I'm too hungry and thirsty to sleep. Every time I closed my eyes, I kept dreaming of finding pools of fresh, cold water, but when I got near, they had all dried up," complained Rose pitifully.

"It's your body Rose. It's not normal for us to be asleep this long; our bodies are startin' to suffer. I don't know how long we can keep goin' like this, it's ridiculous." snapped Scarlet moodily, poking the sand with a dead twig which just so happened to be by her feet on the ground.

"You're right Scarlet," said a voice which suddenly appeared from nowhere, in the dome with them.

Swinging round in fright, Scarlet was relieved to see Emberleigh had finally broken through.

"Emberleigh you're here. We were beginning to think you might not get through the barriers," said Scarlet through a croaky voice mixed with joy and tears.

"Scarlet keeps sayin' we might die here if we can't wake up," said Rose tearfully, wrapping her fingers around her guardian's arm in a childish, needful way, indicating her fear that Emberleigh may disappear again if she were to let go.

"I'm afraid Scarlet's right. If you stay away too long your bodies will die without the basic fundamentals of life, that's just biology."

Scarlet smiled slightly to herself, she couldn't help feeling just a little bit smug. Biting her bottom lip and folding her arms tightly together she turned away furtively so as to not antagonise Jamie further.

"The only way I think you're going to get out of here alive is if you muster up the courage to aggravate Abaddon," continued Emberleigh. "The same way you did last time you actually saw him."

Jamie's face turned an acrid grey colour. "You're actually tellin' us to face up to him? You want us to expose ourselves, here – where the Sand Demons live?"

"Exactly!" said Emberleigh with a smile.

"You've got to be kidding, we'll never outwit those Sand Demons. They nearly killed us last time we saw them." said Jamie in disbelief.

"But here you are," replied Emberleigh proudly. "Somehow you survived, you managed to escape with your lives and at the same time learned a little bit about them. You will need to use each other's strengths to get through this, much in the same way as you've been doing already, but without the fighting. You've all got different gifts so if you work together, you'll come out on top."

"Will ya stay with us Emberleigh?" begged Rose. "I feel safer when you're with us."

"Of course I will, I didn't fight my way through just to leave, did I?" she replied gently, taking Rose's hand in her own in a reassuring grip. "So Rose, these animals that you were talking about – shall we have a look at them?"

"Can I really?" asked Rose in excitement.

"Of course you can. You're going to have to start somewhere, why not here? Are you ready to drop the shield Scarlet?"

Scarlet nodded, relieved that Emberleigh was here to help a little. The arguing and animosity were becoming too much to bear, especially since she felt responsible for everyone's safety.

Cautiously Scarlet dropped the protective bubble which encapsulated them. She trusted Emberleigh implicitly, but since both Jamie and Rose thought it to be a bad idea, she was feeling less certain of the idea. It seemed suicidal now, uncovered and extremely vulnerable like lambs to the slaughter.

"Go on then Rose, give it your best shot," encouraged Emberleigh again.

With her mood lifted and with Emberleigh's permission it felt easy for Rose to conjure up the animals which were locked in her head. They were completely formed in her mind's eye right down to the last detail just waiting to be released.

With a swish of her hand and a bright smile on her face, Rose produced the weirdest, most ridiculous looking creatures imaginable.

There in front of them, were around fifty burnt orange coloured beasts which significantly resembled large lizards, only these had a few differences. Instead of having four legs, these had six, each with four toes on every foot. A stubby short tail extended out from their behinds which came to a sharp needle-like point at the ends.

Their heads appeared to be better suited on a snake's body with square teeth lining their mouths in several rows. Each had a long purple tongue rolled up like a slim carpet inside their gaping mouths and a pair of brilliant green eyes was set in either side of their heads. Two rows of parallel yellow spines adorned their backs, while a thick collar of bony horns decorated their necks like jewellery.

They began roaming the land, looking for specific shaped and sized rocks which they promptly began dining on, firstly grinding them into a chalky concoction with their perfectly adapted teeth, before swallowing the gritty mix in their mouths.

Emberleigh smiled. "Lizards, right?"

"Dippidocus Lizards actually. D'ya like them?"

"They're very unusual Rose, but yes they are rather splendid," said Emberleigh trying not to laugh at the outrageous looking beasts. "I can certainly see where they get their name from."

"D'ya want ride one then?" asked Rose expectantly.

"Actually Rose, I think we will all ride one. I've got an idea which if it works, will get us all back to a place you're comfortable with. Didn't you create a lovely lake in the Shadowlands Jamie?" asked Emberleigh, lightly touching his shoulder.

He smiled timidly; he wasn't used to receiving compliments.

"Yeah, I did. And Ruby created some fantastic creatures to live in there – didn't you Ruby?" he said quickly, in an attempt to turn the limelight away from himself.

Ruby blushed with pride and smiled with acknowledgement. "Yeah, I made several actually."

"That's where we're going. I'm hoping that my default setting if you like, will get us back to my homelands. There's no way I can get you to Elysium though, not with the lands being jumbled so badly. My instincts can only take me so far. After that we have to work on a way to get you home."

That was good enough for the children, a start was certainly better than nothing and at least this time their efforts would not be in vain.

"Is there any special way we get the lizards attention Rose? I can't say I've ever ridden a Dippidocus Lizard before," said Emberleigh curiously.

"Ya just climb up, like this!" replied Rose as she demonstrated the simplicity in her actions.

The lizard looked down at Rose standing by its side and bent its enormous knees, sinking to the ground to assist her. Grabbing a hold of its spiny collar, Rose pulled herself up using its leg joint as a footing, hoisting herself into position.

"Okay, looks easy enough," said Jamie as he lunged forward enthusiastically ready to take a seat on his own Lizard.

The Dippidocus Lizard stared down at him, ignoring his efforts and refusing to cooperate.

"Wha' am I doin' wrong?" he called to Rose in frustration as he continued in vain to coax the animal down to his level.

"Pat his front leg. Ya need to take control, show him who's boss." She called back proudly.

Jamie slapped its leg with authority half expecting it to kick him effortlessly aside, but much to his surprise and relief, the beast dropped to the ground at his touch allowing him to climb up.

"Follow me everyone, stay close," said Emberleigh when everyone had chosen a Dippidocus Lizard. "If the Sand Demons come back, I might need to defend you all and I can't do that properly if you're lagging behind."

The beasts began to move. Their heavy feet plodded through the dusty land, making deep imprints into the ground. They were quite bumpy to ride with the movement of six legs, but they travelled fast across the plains, reaching the Ebony Lake in short time without any hindrance from the Sand Demons.

The familiar sight of the Opal Mountains appearing on the horizon jerked at Scarlet's heartstrings. She hadn't realised just how beautiful it was up until now, but as the Ebony Lake broke away from the sky, she felt her emotions were incapable of remaining locked away and her tears fell. She wasn't sure if they were tears of relief or of exhaustion, but she didn't care, all she knew was that she hadn't felt so good since being trapped here. The entire landscape although entwined with the oddities of a collided world, really was on this occasion an exceptionally beautiful sight to behold.

The group slipped down from the animals' backs and glided gently to the ground. It was surprising how exuberating it felt to be back in the Shadowlands and in sight of the Ebony Lake.

Chapter Thirty-Eight
The Shadowlands

"We can't waste time children," said Emberleigh forcefully. "As wonderful as it is to be in familiar territory, we still have no idea how long you may be trapped here, or how long Abaddon wants to play his pernicious games. We need to set up camp and make ourselves as comfortable as possible for the foreseeable future."

"Foreseeable future? What does tha' mean exactly?" asked Ruby sharply. "I thought by comin' here, we were on our way home!"

"You are. But until we can come up with a way of getting you all home safely, we have to be prepared for everything and more importantly ready to seize the chance of escape when an opportunity arises. It's best to know when to fight and when to stay out of sight."

"It doesn't sound very promisin' if ya ask me," said Jamie dubiously. "Ya already told us tha' we can't stay alive back in the wakin' world without our spirit. I hardly think stayin' here is gonna be doin' us any favours is it?"

"I know it sounds all very worrying children, but I can assure you, it won't come to that. I promise. There are ways around these kinds of things. I'm a guardian, it's my job to keep you safe remember."

Without fully understanding how Emberleigh could be certain their lives would not be at risk, the children trusted her nonetheless. The guardians hadn't given any reasons to believe they were untrustworthy after all.

"So where do we start?" said Jamie apologetically.

Emberleigh smiled, "See those rocks at the base of the mountain?" Jamie and Scarlet looked across to the far side of the lake where Emberleigh was pointing. There were several very large boulders at its foot which had fallen from the mountain at some point, perhaps during the movement of the land. "I think that would be a good place to make camp."

The ground in this area was scattered with rocks, almost as if they were waiting to be used for construction. With Emberleigh's approval, Jamie's mind got to work immediately, processing the information in the exact way the girls had seen him sift through his Lego bricks.

There were two very large pieces of rock which Jamie used to his advantage. They were positioned slightly behind each other so that from a frontal perspective it was virtually impossible to see that there were in fact two boulders rather than the one which appeared, giving it an optical illusion.

"Give me a hand movin' some of those rocks will ya Scarlet," said Jamie forgetting where he was.

"Are you insane? Ya want me to actually, physically help you move rocks?" she snarled incredulously, staring at him until he looked up from his thoughts.

"What? Why ya lookin' at me like tha'?" he said blankly, when he caught her eye.

"Jamie, use your head will ya. I'm not helpin' you or anyone else move rocks when you can quite easily move them with your mind. I'll see you later, I've got better things to be doin' with my time."

Scarlet marched away leaving Jamie to construct the stone house himself. She had been going over a few things in her head, particularly the food related thoughts.

They were all beginning to suffer now from thirst and hunger. The reality of the situation though, was that no matter what they did here to relieve their symptoms, their bodies would still be left starved without the proper nutrition in the waking world.

However, regardless of the reality, Scarlet still felt she had to do something to at least trick their minds into feeling better. Make believe food had to be better than nothing, *"mind over matter,"* that's what her mother used to say when things got tough.

It wasn't difficult to make plants grow. By now it had become relatively easy producing life from barren ground, it was the depravation of real nutrition that made it hard for Scarlet to concentrate. Materialising imaginary food into something that resembled the real thing was almost cruel, it made her hungrier and producing it only made her angry. It was only imaginary and therefore of no real value, but it looked perfect if that counted for anything.

Ruby was sitting by the water's edge throwing in small pebbles as she considered other creatures which would be suited to these waters. Every so often,

Scarlet heard the splash of another pebble hitting the lake before sinking to the bottom. Other than this slight disturbance, nothing stirred. It seemed too still, too quiet and far too peaceful in retrospect of where they were and the trouble they had been in previously.

Something didn't add up. She expected to at least see half a dozen dragons circling overhead on Abaddon's command, or some kind of weird beast come hurtling out from a hiding place unexpectedly.

Emberleigh was sitting high above the lake on the cliff ledge observing the children, her hand propped up her chin as she rested peacefully, unfazed by anything. Scarlet put down the food she had collected and climbed up to where Emberleigh sat, certain that if there was a problem, she would know about it.

"It's very calm here Emberleigh. A bit too calm wouldn't you say?" probed Scarlet cautiously as she took a seat next to her.

"You noticed too then?" said Emberleigh without moving. "Have you given any thought as to why that might be?"

"No, not really. I'd 'ave thought Abaddon would've come after us by now, it's not like we've hidden ourselves away is it? He couldn't wait to play games when we first arrived, but now you're here –" She stopped as the penny dropped. "Oh, I see…"

"Yes, now I'm here," repeated Emberleigh thoughtfully. "That's precisely the reason he's staying away, he knows you're being protected. There's little point attacking when his efforts are likely to be thwarted. Its wasted energy, he's got all the time he needs to plan his attack and he'll do it when it suits him."

"Do we want him to attack us?" asked Scarlet with a slight shake in her voice, uncertain that the idea of attack ever felt like a good suggestion.

"Not yet, but soon. Definitely soon." She turned to look at Scarlet now, her tone shifted to one of urgency. "I didn't tell you before, I didn't want to frighten Rose, but your bodies are not in a good way. You've been asleep for about five days in the waking world, and in that time you've gone unnourished. Abaddon doesn't care how you die, he doesn't care how long it takes, he has all the time in the world. All he's done is torment you while you've slept because that's what he does best. He's not worried about you waking up because he knows you can't. As soon as you have a place of shelter, we need to make Abaddon care, and the only way you have any chance of getting his attention is if I'm *not* here to help."

Scarlet's face turned pale. "You said we wouldn't die, you promised us that we'd be safe. Now you're tellin' me you're leavin' and that we can't wake up anyway. It was all a lie to keep us positive wasn't it?" she spat in anger and disgust as she stood up to leave.

Emberleigh grabbed Scarlet's arm and pulled her back to the ground.

"You listen now," she said firmly. "I am doing everything I can to help. I've never lied to you, to any of you. If you want to get out of here alive then you better start trusting me. Abaddon is keeping away because I am here; you've worked that out for yourself and for the moment that's a good thing because you need a place to stay, particularly if it takes longer to coax him into a trap.

"I will help you to come up with a plan but the rest is up to you. You've all got the powers you need to work this one out together. I can't fight this battle for you; this is one you have to fight yourselves in order to regain your confidence and strength. Now, I'm not leaving entirely. I will be guarding your bodies at home so that if the time comes where your lives are in critical danger, I will ensure the right help comes at the right time. Do you understand?"

"We will wake up though, right?" asked Scarlet more calmly.

"Yes. But only if you manage to draw Abaddon into battle and win."

"How do we get Abaddon's attention? If he doesn't care about us being here, if we're not a threat, why would he bother with us?"

"You're not any threat to him at the moment, but that can change. Challenging his authority is a good place to start. Anyone who's in a position of power will defend that right if they feel threatened enough, that I know for certain." Emberleigh gazed across the lake to the South side where Jamie was busy building the house. "It's looking good from up here. It looks like he's almost finished wouldn't you agree?"

Scarlet's eyes settled on Jamie's new creation and smiled. "He's always been good at building. I bet he's made it really cosy inside knowing him."

"I think it's time for us to go back and talk to the others," continued Emberleigh getting to her feet. "Don't forget your mind feeding boost; I think the others will appreciate it even if it does nothing for you."

Chapter Thirty-Nine
The Plan

The two walked together back towards the stone house. It was a beautiful building, obscured from view and perfect for their requirements.

Scarlet laid the food down on a small dining table. Six wooden chairs sat neatly underneath and on the far side of the room, a spiral staircase caught her eye. It opened up at the top of the house into an open plan bedroom complete with a bed for everyone.

"It's almost a shame we don't intend to stay for long!" said Scarlet quietly under her breath.

Emberleigh gathered everyone into the house. As soon as Rose saw the food on the table, she hurried towards it, greedily indulging herself on the fruits and berries, extinguishing her hungry thoughts from her head for a little while longer.

"I've brought you in because I need you all to understand what's going on here right now," said Emberleigh when Rose had eaten her fill. "You've probably noticed that Abaddon's presence seems to have disappeared, he's not watching you, and he doesn't seem to care that you're here anymore."

The children hadn't thought about it if truth was known. Ever since Emberleigh had arrived they seemed to forget the danger they were in and dismissed the idea of being in any kind of trouble at all.

"Scarlet and I were talking," continued Emberleigh. "It appears that while I am here watching over you, Abaddon isn't interested, he won't show up. So, I'm going to help you come up with a plan, and afterwards I will have to let you get on with it alone. Now I know this sounds scary, but if you work together, I know you can win the battle and free yourselves."

The children were speechless; the idea of being alone again did nothing to comfort their fears, but Emberleigh gave them no time to react.

"We are going to trap him in a cage," she continued.

"Sorry? A what?" said Jamie, now managing to find his tongue if only to protest briefly. "You think a cage will hold Abaddon? And more to the point, ya reckon we can lure the world's most evil – demon – creature – thing or whatever he is, into a cage? We're more likely to get him to go in voluntarily if we ask nicely!"

"Have you ever heard of Blayne Jamie?" asked Emberleigh in a composed, confident kind of way.

"Err, no," he muttered.

"No, I didn't think so. Blayne is a metal found only in Dreamworld. Its properties make it unbreakable, even to Abaddon. I will fashion a cage using Blayne and then you children will use it to trap him. How you do that is up to you. Now, if you all follow me, we can get started. When the cage is built, I will leave."

Jamie didn't argue again, even though he thought her idea was completely insane.

The children followed behind as Emberleigh took the lead marching them towards the Ebony Lake. She stopped in front of it, standing on the ledge she had earlier been sat on as she had gathered her thoughts together.

The lake looked cold and unforgiving from up there. Its dark, murky waters rippled in the breeze, hiding the mysteries which lurked beneath. Scarlet shuddered. There was an odd sensation that oozed from its surface which made her feel uncomfortable.

"When I'm done with the cage, you will need to cover it over with your camouflage shroud Scarlet. Abaddon mustn't get wind that it's here."

Scarlet shivered again and nodded nervously as Emberleigh got to work.

"Now watch!" said Emberleigh suddenly full of excitement.

Her eyes started to change colour. The orange ring around her iris's brightened until they glowed white, spreading entirely across her eyes, transforming the chestnut brown as her gaze fell over the Ebony Lake.

The wind picked up in recognition of the magic being performed, blowing her long red hair out in waves behind her back and forcing the children's garments to cling desperately to their bodies as though they were in danger of being torn to shreds.

Emberleigh's hands lifted slowly from her side, bringing them together in front of her chest as if she were holding an invisible sphere.

The strong wind persisted for a moment longer and then seemed to gradually disappear with the arrival of a strange sound.

It was a strong, hollow sound, and it was coming from Emberleigh. She was actually drawing the wind into her body so that the air outside fell dramatically still. Then to the children's surprise, Emberleigh blew the wind into the something she held in her hands, releasing it with control so that it now swirled steadily. They could see it perfectly, Emberleigh had harnessed the power of the wind, encapsulating it inside a bubble, or at least that's what it looked like.

She held it there effortlessly, her hands hovered around the orb compressing it into a compact force, and then gently, she let it float away, controlling its flight path until it reached the edge of the shore.

Once in place, she seemed to inadvertently lose control over the ball, suddenly allowing it to spill out of shape and spin violently on the spot.

Her eyes stayed focused as she held it in place before cautiously pushing her right hand forward. The wind whirled under her control as she gently eased it across the lake, whisking the surface as it went, churning up the silt from the bottom and leaving a trail of frothy bubbles in its path.

Guiding it to the lakes centre, Emberleigh unleashed its power as it now began to cut through the water's surface, driving its head down towards the lake bed. A vacuum opened up as the whirlpools mouth grew in size, sucking even the darkness deeper into its watery belly, whirling tirelessly until it reached the very bottom.

But still the vortex dug, deeper and deeper under Emberleigh's control, drilling into the basin, churning up water and rocks and forgotten time, and still it is twisted.

By now Ruby was becoming very concerned, she couldn't help wondering what Emberleigh was playing at. Her face seemed to be completely focused, lost inside the destructive force she had created, as if perhaps she might have forgotten the plan and unintentionally become wrapped up in some other mission.

She nudged Scarlet and gestured towards Emberleigh. "Wha' she doin? D'ya reckon she's okay?" she whispered weakly.

"She did say that the Blayne was deep in the ground. She's probably just not found it yet," said Scarlet reassuringly. "I'm sure she's fine."

Ruby wasn't so sure. She knew that her own guardian was from the Shadowlands and had quite openly expressed that she also had an appreciation for darker magic. But Rose had never shared where Emberleigh was from, her behaviour and dark mannerisms were not what she expected from an Elysium guardian. Come to think of it, Esperanza had informed the children that neither she nor Breanna could break through Abaddon's defences due to their powers failing while dark forces were gripping the land. Yet Rhomelda and Emberleigh could.

Emberleigh's powers seemed to be strong in these lands, making Ruby certain that the Shadowlands were also where she originated. She came across as very intimidating, but completely fascinating and mesmerising to watch.

Ruby smiled to herself, convinced that she had uncovered a secret that Rose hadn't wanted to share.

The cyclone drilled ever deeper, filling its funnel now with sediment, debris and ash, but still it kept boring down, hunting for the Blayne which was almost within reach.

Fiery molten rock now added to the mix setting the funnel aglow, igniting the insides like a radioactive rod. It was alive with colour, hissing as it made contact with the lakes water before cooling rapidly, returning the lava back into blackened rocks before casting them aside to fall back to the bottom of the lake.

And then the hissing stopped. There was no more rock being dug up, only a thick liquid of brilliant white, whirling around relentlessly inside the vacuum. The children squinted, straining their eyes to see through the brightness. There was something happening in its centre.

A haze of electric blue burst through the brightness, it was blinding, but although difficult to see exactly what was happening, the children were certain this had to be the formation of the cage.

At last the whirling cyclone died down, dispersing its energy into the lake as though nothing had happened. All that remained above the lakes surface was a metallic, pale blue prison, no larger than four metres in diameter and height.

The bars were thick and heavy with a long chain holding it in place, anchored firmly into the earth's core. It still glowed even as the Blayne cooled, hovering in mid-air as Emberleigh suspended it there for a while.

The children hardly dared to breathe as they watched the cage precariously hang, and then gently sailed over the surface as Emberleigh willed it into shore, allowing it to come smoothly to the ground with a soft thud, landing between two large boulders which would serve as a marker later on.

The flames in Emberleigh's eyes burned out, returning to their natural hazel and orange colour before turning to face the children who were still gaping in awe at what they had seen.

"Well. Do you think that'll do?" she said casually as if it were the most normal thing she could have done.

"Yeh. It's great!" said Ruby automatically who was still utterly flabbergasted.

Jamie tried to say something, but nothing came out of his mouth, instead a squeak emerged from somewhere in his dry throat and his mouth snapped shut in embarrassment.

"Any questions before I leave?" asked Emberleigh, after observing their reactions.

"Actually yes, there is somethin'," said Scarlet, managing to find her voice again. "How does it work? The Blayne I mean, how does it work exactly?"

"It burns," she answered in a hurried excited tone. "See how it glows blue. It can cause some really nasty lesions to the flesh if it feels attacked, and of course it's the strongest metal ever discovered, but then it needs to be – considering who it's for," said Emberleigh.

Her voice had a preoccupied tone as she drew the children's attention to its detail. She obviously had a deep fascination with this metal, her desire to leave so quickly moments earlier seemed to disappear as its magnetism pulled her back in.

"Emberleigh!" said Ruby, gently drawing her attention away from its overpowering connection over her.

Emberleigh snapped out of the lure in a daze. "Sorry – yes Ruby."

"Won't Abaddon have heard all the commotion when you constructed the cage? And what do you mean, *Feels attacked*?" she asked in confusion.

"Yes, more than likely," she replied. "But you have to remember that in the Shadowlands there are a lot of strange noises and goings on. It's quite normal to see winds miraculously appear and monsters just get up and roam around. Don't worry about that though, as for the Blayne feeling attacked, it's a sensory metal, it is capable of feeling, so if Abaddon uses his powers to try and break free or force the metal against its will, it *will* fight back."

"And with you being from the Shadowlands, you'd know that strange things happen often, wouldn't you? I mean, we're not ready for Abaddon to know about the cage yet." Said Ruby, probing a little to discover if her assumptions were correct.

"Absolutely," answered Emberleigh proudly. "The Shadowlands are full of curiosities."

Rose blushed bright pink, embarrassed that her siblings had discovered her secret this way and hung her head in shame.

"There's nothing to be ashamed of Rose. Magic is a beautiful gift, not something to be ashamed of, not an evil that should be shrouded with secrecy. Our gifts, whatever they may be, whether we have magic or not, should be used for good, for helping those who need our support. It only becomes a problem when our gifts and our minds are used to harm others." Emberleigh smiled reassuringly.

"Anyway, if there's nothing else, I really ought to go," she said, excusing herself. "Don't forget to cover it Scarlet," she smiled warmly before fading away and disappearing.

It was suddenly less comfortable without Emberleigh. The Shadowlands seemed more threatening than ever before, and the cool air felt more devious.

This was no time to fall apart though. With Emberleigh's words still fresh in her head, Scarlet threw her shrouding spell over the cage, hiding it completely from sight – and then the children stared blankly at one another, hoping that one of them might know what to do next.

"Now what?" said Jamie after a few moments had gone by and nobody had spoken. "I don't think Abaddon will accept an invitation, and I'm not convinced he's jus' gonna walk into the cage accidently either."

Chapter Forty
Scarlet's Plight

The children shut the door behind them as they entered their house. Their stomachs bubbled and twisted into nauseating knots as hunger took a firm hold over them. Some of the food Scarlet had conjured up was still spread over the table, but its presence only seemed to heighten their hunger pangs.

"Can you get rid of that stuff Scarlet?" asked Jamie eyeing it up as though it were offensive. "I can't concentrate with it all over the place like that."

Scarlet gathered it together and shoved it inside one of the cupboards so that it was out of sight before sitting down at the table with the rest of the children.

"What if this all goes horribly wrong?" croaked Jamie, now that he was able to think about the task in hand without the temptation of food teasing his thoughts.

"It won't. We're in this together and we'll get out together," said Scarlet, putting on a brave face. "Emberleigh told us that we could win this fight so long as we work together. When we get outta here, this'll be just a distant memory and one which will have made us stronger."

For a moment nobody said anything. None of them were particularly comfortable with what they knew needed to be done, especially now that they were alone.

"Okay, work together she says," murmured Jamie quietly. "If we go back outdoors now without Emberleigh around to protect us, we are bound to get Abaddon's attention pretty quickly. The question is, is everyone okay with taking that risk? We have no idea what trouble we might get ourselves into and no real plan in place as to how we're going to fight him, apart from fighting him with the gifts we have. I guess the best thing to do is to stir things up a bit and see what comes of it."

"I'm okay with that," replied Scarlet defiantly. "We have to do something; it may as well be now. What about you two? Are you game?"

"Me too," said Ruby getting to her feet.

Rose nodded gingerly more because she knew they had little choice, and staying with her siblings seemed like a better option than being alone.

"Good, that's settled then," said Jamie confidently, standing up purposefully and heading boldly straight out of the door.

"What ya goin to do?" asked Rose leaping to her feet and running after him.

"We're gonna annoy him; make him angry enough to do somethin' about it. I thought we just agreed on that!"

"I was going to make some more creatures earlier before Emberleigh called us together," said Ruby breathlessly as she chased after him. "D'ya reckon I could get back to wha' I was doin?"

"Yeah, I don't see why not," replied Jamie casually, without stopping.

"I wonder if the Horsehawks migh' be able to find their way to us if I called them?" said Scarlet now becoming very animated at the idea that this might be a possibility.

"Dunno Scarlet. Why don't ya see wha' happens. If we all jus' do wha' we can to get Abaddon's attention, then we're doin' somethin' right, aren't we?" said Jamie who was still pacing purposefully away from the house at speed.

"You don't understand Jamie. The Horsehawks might be able to help us too."

"Yeah? How d'ya work that one out?"

"Jus' stop and listen fer a minute will ya!" she barked, grabbing his arm impatiently.

"What Scarlet? Why are the Horsehawks so important all of a sudden?" said Jamie coming to a stop. "We're runnin' outta time here, we don't 'ave the luxury of standin' around discussin' Horsehawks."

"Really? You don't see what I'm getting at?" said Scarlet incredulously, staring at him as though he were suffering from some kind of insanity.

Jamie stared back blankly at her. "If you've got somethin' to say jus' get on with it will ya. This is exactly what I meant the other day. You always seem to talk in riddles instead of gettin' to the point and it's something you always seem to do at the worst possible time."

"The Horsehawks could fly us back to the treehouse. I mean after we imprison Abaddon, hopefully the land should stabilise so that there will be a

300

definite way out of here," replied Scarlet, now almost delirious with exasperation.

Jamie's face changed, brightening dramatically as it dawned on him that this wasn't a bad idea after all. He'd been so focused on trying to get Abaddon's attention that finding their way back home had completely vanished from his thoughts.

"Brilliant, do it. See if you can bring them in," he said patting her on the head as he hurried on by.

"I'm only guessing," she shouted after him. "It might not work."

"TRY!" he shouted back over his shoulder as he marched away, disappearing over the hill.

Ruby sat down by the lake, submerging her feet into its icy water and dragging her fingers along its surface. The water rippled in a trail behind as her thoughts travelled through her finger tips.

The watery trails thickened, expanded and grew larger as the creatures Ruby had begun to create, grew fleshy and heavy, expelling the fluid from their bodies until their dark shadows lurked menacingly beneath the surface.

With robust, but agile frames, the creatures continued to evolve. Their noses and jaws elongated into slim, pointed mouths, lined with row upon row of backward tilting, razor sharp teeth. Heavy prehistoric armour grew rapidly over their slim-line bodies, tapering off to form whip-like tails. Two long dorsal fins protruded from their hindquarters which closely resembled those of a blue whale, while two shorter fins sprouted underneath their tummies for buoyancy.

They glided through the water like torpedoes, cutting the surface with ease and elegance without making a splash, silent and beautiful. Arching their backs, they dived down into the inky abyss, flicking their tails as they left Ruby staring in wonderment at their enchanting display.

With Jamie out of sight, Scarlet focussed her attention on the Horsehawks, reaching out to them with her mind as she probed for their presence. It was difficult finding them at first, much like the interference on a radio wave causing the signal to become broken and noisy. It was hardly surprising though; the lands borders had been corrupted to such a point that even the guardians had difficulty reaching the children.

The moment she made contact, her voice echoed out to them, calling them to her assistance. Now with a guide line in place, the Horsehawks were able to grasp the end, tracing it back to where the children were waiting in the Shadowlands.

It was a relief when the four Horsehawks came into view, appearing first as small dots on the horizon, growing larger as they approached then finally touched the ground in a running gallop. Their giant feathered wings which were spread in flight, elegantly bent at the elbow as they folded them away on landing.

Scarlet held her hand out to Ossaro, luring him to her side. His head lowered as he approached before resting his muzzle in her outstretched palm. Scarlet tenderly wrapped her other arm around his neck, patting him with elation. Ossaro kneeled, lowering himself to the ground as Scarlet slipped her foot into his wing joint, hoisting herself onto his back. Her knees rested comfortably inside the wing crevice holding her perfectly in place.

Sensing what Scarlet had in mind, Ossaro broke into a gentle trot, gradually gathering speed until he galloped along at full pace kicking up dust as he ran, until at last he left the ground rising higher as he soared into the air.

His beautiful long wings stretched out in mid-flight as the breeze swept beneath, lifting them effortlessly and gracefully like a phantom gliding through the night. Scarlet clung onto his mane, her knees lodged firmly in place as Ossaro continued to fly higher and higher into the sky. The clouds were still heavy and thick, but somehow up here nothing seemed so severe.

It was so peaceful up here that Scarlet forgot her worries; she didn't notice the dark shadow creep in over her from above. Its wispy form slipped behind her unnoticed, before whirling around her like the ink from a startled squid, and then without warning, it dashed into her with open jaws, suffocated her spirit with its noxious mass.

Scarlet grappled with the air in desperation, her hands flayed hopelessly through the toxic vapours as she anxiously fought to keep it away, but her efforts were futile. The black mass simply collided with her spirit, suggesting it could become part of her just as easily as it could pass through her.

Back and forth it glided, crashing into her time and time again seemingly attacking her airways so that she had no choice other than to breathe the Shade into her weakened lungs.

The air thickened now – Scarlet could hear her heart beating in her ears, her thoughts closed in and began to spin out of control making her eyes grow heavy. She was suddenly aware of a high-pitched humming inside her oxygen depleted head, and then a blackness fell over her, cloaking her from her senses.

Scarlet's lifeless body fell limply forward over Ossaro's back, her hand flopped over his wing and her heart slowed to a gradual standstill.

Gliding down from the sky, Ossaro spread his wings wide as he came into land, slowing himself quickly to bring Scarlet back to the ground.

Ruby's stomach lurched forward. She had seen the sudden appearance of the Shade, and she'd seen Ossaro pretty much freefall out of the sky. Frantically she ran to Scarlet's side, dropping to her knees as she came to her sister's aid.

Scarlet had slipped from Ossaro's back and was now lying flat on the ground with her face buried in the dirt.

Ruby scanned the lifeless body, hardly daring to touch her. She wasn't sure if her sister was even breathing, and to make matters worse, Ruby seemed to forget how to help.

Realising there was nobody else to assist, Ruby managed to calm herself enough to hear the voice of reason whisper in her mind. She turned Scarlet onto her back and pressed her ear against her chest hoping to hear a faint murmur from Scarlet's heart – but there was nothing.

Automatically panic took over again sending Ruby into a fit of anxiety. Her own heart beat heavily like a bass drum echoing in an empty room, chasing any thoughts of trying to resuscitate her sister completely away. Her sister was dying and Ruby was utterly helpless.

Ruby's eyes flicked frantically over the horizon, hopeful that someone else might be able to assist, but her hopes remained just that, she was alone and it was down to her to do something.

"Help!" she wailed weakly, her voice broken and croaked.

The wind picked up a notch sending particles of dust into the air so that her already tearful vision clouded.

"Scarlet, please wake up," she sniffed. "I don't know what to do."

The wind blew harder, whipping Ruby's hair into her face while the sandy grains raced towards Scarlet's body on the ground. Ruby watched as they piled up around her sister, almost as though the earth was already trying to bury her.

"Stop it," croaked Ruby, desperately pushing the earth away with her hands. "Go away, she's still alive," but the wind took no notice as it continued relentlessly building small piles of sand around her body.

The time seemed to drag by, and all the while Ruby stayed by her sister, pushing back the sand and occasionally calling for help until at last a small figure appeared on the horizon.

Ruby rubbed her eyes dry and squinted through the clouded atmosphere. She couldn't be certain that somebody really was coming, but she got up immediately, glancing down at Scarlet briefly before running towards what she thought was help.

The figure drew nearer, and Ruby wiped her eyes dry again allowing her to focus. It was Jamie.

"JAMIE!" she screamed, running towards him with a sense of urgency, her arms waving uncontrollably. "JAMIE, HELP!"

Recognising Ruby's distress, Jamie burst into a full sprint nearly stumbling over his own feet from the added exertion he had suddenly thrust through his legs.

"Wha' is it? What's wrong?" he panted, as he approached.

"Jamie, you have to come quick! It's Scarlet, I think she's dead!" she spluttered through broken tears.

Without listening for an explanation, Jamie pelted away faster than he had run before, leaving Ruby to catch up. His heart pounded in fear, anxious of what he might be met with, the nearer he got.

As he got closer, he could see Scarlet lying lifelessly on the ground while Ossaro stood vigilant by her side. He skidded to an abrupt stop – his hands trembled wildly as he fell to his knees.

Her face was pale, her lips were blue and her eyes were closed. The prognosis didn't look good, but he still had to try and help.

"How long has she been like this?" he trembled, questioning Ruby the instant she came near.

"I don't know," she answered. "Ages, I think – I can't be sure – it seems so long ago. I didn't know what to do Jamie. Is she dead?"

"Scarlet! Can you hear me?" he shouted, shaking her violently by her shoulders. But her head fell unresponsively to her side.

Jamie pressed his ear to her chest, but couldn't hear anything.

"Is she dead?" Ruby asked again, trembling frantically.

Jamie didn't answer. He was already placing Scarlet's body onto her back, tilting her chin up so that her mouth dropped open. Then he counted – "One, two, three, four..." pushing on her chest rhythmically – thirty compressions to two rescue breaths, over and over he worked until at last Scarlet spluttered...

"You okay Scarlet?" he asked quivering nervously.

"I think so," she croaked weakly.

"What happened Ruby? Did you see anything?" he asked.

"I don't know what it was. It was like a big, black, cloudy, gas thing. One-minute Scarlet was riding Ossaro, and the next I could see this shadowy thing sweeping around her like it was trying to suffocate her or something. It might have been Abaddon but I'm not sure." Ruby shook fearfully.

"She struggles to breathe at the best of times, he knew that. He meant to kill 'er," hissed Jamie angrily. "We need to take her to the house Ruby. We have to take control of this, turn it into a game we play under our conditions, where is Rose by the way?" he asked, suddenly troubled by the realisation he hadn't seen her for a little while.

"She said she was goin' to practice shape shifting. I did see her just before Scarlet fell, I was coming back from the lake, she wasn't far from where I was," said Ruby now afraid that Rose may be in danger.

"Stay here. I'm goin' to get her." Jamie launched from the ground leaving Ruby and Scarlet alone on the hilltop.

He came back a short while later, jogging gently with Rose by his side.

"Right, she's okay, but we still need to take Scarlet back to the house," he said, trying to catch his breath.

Grabbing Ossaro by his mane, Jamie lowered him to the ground next to Scarlet and lifted her frail body over his back.

"C'mon Ossaro, Scarlet needs you," he said, as he led the group back to the house, this time unhindered.

The children sat around the table as they drew up their new plans.

"When we go back out, we'll have to stay together. Abaddon can't be allowed to pick us off one at a time like he has tried to. We work together, we stay together and we look after each other," said Jamie firmly. "If it hadn't been for Ruby seeing what happened then goodness only knows what might have been."

Scarlet's breathing rasped, her lungs bubbled as she lay silently in sleep, unaware of the new plans the others were making without her.

"Will she be okay here alone?" asked Ruby pitifully, staring upstairs to where Scarlet slept.

"She'll be fine. We'll be keepin' Abaddon occupied anyway, and besides, the house is hardly conspicuous is it?" replied Jamie confidently.

"Do you have a plan Jamie, or are we just goin' to muddle through?" asked Ruby nervously.

"Do plans ever work the way you expect them to?" he asked dubiously.

"Not really, bu' we still ought to have some kinda strategy, didn't we?"

Jamie smiled. "We do," he said soothingly. "We'll carry on as though nothin's changed, our plan was to aggravate him and ultimately to trap him. So we work as planned, exasperate him and draw him as close to the lake as possible and with luck, something will fall into place which gives us the chance to trap him."

"As easy as that, hey?" said Ruby unconvinced.

"Unless you 'ave a better idea?"

"Not really," answered Ruby. "I'm jus' worried it might all go wrong and we end up like Scarlet," she replied, pushing away a tear from her cheek.

Jamie felt suddenly ashamed and guilty. "Sorry Ruby. I dint mean to make ya cry. I'm just worried about Scarlet, it's all my fault. This whole thing is my fault. I have to make this right. It's because of my Dad this has all 'appened, and it's cos of me that we're here where we are now. If I hadn't encouraged ya all to follow me into the Abstract Forest, we'd 'ave still all bin safe."

Ruby looked up at him. He was just about holding himself together, but she could see how responsible he felt. His eyes were dull and he looked so tired, his skin had even greyed over during the time they'd been trapped in Dreamworld making him appear older than his years.

"Don't be daft. How could you 'ave known your dad was goin' to turn into a monster? No one blames you Jamie, least of all Scarlet." She draped her arm around his waist. "C'mon, we best go and play, Abaddon's waiting."

Chapter Forty-One
The Battle

The children slid silently outside, shutting the door as quietly as possible and sidled away from the house. The sky was still swirling angrily above them, signalling that Abaddon was near, but the children were not deterred, in fact it made them more determined to put an end to their nightmare and make sure they could return home safely.

Holding their nerve, they courageously walked on, leaving the South side of the lake where their stone house stood, and trekked up over the steep gorse banks towards the forest that stood between them and the cage on the West side of the lake.

The wind picked up aggressively, whipping their hair and clothes around them like kites, but undeterred they walked on. They could see through the trees where they wanted to be, the hill dropped down hard towards the lake leaving a small ledge just in front of its waters where Ruby had been sitting earlier. If they could make it to that hill, they had a good chance of getting Abaddon exactly where they wanted him.

Without drawing attention to themselves, the children pressed on, ignoring the wind and ignoring Abaddon's presence, but this only exacerbated the situation.

Before they could position themselves, a dark green wing swooped out from behind the thick clouds, stopping the children in their tracks. They knew precisely what stood in their way without giving it too much thought, it was a dragon, and there perched majestically upon its back sat Abaddon.

He was wearing the same outfit they had seen him wearing on the occasion that Scarlet had transformed his ferocious dragon into a lovable, pink, fluffy one. The image projected itself back into Jamie's mind encouraging a small grin to creep across his lips so that he had to fight the urge to laugh.

Abaddon stared hard at the children, but he did nothing. He seemed to be having a problem as to what his next move should be, now that he finally had them, where he wanted them.

"What's he doin'?" whispered Rose. "Why's he not doin' anythin'?"

"Sshhh," replied Ruby in a hushed voice.

Abaddon pulled on the reins, deliberately lowering the dragon so that he now hovered in front of the children at eye level.

The children stood still, transfixed and baffled as to what Abaddon was trying to do, uncertain if he was challenging them to make the first move or if this was just another game he wanted them to play a part in. And then for some peculiar reason, Abaddon suddenly made his move.

He pulled off his long, dragon-hide jacket, placing it neatly over the front of the saddle. The children were surprised to see he was wearing an ordinary black, V necked, T-shirt under his coat, and his body looked remarkably like a normal man.

"Why's he strippin'? Does he think he looks good or something?" scoffed Jamie, feeling a mix of slight annoyance with surprised humour. "Why is he flexing his arms like that? What an idiot!"

His arms were muscular, almost distracting the children from what Abaddon meant for them to see.

"It's his arms. Look at his arms! That's wha' he wants us to see," croaked Ruby frantically.

"I kind of guessed that. He really loves himself, doesn't he?" said Jamie slightly enviously. "Although I'd have thought that you'd be more concerned about the bloody great dragon hovering in front of ya," he continued in disgust.

"No stupid, his tattoos. They're the same as Dennis's," she spat back in disdain, annoyed he would even suggest what she thought he had meant.

Abaddon let out a hearty laugh as the realisation hit home. "WOULD YOU LIKE TO MEET MY PETS?" he growled, using the same expression Dennis had done on a few occasions before.

He held out his right arm, sweeping his left hand over the tattoos, releasing them from his skin. The inked panthers took on a life force, skulking down his arm then leapt from his skin, soaring over the children's heads, only just missing them by inches.

The children threw their arms into the air in an attempt to protect themselves from his attack, but lost balance. They stumbled backwards, catching a fleeting glimpse of the beasts as they disappeared into the forest behind them.

An unsettling, thunderous roar of laughter erupted from Abaddon as the children fell ungainly onto the floor, before removing his helmet. This move was to be his cruellest yet.

Keeping his head and identity low, he shook his thick black hair free – then slowly lifted his face. His eyes sparkled an excellent sapphire blue and his square chiselled face defined his identity.

"Daddy," murmured Rose with a mix of disbelief and hope.

Both Jamie and Ruby sat transfixed – their mouths ajar and gawping, unable to do or say anything.

"DADDY!" shouted Rose again, certain that now it really was him. Before there was time to think, Rose had leapt to her feet and was running towards him, her arms open ready to embrace the father she feared had died.

Jamie made a grab for her arm, but his fingers slipped over as she slid through his grip, straight into Abaddon's trap.

Abaddon jumped down off his dragon landing heavily on the ground to meet Rose, swiftly scooping her up into his arms, holding her tightly so that she was unable to wriggle free.

"I thought you had died," wept Rose, nuzzling her face securely into his neck.

"I know baby," he cooed softly before allowing his real voice to take over. "He did!" he growled.

Rose slowly pulled her face from his neck realising she had been fooled, in time to see the face she cherished, dissolve into the monster he had been hiding.

Abaddon's head rolled backwards so that he looked straight up into the sky while his disguise peeled away, melting like hot wax, producing a face which the children thought suited him perfectly.

His skin had an unhealthy yellowish tone making him appear to have some kind of kidney failure setting his thinning, greasy hair off like straggly parasitic worms around his pitted, bumpy face. Huge, crusty, green, scab like formations sat deeply embedded within some of the wounds scattered over his face, giving the impression he was being eaten alive by some nasty pox-like disease.

His small, bright yellow, piggy eyes were set deeply in his skull surrounded with dark folds of heavy browning skin framing his sockets like puffy bags. A thin, broad, laceration like mouth had been slashed into his face almost as if it had been attached as an afterthought. It looked tight and rigid as though it might rip the entire length of his face if he dared to move or express any emotion at all. His body, although remaining largely built with heavy muscle, had turned the same horrid, sickly, yellow colour.

The children hadn't expected him to be quite this devious. Somehow this kind of cruelty seemed unthinkable, but on top of this shockingly, brutal hoax, his appearance was so hideous that their minds had still not quite registered what had surreptitiously crept up on them.

A snarl from behind snapped them back to the situation which had escaped their attention. A cold shiver writhed down their spines as they suddenly understood what was going on.

Instinctively, Jamie spun round taking the element of surprise, immediately grabbing the panthers telekinetically with his mind and whisked them out of harm's way high into the air.

Seeing her chance to help Rose, Ruby charged towards Abaddon with her finger outstretched, pointing it toward his head like a wand. Then with a quick flick from one side to the other, she cut a deep gouge across his face, opening his flesh so that the inside of his mouth gaped through the wound, exposing his blackened tongue.

Abaddon growled angrily thrusting Rose to one side. Her small body bounced like a rubber ball and landed under a tree – then slowly his attention turned to Jamie. He could see his pets clawing and scratching at the air as they floated, suspended out of reach.

Jamie smirked; a plan seemed to be coming together now as the advantage shifted from Abaddon and into the hands of the children.

Without giving the game away, Jamie hurled the animals across the sky, directly over Abaddon's head so that for a moment he actually looked concerned as they whizzed by. They landed in the centre of the Ebony Lake disallowing any time for Abaddon to respond.

Ruby's mouth twisted deviously, submerging her thoughts deep into the lake, scanning the waters for the Leviathan. They were lurking in the murky depths within easy reach of the panthers, waiting for her instructions.

"SAY GOODBYE TO YOUR PETS!" she mocked vengefully, staring insolently at him with hardened eyes.

Gliding up silently in answer to her call, the Leviathan opened their vast jaws swallowing the distressed animals whole – then with a gentle splash, they elegantly flicked their tails momentarily above the water, returning from where they had come. The surface of the lake stood still and calm, as though nothing had happened at all.

Ruby felt smug now as the tell-tale signs of anger writhed visibly on his face. This was all as much of a surprise to him, as his own tricks had been to the children.

Abaddon leapt forward in a fit of rage, his eyes galvanised steel as he glared sadistically at her, thrusting his scabby, yellow hand towards her throat. But Ruby had expected this attack and dodged his aim at the last moment. His fingers marginally missed, leaving him grasping the air, as she stumbled to the ground.

Jamie and Rose understood what Ruby was trying to do, so begrudgingly they left their sister to keep Abaddon entertained while they prepared themselves for the next move. Ruby's main objective was to now entice Abaddon nearer to the lakes edge. If her intuitions served her correctly, that is where her siblings would be waiting, ready to support her in their strategy.

Turning in a spontaneous twist from the ground, Ruby bounced to her feet and ran into the forest, deciding that her ploy to run might take him by surprise, leaving him too stunned to follow.

Her plan worked. Abaddon hadn't expected her to run away, it took him a moment to realise what she was doing. But to her delight, he raced back to his dragon, choosing to pursue her in flight, antagonising her as she ran, in the belief that she was afraid.

"THAT'S IT LITTLE WORM – FLEE," he roared, causing the ground to tremble as she ran.

The Ebony Lake was visible, the rocks marking the prison stood out clearly, but her siblings were nowhere to be seen. She had hoped she might see them, but now she wasn't certain how her plan would come together. Realising that unless they came out of hiding, she couldn't tie up her idea, Ruby was forced to make a scene. She held her breath and made a dash out from the trees' coverage and into the open, screaming for help, more to signal to the others she was in the vicinity than for actual assistance. It was risky, but she hoped it would be worth it.

As expected, a high-pitched squeal overhead alerted Ruby to the fact that Abaddon was above her. The time for games was over. He guided his dragon down in front of her, stopping her dead in her tracks, allowing him to think he had won.

Abaddon jumped to the ground and grabbed Ruby by her neck, suspending her in the air like a rag doll. Her body hung from his hand as she struggled to breathe, her hands clasped over his as he dangled her mercilessly above the ground.

"I'm through with playing games," he hissed through clenched teeth. "Where are the others?"

His face gaped open from the injuries she had inflicted upon him allowing a trail of black blood to ooze from the wound and trickle down his cheek, but she said nothing – she didn't even try. If it meant she would die right here, then so be it, but there was no way she was going to make it easy for him.

A sudden, frantic, splashing noise from the lake caught Abaddon's attention. His beady eyes flicked from Ruby and focused on something black within the lakes centre.

An injured panther trod water in an effort to keep its head above the surface. Its paws moved in a weak, doggy paddle, whimpering feebly to its master. Abaddon was too dumb struck to do anything, he stood unanimated staring in disbelief at the half-drowned beast which continued pleading with the most pathetic groans of self-pity Rose could muster up.

Ruby intuitively grasped what was happening and smiled through her pain. Her thoughts travelled through the water again, this time ordering the Leviathan to stay away.

Rose's pride had never allowed her to wallow in self-absorption, and so to act this way now wasn't easy.

Abaddon wasn't budging though. Ruby still dangled from his strong grip, so with more urgency Rose whimpered again. A ludicrous yelp begging her master for help emanated from her mouth, the sound of cats screeching in fight bounced across the water reaching Abaddon's ears. It sounded genuine, desperate and wretched; she just hoped it was enough to coax him into action.

Rose continued to paddle in the lake, splashing as much as she could to hold his attention, but now the shore was in sight and her little legs touched the rocky bottom. She dragged herself pitifully from the water flopping helplessly on the bank.

God this is embarrassingly painful, she thought quietly, but at least it seemed to be working. He was watching her every move, she had his complete attention, she just hoped her sister would be strong enough to hold on.

Ruby clung on, her heart pounded hard as it fought to keep her alive; her head pulsed with a thickness that curdled in her thickening blood, rapidly congealing as the life plummeted from her body. She didn't know how much longer she could fight the desire to let go. A numbness washed over her entire body now as her mind clouded and a soft humming sound filled her ears. She was dying and she knew it.

And then quite miraculously, as if a button had been switched in his head, Abaddon dropped her, keeping his eyes fixed on Rose's performance.

Ruby gasped. The sudden rush of oxygen rich blood pulsed quickly through her released veins which in itself felt peculiar, sending another wave of overwhelming dizziness through her body as it soaked up the nutrients like a sponge soaking up water. And now her anger flared inside her, bubbling ferociously – she wanted to chase after Abaddon, hurt him or send something after him to attack him, but she was too weak. She had little choice but to remain down, allowing Rose to play out her act.

Rose lifted her phoney body from the ground and slumped a few inches before dropping back to the ground, remembering to make the most ridiculous noises she could muster. She dragged herself a bit more, slopping her weight down in front of the prison door.

Abaddon marched heavily towards her, his legs displaying the fury he felt in every purposeful stride he took, growling angrily while demanding she return to his side.

She lifted her head feebly – and dropped down again just as quickly, emphasising the gaping wound that she had conveniently managed to mimic on the side of her leg.

God how long do I have to keep up this charade? she thought to herself as he got enticingly nearer to the prison entrance. Rose tried another sickly attempt, and another pained whimper brought her to the ground, howling in distress as she collapsed.

Rose's life hung precariously close to the edge as she lured him ever nearer to his incarceration. There would be no telling how he might react once within her range, but she didn't care. All she wanted was the safety of her siblings and to see Abaddon locked away where he belonged.

The children were all running high on adrenalin, they hardly dared to breathe in case he caught wind of what was happening and turned away. At some point though, he would have to realise that he had been tricked, and having Rose in range made her a prime target for him to vent his anger.

With the danger growing, Jamie made up his mind to come out of hiding, sneaking quietly towards Abaddon, using the trees as camouflage. He had no weapons, he didn't really have a plan either, other than to push him as hard as possible and hopefully catch him off guard.

Abaddon was on top of Rose now. He stared down at her, his cold eyes cruel and burning. There was no empathy, no sympathy, just anger at her pathetic attempts. His anger raged apparently in his face, his voice bellowed at her, forcing the veins in his temples to pulse impressively hard under the pressure of his outrage.

"Get up you imbecile, you pathetic excuse for a beast." His foot landed heavily in her side as he dug it in with a swing. "GET UP I SAID."

Rose winced as his foot embedded in her side for a second time. This was getting too much; her elegant animal body taking the brutal force of his kicks couldn't tolerate this harshness for long. Despite what she looked like, the reality remained that she was still only a child, and a child who was already weakened from starvation. She began to worry what he might do next, she knew he was ruthless, but had expected a bit of empathy considering he believed her to be one of his beloved pets.

"YOU'RE NOT WORTHY OF SERVING ME, YOU'RE A WEAK, USELESS, WRETCHED, PATHETIC PIECE OF SCUM." He bent down grabbing her scruff and lifted her from the ground. "I may as well just throw you back into the lake. You're only fit to feed those – those – THINGS."

This was the moment Jamie had been waiting for. Abaddon was now completely distracted; it was now or never if he were to knock him off balance.

Launching himself into a sprint, Jamie bounded out from behind the trees and charged, plunging his weight into him as hard and as forceful as he could. "LEAVE HER ALONE!" He shouted as he lurched himself into Abaddon's side.

Abaddon was knocked slightly to one side. But other than that, his efforts had absolutely no effect on him at all. He barely moved; Jamie however fell flat on the floor like he had just run into a wall.

Abaddon turned idly from Rose in a nonchalant manner, reluctantly facing Jamie on the ground.

"There you are! Ya worm," he snarled, pushing his heavy foot over Jamie's arm, pressing him to the floor spitefully, before bursting into a cruel laugh still holding Rose by the scruff. "Her is it?" he laughed. "You thought you could just push me into the lake to feed your monsters, did ya? Ya pathetic, the lot o'ya. Nothin' but filthy bottom dwellers. You had no chance against me. Didn't ya see what I did to the other one?"

Rose saw no point in staying in her disguise. Hanging from the scruff was not at all comfortable. But, returning to her normal form, found herself dangling in the air by her cardigan.

"PUT ME DOWN," she demanded angrily.

Abaddon cackled in surprise as he watched her squirm like a worm on a hook.

"And why would I want to do that?" he said through a snigger, the cruelness in his voice apparent.

By now Rose's options were running low; she had to get out of his grasp as a matter of urgency if they were to complete their mission. Using her trump card and the only available option left, she slipped away into thin air leaving him grasping at nothing while she made her escape.

His jaw dropped in utter bewilderment as Jamie seized perhaps his final opportunity to incarcerate him.

Weak and writhing in agony, Jamie focused all his remaining energy, lifting Abaddon slightly into the air and hurling him backwards into the open prison. With an easy push, the door swung shut with a tell-tale 'clunk', locking it firmly into place.

Jamie played his final card. The sound of several cogs turned inside the prison door as his mind turned the lock within his imagination. A lock without a key, a prison he would be detained in until Jamie found a time fit for his release – which in his opinion would be never.

Ruby removed the shroud from the cage so that for the first time Abaddon was able to see his confinement. The thick, heavy metal bars stood between him and the outside, but he wasn't ready to give in yet.

Dumbfounded and stupefied that he had actually been captured by the children, Abaddon idly got back on his feet, brushed himself down and began to chuckle.

"Well played. But you can't possibly believe you can hold me here, you must know that?" he said calmly, unaffected by the situation he found himself in.

The children remained silent allowing him to slowly take on board the full understanding of his plight.

Plodding care free to the door, he grabbed the bars expecting them to buckle under his strength, but instead he howled in agony. His hands had melted into the pale blue metal.

Violently he ripped his hands free, nursing his injuries magically while the consequences of his imprisonment spread across his abhorrent face.

The bars began to rattle aggressively as Abaddon changed tactics, now using his own telekinetic powers to force the bars open. But they stood strong, unbending and as Emberleigh had said - unbreakable.

Ruby smiled as her plans to incorporate the Ebony Army fell into place.

The lake stirred and bubbled, disturbing the sediment into cloudy masses. Dripping with silt, the Ebony Army emerged from the lake, reforming while the water poured from their bodies.

Abaddon stood dumbstruck as he watched the army surround the cage. This went way beyond what he'd expected from the children, he had never been physically attacked, not by creatures and certainly never by children.

"You've lost!" said Ruby calmly in a factual way as she cautiously approached the cage. "Take him away."

A heavy metal clonking sound echoed from the lake as the chain attached to the prison tightened from somewhere in the depths, then slowly the cage slid down towards the banks of the Ebony Lake.

The water edged in with each pull, licking the metal sides tantalisingly slowly as it immersed beneath the surface. Unable to stop the progression, Abaddon stared blankly at the children, unmoving and unresponsive. His widened eyes stayed open even as the water lapped around his face, then covered his stare. The children held their ground, defiantly staring back at him until at last the prison tumbled over the ledge of the lake, deep into the abyss.

A sense of relief immediately fell over the children, and with that the boundary walls broke, allowing the guardians to finally get through. Out of nowhere their guardians appeared by the children's side.

"You did good," said Emberleigh smiling. "We need you to get back inside your bodies now. There's no time to lose."

"Scarlet? Is Scarlet okay?" said Jamie anxiously.

"Esperanza has already taken her home. Now you all have to leave," said Breanna pressing them to take action.

"Wha' about Dad?" said Jamie nervously.

"You'll find he's no longer a threat, but you have to go now," she insisted.

From the other side the guardian's voices reverberated in their heads calling the children home.

"Open your eyes. Wake up. Wake up. Wake up…"

They listened, unmoving, then their eyes flickered.

Sitting up painfully slowly and stiff from sleep the children felt the exhaustion their weakened bodies had suffered. A painful, sore dryness cut their throats as they shook uncontrollably from head to foot from severe dehydration.

A large glass jug of slightly blue water stood on the girls' dressing table with a little note.

Toby x.

A sudden burst of energy moved the children into pouring a glass, quenching their thirst over and over until at last the children were strong enough to stand up.

Chapter Forty-Two
A Punishment for Dennis

Downstairs, a figure rocked back and forth scrunched into a foetal position. A gentle repetitive humming sound purred from his lips as he swayed rhythmically.

His remaining hair hung in strands displaced over his left eye leaving his bald head shining like a polished stone in the sunlight which filtered through the large front rooms bay window.

Scarlet noticed his tattooed arms and pointed at them. An inky mess was splattered across his skin where there had once been the deep, clean impressions of the tattooed, black panthers. Now all that remained were washed out, smudged marks of the images which had been imprinted onto his skin. They were barely visible as anything at all, just dirty black smudged ink, like someone had tried to wash off Indian ink from parchment.

The children couldn't take their eyes off him, he suddenly didn't have a name, he was empty, unrecognisable as the man they knew before now that Abaddon had finished using him. You would have been forgiven if you had felt sorry for the wretched state that he had become. The children though, felt nothing for him, no empathy at all – just a numb, cold, hatred reserved only for him.

He looked pathetic and weak, like a diseased, dying man. He was petrified of who the children had become, strong in their own rights, individuals who had learned to stand up to him.

His hands trembled over the tops of his knees, and the fear in his grey eyes betrayed the sorry excuse for a man he actually was. He had become nothing more than an empty shell, void of any emotion other than depraved fear for what might come after him in years to come. His former strength had completely drained leaving nothing but a crazed, mentally disturbed wretch.

"Your pets aren't lookin' too well!" jeered Scarlet, kneeling down next to him, staring him straight in the eye. He tried to look away, uncomfortable with how his victims were now able to speak directly at him. But Scarlet refused to let him turn; grabbing his face in her hand she pulled him round, forcing him to look at her. "I hope you enjoy the rest of your miserable, lonely life as you rot in a cell somewhere." She stood up and walked away, turning her back on him.

Dennis said nothing as he continued to shake with fear, rocking in his perpetual rhythm, even when Jamie approached and squatted by his side for a moment.

Jamie wanted to tell his father how badly he had let him down, and how for so many years he had ruined his childhood, that he was still his dad, and that he cared for him if only for that one reason. But nothing came out of his mouth. Jamie was so full of rage and anger that he couldn't say a word. He shut his mouth again; nothing was going to come out. For years he had wanted to tell his father how he felt, but now that he had the chance, there were no words to describe his pain. He felt frustrated that nothing seemed to fit his emotions, and so he whispered the only thing that he really felt able to tell him.

"You reap what you sow, isn't that what you always taught me Dad? And you're getting exactly what ya deserve right now. Don't worry though; we won't leave ya to suffer alone like ya did to us. We'll send ya some help; the doctors from the mental health unit will be round soon. They'll know exactly how to help you."

The children stood up together and walked away leaving Denis alone with nothing but his thoughts.

Scarlet stopped talking and looked up at Pam. "You think I'm nuts, don't you?"

Pam stopped writing and looked Scarlet in the eye.

"Have you ever heard of psychic connection Scarlet?"

"No, not really. Only in my dreams I guess."

"It's something that happens when people are close. They tend to experience the same things, feel the same things and sometimes like in your case, dream the same things. From what you've told me, it sounds like you've all had a very traumatic childhood, so you created a world in your head where you felt safe. If you think about certain aspects of your story, you'll find connections.

"The first one that strikes me as completely plausible is your magic key. Do you have any ideas why this came into your imagination the way it did?"

"I don't understand what ya mean." said Scarlet in confusion.

"I think you'll find that metaphorically, you *are* the key Scarlet. You didn't fit the life you were forced into living so you found some place else where you would fit – your mind, which is also a reflection of the willow.

"Your mind is the willow. You opened your creative mind with a key you found hidden away inside yourself, turning it into a place of safety, a place you escaped to when you most felt threatened. So in theory, you really have unlocked the willow.

"Lots of people do that, even as adults. They go inside themselves and hide away when things get too much to cope with. You're a bright child, full of hope and ambition, but you've been through some very tough times making you appear damaged, less shiny and in need of redefining yourself again, just like the key you described. Once you convinced yourself that you were able to fight the troubles you faced on a daily basis, your eyes were opened to the strength you held inside.

"You told me about your grandparent's house, how you felt safe there. It had a magical feeling about it, particularly the 'shop' under the stairs and the rocking horse in the attic. You'll find there's a strong similarity to the door in the willow and the Horsehawks you created in your dream.

"You talked of Abaddon and you automatically connected him with the evil in your stepfather. Then there's Toby; it sounds like you're describing the maternal relationship with that of your grandmother.

"There's the matter of how you've grown up with a strong religious background, it taught you to fear the unseen which is why you see demons in your dreams.

"So you see Scarlet, everything you've told me; the fire, your father's murder, the loss of your mother, even the magic you experienced living with your grandparents, are all reflected in the world you created. You've become confused, combining a perfect world you crave with the hardships you've endured, and turned everything upside down.

"It's not until we analyse every piece of the jigsaw puzzle that we can fully understand and make sense of the bigger picture. You know, I could go on with different connecting resemblances Scarlet, so my short answer to '*do I think you're crazy?*' is quite simply no, I don't."

Scarlet stared back aghast. She hadn't considered this before, it sounded plausible, but something told her there was more to it than what Pam understood. It felt real.

320

"We were asleep for days though! How do you explain that?"

"Sleep paralysis is more common than what you'd think. Granted, I've not come across a case which has lasted so long and there are certainly questions to be asked, particularly as to why you weren't taken to hospital if Dennis was unable to wake any of you. He will be questioned and cautioned for child neglect offences. On top of that, until we can speak to him the police have to take your accounts seriously. From what you've told us already, there's reason to believe he may be involved with arson, murder and may have information regarding a missing person."

"Where is he now?" asked Scarlet with curiosity.

"He's in a high security hospital at the moment. We haven't been able to communicate with him yet. He's unresponsive apart from the occasional outburst where he has delusive ideas that something's coming for him."

"You don't believe me then, do you?"

"We have to be realistic Scarlet. This is the real world; there are no monsters here, just your imagination."

Scarlet's fingers curled around the warm Transportation Stone in her palm and she smiled knowingly, but said nothing.